SPELLS, SALT, & STEEL
SEASON 1

SPELLS, SALT, & STEEL
SEASON 1

GAIL Z. MARTIN

LARRY N. MARTIN

PART I

SPELLS, SALT, & STEEL

1

W hen all else fails, the ass end of a carp makes a damn fine weapon.

I'd been lying in wait for the ningen to show up, and by the wee hours of the morning, I was tired and cranky and out of coffee. As soon as the sun went down, I pulled in to the Linesville, Pennsylvania, spillway. The tourists were gone, and the concession stand's gates were closed. Still blows my mind how many people will come look at a bunch of fish. Even if those fish are a boiling, writhing mass of three-foot long, twenty-pound carp that look like something out of a Biblical plague.

I'm Mark Wojcik, mechanic—and monster hunter. I gank things that go bump in the night so that most people never have to know supernatural uglies exist outside of bad horror movies. No one chooses this life; it chooses you, usually in a violent and awful way. In my case, a deer hunt turned into a wendigo hunting us. I survived—barely—but my father, brother, uncle, and cousin didn't. Neither did the wendigo, when I was done with it.

The carp weren't my problem. Tourists loved throwing day-old bread into the water to watch the carp roil over each other, mouths gaping. Tonight, they weren't the only ones with an unnatural interest in big fish.

A corpse-pale creature balanced on the low concrete rim of the spillway catch basin. It stood about five feet tall, slender with long arms, and a body that looked like a giant white tadpole with arms and skinny, short legs. Ningen can get as big as sixty feet, or so the cryptid sites say, but then again, they say that ningen are only found in Japan, so I don't put much stock in them.

"*Koko ni sakana no kao ga kuru,*" I called to it, betting that a Japanese monster might understand Japanese. Then again, I'd looked up key phrases on Google Translate, so God only knows what I actually said. "Come here, fish face," I repeated in English, in case the ningen was bilingual.

The ningen cocked its round head and blinked its solid black eyes. I leaned over the railing and waved my bait at it, a nice piece of salmon I'd paid fifteen bucks for at the supermarket, thinking the creature might want an upgrade.

"That's it," I coaxed, dangling the prime wild salmon and giving it a shake. "That's a good little *sekana no neko.*" That's the magic of translation: "fish fucker" sounds classier in a foreign language.

If the ningen felt offended, it didn't look it, although for all I knew, maybe I'd been descriptive instead of insulting. The ningen raised its head and opened its mouth, scenting the air. It shuffled toward me on its stubby legs, like it had its pants down around its knees. I grinned, keeping the sharpened iron harpoon blade concealed behind my back in my right hand.

At the speed the ningen hop-walked, it might take it ten minutes to get to me, but once I ganked him, I'd be back home relaxing with a nice cold beer.

That's when the damn thing leapt into the air like a horny salmon going to spawn and grabbed the filet in my hand so hard he pulled me over the fence and into the carp-filled water.

I lost the piece of fish, but managed to keep the harpoon. When I fell in, fully-clothed and in my steel-toe boots, I thought I'd sink, but I fell onto the roiling carp that made a moving, lumpy net beneath me. They buoyed me along just long enough for me to regain my wits and scramble onto the small stretch of rocky shore between the overflow basin and the wall below the fence.

The ningen crouched, eyeing me as it shoved the raw salmon into its mouth, and I got a look at its jagged, sharp teeth—something else the cryptid reports had been less than accurate about. I realized then that the small strip of land around me was covered with fish bones. Those all-black eyes kept staring at me, and although I'd heard long pig tasted like chicken, this jagoff looked like he was wondering how much I'd taste like fish.

It sprang for me, and I rolled, gritting my teeth as the sharp stones and fish bones jabbed through my jacket and jeans. I brought up my harpoon gun and got off a shot. The barbed iron blade hit the ningen in the shoulder instead of the chest like I'd hoped, but it must have hurt like a mother since the thing let out an ungodly howl that would have put any loon to shame.

I yanked on the rope attached to the base of the blade with all my might. The ningen stumbled toward me. Then it grabbed the rope and *pulled*. And I found myself face down in the water, getting smacked in the head by carp the size of toddlers.

I scrambled back onto the rocky bank. What little I could find about ningen, that was written in English, said it would have less power on land. I yanked the rope again, getting angry now, and the ningen bared its barracuda teeth at me and gave another ear-splitting shriek.

The iron had an effect on it; I could see black veins radiating from where the blade lodged in its shoulder, spreading across the once-perfect white skin. I just didn't know how long the iron blade would take to kill the creature, or if it would do the job completely. My gun was safe and dry in my truck, since I'd figured going for a forced swim was likely. But I had a couple more tricks up my soggy sleeves.

The ningen closed in on me, and I grabbed a kada, one of those martial arts sickle blades, from a scabbard on my back. I didn't know if Japanese weapons were extra-lethal on Japanese monsters, but I fully intended to go ninja on its ass for leaving me soggy and freezing and smelling like carp.

"Let's see you *shi'ne*, you piece of fish shit," I muttered. I watched as much anime as my Crunchy Roll subscription could handle, and I'd picked up on a few overused phrases. "Die" seemed like a good one.

Except that the ningen didn't seem to take it the way I'd intended and jerked me back into the water.

I managed to roll so I got the kada blade between us and swung as hard as I could, sinking the point of the curved blade into its chest where I hoped its heart might be. The black veins from the iron blade had spread across its entire torso, up its fish-belly white neck, and down its overly long arms.

But it wasn't dead yet, and it came at me again, forcing me to fall backward in the water into another mass of carp. I kicked with my legs to get some distance between myself and the ningen. The carp weren't pleased to have me land on them, and one of the fish jumped out of the water and landed in my arms, all thirty pounds of him.

Instinct took over, and I wrapped both arms around the carp's middle and thrust its powerful tail toward the ningen. The fish wriggled wildly in my grip, its tail slapping back and forth with sharp scales and fins. It knocked the harpoon deeper into the ningen's chest, as the black lacework of the iron's poison spread across the rest of its skin.

I got my feet under me and dragged myself onto the shore, still holding a pissed-off carp between me and the monster. The ningen lurched forward, grabbing for me with its long, skeletal arms and clammy, dead white hands. Then it fell over and lay face-down amid the carp, completely covered by the deadly pattern of the iron's taint running through its veins.

"Tora, tora, tora that, fish fucker," I muttered. I dropped the carp, and it disappeared into the roiling mass of its companions.

I hauled myself back up on the rocky shore and caught my breath. The night was warm, but that's a relative statement in this neck of Northwestern Pennsylvania, and I started to shiver. The ningen lay where it fell, and I was just about to pull it out of the water when I saw its body twitch.

"Oh, no you don't!" I growled, but before I could climb up the wall to get my gun out of the truck, the carp began to thrash. My stomach turned as I realized that the ningen wasn't moving on its own; its body jerked and moved because dozens of carp were nibbling at its flesh.

In the next moment, the ningen's form sank lower, pulled down by the fish. The pale body vanished beneath the water, and the fish fought each other to get closer, obscuring it from view.

"Hey buddy! No fishing!" I turned and got a face full of flashlight beam, blinding me. The perfect end to a lousy evening would be getting arrested for monstercide. Or in this case, fishing without a license.

"Oh, it's you, Mark."

I blinked and recognized a familiar voice. Louie Marino, a guy I'd known since first grade, and one of Linesville's Finest.

"Not fishing, Louie. Honest. Just business." Louie's one of the few area cops who know what I really do. He gets it—mainly because when he had a nasty little infestation of demon-possessed rabid raccoons a few years back, I took care of it for him, no questions asked.

"Keeping busy?" he asked, angling the flashlight so I could see again.

"Always. They pay you enough to be on fish patrol at this hour?"

Louie shrugged. "Workin' nights this week. Drew the short straw. Just another day in paradise." He wrinkled his nose. "You stink like carp."

"I've heard of 'swimming with the fishes,' just didn't intend to take it literally," I replied, wringing out the water from the hem of my flannel shirt.

"Do I want to know?"

I shook my head. "Probably not. If the rangers at the Spillway say anything about their fish count being down, tell them it's been taken care of."

Louis grinned, taking in my utterly disreputable condition. "You're just lucky I was on duty tonight, or you'd be going from the fish tank to the drunk tank."

"Ha, ha. Very funny," I mumbled, although I knew he was right. "Oh, and Louie?" I said as we headed back to our vehicles. "If I were you, I wouldn't eat any carp out of the lake this season. I think their diet's been a little…off."

Regular soap didn't get the carp stink off of me, so I opted for the canned tomato juice I keep around in case of skunk. That made me feel like a Bloody Mary, but being a brunch drink was better than smelling like day-old catch.

I knew when I ambled in to Hamilton Hardware the next day that I'd be in for a ribbing.

"Whoa, Chick!" Blair Hamilton called, her affectionate mangling of my last name. I'd long ago quit correcting her—since it only made things worse—but for the record, it's pronounced "voy-chick." I'll answer to anything close. Most people who can't figure it out just go with "Mark."

"Whoa, yourself," I replied. "What's the word on the street?"

Blair blew raspberries. "This is Conneaut Lake. Nothing ever happens here." Blair is five-ten to my six-two and with her military background, I'd put my money on her in a fair fight. She inherited the family hardware store, the third-generation Hamilton to supply the good folks of Conneaut Lake with all their hunting, fishing, shooting, and hardware needs.

She gave a knowing grin. "Except that I hear there was a commotion over at the Spillway in Linesville last night. Poachers or something."

"That so? Can't trust anyone these days," I replied. The store was fairly empty. I'd intentionally waited until the "dawn patrol" of DIY-ers and contractors filled their urgent orders and I knew Blair would have time for some less conventional requests.

"I got a job coming up," I said when the few remaining customers were out of earshot. "Gonna need another big bag of rock salt, a case of shotgun shells, and about fifty feet of hemp rope." I paused. "Oh, and can you let Chiara know I need her help on something?"

"How about you tell me yourself?" Chiara Moretti Hamilton slipped behind the counter and threw an arm around Blair's waist.

"I need some intel," I replied.

Chiara gave her wife a squeeze and then beckoned for me to follow her. "Step into my parlor," she said.

I followed her through a doorway Blair had cut into one wall of the hardware store that led to the adjacent building, which had been many things over the last century. Now, it housed Crystal Dreams, Chiara's New Age bookstore, café, and gift shop. In the renovated office upstairs, Chiara also ran a website development company. On the sly, she did Dark Web research for me and other hunters, and there was an invitation-only back room behind the hardware store that carried a variety of silver, iron, spelled tools and weapons, holy water by the keg, and other hard-to-find herbs and items necessary for hunting or warding off ghoulies and ghosties and long-leggedy beasties. She and Blair weren't even thirty yet, and they made me feel like a slacker, even though I had less than ten years on them and owned my own car repair shop.

"Coffee first," she said, holding up a hand to stop me before I got on a roll. "And sugar." She poured me a cup of joe, black, and started a latte for herself. Then Chiara reached into the display case and pulled out a couple of *sfogliatelli* pastries fresh from her family's bakery.

"Good, right?" She nudged as I bit into the lobster tail-shaped flaky bit of heaven and gave a pornographic groan of sheer bliss.

"You're not going to make Blair jealous, you know," she joked. "I don't bat for that team."

"Shhh," I joked. "Don't ruin the moment. This is between me and the pastry," I said, and rolled my eyes back in my head with another groan.

"You better not try that if you ever stop by the bakery," Chiara warned. "Grandma won't put up with any 'lascivious goings on.'"

"Spoilsport," I retorted. Chiara treats me like one of her older brothers, and considering that she's got five of them, she can dish it out and take it with the best of them. I chugged the coffee, still groggy from the late night, and Chiara obligingly refilled it before taking a seat at the bar next to me.

"So what is it this time?" she asked. At the moment, the cafe was unusually quiet. That wouldn't last. Tonight, the Tuesday night Bunko group would be gathering in the social room in the back, and no one aside from a privileged few would realize it was really the local coven. There aren't a lot of people in the supernatural community around these parts and mostly, we look after our own.

"I need everything you can find on the old Keystone Ordinance Works plant," I said, sipping the coffee to make it last and savoring the caffeine buzz.

"You mean the KOW?" She pronounced it "cow" and laughed when I looked puzzled. "The old TNT plant in Geneva?"

I nodded. "Yeah. You've heard the story about the Nazi sniper that got shot off the water tower?"

"Hasn't everyone?"

"Yeah, well apparently it's true, and something's got his ghost riled up."

"You know that place is dangerous, right?" Chiara cautioned. She tucked a strand of dark hair behind one multiply-pierced ear. Chiara's thin enough to qualify as "waif-ish," but she'd hit me if I ever called her that. With long dark hair, big brown eyes, and a light olive complexion, Chiara's a looker, but she's been heart-and-soul for Blair since high school. "Part of it's owned by a big corporation that doesn't like urban explorers, some of it's still military—and lord knows, they're not friendly —and the other piece is owned by a local guy who's put out the word that trespassers will be arrested, or maybe shot."

9

"Nice," I muttered. "Actually, I've got the invitation from a guy in the corporation, and they're paying me. I did a job for his uncle—got rid of a ghost that was hanging around his hunting cabin, scaring off the game—and got me access."

"Not going to help you if your Nazi spook Heil-Hitlers over onto private property and you get your butt filled with buckshot."

I shrugged. "Won't be the first time, probably not the last either." I drained my coffee cup and met her gaze. "Can you see what you can dig up? I've got all the easy stuff Google can give me."

"You want what's in the old records—old *government* records —don't you?"

"Something powered this ghost up after seventy years, and he's been poltergeisting around the place, vandalizing corporate property."

"You sure it isn't kids?" Chiara asked. "Every high school kid around here knows the story, and a 'no trespassing' sign is an open invitation for anyone who wants to impress a date enough to get lucky."

My eyes narrowed. "Do I sense a story here?"

Chiara grinned, though her cheeks colored a bit. "Maybe. Blair hopped the fence and brought me back a souvenir when we were first dating."

"And did she get lucky?"

Chiara's blush deepened, as if I hadn't already guessed the answer. "Shut up," she protested in jest, and smacked me on the arm. "When do you need the intel?"

"As soon as you can get it," I replied. "Apparently the company is plan- ning to refurbish some of the old buildings on its land for labs and product testing. The planning team that went out to look at the buildings thought they were being shot at. They called the cops, reported gun shots, and holed up like they were under siege."

"And when the cops came?"

I shook my head. "Nothing. No spent shells, no footprints or tire tracks, no bullet holes. Now the architect and the designer refuse to set foot on the property until it gets 'exorcised,'" I added, making air quotes.

"Are you trying to put Father Minnelli out of a job?" Chiara teased.

I put my hand over my heart. "As God is my witness, and much to my grandmother's sorrow, I've got no interest in being a priest," I swore. "I just didn't have time to waste explaining that 'exorcising' ghosts won't do a damn bit of good. Demons, yes. Ghosts, no."

"Is it actually dangerous?" Chiara finished her coffee.

"Don't know, don't want to find out the hard way," I replied, draining the rest of my cup. "That's why I need anything you can find for me. If I've got to chase the damn thing, I want to know everything about that property, and that ghost."

Chiara looked up as the door chimed and a customer walked in. "I can work on it tonight, after we close. Should have something to you first thing tomorrow."

I grinned. "Blair's got fine taste in women. You're the best!"

Chiara punched me in the shoulder, just enough to twinge. "Gotta go. I have to set up for the Bunko meeting tonight," she added with a wink.

Shit. That meant she'd be closing late. I was in a hurry for her data, but not enough to piss off a coven of witches. I sighed, carried my empty cup up to the counter, and ambled back to pick up the rest of my purchases from Blair before I headed home.

I pulled into my driveway with a truckload of supplies and a hot pizza. "Home" is a cabin down a gravel lane in between Adamsville and Atlantic, two towns with a combined population of less than two hundred. Suits me fine, although now and again I still have to go out and handle restless ghosts from the big tornado twenty years ago that damn near took out both towns and a couple other 'burgs, too. I reckon we've got more residents under the ground than above it, and since I keep the local cemeteries blessed and ghost-free, it makes for a nice, quiet place to put my feet up between hunts.

Chiara pulled some strings—legal and not so much—to get me better internet out here than anyone would ever believe. I popped open an Iron City beer and fired up my laptop to go over everything again. Demon, my big softie of a Doberman, planted himself next to me and dropped his head into my lap for attention. I scratched his ears as I read over my notes.

If I'd have put as much effort into my homework back when I was in school as I do getting ready for a hunt, I'd have the grades to be a brain surgeon. Sadly, I couldn't see my way past anything that didn't have to do with cars or girls back then. Girls broke my heart; cars didn't, which is one reason I'm still a mechanic after all this time, but my love life's deader than most of the things I hunt.

It's not that I'd mind having a good woman in my life. It's just that finding one who would put up with my anime and comics collection, my poker nights, and the odd hours I keep at the shop would be rough enough, without the monster hunting stuff on top. My wife Lara left me after the wendigo incident. Blair and Chiara are lucky—they didn't have to convince each other that the supernatural shit is real. Blair saw stuff that can't be explained when she was military, and Chiara's brothers offed a werewolf when she was in high school. Most of the time, I'm too busy to think about finding myself a girlfriend.

Or maybe I'm just chickenshit.

I finished the beer and pizza and powered up my secured search engine. There are many times when my browsing might raise a few questions, so I figure it's better not to take chances. Urban explorers have done a pretty fine job of taking pictures despite Keystone's "off limits" status. The photos revealed dilapidated two- and three-story brick buildings with their windows long broken out, rusted machinery, junker trucks from the 1940s, storage silos, and the famous water tower—still standing after all these years. According to the blog posts, someone had thought it was a good idea to raise cattle on what had to be a Superfund site. I wondered if the cows still ran loose at KOW, and if the sniper cared.

I'd heard the story about the Nazi spy at the TNT plant when I was growing up, but now that I needed details, they were hard to find or were classified, and any eyewitnesses were either over ninety or dead. Still, I pieced together what I could. It wasn't a pretty picture.

My phone rang at the same time a chime on my computer indicated that I had new email. "Did you get what I sent?" Chiara asked as I juggled the phone and logged in to the Dark Web, trying not to get pizza sauce all over my keyboard.

"Give me a minute," I growled, wiping away a stray bit of sauce as I pulled up her file on the anonymous file-sharing network and looked at the results. "All right, walk me through it."

"The spy's name was Helmut Zinzer, but he infiltrated the plant back in 1944 as Hank Stump. His job was to sabotage the production of ordnance in any way he could, and also to find out about the secret projects German high command suspected were taking place at the plant,"

Chiara recapped as I scanned the old documents she sent. Even though they came from government servers and over seventy years had passed, parts were blacked out for security reasons.

"Secret projects?" I took a swig of IC and peered more closely at the old files.

"Pittsburgh manufacturing was hot stuff back then, some of the best engineering in the world," Chiara said with pride. "There was a big glass company that tried to build an invisible plane."

I let out a low whistle. "You mean, like Wonder Woman's?"

Chiara sighed. "You win, Blair," she called out, and I heard snickering. "Yes, comic nerd, like Wonder Woman's. Only they wanted to build it for real, out of super special secret glass. Zinzer was supposed to halt production, assassinate the engineers on the project, and grab the plans."

"Only it didn't work out," I added, still torn between being annoyed and secretly pleased that Chiara and Blair had bet on whether my comic-fu would pick up on the connection.

"Closer than you'd think," Chiara said as I flipped through the rest of the file. "The two lead engineers died suddenly, one with a heart attack and the other from a car accident, both suspicious. An early prototype was destroyed in a lab fire. But the project continued, and rumor has it that a second, improved prototype was not only built, but aced its initial tests. Zinzer stole some schematics and passed them off to an associate, then went back to finish the job. He planned to detonate some of the ordnance, destroy the lab and prototype, and get the hell out of Dodge."

"But someone picked him off the water tower before he could do that, and now he's haunting the place," I said. A long pull finished my beer, and I scowled at the computer. "Bad enough we never got the flying cars they promised, but we coulda had invisible planes, too?"

"Life's a bitch," Chiara commiserated.

"So why now?" I asked, leaning back and debating popping open another beer. "Has ol' Helmut been haunting the place all this time, but there wasn't anyone around to see?"

"You mean, if a ghost haunts in a forest and no one's there, does he make a sound?"

"This is the sound of one finger clapping," I muttered, tossing her the salute. She responded with a chin flick.

"Could be," Chiara replied. "I mean, who would know or care? But get this—the corporation that hired you is the legal successor of the company that wanted to make the invisible plane out of special glass all those years ago. Only now, we've got all kinds of polymers…"

"And so it might actually be possible," I said. "Holy shit…so Helmut's back on the job, different war, same shit."

"That's what it sounds like to me," Chiara replied.

"Okay, thanks. You totally rock. This helps."

"Hey Mark—be careful," Chiara cautioned. "Helmut was a dangerous guy, and he offed a couple of people before he lost his luck. He might be pissed about that, so watch your back."

"Will do." Just what I needed: a pissed off Nazi ghost assassin. Well, I already spent the advance so it's too late to back out now. Guess I'd just have to gank the Jerry and save the invisible airplane.

Funny, I'd always pictured myself more Space Ghost than Wonder Woman.

"And I scored big," Chiara continued.

"TMI," I protested. "I don't want to know—"

"Not like that, perv," she joked. "I was talking about the whole TNT plant thing with Blair, and she reminded me that her aunt's neighbor used to tell stories about working there during the war. Want to go see what he remembers?"

Which is how I ended up standing on a stranger's doorstep to see a man about a ghost. I'd like to say my innate charm opened the door, but I'm betting it was Chiara's box of homemade Italian pastries that did the trick.

Despite being over ninety, Eugene was sharp as a tack, and he told us plenty of stories, including a first-hand account of the night his Army patrol shot the sniper off a water tower.

"Thank you so much," Chiara said, after Eugene's story came to an end. "We've taken up enough of your time."

"Would you like to see the stuff I kept from when I worked there?" Eugene's rheumy eyes sparkled, and I bet he was having more fun flirting with Chiara and eating the pastries than he'd had in a long time.

"We'd love to!" I replied before Chiara had a chance to protest.

Eugene got to his feet and reached for his cane. "Be back in a moment," he promised, setting off down the hall.

"Blair is gonna kill me," Chiara murmured. "I'm late opening the shop."

"Wait 'til she finds out you've been flirting up a storm," I joked, elbowing her.

She rolled her eyes. "Blair knows better."

Eugene shuffled back with a box in one hand and put it on the coffee table before settling back into his worn recliner. "I kept a little of this and a little of that over the years," he said. "This is the box from my time in the Army." He opened it, revealing a collection of badges and medals, hunting licenses, snapshots, and…buttons. Dozens of buttons of all kinds.

I must have looked confused because Eugene laughed. "My mother was quite the seamstress when I was a boy, and I used to amuse myself playing with her button jar. Never quite got over my fascination, so I've always picked up the odd button when I saw it and added it to my collection."

Then he held up a pebbled black button. "You know where I got this?" Eugene asked. When Chiara and I shook our heads, he chuckled. "Our Jerry spy ripped his jacket when he took a header off the water tower. We found the button in the grass. German-issue. I pocketed it, since I figured it didn't matter to anyone else, and I'd been part of the team that got in the lucky shot."

I felt a chill go down my spine. "Mr. Sprake—"

"Eugene," he corrected.

"You probably aren't going to believe me, but that spy you shot came back as a ghost."

To my surprise, Eugene nodded. "That's old news, son."

"You know?"

"Yep," Eugene replied, and helped himself to another pastry. "We'd see wisps up on the catwalk around the water tower after he was shot and hear a voice muttering in German. Never came to anything, and then we all cleared out, and the place stood empty for a long time. Figured it served him right, being stuck as the last sentry after trying to kill us."

"He's back, and a lot stronger—strong enough to cause trouble," I said. "I was wondering, I know it's a lot to ask, but may I have that button? I need to make sure he doesn't hurt anyone else."

Eugene fixed me with his gaze, and I felt like a teenager caught breaking curfew. "You're that monster hunter guy, aren't you? I've heard about you."

I tried not to cringe. For obvious reasons, I didn't advertise my side

GAIL Z. MARTIN & LARRY N. MARTIN

job, figuring that people who needed my services would find me on their own. Still, word gets around, and I hated to think what he might have heard.

Eugene chuckled. "None of that now," he chided. "Blair's older brother was at the VFW and had a bit much to drink one night, started telling stories, and got to the one about that werewolf he and his brothers took care of. Said there was more stuff like that out there, and that you were one of the guys who got rid of it." He shrugged. "At the time, I blamed it on the whiskey, but I saw him later, and he swore it was true."

"It's true," I confirmed.

Eugene nodded. "I've seen a strange thing or two in my time as well," he said, and dropped the button into my hand.

"I won't be able to return this," I warned.

He shrugged. "You gonna use it to get rid of that Nazi bastard once and for all? Keep it, with my blessing." His eyes blazed with the fire of the young soldier he once had been. "And when you send the son of a bitch to hell, you be sure to tell him that's for my brother Mickey and his friends, the guys who never came back from Normandy."

My fingers closed around the button. "It would be an honor."

The old Keystone Ordnance Works looked even more ominous in the dark. The full moon should have let me navigate easily, but the cloud cover kept blocking the moonlight. We're in one of the spots in the US that has the most cloudy days, and I'd been told that was one reason the TNT plant got located here—because aerial surveillance didn't work well. Tonight, it made my job that much harder.

Forget about climbing the fence. I found a hole in the chain link and crawled through. Apparently, I wasn't the only one who'd decided to ignore the warnings. Thanks to the maps and Chiara's research, I'd come in near the old water tower instead of near the front, because the site covered acres and I didn't want to hike through tick-infested scrub or fall into a polluted catchment pond.

The clouds broke, and I could see clearly. In the distance, I could make out the silhouette of one of the larger buildings, like a hulking shadow. Ahead of me, I saw the water tower, and to its right, a stand of trees.

I've got to admit, I was feeling pretty jazzed about this hunt. My grandad fought in "Dubya-Dubya-Two" as he called it, and now here I was, picking off a Heinie sniper. I felt like Indiana Jones and the Hunt for the Last Nazi.

Shoulda known it was all gonna go right to hell.

The weeds tangled around my legs like tripwire, dragging at my jeans with burrs. Mosquitos rose into a fierce, bloodsucking cloud, and I wondered if I could get turned into a mutant superhero by getting bitten by one, considering the stuff that probably got dumped in the shallow ponds. The ground beneath my feet felt rutted and squishy, probably from the rain we'd had lately. Bats dive-bombed me, swooping out of the broken windowpanes like a squadron on a mission.

Great. Bats, mosquitos, ticks, *and* Nazis.

That's when I tripped over a rusted piece of equipment, landed flat on my face in the mud, and added "lockjaw" to the list. I got to my feet, and then I realized there were *two* water towers and I had no idea which one held the ghost of Helmut the sniper.

A shot rang out. I heard the cha-ka-ching of the bolt and guessed Helmut had a Mauser K98k, one of the deadliest guns of the war. Ghost or no ghost, I ducked and ran for cover. Another shot, and son of a bitch if the dirt didn't kick up close to me. Fucking ghost sniper was shooting fucking ghost bullets.

I didn't intend to find out whether or not those shots would kill me. I dodged into the stand of trees between the water towers and weighed my options. The clouds parted again, and I could make out some cattle far down the field, apparently oblivious to the spectral sniper. Then I looked from one water tower to another and spotted my quarry.

"Gotcha," I murmured, watching the silvery shape of a man in an outdated uniform scan for his next shot, with his rifle sighted and ready.

Except, I didn't have him, not yet. I knew where Helmut was, but I had fully expected him to come down from his perch and hunt me like a man. Fortunately, I'd come prepared. I shrugged out of my backpack and pulled out my paintball grenade launcher pistol. I grabbed a paintball shell I had repurposed, pre-filled with salted holy water and an iron BB inside, and let fly.

The first shell hit the tower just over Helmut's head, and I heard cursing in German as the water splashed the rusted catwalk where the sniper had just been. His ghost winked out, only to reappear at a better vantage point to take a shot at me, and I threw myself out of the way as a bullet cracked against the tree trunk behind me.

I popped up, got off another shot, and this time, the shell went right through Helmut's chest before it hit the tank behind it and splashed all over everything. The yowl of pain might have been from the salt, iron, or holy water, or a little of all of them. Damn, this was even more fun than firing holy water balloons with my hunting slingshot.

Helmut showed up again, a few feet to the right along the walkway by the tank, and I nailed him again with another paintball shell. His shot nearly parted my hair, forcing me to scramble to change positions before I discovered whether his bullets were "real" enough to do damage. I had the feeling we could shoot at each other all night and still be at a draw come morning.

According to what Chiara and I had found in the records, the Feds took Helmut Zinzer's body away and disposed of it, so salting and burning his bones wasn't an option. But I had Eugene's button, and a half-assed plan, and that was as good as any of my jobs ever got.

First, to distract Helmut. I had made a run over the Ohio line earlier in the day and came back with a trunk full of fireworks I couldn't buy locally. I pulled out a string of firecrackers, tied it to a stone so it would fly when I threw it, then lit them and tossed them so they hit to the right of the water tower.

They went off like a series of loud *pops*, and in the distance, the cows *mooed* their annoyance.

Then I pulled out a big cylindrical container of salt that I had duct taped onto an M80, lit the fuse, and lobbed it under the water tower where Helmut's ghost was still firing at my dummy shooter.

The M80 exploded, tearing the canister to bits and spraying salt in a wide radius that effectively trapped Helmut on the tower. I used my grenade launcher pistol to send another holy water paintball shell through Helmut, momentarily dispelling him and buying myself enough time to run headlong for the safest place—directly under the water tower. Helmut couldn't come down to ground level because of the salt, and he couldn't see me from the catwalk. The water tower tank and its catwalk might be steel, but the rusted support structure was iron, which ghosts hate.

I pulled out the old button and clutched it in my palm. Ghostly footsteps paced above me, and the cows sounded downright pissed. I had to hurry because the firecrackers had been loud and I didn't want to explain myself to either a local cop or a security guard.

I put the old button in a tin can that I'd brought for that purpose, filled the can with kindling, gave a squirt of lighter fluid, and dropped the button into the flames, followed by a generous handful of salt and iron shavings.

Overhead, I heard a man's shriek followed by what I guess was some creative cursing—everything sounds worse in German. All the research Chiara and I found said that burning a personal possession in the place where a troubled spirit manifested with plenty of salt, iron, and holy water should do the trick if the bones were not available. I hoped that was right because I'd sure as hell had enough of the KOW to last a lifetime.

Once the fire burned out, I dusted off my hands and stared up at the catwalk overhead. The clouds slid free of the moon, but I did not see any trace of Helmut's ghostly silhouette. Cautiously, I edged out from under the water tower, ready to dive back to shelter if a shot rang out, but nothing happened, and I sighed in relief.

The galloping hoof beats echoed in the quiet night, and I looked up to see a wild-eyed, full-grown, big as fuck *bull* coming right at me like a hellhound with horns.

I grabbed my backpack and ran. I'd faced down wendigo and werewolves, vengeful ghosts and possessed raccoons, but right now, I was reenacting the Running of the Bulls in Bumfuck, Pennsylvania, in the middle of the night, and my money, if I were a betting man, was on the bull.

I lit a cherry bomb and threw it behind me, barely slowing my pace. It exploded, and the bull made a noise between a snort and a whinny that told me it intended to have Wojcik-kabob for dinner.

The fence loomed up ahead of me, and now that I looked at the cut I had used to enter, I wondered whether or not the bull could tear right through after me. I'm thirty-five, so I've slowed down a bit since my teenage years, but tonight, my legs ran like I was seventeen again. I threw myself at the fence like a two-strikes junkie caught with a pocket full of dime bags and scrambled up the metal links before my manly ass could get deflowered on the point of that bull's pointy horns. As I flipped over the barbed wire at the top and shredded my jacket, I thought about how easy they make this look in the movies.

Just before I could let go, the bull hit the fence full speed, catapulting me free. I might have pissed myself, just a little. Or maybe I landed in a puddle. Either way, I came down hard and landed with an inglorious *splat.*

The bull stared at me with pure malice in its beady black eyes, huffing and snorting on the other side of a chain link fence that looked as delicate as lace to me right then. It backed up a few steps, and when I saw how the fence support posts had tilted after its last charge, I had visions of it chasing me all the way back to Adamsville.

Screw that. I reached for my grenade launcher, grabbed another paint-ball shell, and took my shot. The shell hit the chain link fence and exploded all over the bull, spraying holy salt water in its eyes and pinging it on the nose with the iron BB. I didn't wait; I ran for all I was worth, legs pumping, chest heaving, and I didn't stop until I collapsed next to my big, black Silverado pick-up, Elvira. I damn near threw up on my boots, and I sat on the running boards until I could breathe without gasping, then I hauled my ass into the driver's seat and spun out on the gravel, before that bull could follow.

2

———

Snow covered everything, thick and cold. The trees hung heavy with it like something on a Christmas card, and the woods were quiet except for the creaking of branches beneath the extra weight.

Inside the cabin, a roaring fire chased away the chill. My father and my Uncle Christoph still sat at the table in the kitchen, finishing their coffee and laughing about something. So many in-jokes between them and they'd rarely explain, just share a knowing grin and a guilty chuckle.

"Don't encourage them." My cousin Greg came down the ladder from the loft buttoning up his flannel shirt. He looked at our fathers behaving like teenagers and shook his head with an affectionate smile. "You know they'll get worse tonight, after we tap that keg."

"You mean, my keg." Sean, my younger brother, looked up from where he sat in one of the worn chairs near the fireplace. "Since I'm gonna be the one who gets the buck with the biggest rack."

"What's the rule again? No drinking before the hunt?" I needled him. The keg was a long-standing Wojcik tradition. We all went up to Grandad's cabin on the first day of deer season. The hunter who shot the buck with the most points had the honor or being the first to tap the keg. The first round of drinks went in order of points, and whoever either didn't get a buck or got the smallest rack had to serve.

21

"You got lucky last year," Sean replied, competition keen in his eyes. *"Pay-backs, Mark. Paybacks."*

Just before sundown, the dying started. I'd heard all kind of wild animals out in those woods: bears, mountain lions, wild dogs, bald eagles. I'd never heard that noise before, a shriek like a cat in a blender, and before we even had a chance to look around, the creature was on us.

Dad and Sean shot first, but the bullets didn't even make a dent, ammo that could drop a two-hundred-pound buck, and I know they didn't miss. I took my shot, just as Uncle Christoph and Greg fired, and the bullets just seemed to bounce off the thing's hide.

It stalked us, as if it wanted us to get a good look. Coarse, dark, matted hair covered its body, and its head looked like an elk's skull without the skin, but with razor-sharp teeth and at least a twelve-point rack of antlers that didn't look like anything I'd ever seen in a fish and game magazine. I learned later to call it a wendigo.

We kept on shooting, and it just kept coming. The creature stood on two legs, but its long arms made me think it could drop to all fours and outrun us. It lurched forward and caught Uncle Christoph across the throat with the long claws on its huge paw, and he went down, burbling blood.

"Chris!" Dad yelled, but the beast swiped once across his chest, opening him up to the ribs from throat to belly, spraying blood across the white snow. Sean shot the thing point blank, but it never slowed down, and it grabbed him with one hand while its teeth sank into his throat and Sean went still.

"You son of a bitch!" I shouted, dropping my rifle and pulling my utility knife. Greg did the same, and we tackled the creature. We each weighed about two-twenty, and we jumped that beast at a full run, but it took our weight like it was nothing. Up close, the stench made my eyes water. Greg and I stabbed with our knives, but its hide was so tough we couldn't cut deep enough to wound it.

The creature fixed its blood-red eyes on me and ripped me away from its body with one hand, throwing me across the clearing before it swung its claws and took Greg's head right off.

My knife was useless, my gun was empty, and I was the last one left. I scooted backward like a crab and felt something hard press against my back. I still had my flare gun, and as the creature loomed over me, I pulled the trigger.

The flare hit square in its chest, and the matted hair ignited. The wendigo screamed, in pain this time instead of dominance, and the flames engulfed it. It backed up, beating at its burning pelt, back arched, howling, and the woods filled with the smell of burning flesh and hair. It kept on screaming, and I collapsed back into the snow, too battered to move, and too heartsick to want to.

I sat up in my bed, gasping for air, the wendigo's shrieks ringing in my ears, and the smell of stinking smoke in my nose. I swallowed hard and guessed I'd been screaming in my sleep. Again.

I ran a shaking hand back through my hair and wiped away cold sweat. Ten fucking years, and when I closed my eyes, it was just like yesterday. The alarm clock read three a.m. I sighed and got up, stumbling to the kitchen to pour myself a drink. I wouldn't get any more sleep tonight.

On the way, I saw the picture of the five of us on the mantle. Dad, Uncle Christoph, Greg, me, and Sean, all with our arms slung over each other's shoulders in front of the fireplace at the cabin, holding our hunting rifles, big cheesy grins on our faces. We'd taken that photo the morning of the hunt, and it hurt every time I saw it, but I couldn't bear to put it away. I needed a reminder of how badly I'd failed.

If bullets didn't hurt it, I should have known knives wouldn't either. I forgot all about the flare gun, until it was too late. I lived, but that screw-up cost me everything.

I made myself turn away from the photo. The cuts on my shoulder where the wendigo slashed me burned, and I chalked it up to imagination. Then again, with supernatural creatures, maybe it did leave some of its taint behind. If so, it wasn't merciful enough to finish the job it started.

I made a pot of coffee and sat down at the kitchen table until it brewed. It had been a while since I'd dreamed of the wendigo, and I wondered if the Nazi ghost stirred up old memories. I fired up my laptop while I waited on the coffee and started looking for new cases.

By seven a.m., I'd started on my second pot of coffee and made notes about several promising leads. All that research hadn't completely pushed the dream from my thoughts, but denial is one of my specialties, and I'd managing to get this far into the day without spiking my coffee, which I took as a win.

I leaned back in my chair and closed my eyes, which felt like I'd poured sand in them. Damn, but I needed some time off. And I was going to take it, too. I had a whole week of vacation written onto my calendar in red ink. I'd lined up someone to cover for me at the garage, made sure my fishing license was current, and made a list of everything I'd need. Spend a few days by myself fishing and watching movies on my laptop and tramping around the woods, and then my poker gang were going to come up on the weekend. Nice, simple, relaxing.

My phone rang, and I grabbed it without looking at the number. "Mark! Did I wake you?" Father Leonardo "Leo" Minnelli sounded far too chipper.

"No, I was up," I managed, running a hand over my face and realizing I needed to shave. "Look, Father, if this is about what I owe you for the poker game—"

Father Leo chuckled. "You do owe me—or, I should say, you owe the Poor Box—but you can pay me on Friday before we start the next game."

Nothing is normal about my life; why should my poker buddies be any different? My regular group includes Chiara and Blair, Dave Ellison from Ellison Towing, Tom Minnelli and his brother Leo—the priest. Father Leo's winnings go to the parish poor fund. He said he learned to play in seminary, and I guessed all that unrequited libido had to go somewhere, because he's probably the best player at the table, and we're all pretty damn good.

"You called me about poker at this hour?"

"No, I called because I need your help. Can you meet me at the diner? I'll buy breakfast."

Considering that I'd been up for hours and only had coffee and a day-old donut, he had me at "hello." "I'll be there in fifteen," I said.

"I'll be there in twenty," he replied. "Get us a table and a pot of coffee, and I'll join you." He paused. "Take a spot in the back, where we can talk."

I closed down my laptop, set my notes aside, and shambled to the bathroom for a quick shower and a shave. I planned to go straight from the diner into the garage, so I dressed for the shop. Pete Kennedy, my shop manager, would open, so if I came in by nine, I wouldn't miss much. And I figured having breakfast with a priest came with a side of automatic atonement.

The Original Best Lakeview Diner was a local institution. It sat on stilts at the very edge of Conneaut Lake, with a great view and even better food. Pictures of local celebrities dining in the booths hung on the walls, as well as framed restaurant reviews spanning sixty years and vintage ads and placemats from the diner's long and storied past.

"Hiya, Mark!" Sandy called from the register when I walked in.

"Hey, Sandy," I replied. "I'm meeting the padre—got a table for us someplace quiet?"

Sandy rolled her eyes. "If you're going to start confessing your sins, Mark Wojcik, you'll be here all night."

"Good thing you're open 24/7," I quipped. Sandy went to high school with me; we go way back. Sandy had short dark hair, blue eyes full of mischief, and a figure that, even now, could stop traffic. She and her husband Vince run the diner now that her parents are retired. That's the thing about living in the town where you grew up. Everyone knows where the bodies are buried. In my case, that's not even a joke. I tried to leave after the whole wendigo thing, but that didn't work out, and now I'm back.

"Take the back table on the right," Sandy said with a jerk of her head. "I'll get Amy to bring out coffee and menus, although I don't imagine either of you will look at them."

I wended my way toward the rear of the diner, nodding to people or stopping to say hello as I went. The early morning crowd here doesn't change much, and most of us have been coming in for years. I was just lucky that the table in the back didn't "belong" to a regular.

I'd barely poured myself a cup of coffee before Father Leo slid into the booth across from me. "You look like crap, Mark."

"Need to work on that bedside manner, Father." I didn't take offense. He was right.

Father Leo is Tom's older brother, which makes him about four years my senior, or just shy of forty. He looks younger, with wavy dark hair and big brown eyes. I bet he was the guy who got carded until he turned thirty. Leo was ahead of me in school, and the way Tom tells it, he left a string of disappointed girls in his wake when he announced his intention for the priesthood. He's funny and easy to talk to and has the boy-next-door looks women seem to fall for. I wondered if that made for better attendance at Mass.

On the other hand, I had my dad's straw-blond hair and light green eyes, with the high cheekbones and broad forehead that mom always said was like having a "map of Poland" on my face. Whatever that meant. The solid, stocky build came from mom's side of the family and made it clear I came from a long line of farmers and laborers with big hands and strong shoulders. I'm not the guy any of the girls notice first in a room, but back in the day, it'd been enough to get Lara's attention. For a while.

Father Leo cleared his throat, and I hurriedly sipped my coffee. "Sorry, didn't sleep well last night," I muttered.

He gave me a look that said he gathered far too much from my appearance. I often wondered if he didn't have a little psychic mojo that he kept on the down-low. Might not fly well with the Vatican boys, but I imagine that a little enhanced intuition could be a help in his line of work. Right now, it made me squirm. "Bad dreams?" he asked quietly.

I blew out a long breath. "Yeah. Same old, same old." When I looked up, I pasted on a smile neither of us believed. "You have a case?"

Father Leo took the shift for what it was and nodded. "You know Sam Roundtree?"

I nodded. "Yeah. Worked on his sports car a while back. Owns some kind of plastic molding company out near Conneautville, right?" If it was the same guy I was thinking of, he had made a fortune with a couple of lucky government contracts and became a hometown hero by keeping the factory here, where good manufacturing jobs were scarce.

"He's involved in a lot of local philanthropy projects, including some where I'm on the board," Father Leo went on. "Like the Tracks to Backpacks initiative."

I'd heard of that. Back in the day, when this area had more tool and die shops than anywhere else in the country, a lot of railroads came through to take those machine parts to Pittsburgh, Detroit, Chicago, and elsewhere. Then the big factories closed or moved overseas, and most of the trains stopped coming here. Now, Tracks to Backpacks raised money to buy up those old abandoned railway easements and turn them into hiking and biking trails. I'd tried out a few and loved the way they wound through countryside that usually went unseen. "I don't understand—"

"They've been getting a new trail ready, and there've been problems," Father Leo said. "Your kind of trouble."

Oh. I guess I shouldn't have been surprised. The railroad was a dangerous place to work, and back in the day, safety standards were often non-existent or poorly enforced. I'd heard tell of men who got burned in boiler accidents, who fell beneath the cars, or were crushed between them. Of hobos who got hit on the tracks, tumbled out of freight cars, or motorists broadsided by engines at lonely crossroads. "Restless spirit?"

Father Leo nodded. "There've been delays throughout the construction, and while the official paperwork says otherwise, the workers claimed to see strange things, hear weird noises. The phenomena got stronger as the work went on and started to knock over tools, spill materials, and hide things. Then the workers said the manifestation got hostile, shoving people, tripping them, and throwing objects. They reported cold spots, a shadow that didn't have a source, or a gray man walking along the tracks who suddenly disappeared. They began to feel unwelcome, like something was trying to make them leave. It got serious when a flying hammer hit a man in the head and everyone swears there was no one around to throw it."

I frowned. "You sure it isn't just pranks gone awry, or maybe the work crew has been drinking?"

Father Leo sighed. "Believe me, the organization tried every other explanation before they took any of the stories seriously. But the workers have walked off the job, and the organization is supposed to do a big ribbon-cutting in a few weeks, where they expect to take in enough donations to fund the second half of the project. But if the first portion isn't finished—"

I got the picture. Bad press, donors might bail, and a worthy project would founder—and with it, jobs that the trails would bring to the area. "And I guess they can't do a big fancy event with a renegade ghost on the loose."

Father Leo leaned forward. "There are men who would, regardless, just to avoid embarrassment. Even if people got hurt. Sam isn't like that. He's done a lot for this area, and he's got his own money donated to this. He wants it to succeed, but he doesn't want anyone harmed." He tugged at his collar. "I said I knew someone who could look into it, discreetly."

"Do you know where on the trail the ghost shows up the most?" I was already guessing at probable causes, and narrowing down the location would help a lot.

Father Leo slid a paper with coordinates over to me. "From what the witnesses say, that's the epicenter. Sightings and phenomena occur within a couple hundred feet of that spot, but it's apparently Ground Zero."

I sighed and slipped the paper into my pocket. Father Leo was a good guy, and a friend. "I've got a couple of appointments this morning at the garage, but I'll go out this afternoon and see what I can see," I said.

"Thank you," Father Leo replied. "I don't want anyone to get hurt—and the trails project is important."

We finished our meals talking about the Steelers' defensive line, the Pirates' batting averages, and whether the Penguins would be in the running for the Stanley Cup again. Everybody around here pretty much bleeds black and gold for the Pittsburgh teams, or blue and white for Penn State if we're talking about college ball. People might pretend they don't care, but when the playoffs come, fans get rabid. Someone told me once "there are no atheists in football" meaning everyone really has a team they believe in. I'm pretty sure the phrase is "no atheists in foxholes," but it seemed accurate either way.

The morning passed quickly, and for a while, I quit thinking of railroad ghosts and wendigos as I got my hands dirty working on engine blocks and carburetors. Some people knit; others do yoga. For me, the best therapy in the world happens with a wrench and some motor oil. My garage works on all kinds of cars, but I love working on old classics and helping out when one of our local car nuts is rebuilding one from the frame up. Before hunting took up so much of my time, I used to help out at the local rallies and race tracks. Spending a nice summer night with a cold beer and the smell of gasoline and burning rubber at the track is my kind of heaven.

I worked through lunch, stopping just long enough to wolf down sandwiches Pete fetched from the place up the street. The afternoon got slow, and by three, I left Pete to close down, since I wanted to go check out the trail well before dark.

Both ends of the new trail were completed, but the ghostly disturbances had shut down finishing the middle. I had checked out the project's website. It would be a wonderful local destination when it was finished, with a smooth asphalt trail perfect for walkers, joggers, cyclists, even wheelchairs and strollers. Local bird watchers, garden groups, and the botany department from the college had all signed on to tag plant specimens, erect informational signs, and create guide books. Groups from the Rotary to the Daughters of the American Revolution pledged money for benches along the route. Schools were already planning nature hikes.

And one grumpy ghost threatened to shut it down.

I parked at the midpoint construction entrance and pulled my gear bag out of the back. It was full of all the stuff I usually needed for a job like this: salt, holy water, lighter fluid, iron, and wooden stakes, a crow bar, an EMF scanner, a shotgun with a choice of shells filled with iron pellets or rock salt, and a shovel, just in case.

No one Father Leo had talked to seemed to know who the ghost was, which made it tough. Some of the witnesses thought they saw a man wearing a Fedora, which only narrowed it down to the first half of the twentieth century. My internet search turned up bupkis on railroad fatalities linked to this stretch of rail. I was going in blind, and I hated it. That kind of thing gets hunters killed.

The middle stretch of trail had a gravel base, but no asphalt yet, and one end was just scraped dirt. The long, straight vista made it easy to envision tracks, with freight trains rumbling down the rails at full speed, blowing their whistles when they passed neighboring farms. Trees and marshland stretched on both sides, with nary a farm in sight, making this spot either peaceful or lonely, depending on your perspective. Tools and machinery looked like they had been abandoned by a crew that went to lunch and never came back, which wasn't far from the truth.

Wind rustled the treetops, but otherwise, the woods were eerily quiet. I should have heard birds chirping and seen squirrels and chipmunks scurrying, maybe even spotted a rabbit or a deer. Other than the leaves rustling in the wind, nothing moved. I felt the hair prickle at the back of my neck.

The EMF reader stayed quiet, its needle still in the green range. I poured a salt circle and set down my gear bag inside, although I doubted any ghost could get past the sigils and protective runes painted and stitched on the bag itself. I had my Glock tucked in my belt at my back like always, but I grabbed a crowbar, a flask of holy water, and some salt. Then I went for a stroll.

The longer I stayed, the more I could feel someone watching me, though there was no one in sight. The EMF reader gave a few hiccups, but no piercing squeals. I walked along the dirt portion, but saw no sign of recently dug up bones. Still, the unnatural silence gave me the heebie-jeebies, and I had the feeling something was biding its time.

Out of the corner of my eye, I caught a glimpse of movement, but when I turned, nothing stirred. If this son of a bitch ghost felt like playing games, I refused to play nice. I made another slow pass, and this time, the

EMF reader twitched more, jumping up from yellow to red and swinging back and forth wildly.

"Come out, come out, wherever you are," I murmured, holding an iron crowbar in one hand and the EMF reader in the other. A loud squawk from the meter froze me mid-step, and I turned in a slow circle, on guard. Nothing stirred, but the meter definitely made more noise when I pointed it off to the right, so I stepped down from the rough asphalt and walked straight toward the edge of the woods.

The trees had surely been kept farther back from the rails when trains were running, so I figured that the old tree line was probably at least two or three feet in from the current edge of the woods. My foot hit something solid, and I kicked at the covering of leaves, unearthing a steel spike sunk into the ground and rising out of the dirt by a few inches once the debris was cleared.

The meter went wild. I could see something etched in the domed head of the spike, and bent for a closer look. Someone had carved a symbol in the steel, but I didn't recognize it, so I dropped the meter in my pocket and took a picture with my phone. I lost my balance as I got to my feet, and when I put out a hand to steady myself, my palm brushed the spike.

An unseen force picked me up and threw me beyond the trees on the grass at the side of the trail. I landed hard on my back, knocking the breath out of me and knocking the crowbar out of my hand. Before I could get up, a man loomed over me. He wore a long top coat, a scarf, and a Fedora. The style of his coat and the suit jacket lapels I could see under it made me think Swing era. With a beak of a nose, dark, accusing eyes, and thin, tightly pressed lips, he clearly didn't look happy to see me.

And, oh yeah, he was gray and translucent.

Fedora Man reached for me, and I rolled to one side, scrabbling for the crowbar. I came up swinging, and one pass of cold iron sent the ghost packing, but I knew he wouldn't be gone for long. I grabbed my gear bag and ran. Behind me, a man's laughter filled the air, cold and mocking.

When I reached Elvira, I threw one arm over the side of the bed and heaved for breath, never taking my eyes off the spot where I came out of the woods. Nothing followed me, and I wondered if I had imagined the laughter.

No, I didn't. But what the fuck? What was a guy dressed like he was going out for dinner, back in the Glenn Miller era, doing next to railroad tracks that at the time they were in use would have been in the middle of woods and cornfields? Who the hell put that funky stake in the ground, and what was that symbol? Did Fedora Man throw me on my ass, or was it bad juju from that stake?

Too many questions and not enough answers. I stowed my bag and got in, happy to peel out of the gravel access road and get away. One thing I did know: whatever haunted the rail line had serious mojo. Someone was going to have to put it down, and I knew in my bones that "someone" would be me.

F riday evening at Crystal Dreams was Cards Against Humanity (CAH) night for the eighteen to twenty-one crowd. Everyone was welcome, but those in the know knew the group was also a safe space for the LGBT teens in the area—a popular haven. Chiara put out cookies and punch, and then hung out in the main section of the store until game night ended at nine.

I strolled in just as the game must have gotten underway because I could hear loud laughter and picked out some definitely NSFW phrases.

"Didn't think I'd see you here on a Friday night," Chiara said, moving out from behind the counter. A few latecomers browsed the bookshelves, but Conneaut Lake's nightlife tends more toward the local watering holes like my favorite, The Drunk Monk. "Thought you'd be holed up with a six-pack of IC and that *Ice Road Truckers* marathon on the History Channel."

"Bite me."

"So not appropriate." She rolled her eyes and grinned. We had a long history of inappropriate humor, and the games of CAH she and Blair and I played were spectacularly politically incorrect.

I pulled out my phone. "Got a picture to show you."

She grinned. "Please tell me you aren't going to show dick pics to a lesbian."

It was my turn to roll my eyes. "I don't show dick pics to anyone," I replied, looking heavenward for patience. "Although the ghost who threw me across the tracks acted like a dick and may, in fact, have been named Dick. I didn't know."

That got her attention. "Really? What've you got?"

I showed her the symbol carved on the stake, expecting a wisecrack. Instead, she paled and her eyes went wide. "Sweet Mother of God," she murmured. "That the mark of a *stregone*."

It took a lot to get a reaction like that out of Chiara. "That sounds like a type of pasta. Enlighten me."

Chiara blinked and regained her composure. "Not pasta, not pastry. It's a male witch from Italy. And in these parts, likely to be more Mob than Mephistopheles."

"No shit. The Mob has warlocks?"

Chiara cringed. "Normally, I'd school you that 'warlock' is a pejorative, outdated term, and 'witch' is preferred regardless of gender, but in this case, you're dead on. *Stregone* are bad news, especially the Sicilian ones." She shook her head. "When you step in it, Mark, you go hip-deep, don't you?"

"It's a talent," I replied.

Chiara looked up as her last two customers left without buying anything. She flipped the sign on the door to "closed," and then went behind the counter, pulled out a bottle of whiskey, and grabbed two Styrofoam coffee cups before leading me over to a couple of arm chairs out of sight of the front windows. Once she had poured us both a couple of fingers-worth of booze, she took a slug and sat back.

"From the stories Nonna Lucia tells, I thought the last real *stregone* vamoosed from around here after the Yablonski murders down in Clarksville back in the late sixties made national news."

I wasn't born then, but like everyone in these parts, I knew the stories. Nearby Meadville was conveniently located between Youngstown, Ohio; Buffalo, New York; and Pittsburgh, all allegedly hotbeds of Mob activity back in the day. People whispered that *capos* and lieutenants came out here to "cool off" when things got too hot to handle, either from law enforcement or rival Mafiosi families. That *Sopranos* shit doesn't just happen in Chicago and New York; my dad had stories to tell about dirty deeds done dirt cheap in these parts that could curl your hair.

Mob connections around here were something everybody "knew," but no one could or would prove. Most of the time, the local Don kept his boys on a tight leash. Civilians didn't get hurt, paybacks happened in private, and everyone was happy to look the other way.

"So, of course, this is all just hearsay," Chiara prefaced her tale, as everyone did around here. Just so I wouldn't ever think she might have heard it from a member of her extended family who might have been in the "family business."

"Of course."

She gave me a death stare, and I stuck out my tongue at her. The evening was just getting started.

"So the Families around here did well for themselves during Prohibition and 'reinvested' in a lot of legitimate businesses."

In other words, *laundered the cash*. But whatever.

"The forties, fifties, and early sixties were the heyday," Chiara continued, sounding almost nostalgic. "The steel mills and factories in Pittsburgh, Youngstown, and Buffalo were booming, Union dues were big money, and the cops were the best money could buy. Life was good. But now and then, someone got out of line—"

"And needed whacked."

"Yeah."

"So, these *stregone*, why use a witch when you could just call in a hit man?"

Chiara took another swig of whiskey. "No one would, unless the hit man didn't come back."

I stared at her. "Damn."

She quirked her head to one side. "Hey, the Family plays rough. Hit men and witches don't come cheap, so whoever needed to be taken care of had to be a big fuckin' deal. A made man, probably high up, maybe with connections to the big-city Families."

"So who do you think Fedora Man was? The witch or the target?"

Chiara grimaced. "No idea. But…why don't you come to dinner with Blair and me tomorrow night? I'll sit next to Nonno Carlo and make sure his wine glass never goes empty. By dessert, he'll be telling you all the 'good old days' stories you can handle, and I might be able to nudge him in the right direction."

I weighed my options. Dinner with Chiara's big, rowdy Italian family —some of whom were still willfully in denial about her "good friend" Blair—was sure to be full of loud family drama. On the other hand, the Morettis owned not only a bakery but the best damn Italian restaurant in the tri-state, and I knew from the leftovers Chiara brought back that the food at home was even better.

"All right, you made me an offer—"

"Oh, don't even go there."

I held up my hands in surrender. "I promise to be on my best behavior."

She snorted. "That's rich, coming from you."

"Do I get a cheat sheet ahead of time to know which ones believe you're actually married, and which ones might be trying to foist you off on me?" Chiara's very conservative Italian Roman Catholic family had not completely accepted her relationship with Blair. On the other hand, Father Leo not only sent a wedding present, he included a bottle of bubbly. Go figure.

Chiara let out a string of curses in Italian, and while I'm not fluent, what I could pick up made my eyebrows rise. "Listen up. Nonna and Nonno figure if they don't see it, it's not real. Mama says novenas for me every day. Daddy's surprisingly cool with everything, says he doesn't care as long as we're happy. Ditto for Tony, Eddie, Carmen, and Frank," she added, naming off her brothers, all except one. "Michael—he's the family hard-ass. Missed his calling with the Inquisition." She wrinkled her nose. "God, I love him, but he's such a prick. I told him that he was probably gay himself since he was so hung up on it." She chuckled. "Thought he was gonna pop an aneurysm."

Chiara knocked back her drink. "But at the end of the day, he loves me as much as the rest of the family."

I got the feeling that was a loaded statement, and I wasn't touching it with a ten-foot pole.

"What time?" I asked.

"Dinner's always at six," she replied.

"No, I meant, what time should I start drinking before I get there."

She punched me in the shoulder. "That depends. Do you intend to drive home? Cuz calling a cab in Conneaut Lake is gonna be a long wait."

3

I knew the Moretti brothers by reputation long before I met Chiara. One of the first stories I heard when I moved back after my brief absence was how five local boys took out a werewolf that tried to kill their sister and her date. I'd been surprised because I thought that a secret government agency had taken out all the local werewolves back in the 1890s, but I guess one or two always slip the net.

Anyhow, the Moretti brothers handled the werewolf with extreme prejudice, and that's what got Chiara into the business of hunter support. Yeah, the cops tried to tell them that it was really just a hippie high on meth, but all the therapy in the world wasn't going to change their minds about what they saw that night.

Apparently, Chiara had told her brothers about me because I got a warm welcome when I walked into the house. The Moretti's home was one of the two-and-a-half-story WWII vintage houses that are every-where in these parts, solidly comfortable and middle class, like their owners. I knew Chiara's mother was devout, and from the Virgin Mary statue in the front yard to the religious bric-a-brac, that hadn't changed.

I'd had a bit of a chip on my shoulder before I arrived, knowing that not all of Chiara's family accepted her marriage to Blair. But I was blown away by how friendly everyone was and how easily I got sucked into the jokes and chit-chat. If Blair felt uneasy, she hid it well, lounging on one of the well-worn couches with an arm slung over Chiara's shoulder talking hunting gossip with Eddie and Carmen.

Nonna Lucia sat straight-backed and imperious in a rocking chair, with her dark gray hair swept up in a bun and a shawl around her shoulders. She might have been pushing eighty, but I had the feeling she could still put me in my place like a whelp. Nonno Carlo sat near her on the couch, holding a dark-haired toddler who was sucking her thumb.

Chiara's mother, Maria Louise, bustled around the kitchen and dining room like a general in an apron, directing her daughters-in-law who snapped to do her bidding. She was a wiry woman with classic good looks that did not wilt even in the heat of a hot kitchen, and I respected the work she and her husband had put into maintaining their foodie empire. Jimmy Moretti, Chiara's father, stood in the doorway to the dining room holding a beer, deep in conversation with Michael.

I drifted over to the side, observing and feeling a little unsure. Part of me felt a sudden, unexpected stab of loneliness. Lara and I didn't have kids, and her family lived out in the Eastern side of the state, but before that damned hunting trip, Sunday dinner at my dad's place wasn't that much different. My mom died when Sean and I were in middle school, but Dad had been a cook in the Army, and he enjoyed a good pot roast as much as anyone. Sure, he could only cook about three different meals and grill steaks or burgers, but no one ever left the table hungry, and his homemade pierogies were to die for.

"Drink up." Tony pushed a beer into my hand and grinned. "I see Chiara finally dragged you into our dramatic family dinners. God, I hope you took Valium before you left home."

I took a long pull from the cold beer and sighed in contentment. "I think I'll manage."

"Chiara tells us all about you, you know," Tony confided. "Mama and Papa don't know about her side business, but we do. Baby Girl doesn't keep secrets from us."

I chuckled at the thought that anyone got away with using that nickname for Chiara. Then again, her brothers—even Michael, the prick—seemed pretty hard-core about family. I could respect that. "I imagine she makes it sound much more interesting. Mostly, I end up covered in mud and bleeding like a stuck pig."

Tony looked like he would have said more, but Jimmy had moved to the end of the dining room table and clinked his spoon against his wine glass. "Dinner's served!"

Everyone scurried to their places as if the food might run out, although from the bounty of dishes on the table, I couldn't imagine how we could ever make a dent. It looked amazing and smelled like heaven.

Chiara winked at me and settled in next to Nonno, with Blair to her right. I sat next to Blair. The meal was raucous, filled with good-natured jibes, family gossip, updates on a dizzying number of cousins whom I didn't even try to keep track of, and some heated banter about the Steelers' draft picks. I took it all in, shoveling food into my mouth like a starving man, because damn, this was fine fodder. Lucia and Maria Louise noticed and gave me an approving nod. If food was love, then I felt utterly embraced.

Of course, dessert was as magnificent as the meal. The Moretti bakery hadn't built its reputation for nothing. Plate after plate of fresh-baked treats came from the kitchen, and I might have had to unbutton my pants, but I enthusiastically indulged.

Throughout it all, Chiara and Blair chatted up Nonno Carlo, asking about his weekly dominos game at the Italian Club, and how his friends at the Masons or the Elk Club fared, all the while keeping him plied with wine. Lucia looked on with an eagle eye, not missing a trick, but permitting it to happen. I didn't want to even start to plumb the complexities of Moretti family politics, but despite her family's ambivalence about her partner, it was clear that Chiara was the cherished baby girl of the family, a super-power she wielded with clear knowledge of its devastating effects.

Once we were all sated with food and wine, Chiara leaned forward, resting her chin on her interlaced fingers. "Nonno," she said, "I heard a rumor that back in the day, a *stregone* whacked a guy out on the old Erie-Lackawanna line. Is it true?"

Carlo leaned back and slid her a sidelong look. "Well now, that's going back a while," he said, folding his gnarled hands in front of him. "Not that I know anything I didn't hear secondhand, you understand—"

"Of course," Chiara replied with a completely straight face.

"But depending on how far back you go, the only guy I ever heard might have pissed people off enough to call in a *stregone* would be Vinnie Three-Nuts."

I nearly choked on my wine. "Did you say—"

Carlo nodded. "Yeah. Might have been because his last name was Trinotti. Or maybe he was just especially blessed. Who knows? But he was brash and loud, always calling attention to himself, getting into trouble." His voice dropped to a confidential tone. "The bosses, they don't like that, you know."

I'd seen *The Godfather* and *Goodfellas*. I knew that wasn't good.

"So what happened?" Chiara asked with rapt attention. No stretch of the imagination to guess she had Nonno wrapped around her little finger. Also no stretch to think perhaps the story might not be as hearsay as the old man wanted us to think.

"Vinnie kept getting in fights, roughing people up who didn't need it, and the Don finally got tired of it. Because Vinnie, he wouldn't listen to the warnings, and the Don didn't like to repeat himself," Carlo said. "But Vinnie was a hit man, so how do you hit a hit man?"

"With a witch?" I asked.

Carlo pointed thumb and forefinger at me like a gun, and for a second, those watery blue eyes had perfect clarity. I tried not to shudder. "Got it in one," he replied, and I wondered if he guessed that I had primed Chiara to ask.

"And then what happened?" Chiara prompted, and Carlo's attention returned to her. I felt like I'd gotten a reprieve.

"Well, it depends on who you hear tell the story," Carlo replied. "According to what I heard, and this was back around the time it happened, Vinnie went out to do a job on one of the trains that left outta Meadville. Back then, trains were comin' and goin' day and night, 'cause of the War, you know? Lotsa places up here made parts for the military or tools or nylon, so the yards were always full o' trains. So Vinnie goes to do the job, and he doesn't come back."

"They ever find his body?" Tony asked.

Carlo shrugged. "A few days later. The Don made sure he had a nice funeral, lotsa flowers, a nice gift to the Church in his name, and a 'bereavement gift' to his wife."

"So the guy who fixed his hit sent flowers to his funeral?" I sputtered.

Carlo looked at me like I was slow. "That's how business was done. People had class."

Chiara kicked me under the table, and I took a mouthful of wine. "What happened to the *stregone*?" she asked, once again diverting attention from my inappropriate question.

"Don't know. Don't want to know. Guys like that, you wanna stay as far away from as you can." He turned to address that last sentence to me. I gulped more wine.

"Why do you ask, baby girl?" Carlo said after a long, uncomfortable silence.

"They're tearing up one of the old rail lines and making a walking trail. People got telling stories, and I heard bits and pieces. Figured you'd remember," Chiara replied, managing to look big-eyed and innocent.

Carlo didn't look like he believed her for one second, but he let it go. "I've always been a good Catholic," he said, lifting his chin. "But in my time, I've seen some things that they don't talk about in church. The *stregone*, they're real. Nothing to fool with. Some stories are better forgotten."

With that, Lucia and Maria Louise rose to get fresh coffee, and I tugged at my collar. The conversation drifted back to local gossip and sports, and before long, Chiara and Blair rose, which was my cue.

"Gotta get back home. Store opens early tomorrow," Blair said. Chiara gave a round of hugs and kisses to her family, some of whom embraced Blair as well, while others just nodded and kept their distance. Their loss, I figured. I shook hands with the men and complimented the women on the food.

Carlo held my hand a bit more firmly and longer than necessary. "You're the ghost hunter guy," he said in a voice pitched low for me alone.

"That's me."

"The *stregone* who killed Vinnie was Johnny Vasili. If he's still alive, Don Giordano will know. He'd be older than me. But still dangerous, you hear?"

I nodded.

"You didn't find none of this out from me," Carlo continued in a smoker's rough whisper. "But Vinnie was a friend. Batshit crazy, but he did me a good turn now and again. He didn't deserve what he got from that witch. Send him on, and tell him Carlo said 'hello.'"

"I'll do my best," I replied, hoping I sounded less freaked out than I felt. Carlo slapped me on the shoulder with a big paw that almost made me stagger.

"Good for you," he said, and then passed by me to go light a cigar on the back stoop.

4

___

W hat do you wear to meet with the local godfather?

Make that "alleged" godfather.

Simon Giordano ran JASG, Inc., the company named for family patriarchs Joseph, Anthony, and Saul Giordano, from an unassuming brick office building on the outskirts of Meadville. I'd seen his picture in the paper for ribbon-cuttings, charity donations, golf outings, and black tie dinners in what passed for local high society. From the photos, I figured he was in his mid-forties, so the Don who whacked Vinnie would have been his father or grandfather, not him. Still, I figured that if anyone knew more about Johnny Vasili, it would be Simon G.

Chiara, Blair, and I had talked the whole way back to their shop, where I had parked my car, and then we went into Crystal Dreams' back room, made some espresso, and talked some more. Chiara had found out enough about the strange sigil to know that it wasn't just used to kill Vinnie—it cursed him. She couldn't tell how or whether that had something to do with him being a restless—and vengeful—ghost, but it made the whole thing a lot more complicated than the average salt and burn.

By the time I finally headed back to my place, we had talked through the options and decided the best approach might be the simplest. Father Leo would get Sam Roundtree to ask Simon to see me, about "something vital to the project." Apparently, Tracks to Backpacks was one of Simon's community causes, and Sam was a golfing buddy. Small towns—everyone knows everyone.

So here I was, tugging on my too-tight tie feeling like a chump in a blazer and khakis, screwing up my courage to go ask the (alleged) head of the local *Cosa Nostra* how to find a witch-assassin his grandad might have hired.

Awkward.

The reception area had big windows on one side, lots of natural light. A receptionist looked up as I entered, and when I gave my name, she told me I had been expected and led me back a corridor past closed offices to a pair of double doors at the end of the hallway. She opened one of the doors and stood aside, my cue to enter.

"Come in, Mr. Wojcik."

To his credit, Simon pronounced my name right. I remembered what I'd read about him. Undergraduate degree from Gannon University up in Erie, MBA from Penn State. Came home to run the family business, worked his way up from small operations to bigger ones in the conglomerate of local companies that made up JASG, Inc.

If he was Mob, he was more John Gotti than Al Capone. Slim, tanned, with a haircut that probably cost more than my car payment and a suit that came from New York if not Rome, he could have walked into any big city corporation and fit right in.

"Please, sit down."

I sat. Simon seated himself behind a massive inlaid wooden desk. I wondered if it was bullet proof, and if he had a gun in the drawer. Even I knew better than to ask.

"Sam Roundtree asked me to see you, told me you were handling a problem that might put the trails project at risk."

I cleared my throat and tried to find my voice. "Yes, sir. There've been disruptions that might slow down or stop the rest of the construction, and Mr. Roundtree hired me to take care of it, because they fall into my... area of expertise."

"Which is?"

Usually, I have no trouble running my mouth. Ask anyone. Right now, I was spitless. "I get rid of supernatural problems." That sounded a little classier than "monster hunter," less sensational than "ghost hunter."

Simon stared at me in silence, tenting his fingers, considering. I only barely managed to keep from looking behind me, in case any large body-guards with bulging, ill-fitting jackets had come in to eliminate me.

"Your reputation precedes you, Mark. I can call you Mark, right?" He had the power, and we both knew it. On the other hand, I'd killed wendigo and werewolves, and if he had sources, he knew that was true. That made this the part of the interview where we vied for dominance, like two bucks in rut scraping their antlers on trees. So I squared my shoulders and held my head high. "That's fine."

"If you came to me, you have a very specific question in mind. Go ahead. Ask."

I kept my gaze level, not a challenge, but not backing down either. "Mr. Roundtree hired me because a vengeful ghost was tearing up his worksite and threatening his crew. It's escalated since they reached the midpoint of the trail—the old Erie Lackawanna line. People have gotten hurt. I went out to lay the ghost to rest and found this." I unfolded my drawing of the sigil and leaned forward to slide it across the desk.

Simon hid a shudder, but I saw it in his eyes. He recognized the symbol, and feared it. "I think the ghost is Vinnie Trinotti, and I think something Johnny Vasili did cursed him to stay here and now his ghost is insane—and dangerous."

"If you've done your homework, you know Vinnie Trinotti was prob-ably always insane," Simon said quietly. "He wasn't a nice man."

I held up both hands in a gesture of appeasement. "I don't care what happened or why—but I do care about laying him to rest so no one gets hurt and the project can be finished. To do that, I need to know if Johnny Vasili is still alive, and if so, where to find him." My voice had gained conviction as I spoke. I'd fought off a fucking Nazi sniper and bagged a Japanese fish-eating monster. I wasn't going to piss myself over a mobster in a suit—alleged or not.

"You've got balls, Mark. I respect that." He leaned back in his chair and drummed his fingers on the arm. "If you find Mr. Vasili, what do you intend to do? He's an old man in a nursing home. Staking him through the heart would be...messy." His lips smiled, but the humor never reached his eyes.

"I'm going to offer him his freedom," I replied.

Simon's eyebrows went up at that. "His freedom?"

I nodded. "For a curse to be so potent after seventy-five years means that the witch who worked it sealed the deal with more than a measly spell. I'm betting that Johnny didn't realize that somehow, he got himself tangled up in the magic, and it's holding Vinnie here—but it also won't let Johnny go, either."

That seemed to mean something to Simon because his eyes narrowed like I'd spoken an unexpected truth. "And you could break that?"

"I'll do my damnedest," I said, and hoped that didn't turn out to be literal. "But I need to know what Johnny did and how he did it. Poking around blind on something like this is likely to get a whole lot of people killed—including me."

I watched Simon debate with himself and come to a decision. "I have no knowledge about any crime against Mr. Trinotti, nor do I have reason to believe Mr. Vasili is anything other than a respectable senior member of our community," he said in the kind of voice that carries well at big event speeches. "But such rumors may weigh heavily on a man's mind, and I would not like to see Mr. Vasili be uncomfortable in the time remaining to him."

"Meaning?"

"Mr. Vasili is in the Serenity Acres nursing home," Simon said. "I'm told that his health is fragile, but his mind is still sharp. He's in his late nineties—quite old for a man in his line of work—and he may be willing to hear you out if it eases his mind."

"Thank you."

"Don't be too quick with your thanks," Simon warned. "Mr. Vasili is in full command of his faculties—*all* of them," he added, "though his body is failing him. If he is not amenable to your offer, I cannot be responsible for the consequences."

Okay, then. I'd just been put on notice by an alleged Mafia Don that an elderly witch/hit man might not be ready to let go of a three-quarter-century-long vendetta, and I might find myself turned into a toad. No pressure.

"I understand. How would you prefer I contact Mr. Vasili?"

"Nikki will accompany you," Simon said, and I looked to my right to see an extremely large man with no neck and an unmistakable bulge under one arm. "He'll bring a letter of introduction from me. If Mr. Vasili declines to see you, there's nothing I can do."

"I appreciate your time and your help."

Simon rose, and I knew when I was being dismissed. "When should I go?"

"I'll make the call now. They'll be ready when you arrive."

I knew the place. Peaceful, quiet. Expensive. Either being a hit man had great retirement benefits, or Vasili's bills were being paid by a grateful friend.

"Thank you."

"You're welcome." Simon turned away. "And Mr. Wojcik? I hope we don't have to meet again."

Nikki No Neck drove, and I followed in Elvira because no way in hell was I riding with a Mob enforcer. Serenity Acres was a pretty campus of modern, one-story buildings and lovely gardens that looked more like a resort hotel than a waiting room for the afterlife. Nikki led the way in, and the greeting he got from the ladies at the front desk made it clear he had been here before.

I hung back and observed, also noticing possible exit routes, just in case. Chiara had made me a curse-deflecting amulet and given me other protection charms, which I had hidden in various pockets. Still, as I followed Nikki down the corridor, I tried and failed to sense any bad mojo. Mostly, I just noticed how the place smelled like piss and baby powder.

Nikki's shoulders practically brushed the walls on both sides. He stopped in front of a door and held up his hand for me to wait outside. A man of few words, that Nikki. He went inside and closed the door in my face. After a few minutes, he opened it again and stepped aside for me to enter.

I expected a hospital bed and oxygen equipment. Instead, I found a comfortable studio hotel room and in a chair beside the window, looking out onto the garden, and a very old man with a fancy crystal glass in his hand, probably full of top-shelf whiskey.

"So you're the monster hunter," Johnny Vasili said without even turning to look. "Come to hunt me?"

I stopped a few feet away from where he sat and clasped my hands in front of me. "No sir. I'm here to talk about your release."

Vasili gave a wheezy chuckle and drew in his breath with a rasp that suggested a pack-a-day habit. "What would you know about that?"

"I know that neither Vinnie Trinotti nor you can move on. Something went wrong that night seventy-five years ago, and now you're both trapped here. All that's left of Vinnie is an insane, murderous ghost. And all that's left of you is right here."

"I don't want your pity, boy."

"You don't have it," I snapped. "I thought we might make a deal."

Johnny looked like a corpse. His skin had a bluish-gray cast to it I'd only seen in the morgue, and it hung on his bones, stretched so tight that his face looked like a Death's Head. He must have been a big man, long ago. Physically powerful, in addition to his magic. Now, he resembled a concentration camp inmate, hunched and emaciated. Then he turned to look at me, and his hard gray eyes bored into me, merciless and shrewd.

"Come closer, boy. Tell me about this deal."

I had the sudden urge to make damn sure we weren't at a crossroads because if Johnny Vasili wasn't a demon, then God didn't make little green apples.

"Come with me back to the railroad line, where you did the spell on Vinnie. I need your help to break the magic and send you both on."

Vasili gave a wheezy, bitter laugh. "On," he repeated. "And where, exactly, do you think someone like me will go?"

"No idea," I replied, although I had my own suspicions.

"Liar." Vasili turned to look at me, and while the body was that of a frail old man, the eyes were flat and cold, an unrepentant killer.

"Mr. Vasili—"

"That's why I let it go this long, you know," he said, speaking to me, but not really. "It worried me, where I'd go. What might happen..." He made a dismissive gesture with his hand. "Oh, the priests will tell you about confession, but they'll also talk about mortal sins. I used to care. Now, I'm just tired. Ready to go."

"Then help me," I said quietly. "End it—for both of you."

Vasili caught me again in his killer's gaze, and I felt like he could see down to my bones, pondering the best way to snuff me out. "If you'd have come to me ten years ago, I'd have killed you on the spot," he said matter-of-factly. "Just for bothering me."

I remained silent, refusing to take the bait.

"I'm fucking done," Vasili said in a whisky rasp. "Tired of it. Ready to take my chances. Never meant to get stuck here over that fucker." He took a sip of his whiskey and swore quietly in Italian. I didn't need to know the language to pick up on the gist of it.

"Then you'll come with me?"

"Don't give yourself credit," Vasili muttered. "I'd been thinking about doing it for a while now." He pushed up from his chair. "I need to gather a few things. Come back in an hour. Bring a priest."

When I picked Father Leo up from St. Gemma Galgani church, he had a tight-lipped expression that usually meant he was ready for a fight. I hoped it wasn't with me.

"Everything okay?" I asked as he got into Elvira and closed the door.

"It will be as long as we're back in time for the Ladies' Auxiliary meeting at eight," he said. "Mrs. Guthrie just called with an extensive list of potential projects she'd like to discuss."

"We could always pick up some beer on the way home," I offered helpfully.

Father Leo leaned back and closed his eyes. "I think whiskey's a better bet," he sighed. "She's very ambitious."

Father Joe's parish might have fifty families on the books and about ten old ladies who come for morning Mass. Everyone wonders why the church hasn't been shuttered, but the truth is Father Leo holds down this area's outpost for the Occulatum, a secret Vatican organization that battles supernatural and demonic activity. I'm his designated first responder, and while there are some other hunters in the area, Father Leo and I make a pretty good team.

"Still on for the poker weekend?" I asked, hoping to cheer him up.

"Assuming we survive our stroll with the hit man and the *stregone*?"

"Unless you have it on good authority that there's beer and poker on the other side of the Pearly Gates."

"Dear Lord, I hope so. I hate harps, and I can't carry a tune in a bucket." He sat up and rubbed his eyes, accepting the cold energy drink I fished out of the cooler on the floor of the back seat. "Yes, I'm looking forward to it. Given what's on my calendar for the diocese and the parish committees, that poker weekend is pretty much giving me a reason to live."

I laughed. "If you can weasel out of your responsibilities, you're welcome to come up early and fish."

"Don't be surprised if I do," he replied. "Fishing sounds like a little slice of heaven. They don't tell us about this kind of thing when we sign up, you know. We think it will be blessing babies and Last Rites and weddings and funerals. And it turns out to be mostly committee meetings and administrative paperwork."

I almost made a smart remark about celibacy, but given how long it had been since I'd gotten lucky, I figured I should keep my trap shut. "Did they say much about witches and ghosts?"

"Nope. Which just further proves my point." Father Leo might gripe about the paperwork and his more difficult parishioners, but he's one of the few men of the cloth I actually thought was suited to the calling. If he didn't believe what he peddled, there's no way in hell he'd have stared down some of the stuff we've handled. Not to mention the fact that my Latin sucks, so he comes in handy for exorcisms.

I glanced at him as I drove back to pick up Johnny Vasili. "So, do you have a plan in mind for this?"

He gave me a look. "Do you?"

"I've got salt, holy water, and cold iron in my bag. None of those worked the last time, but I'll bring them again, just in case. Otherwise, I'm hoping Vasili holds up his end of the bargain."

I half expected Vasili to have changed his mind, but he and Nikki were waiting when I got to Serenity Acres. Father Leo got in the back, and Nikki No Neck helped Vasili into the front seat, then climbed in behind him. We drove in tense silence to the trail parking lot. Nikki offered a meaty arm to help Vasili down, but after that, the elderly hit man refused any assistance.

"Things sure look different," Vasili said as we reached the construction site. "It was dark and real smoky the night I capped Vinnie, good night for that kind of work, you know?" he reminisced. "He was expecting to pick up a drop from one of the trains. That's how things were done back then. Thought he was going to retrieve a suitcase full of money, payment for a job. Only, surprise! There wasn't any suitcase, but there *was* a job."

Even now, after more than seventy years, knowing he was about to meet his Maker, Vasili didn't sound sorry at all. It made my flesh crawl.

"What was the spell supposed to do?" I couldn't help asking.

Vasili looked down the long straight path where the trains used to run, and I could tell he was seeing a different era. "It was a binding spell. Vinnie was a city guy. Hated the woods. Didn't like to get mud on the cuffs of his trousers. So the spell was gonna keep him out here, in the middle of nowhere, 'till Kingdom Come. See, that's where I went wrong," he said, shaking his head. "I shoulda kept it simple. Couldn't stand the guy when he was alive, finally have a chance to get rid of him, and what happens? I'm stuck with his fucking ghost for seventy-five fucking years."

"No time like the present to fix that," I said, biting back anything I might have thought about poetic justice.

Vasili fixed me with his cold, killer stare. "Don't rush me, monster boy. It's my funeral." He looked to Father Leo. "You gonna say Last Rites for me? Not that I think it'll make any difference on where I go, but hey, it's the thought that counts, right?"

Father Leo managed a pained half-smile. "If you want me to, I'll say them. Do you wish to make a Confession?"

Vasili gave a laugh that sounded like sandpaper, rough with hard liquor and cheap cigars. "How long you want to be out here, Father? I might be damn near immortal, but I don't think you've got the time to hear all I'd have to say."

Father Leo's expression remained carefully neutral. "You asked for a priest to attend. I want to make the…transition…for Vinnie and for you as easy as possible."

"Ain't you a Boy Scout," Vasili said, and patted Father Leo on the cheek before he turned away, walking down the rail line.

"Should be right in here," Vasili said. He paused as if he were listening for something only he could hear, and perhaps he was, because after all this time, he moved unerringly to the spike, and lifted his head.

"I know you're out there, you son of a bitch. Show yourself!"

The woods around us stilled, and the temperature plummeted. I'd already pulled out my iron crowbar from the gear bag, and I had my holy water flask and a canister of salt in my pockets, plus the charms Chiara had given me and a sawed-off with rock salt shells. Father Leo had a rosary in one hand, and he had the other in the pocket of his suit coat, which I'd be willing to bet money contained a relic.

A cold wind gusted through the trees, whipping up the leaves around the stakes.

"Still a prick after all these years, Vinnie? You want out or not? 'Cause if I came here and you don't show, I'll wait another seventy years. And so will you."

The air shimmered several feet behind the stake, and the figure of a man solidified from mist. I got a better look at him than I did when he'd rushed me the last time. Vinnie Three-Nuts looked like he stepped out of Hollywood casting for a Mob enforcer, with a pinched, rat-like face and dark, furtive eyes.

"About time you showed up, you muther—"

Father Leo cleared his throat. Vinnie glared, but adjusted.

"You clap-tongued son of a whore," he finished.

"Same old Vinnie," Johnny said. "Didn't learn a thing in all these years, did you?"

"Oh, I learned plenty," Vinnie said with a very unpleasant smile, right before the wind picked up, pelting us with sticks and rocks from the forest floor. A strong gust forced us back a step. The frigid air numbed my nose and cheeks like a blizzard, and frost began to form on the ground around us, although the autumn day had been mild.

"Is that all you've got?" Johnny raised a hand and muttered. I couldn't catch what he said, but Father Leo began murmuring a litany I recognized as protection against dark energies. The gale died, the frost vanished, and a flash of green light seared from Johnny's palm and arced to hit Vinnie in the chest. The ghost staggered, and his face twisted in pain.

"Watch and learn, old man," Vinnie replied, moving in a blur right at Johnny, arms stretching out impossibly long, with grasping, clawed hands. Nikki stepped between them. The spectral hands went right through the big man's chest, and Nikki grunted in pain, paling as a death rattle sounded from his throat. Johnny jumped backward, suspiciously agile for a man his age, and Vinnie stepped right through Nikki's dying body, intent on finishing the fight.

Johnny shouted words of power, and a lattice of green fire sprang up from nowhere around Vinnie, momentarily trapping the spirit. Vinnie's form disintegrated, materializing outside the cage and hurling a ball of gray energy at the old witch. "Eat shit and die, old man."

Johnny sidestepped the energy, which careened past him, forcing Father Leo and me to throw ourselves out of the way, and the gray power blasted a tree behind me. Vinnie threw another mojo-ball that went zinging through the trees, and Johnny threw up a translucent shield that sent it careening into the woods where it took out two saplings.

"Do it!" Father Leo yelled. "Send him on!"

Vinnie's ghost hurled a thick limb like a javelin. It barely missed me and bounced off Johnny's wardings.

"I warned you, Johnny!" Father Leo said, and his posture straightened. "John Vasili, we find that you are legally convicted both by the evidence of credible witnesses and by your own repeated confession, that you have fallen, and fallen again, into the heresies which you abjured," Father Leo recited, and Vasili recognized it at the same time the words clicked in my memory as being from the *Malleus Malificarum*, the "Hammer of Witches" used by the witch-finders in the Middle Ages.

Vinnie threw a rock the size of a grapefruit. Johnny's attention was on Father Leo, until the rock struck his left shoulder and he cried out in pain.

"End this!" Father Leo commanded. "Or I will. I'll send you on, John Vasili, condemned by the old words, and Vinnie will remain trapped here for all time."

Vinnie was so obsessed with Johnny he didn't see me raise the sawed-off. I pulled the trigger and hit him right in the chest with the rock salt. The ghostly image blew apart. "I'll cover you," I snapped, glaring at Johnny. "Just quit screwing around."

For a moment, I thought I'd pushed my luck too far. Johnny's gaze was murderous. He dropped to his knees next to Nikki's body. "Watch my back," he growled, as he rolled the dead man over and patted down his pockets without the slightest indication of concern or remorse. Johnny found what he was looking for and rose, scanning the woods for Vinnie.

"Keep him off me. He'll be back."

I kept the sawed-off in one hand and the iron crow bar in the other. Father Leo stepped closer, fixing Johnny with a no-nonsense glare. Or maybe, no-nunsense, since a ruler across the knuckles or a slap up the side of the head seemed to be in Johnny's future.

"Keep your collar on, padre. I'm working." Johnny took a swig from a flask in his pocket, and then pulled out a cigar and lit up. "For old time's sake," he said with a crooked smile.

Vinnie started to pull himself together, and I fired again, scattering his atoms. "Hurry it up," I griped, loading more shells.

Johnny replaced the flask and lighter and held up a glass bottle filled with a foul-looking concoction. "Lightning in a bottle," he said, and began to walk counter-clockwise around the prong, dripping out a thin line of the awful-smelling liquid. When he closed the circle, he stood inside it next to the stake, and as the last drops hit the ground, a phosphorescent green light flared, like the glow of rotting plants.

Vinnie re-formed. I shot him in the balls. He vanished. Father Leo cleared his throat menacingly. Johnny swore in Italian and pulled out a ritual knife with a bone handle and markings scribed down its curved blade. I don't have a magical bone in my body, and I knew I was watching dark power at work. Father Leo crossed himself, but continued to bear witness.

Vinnie popped up to my left. I wheeled, and the rock salt blasted through his head, taking off his skull above the eyebrows and his damned Fedora before he winked out.

Johnny rolled up his sleeve, his arthritic hands moving with surprising dexterity. He drew the knife down his forearm and dripped a steady trickle of blood onto the stake. A sickly red glow answered, and Johnny continued his chant without a hitch, though the deep cut must have hurt.

Vinnie materialized between me and Father Leo. "Duck!" I yelled, and fired. The blast went through Vinnie's neck and chin, and sailed over Father Leo's back as he dropped to all fours.

"Are you done yet?" I yelled at Johnny.

"Almost," he replied around the cigar he chewed as much as puffed. "One more element." He fumbled with the belt on his trousers.

"Oh, hell no," I growled, but by then, Johnny had dropped trou to reveal baggy striped cotton boxers so thin I could make out a mole on his butt cheek. Some things can't be unseen. He pulled out his wrinkled willie and held it limply over the stake.

"Seriously?" I said. "You have to piss on him?"

"Don't interrupt. I gotta concentrate." A few drops fell, and Johnny shook his limp lizard. "Come on," he muttered. A yellow light around the stake stuttered and vanished.

Vinnie popped up behind me. I felt the shift in temperature, dropped and rolled before he could get his grubby hands into my chest, and came up shooting.

"Watch it!" Father Leo yelled as the rock salt flew.

"Aren't you done yet?" I shouted at Johnny.

"Hey, I got prostate problems! Have some respect!"

"Mark!" Father Leo warned.

Vinnie, the crafty little fucker, materialized in the branches overhead. I filled his belly full of salt as he fell toward me and smirked when he winked out just as I swung my iron crowbar at his head for good measure.

I chanced a look at Johnny and couldn't tell whether he was coaxing out more pee or having a last round of "alone time" before the great hereafter. Father Leo opened his mouth for what I was sure would be the next section of the *Malleus Malificarum*, just as Vinnie popped up from the ground—just from the waist up—wrapped his arms around my legs, and pulled. I went down hard, but as I fell, I sighted the shotgun between my knees and over my nuts and got Vinnie right in the face.

Piss-yellow light flared. The woods smelled of old blood, fresh pee, and cigar smoke. I got to my knees in time to see Vinnie forcibly pulled into the circle, and this time, his form looked as solid as Johnny's.

"Well fuck me sideways," Johnny muttered, looking beyond us and Vinnie to something distant across the Veil, something the living could not see. "That's a helluva thing to spring on a guy."

The light flashed, and they were gone.

Father Leo put the rosary back in his pocket and withdrew a thin purple stole, which he placed around his shoulders as he began to say the Last Rites. I got to my feet and tried to pretend I wasn't shaking. Still wary, I advanced slowly on the place where Johnny and Vinnie had disappeared, cocking the shotgun just in case.

The stake looked like it had been struck by lightning, and nothing remained of the rounded dome where the binding sigil had been except a melted, twisted lump of metal. I caught a lingering whiff of cigar smoke and something that smelled like a backed-up toilet. I racked another shell and shot the ground, just because.

Father Leo finished his litany and removed the stole. "Feel better, shooting an innocent lump of dirt?" he asked with a bemused look.

"Maybe. Let's go," I said, turning away.

"You're just going to leave him here?" Father Leo asked, with a nod toward Nikki No-Neck's body, which I'd totally forgotten about.

"Yeah, unless you feel like digging a shallow grave," I replied. "I'm not calling Simon Giordano to tell him one of his goons is missing. He's a smart guy. He'll figure it out." I took another look at the twisted stake and shuddered. "You want to make an anonymous call to the cops, I won't stop you. Right now, I want a shower, a chance to bleach my eyeballs, and a bottle of whiskey. Not necessarily in that order."

5

For a guy who misses a lot of work, I don't take much vacation. Good thing I own the shop, or my ass would be fired. I've been lucky enough to hire good people who can take over when my other job—the one that pays squat—calls on the Batphone with another monster to gank.

But I'd taken out a Japanese fish-eating monster, a Nazi sniper ghost, a vengeful hitman's ghost, and an Italian witch, and I was ready for a real vacation. And maybe some alone time.

I'd started gathering what I planned to take with me in the extra bedroom. My cabin isn't big, but it's got plenty of room for me and Demon, my Doberman Pinscher. Demon watched me bring one load after another into the bedroom and stack supplies on the floor and on the bed. He padded out of the room and returned dragging his favorite blanket, then sat down and stared at me as if daring me not to pack his stuff as well.

I scratched him behind the ears, which made my terrifying watchdog flip over onto his back, bare his belly, and kick his legs into the air. I didn't name him, the pound did, and if ever there was a case of false advertising, Demon was it. Worse, he made happy little grunts as I rubbed his belly and rolled his eyes back in a total state of doggy bliss.

"You want to go fishing, too?" I asked, and Demon looked at me, tongue lolling, like he knew what I said. "Good. You can clean up when we spill the snacks playing poker." Demon's tail wagged harder. Maybe he did understand.

My fishing rods and tackle box were in the garage. In here, I stacked cases of beer, a couple of bottles of whiskey, and some twelve-packs of pop. I had a fridge full of sandwich meat and cheeses. Stuffed into a big cardboard box were bags of chips and bottles of salsa, loaves of bread, boxes of breakfast cereal, and the seasonings necessary to grill any fish I caught. I had a bag of potatoes, and I'd stop on my way to the camp for sundries like milk. And yeah, my gear bag with my guns, salt, iron, and silver lay with the rest, because I don't go anywhere without it. I'd packed my clothes, grabbed the back issues of several car magazines I hadn't had time to read, and added my laptop and a stack of DVDs. Life looked good.

Then my phone rang.

I thought about not answering, but it was Chiara. She heard me swearing when I picked up.

"Stop that," she said. "I've got a job for you."

"Nope," I replied. "There may be a job, but it's for some guy who isn't going on vacation."

"C'mon, Mark. You've got a couple of days before you leave, and this'll be a cakewalk."

"The last 'cakewalk' job put me in the hospital in traction."

"Steve Louden asked us to do him a favor."

"Shit. And that SOB knows I can't say no."

"Not can't. Won't."

I cussed some more under my breath, and she waited for me to get it out of my system. "All right. What's the job?"

Steve had done me more than one solid over the years. He's a cop up near Kane, and he's the one who hauled my sorry ass out of the woods when the wendigo happened. He's kept me out of trouble with the police and managed to lose evidence that might have attracted too much attention from Homeland Security. I owed him.

"He needs you to take out a were-squonk."

I blinked. "A what?"

"A were-squonk."

"Is that even a thing?" I rolled my eyes. "What next? Zombie cow tipping? Vampire snipe hunting?"

I'd heard of a squonk before. If a Shar-pei and a wild boar had a love child, it would look like a squonk. They're a cryptid that's supposed to be native to the wilds of PA, and said to be so reclusive that nobody's gotten a good photograph. Not only that, but when they die, their body turns to water.

"If the damn squonk liquefies when it dies, how the hell did something make it a were?"

"Maybe that werewolf out near Bradford last year got hold of one and drank it," Chiara said.

Shit. That was crazy enough it might be true. If the "werewolf" was really a shapeshifter, it could happen. Shifter bites squonk, dying squonk turns to water, shifter drinks squonk, and the squonk takes over.

"Is it hurting anyone? I mean, do we care if there's a were-squonk running around if it isn't eating people?"

"Apparently, they're very anxious, and chewing on wooden things calms them down," Chiara replied.

"Good. It's up in the middle of a honking big forest. Plenty of wood to chew, enough for it and the woodchucks, muskrats, and beavers."

"Squonks are bigger. The size of a Mastiff, or a small brown bear," she said patiently. She knows me, and she's good at wearing me down with details. "So far, it's eaten two cabins, a couple of boat docks, and part of a covered bridge."

"Damn. That's a lot of anxiety. Have we considered therapy? Or Prozac?"

"Usually squonks don't do that much damage, but since it turned were, it's hungrier." Chiara huffed out a sigh. "Look, Mark. I'm not trying to screw up your vacation. Just go see what's going on. Maybe you won't find anything. Maybe you go shoot the were-squonk and be done with it. Steve's paying for your meals, gas, and hotel room."

That made me reconsider. I could be up in that neck of the woods in a couple of hours if I left now. Have a nice dinner, stay in a hotel that might have a minibar, go tramp around the woods tomorrow—never a waste of time—look for a were-squonk, and come back with a full day before my real vacation.

"Okay," I said. "But if I can't find the damn were-squonk before Friday, I'm leaving, and I'll try again after I get back from vacation."

"I have faith in you, oh mighty squonk hunter," Chiara said with a laugh. "I'll let Steve know, and he'll email you the details. And Demon can come over for a slumber party with Blair and me until you get back."

When I hung up, I knew I'd been outmaneuvered, but then again, I expected that when I saw Chiara's caller ID. I went to pack an overnight bag and grab my go bag of weapons. I cast a longing look at the pile of stuff ready for my vacation, and promised myself that this time, neither squonks, nor sasquatches were screwing up my fishing/poker trip. Then I threw my stuff into Elvira and took off for the Big Woods.

S teve's email gave me directions to a hotel where he made arrangements for my room, a diner nearby, and the coordinates to start my squonk hunt in the morning. All in all, not too shabby, and I got on the road early enough to enjoy the drive. I took the back roads and reminded myself that this is one of the goddamned prettiest states in the US of A. The big cities, Pittsburgh and Philadelphia, are on either end, and the lower two-thirds of the state has plenty of small towns and mid-sized cities, but the top third, where Interstate 80 runs through and above that to the New York State line, that's mostly forest.

Sure, there are hiking trails and park rangers, but you get out into the backwoods, and it's wilderness. Grew up going hunting out in these parts. Deer—buck and doe—even went muzzle-loader hunting for bear once. It's rugged enough that there hadn't been any stories about that wendigo all those years ago because no one had run into it. Until we did.

I shook off the memories, although they never went too far away. I'd read all about "survivor guilt," and I guess I have some PTSD to go with my ADD, but after everything's said and done, the truth is that losing people you love changes you, and you're never the same afterward. Maybe you keep going, and maybe you don't. But you're different. I tell myself that I hunt monsters so no one else has to lose people they love like I did.

I'm a fucking liar.

I hunt monsters because every time I take one of those fuckers down, it's that mofo wendigo all over again. It's me shooting my nightmares. Shooting my guilt.

Whatever it takes to get you through the night.

I focused on the scenery and forced myself to think about dinner. They say that eating and fucking are what we're most hard-wired to do, but since Lara left me, well—there's eating. I hoped the diner lived up to my expectations. I figured Steve wouldn't let me down.

Then I saw that my "hotel" was an effing bed and breakfast, and I thought about turning the car around, but it was too damn late, and I was tired, hungry, and needed a beer. "Bell's Retreat" the sign said over the front door as I climbed up the steps of a well-cared for white Victorian house that looked big enough for a family of twenty. The broad front porch had wicker chairs and gliders, and the smell of sugar cookies hit me when I walked into the foyer. Antiques were everywhere, from the uncomfortable looking velvet couch in the living room to the vintage sideboard in the dining room. I just bet the pattern on the curtains in my room was going to look like my grandma's floral tea cups.

"Mr. Wojcik. Welcome." A pleasant woman with short dark hair and a nice smile came out from the kitchen, drying her hands on a towel. "I'm Sara McConnell, and I'm the owner of Bell's Retreat." She wore tan slacks, a black blouse, and a red cardigan sweater, and something about her reminded me of an innkeeper's wife in an old sitcom I watched on TV Land.

"Your last name isn't Bell?"

Her smile pinched a bit. "My in-laws started the bed and breakfast. They passed on, and my husband and I ran it until he died a few years ago. Now it's just me."

That's what I get for asking questions, I thought uncomfortably. "Steve Louden said he booked a room for me?"

She nodded, and fortunately, she didn't seem to be upset by me sticking my boot in my mouth. "Booked and paid for. One night, with an option for two if you want it. Right this way."

I felt underdressed for my own damn hotel, but I clomped down the hallway to a room with a huge four-poster bed and more fancy furniture than I'd seen anywhere, except at my pretentious aunt's house. I figured I'd need to shower before I went to bed so I didn't get the sheets dirty.

"Do you like your room?" she asked, and I realized she was waiting for an answer.

I cleared my throat. "I'm more used to Days Inn or Motel 6, so this is really something else," I said in all honesty. It might be frillier than I'd prefer, but even I could figure out that the mattress wouldn't be thin and lumpy and the sheets wouldn't feel like sandpaper and smell like an ashtray. I could ignore frills for a hot shower, thick towels, and—glory be —a mini-bar. "I'm much obliged," I added, and Sara beamed.

"Just let me know if you need anything," she said. "Anything at all." She held eye contact just a few seconds too long, and I felt a flush rise up my neck.

I cleared my throat. "Sure," I lied. "I'll be out early tomorrow. Want to do some birdwatching before the trails get busy."

"Breakfast begins at six," she said, sounding far too happy about anything that early. "Fresh coffee, muffins, fruit, and a different hot item each day. I like to spice things up," she added with a wink.

Lord have mercy, was she actually flirting with me? I was never the fastest to pick up on those kinds of cues. Lara always told me she had to chase me until I caught her, but still—

Yep. That's exactly what she was doing. Suddenly, facing a were-squonk no longer seemed so frightening, and I wished I could get a start on the hunt tonight.

"Thanks for everything," I said, and even I thought the words sounded rushed. "I've taken up too much of your time. I just want to get cleaned up. Long drive." I practically gave her the bum's rush out the door, then closed it behind her and sank back against it, embarrassed at how hard my heart was beating. Some heroic hunter. Or maybe, I just didn't like being prey.

I'm not ashamed to say that I snuck down the stairs and crept out the door, sprinting for Elvira. By the time I reached Patterson's Diner, my heart rate was back to normal, and I had convinced myself that the whole thing with Sara was all in my imagination. Fortunately, Steve's advice on food turned out to be a better fit than his choice of hotel, and I tucked in to a very good homemade meatloaf with a fresh-baked apple dumpling and ice cream for dessert. The waitress looked old enough to be my mother, so I didn't have to even pretend-flirt to get good service, and I left a big tip, figuring being on her feet all day probably put bunions on her bunions.

I crept in like a teenager after curfew, but Sara caught me on the steps. Maybe she was listening for me. I hadn't seen anyone else although other cars filled the parking lot. "Have a good dinner?" she asked.

I told myself I was being stupid and turned to face her. "Probably the best meatloaf ever."

"I don't know about that," she said with a chuckle. "I make an awesome meatloaf and a cream pie that's out of this world."

My mouth went dry, and I wasn't sure I could breathe. "Sounds great," I managed. I might have squeaked a little. "Gotta go." With that, I ran up the stairs like the hounds of hell were on my heels.

I closed the door behind me and ran a hand over my face. God, I hadn't been this pathetic since middle school. Maybe I had just been alone too long, and my subconscious was acting out. That had to be it. No way was the nice lady innkeeper putting moves on me. I felt panicked and embarrassed all at once.

It wasn't that I didn't think about starting over, finding someone new. I did, especially after several shots of Jack on a too-quiet Friday night, but even after eight years, I hadn't quite put the breakup with Lara behind me. I wasn't still in love with her. That was dead and buried. She'd gone off and gotten a new husband and a new life. I was stuck. But then again, that's why she dumped me.

I opened the minibar and poured a couple of the little airline bottles into a glass. The night was young enough one drink would be out of my system by the time I meant to leave in the morning, and the shadows pressed too closely tonight to be completely sober. This hunt wouldn't take me near where I'd torched the wendigo, but the woods up here all looked alike, and I figured that was triggering me.

Lara had come to the conclusion that I should have been faster at getting over seeing my father, uncle, brother, and cousin ripped to shreds. I had been a mess, and while she tried being patient, that was never her strong suit. So, when I didn't straighten up and get with the program on schedule, she moved on.

And here I was, back in the woods, hunting another monster. I knocked back a swallow of whiskey and pulled out my laptop to review what little I could find about squonks. I glanced at the four-poster. The bed looked comfy, but it might be a long while before I'd be able to sleep.

The next morning, I slipped out early. As promised, Sara had hot coffee and homemade muffins ready, and some bacon on a warming tray for good measure. I was almost sad I didn't see her to say hello as I headed to check out the area.

I stopped in a parking lot next to one of the trailheads and got out, walking over to where a large sign under its own little roof showed a map of the paths and pavilions. Police tape cordoned off a badly-chewed group of picnic tables and a small storage cabin that was missing one wall. I climbed over the tape to get a better look. Then a police car pulled in, and guy in a sheriff's uniform climbed out, walking like he'd just ridden in on his horse.

"You got a permit for that, son?"

I tried not to cringe at the glare the local sheriff gave me when he spotted my shoulder holster under my jacket. Thank fuck I'd left the sawed-off in the truck.

"It's in my glove compartment," I replied, and tried to remember whether I'd thought to put my gear under the false back seat in the expanded cab before I'd stopped to take a look at the damage being blamed on the were-squonk.

"Let's walk back there so I can take a look," the cop said in a fake-friendly tone that wasn't fooling anyone. He had me by twenty years and thirty pounds, a pot-bellied, smug bastard who liked to throw his weight around, physically and metaphorically. Bald, sunburned, and sporting a pair of mirrored aviator sunglasses, he was the northern equivalent of every stereotypical pain-in-the-ass cop.

"Suit yourself," I said, and led the way.

"Why'd you say you were out here, on the wrong side of a protective barrier?"

"I didn't," I replied evenly, in a flat voice that stated the truth without looking for a fight. Still, the guy's attitude galled me, and I tried to remind myself that getting thrown in the county jail for mouthing off to an officer of the law was not going to get me to my vacation on time. "I'm an insurance adjuster. Came up to have a look at the damage."

"Been all kind of adjusters through here," he said. "You're late to the party." His name tag said he was "J. Kranmer," but I renamed him "Sheriff Sumbitch" just because.

I shrugged. "You know how it is. Things get kicked from one office to another, and then upstairs. We've heard everything on this one from hungry beavers to rabid termites," I replied, and then thought that might have gone better if I'd switched it around.

"Gotta admit, we've had some odd damage around here," Sumbitch replied, and the knot between my shoulders loosened, just a bit. If I could get him talking, get him to buy my fake insurance story, I might not leave here in cuffs.

"That's why I'm here," I said, forcing warmth into my tone that I didn't feel. "One cabin, that's a freak problem. But more than one, and then a dock, and that bridge—"

"Not to mention two garden sheds and a gazebo," Sheriff Sumbitch added.

"Damn."

I reached Elvira and felt a wave of relief when I saw absolutely nothing on the back seat. Thank God I put the bag away right. I turned slowly back to the sheriff, making sure my hands were always in sight. "My permit's in the glove compartment. You want to get it?"

He shook his head. "You get it. Just—go slow."

I had no desire to end up with a bullet in my back, so I did what he said and handed off my concealed carry permit. He eyed it and gave it back, quickly enough that I knew the whole thing had been about pecking order, not that he cared about the permit itself. Fucker.

"How long are you staying in the area?"

I shrugged. "Probably head out after dinner tonight," I said. "Haven't been in such a fine forest in quite a while—spend most of my time down in Pittsburgh, and there's hardly a tree in sight. Thought I'd check out the damage, take some photos for my report, and play a little hooky out on the trails," I added with what I hoped looked like a goofy nothing-danger-ous-here grin and a wink and a nod about wasting company time.

"Have fun," Sumbitch said in a flat, bored tone. "Don't go in the damaged buildings, and remember—nothing's in season, so I don't care what you see out there, unless it attacks you, don't shoot it."

"I wouldn't think of it," I said. Fake sincerity is something I practice every poker night. My track record of winnings says I'm pretty good.

I watched Sumbitch swagger back to his patrol car, as I lingered on the pretense of fishing out a bottle of water from my cooler and drinking it down. Once he was out of sight, I hiked back to the scene of the crime and wondered how one hungry were-squonk could possibly be anxious enough to chew through the whole eastern side of an entire log cabin. I did, however, decide to spend today checking out the trails and the rest of the damage and tackle hunting tomorrow. That meant taking Steve up on his offer of a second night's stay. I'd still get back in plenty of time for my vacation. And I might have the chance for coffee with Sara.

I grabbed a hot dog at a gas station for lunch and headed back to Patterson's Diner for supper. The diner had good old-fashioned home-made meals, and the fried chicken special with real mashed potatoes and green beans cooked with ham was a treat. Some days I needed comfort food. By the time I came back from the diner, I felt embarrassed. I was a divorced thirty-five-year-old guy; surely if I could snuff zombies and werewolves, I could handle a cup of coffee with the nice lady who ran the bed and breakfast. Nice single, widowed lady who was kind of cute in a preppy sort of way.

Just coffee. To be polite. Give me something to think about before my epic were-squonk hunt tomorrow.

I heard voices when I came into the front hallway. "I can show you to your room, Mr. Conroy," Sara was saying with the same friendly warmth she had put into my greeting. "I hope your sales presentation goes well. It would be lovely if you stayed with us the next time you're in town."

Sara nodded and smiled as she passed me, leading the way for Mr. Conroy, a tall blond in a blazer and dress slacks who had a jaw like a movie star and a build like a hometown football player. I'm over six-two and in good shape, but he looked to be about five years younger and had a couple of inches more height—and way less mileage.

I managed to slide from panic at the possibility of being pursued to a twinge of jealousy at being easily replaced, to crow-flavored chagrin at the unwarranted and somewhat vain conclusions I had jumped to. Sara hadn't been flirting; she was just the kind of person who treated everyone she met like an instant friend. Now that I realized she wasn't interested, I felt disappointed. It had been a long time since I'd looked forward to a cup of coffee with a pretty lady who wasn't Chiara or Blair, and that wasn't the same at all.

Still, coffee or hot chocolate sounded good, so I made my way back to the B&B's kitchen and found the single-serve pod brewer with a rack of clunky pottery mugs and plenty of fancy fixings. I chose a hot chocolate pod and pressed the button, then waited for it to finish.

"Did you enjoy your dinner?"

Sara's voice made me jump, since I hadn't heard her come up behind me. Whether or not she realized I'd been an asshole the last time we talked, I knew it, and I felt awkward. "Very much. I'd say it was like my mom used to make, but her cooking sucked." Not that I remembered it much, since she died when I was twelve, but it seemed like the right thing to say.

"That's why it's been in business so long," she laughed, leaning against the counter while I reached for my hot chocolate. I held the mug like a shield, but I wasn't sure which of us I was trying to protect.

"Steve said you were going to get rid of the thing that's been causing problems," Sara said, going straight for the heart of the matter without any warm-up. "Can you do it?"

Damn Steve for bringing a civilian into this. Then again, the damage the creature caused was plain enough. "I'm going to do my best," I replied, chancing a sip of the chocolate and finding that it was actually good.

"You know it's not a woodchuck," she said, giving me an uncompromising stare. "Or a beaver or termites, or some weird kind of wood rot, no matter what they say. I don't think it's natural, so I hope you came prepared."

I stared at Sara, and my mouth hung open as my brain tried to catch up with my ears. "What do you think it is?" I finally managed, realizing that I'd probably lost any chance to appear reasonably intelligent.

"No idea. But these are deep woods, Mr. Wojcik. Old forest. Lots of places people never go, even nowadays. I've lived in these parts all my life. Long enough to know strange things happen out there, and stranger things live in those woods. I hope you know what you're doing."

I nodded. "So do I."

She gave me an assessing look. I wondered how much Steve had told her about me, but I was afraid to ask. Instead, I took a long pull at the hot chocolate and wished it had a shot or two of whiskey in it.

"You're not the only hunter to come through here, you know."

My head snapped up, and she gave me a triumphant smirk. "I would have made you even if Steve hadn't told me. You've got the look."

That probably meant a big truck, a duffle with suspicious bulges, and an overall sense of being ridden hard and put away wet.

"If you get hurt, let me know. I was a nurse before I became an innkeeper," Sara said, which explained the no-nonsense attitude underneath her friendly exterior. "My first-aid kit is a little more extensive than usual."

"Thanks," I replied, finishing what remained in my cup. "If I do my job right, maybe I won't need it, but that's nice to know." I managed a hesitant smile.

"Offer still stands," she said. "Come by for coffee afterward and let me know how it went. I'll make sure there are muffins out early. Good luck hunting." She turned away, and a few minutes later, I heard the click of a door as she entered the proprietor's suite. I sighed, unwilling to try to identify exactly what I was feeling, and then I rinsed out my cup and went upstairs to bed, knowing I had a hunt in front of me in the morning.

My phone rang as I closed the door behind me. Chiara didn't usually call this late unless something important had happened.

"Mark—glad I caught you. We've got a problem."

"Please don't tell me it's now a *zombie* were-squonk."

"No, that would be an improvement. I've been monitoring the communications in your area—police, EMT, hospital, National Guard," Chiara said like it was no big thing to wiretap their lines in a place that could barely get a cell phone signal or cable TV. "There've been four bodies discovered in different places on the trails out there, gnawed to death with pieces missing." She sounded shook. "Mark—it looks like the were-squonk's got a taste for blood."

"How is that even possible?" I asked, sitting down on the edge of the four-poster bed. "Squonks like eating trees, wood, houses." I had several planks of cedar, redwood, and mesquite from the outdoor grilling section of the hardware store in my bag that I'd brought along to coax the creature into the open. I didn't like the idea of tossing it a steak.

"Squonks do. But werewolves don't," she replied. "Maybe it just took a while for the 'were' part of it to kick back in. I can't find anything in the lore about this, so just be careful. I saw the crime scene photos—they're bad, Mark."

"Shit, we also don't know whether or not their bite is infectious." This hunt had started to go sideways, and I hadn't even gotten started.

"Figure that it will be, and stay out of reach," she snapped. "I mean it, Mark. Blair does not want to have to go up there and shoot your ass full of silver."

"Yeah, yeah. When am I not careful?"

"We don't have time for me to answer that."

I ran a hand back through my hair, mentally calculating what I had in my bag and what I would need for this new-and-improved squonk menace. "All right," I said. "Thanks for the warning. I need to go through my stuff for tomorrow and see how much silver I brought."

"And Mark?" Chiara said. I had the feeling I didn't want to hear what came next. "Just so you know—from the size of the bites, the creature's gotten bigger. Forget Mastiff. Think cow."

Great. A predator cow with proportionally big rodent incisors and a taste for long pig. Whoop-dee-fuckin'-doo.

6

A meat-eating, murderous were-squonk was bad enough, but thanks to the deaths, the woods were crawling with cops. Crime scene tape blocked off the whole lot where I'd met Sheriff Sumbitch, and I ended up having to park a mile away at a tourist overlook and pack in on foot. Good thing I'm a paranoid bastard and had topographical trail maps—real paper, not just on my cell phone, because most of the time, you can't get shit for a signal out here.

My gear bag probably weighed half as much as I did, but it had saved my ass more than once, and I just knew that whatever I left behind to lighten the load would be the one critical thing that I'd need to survive. It held my weapons, salt, silver, holy water, flare gun, ammo, lighter fluid, thermal blanket, cocoon bag, rope, hell—even pitons and a rappelling harness, which I'd used once and hoped never to need again. It also held enough emergency food and water for three days, Sterno, kindling and matches, plus a hand-crank radio/flashlight, and some specialty items I'd packed for hunting squonk. No wonder the damn thing felt like I was carrying a grown adult piggyback.

Enough cops, cars, and noise surrounded the sites where the bodies had been found that I felt certain the were-squonk had retreated deeper into the woods. Rangers would have alerted any hikers or campers in the area to clear out, and I was counting on that making me the most appealing possibility for the creature's next snack.

I circled around all the excitement and tried to think like a squonk. The cops might be looking for a rabid wolf or a crazed bear, but the squonk's prints wouldn't be as familiar. I'd grown up stalking deer in woods like these from the time I could hold a rifle, and I knew that good tracking meant knowing what the hell you were actually looking to shoot. Which left me looking for paw prints for a dog-creature that was the size of a Holstein.

Chiara had given me the coordinates for where the bodies were found, which I'd marked on my map. As far as I knew, squonks couldn't climb trees. Not only did that cut down on places to search, but it eliminated the fear of a cow-sized wrinkly cryptid dropping on me from the branches overhead. Regular squonks kept to the lowlands, where there were plenty of fallen branches and saplings—easy food. If the cops were looking for a mountain lion, a bear, or a wolf, they'd go for the higher elevations and the rocky outcroppings. If I could stay out of their way, I might bag me a squonk.

Once I left the police tape and responder squads behind, I realized they hadn't mobilized search teams yet. Probably wanted to analyze their data and work through the red tape. This was my best chance to get in and out without dodging cops, and to get the squonk before it knew it was being hunted.

I spotted the paw prints just north of the attack site. Squonks had six toes, and a print that was the wrong shape for either a wolf or a bear. I was betting the cops would ignore the strange prints because they were wedded to their idea of what killed the hikers, which could help keep them out of my hair if they did decide to go looking for trouble.

I followed the prints deeper into the woods. Where the overhead canopy blocked the light, brush on the ground was thin, but in the clearings and along the banks of a small creek, plenty of bushes and saplings grew, providing lots of potential hiding places. I found some long, coarse dark hair caught on a bramble, and saw a smear of what might have been blood on some leaves, enough to tell me I had the trail.

This stretch of woods seemed too peaceful to be home to a ravening were-monster, but I knew that some of the most beautiful scenery could conceal the most dangerous creatures, natural and supernatural. Still, I paused for a moment to just enjoy the trees and the setting, and realized that the grotto had grown much colder than it should have been at this time of year. That's when I noticed the deer hunter.

He was dressed all wrong for the weather, in a heavy parka, gloves, and boots, with a Russian style hat that had honest-to-God ear flaps. His hunting rifle would get him in trouble with the rangers for sure, since despite the license pinned to his cap, deer were definitely not in season yet. The man looked to be in his early sixties, with a gray fringe of short hair beneath his cap and a round face that reminded me of my grandfather. I'd bet pennies to pierogies he was Polish, too.

"Hey buddy!" I called. "Give it a rest. Deer season's still a couple months away. Get out of here before the cops see you."

He didn't seem to hear me. Instead, he walked up to a large oak with the kind of thick branches just perfect for a tree stand and stared up into the canopy as if trying to figure out how to climb up there. I followed his line of sight, but tree stands in these woods have to be temporary and can't damage the trees, so there was nothing up in the canopy for him to find.

The hunter turned toward me, his head held at an unnatural angle. That's when I realized I could see right through him.

Shit. A dead deer hunter. And I could guess how it happened, too. Guy probably came out hunting solo, fell out of a tree stand way back here in the woods, and broke his neck. In the winter, with deep snow, a body might not be found until the thaw.

So the guy might be stuck here for eternity, on his last hunt in the middle of a beautiful forest. All in all, not the worst that could happen to a fellow. I wondered about poking around the base of the tree to see if I could find his bones. If so, a quick salt and burn could let him go on to the happy hunting ground in the sky. Then again, from the cut of his jacket, I figured he had probably died back in the fifties, and the bones had probably been carried off by scavengers long before I was born. For no good reason, I found myself calling him "Gus." Gus the dead deer hunter.

He looked straight at me, took in my clothing and bag, and gave me a nod, then tapped his license, either to warn me off from "his" hunting territory, or maybe to let me know he paid his fee. I nodded back, one hunter to another, and he shouldered his rifle and headed off, vanishing into the trees.

Did he hunt ghost deer? I wondered. Or was the poor fellow stuck for eternity taking phantom shots at live buck that would never become his trophies? I hoped he had some ghostly beer to tide him over.

I started to follow the squonk's trail, and suddenly Gus appeared in front of me. He blocked my path, but his expression looked more worried than aggressive. Gus held out his see-through hand and waved me back, warning me to stop.

"You've seen it? The strange creature?" I asked. Some ghosts can hear, and others are just harmless repeating apparitions, memory loops that play out over and over without change. Since Gus seemed to be reacting to me and making up his own script, I figured talking to him couldn't hurt.

He nodded, and I pulled the shotgun out of my bag. "I'm a hunter, too," I said. "I hunt those things. Can you help me find it?"

Gus grinned and nodded. Fuck-freaking-tastic, I had my own spectral Sacajawea. Top that, Lewis and Clark.

Following a ghost isn't like following any other guide. Gus appeared and disappeared with no apparent pattern, sometimes standing disconcertingly half-in and half-out of large trees, hovering over places where the path suddenly changed levels, or going through a large boulder that blocked the path and then having the nerve to glare when I took time to go around. I kept checking for the squonk's footprints, verifying that Gus wasn't leading me into some kind of nefarious deer hunter ambush, but my guide actually seemed worried about the strange new animal in his forest and was eager to help.

The squonk headed north, and so did I. I had a theory and wondered how smart squonks were. The attacks had occurred at trailheads, where hikers and hunters parked and headed into the woods. Easy pickings. Maybe the squonk considered them to be food delivery points. If so, we were just a few miles from the start of the next trail. I had no idea how much of the forest the cops would close off, or whether hikers would listen to the warnings. But if pickings were slim, I might be able to lure the squonk in without too much of a fuss, and then the only challenge was figuring out what to use to take him down.

I reached the gravel lot where the trail began and found it empty. The lot opened onto a two-lane park road, and a wide, flat clearing covered in bark mulch held a couple of picnic tables, a sign with a map and a copy of the park rules, and a modern, cement block one-room bathroom that was really an outhouse with a porcelain toilet. The clearing looked like the perfect place to lure the squonk, not as exposed as the parking lot, or with as many places for him to hide as in the actual forest.

I'd brought some special supplies for this hunt, after thinking about the creature's squonk-ness. I hoped my hunches were right because I had no desire to be the squonk's next dinner or his were-buddy.

Salt wouldn't be much help on this hunt, and iron dispelled ghosts, but it didn't have any special properties against squonks beyond being hard and heavy, which works on most things, at least up to a point. But bashing it over the head might get me close to its big teeth, and I'd prefer to avoid that. I'd also loaded my shotgun shells with absorbent cat litter crystals, the kind that swell and trap water. Squonks liquefy when they die, and I thought those crystals might do damage like rock salt and also soak up excess squonk.

I pulled out some big plastic trash bags and set them to one side, along with a set of thick rubber gloves that reached up to my elbows and a dustpan and whisk broom. I pulled out a coil of netting stuffed with fabric and pink absorbent granules that looked like a roll of sausage as thick as my forearm and made a circle on the ground, leaving an opening on one side. Then I opened a canister and laid down a coating of pinkish sawdust-like stuff all over the inside of the circle. I had to pause a moment and swallow. The smell still brought back unpleasant memories of school, puke, and the janitor's liberal use of the "pink stuff." Finally, I pulled out those tasty planks of cedar and mesquite and laid them down spaced a few feet apart, leading the were-squonk into the circle, toward the big prize—a few sausage patties I'd swiped from the B&B refrigerator on my way out.

I took up my position behind a picnic table I turned on its side for cover. I had silver bullets in my revolver, old school ammo for an old school gun. And in my sawed-off, I had shells I'd filled with my own special squonk mix. Just in case, I had an iron crowbar and a silver-coated tactical knife, but I really hoped I didn't have to use them, and a bag of mesquite briquettes to use as squonk treats if I needed to distract it.

Then I waited.

Squonks aren't the stealthiest creatures in the forest, and their musk is...distinctive. It smelled like a combination of bean farts and tequila barf, and the fact that I know what both of those smell like is an unfortunate commentary on my sorry life. Together, they qualified as a biohazard.

Chiara's intel had the size right: the creature that lumbered into view had the paws and body structure of a massive dog, but the size of a cow, and it looked like it tried to wear an elephant's skin and just pushed it up to make it fit. Next to a squonk, a Shar-pei wrinkle dog looked positively freshly pressed.

It had twitchy little ears on the top of its head that quirked from side to side like its own radar dishes, and big mopey eyes like those awful kitschy paintings of sad-eyed kids. All that might have been cute in a derpy sort of way if it weren't for the razor-sharp rodent incisors that were as long as my hand and as sharp as my blade, and the glint of red in its eyes that reminded me it was were.

For now, the squonk hadn't noticed me. It chomped its way through the treats I left for it, meandering closer to the pink circle. It either didn't smell me or didn't care because it never looked up as it snuffled from one gourmet grilling board to the next, right into the circle. When it reached the sausage, it stopped to take a deep breath and let out a low wuffle of pure bliss. It gobbled down the meat, and I rose from cover, aiming.

Right then, the were-squonk saw me and jerked just as I fired. The bullet should have hit it in the head, but instead, buried itself in the creature's shoulder. I swore and grabbed the sawed-off, trying to make my second shot before the were-squonk recovered from its shock enough to attack.

Too late. That damned thing moved fast. It charged me, and I dropped behind the cover of the overturned picnic table, bracing its wooden cross-pieces with my shoulder. The squonk hit hard, pushing me and the table back several inches and making me wonder if my shoulder would ever work right again. It jarred the shotgun from my grip as I tried to brace the table. Damn, that hurt.

Then I remembered—squonks eat wood.

Two massive top incisors came down over the edge of my picnic table barrier like the squirrel from hell, ripping away at its two-inch thick wood like biting into a sandwich. I scrambled back, managing to snag my knife and the crowbar, but the table had shifted, and my revolver and the sawed-off were out of reach.

I came up swinging as the squonk head-butted the table out of the way, lifting it off the ground and throwing it a few feet to smash against the kiosk with the map. I brought the crowbar down on the squonk's back haunches, but that didn't faze the creature, other than managing to make it madder.

The were-squonk glared at me with its red eyes and snapped its fucking big incisors like it was trying to figure out where to bite me first. I backed up, with my knife in one hand and the crowbar in the other, wishing I could get around the critter to grab my guns.

Between its tough hide and its bulk, the crowbar hadn't made a dent. Iron dispels some magic, and it plays merry hell with ghosts, but it didn't seem to affect the squonk. I doubted the silver on my blade would hurt it more than the knife itself, assuming my left hand didn't stay numb and tingly from the hit I'd taken on my shoulder.

All of a sudden, dead Gus the deer hunter popped up between me and the squonk, with his trusty rifle on his shoulder leveled for a shot right between the creature's eyes. No sound or projectile came from the ghostly gun, although I saw Gus move with the recoil, but the squonk squealed and backed off, warily eyeing me and my ghostly back-up. I gave Gus a thumbs up, and he grinned at me.

I eyed the cordon of the circle, knowing that I needed to get my gun and lure the squonk back onto the powdered surface, and I hoped to hell that my gunshot wasn't going to bring any cops running. I was fucking this up royally enough by myself; I didn't need help.

The were-squonk charged me, and I threw myself out of the way. Not fast enough; one of its big paws swiped across my bad shoulder, opening up my jacket and carving into my skin. I dove and rolled, coming up covered in blood and bark chips.

Gus appeared out of nowhere, standing face-to-face with the squonk, gun leveled so close to its muzzle it would have had powder burns if the rifle were solid. The squonk let out an un-monsterly squeal of surprise and backpedaled as Gus advanced and bought me time to get out of the way.

I scrambled for my bag of mesquite briquettes. The squonk kept a wary gaze on me and Gus, and I wondered when it would figure out that Gus couldn't actually hurt it. I had a new plan, and while it was piss-poor and batshit crazy, I was running with it because the old plan hadn't turned out so well. I grabbed a handful of the mesquite nuggets and tossed one at the squonk's feet.

It wuffled again, sniffing the chunk of wood, before it gulped the chunk down in one bite.

"That's a good squonk," I murmured. I eyed the cement block bathroom, which was really a fancy outhouse. It looked like a single square room with a big steel door, that the last occupant left hanging open. I tossed another nugget to the squonk, forcing him to move a little farther away from me and a little closer to the outhouse as a desperate plan took shape.

I glanced to where my shotgun lay, and then to the pink circle. Unfortunately, the gear I needed to pull this off wasn't close together. I'd have to risk trying to get by the squonk, and it didn't look like it had forgiven me for shooting it.

Another mesquite nugget made the were-squonk forget about me temporarily, and I edged closer to the circle. My original plan hadn't worked, so I grabbed the tube of fabric and swung it around my head, sending it flying over top of the squonk and into the fancy outhouse. Gus looked from the outhouse to me, and I jerked my head at the squonk and the little building. Gus grinned and nodded, telling me he was in on my crazy-ass "plan."

The squonk gave me a baleful look, either remembering that it didn't like me or pissed that I was holding out on the snacks. I tossed it a couple more briquettes, leading it closer to the outhouse, and when it turned to get them, I grabbed the remaining canister of pink powder and dove for my shotgun.

Just as the squonk looked ready to charge again, I hurled a handful more mesquite at it, landing between it and the outhouse, buying me more time. I grabbed an M80 and some duct tape from my bag and slapped it around the canister of pink stuff. The squonk had almost finished the nuggets, and I didn't have many more left.

"Fetch!" I yelled, getting the were-squonk's attention as I hurled the remaining nuggets one-two-three-four over the creature's head and into the cinderblock bathroom. It glared at me, trying to figure out whether to eat me now or later, but the mesquite must have been a real treat because it trotted after the chunks into the cement room.

I leveled my sawed-off and fired once it cleared the doorway, hitting it square in the ass with the cat litter crystals, which made it jump forward, farther inside, as it bellowed. I lit the M80 and threw the canister over its head, and then barreled toward the building to slam the steel door. I braced my back against it, digging in my heels.

The M80 sounded like a cannon in that confined space. Then I remembered that shit gives off methane, and a second boom blew the corrugated tin roof off the outhouse and the door off its hinges, knocking me over with the blast.

Bits of metal roof rained down on top of the steel door that covered me, which had bowed with the force of containing the blast. Chunks of cement block fell like hail.

The forest smelled of roasted squonk and outhouse, pungent enough to bring me back to consciousness without smelling salts. I crawled out from under the door, still bleeding from where the were-squonk had clawed me, and now in some new places where I'd connected too hard with the rocky ground. I'd have a goose egg on the back of my head from the door, but since it saved my life, I counted myself lucky.

I half expected to find gobbets of were-squonk splattered across the remaining walls of the outhouse and hanging in the trees. Instead, it seemed the legends were true about dead squonks turning into water from their tears. The absorbent pink powder and the industrial-strength hazmat "sock" were bloated with liquid—all that remained of the squonk.

"Well fuck a duck, it actually worked," I marveled and took a celebratory swig from my flask. Then I realized that the sound of the shots and the explosion probably carried for miles and I stood in the middle of a disaster zone with glaring evidence of having destroyed park property. So I did the only thing I could do: swept up the powder, used the gloves to gather the squonk-water filled sock, and carried everything to the fire pit, where I doused it in salt and lighter fluid and watched it burn.

Gus appeared on the other side of the fire, grinning broadly, and gave me a thumbs-up. We stood around the fire in silence, just two hunters basking in the glory of a righteous kill. Gus pulled a flask of his own from the pocket of his camo jacket and saluted me, then knocked back a swallow or two. I wondered how many hunts he "helped" with, flushing out deer for other hunters. Maybe this wasn't so bad, as afterlife options went. Gus seemed to be happy, so unless I heard later on about some crazy hunter ghost going all *Cabin in the Woods* on people, I felt good about letting him go on with his eternal hunt.

The fire was nearly out. I fretted about the smoke, but after the gunshots and explosion, it was almost anticlimactic. Still, I was happy to shovel dirt on the last of the embers like the good scout that I never was and get out of there. I'd done my best to bandage the gashes on my shoulder, but I'd lost enough blood to feel woozy, and I figured I'd take Sara up on her offer to patch me up.

That's when I heard voices and figured the cops or rangers were closing in.

I grabbed my bag and looked around, trying to figure out whether to hide or run. Gus blinked from near the fire to at the mouth of the trail and signaled for me to vamoose. I ran in the opposite direction of the approaching rangers, figuring I could circle around on one of the other trails. Before I was completely out of earshot, I heard the most godawful racket and realized Gus was giving the performance of his afterlife, wailing and moaning like a banshee, scaring the bejeezus out of my pursuers to let me get away.

Once things quiet down, I'm going to bring a six-pack of beer back to that old oak tree and leave it for Gus. One good turn deserves another. Hunters take care of their own.

7

"I can't believe you trapped the were-squonk in a hazmat sock," Blair chuckled, when I finally made it back.

"Clearly, you underestimated my creativity under pressure," I retorted, as Chiara popped the top on a cold one and passed it to me.

"Must be because you're so much smarter than you look, Wojcik," Blair replied, getting the last word, like usual.

A week had passed since the were-squonk adventure. I'd hauled my sorry ass back to the B&B, and Sara had taken pity on me, dragging me into the kitchen, pouring me a couple of shots of Jack and patching me up on the condition that I told her the whole story. She knew who Gus really was, a local man who had disappeared one snowy December and whose ghost had been spotted from time to time, unable to pass up helping with a hunt. Sara had poured herself a drink, and we sat up talking for a long while, but injuries, alcohol, and exhaustion meant I was in no condition to suggest anything more. She did slip me her private number before I left. I had already decided to find a reason to head back up there before too much time passed, now that I'd had a chance to go from gun-shy to cautiously intrigued.

"It's a talent," I responded, deadpan. "Protective coloration." I took a sip of my beer, holding my cards in my left hand. The shoulder still twinged from where I'd gotten clawed, but the bump on the back of my skull had gone down, proving Chiara's contention that I had a cast-iron skull.

She and Blair had presented me with an engraved plaque, the kind that usually has a taxidermied deer head attached to it, with a nameplate that said "were-squonk." The rest of the plaque was empty, but it was soaking wet when they presented it to me, all the while swearing up and down it had a head attached to it when they put it in the box. Hardy-har-har.

A week of fishing had done me good, and now the poker party weekend was in full swing. Demon lounged beside the fireplace, having stuffed himself on treats that mysteriously "fell" to the floor. Father Leo sat next to his brother Tom and looked like just a regular guy in jeans and a black t-shirt—no clerical collar. So far, he was beating the pants off the rest of us, as the chips in front of him attested. Chiara and Blair were determined to break the good padre's winning streak, but I wouldn't have bet on it. Louie had gotten the weekend off and came up with a cooler full of his excellent homebrew ale. My buddy, Dave, had also driven up to join us, as well as Chiara's brother, Tony. That would make for a crowded cabin, but the girls got the loft, while the rest of us found space for sleeping bags on the floor. We agreed to let Father Leo sleep on the couch, partly out of respect for the priesthood, but more for the fact that he brought the best booze.

The remains of a six-foot hoagie sat on the counter, along with empty pizza boxes, a cheese tray, and several bags of chips, jars of peanuts, and bowls of dip and salsa. A garbage can overflowed with beer cans and bottles, and in the background, an announcer narrated the Steelers' home game.

I had a crap hand, but I didn't give a flying rat's ass about losing. Father Leo said he had a couple of new jobs for me, and the Occulatum wanted me to explain why they got a request from the good padre to make an anonymous donation to replace a park outhouse near Kane. I'd worry about that on Monday. At the moment, I had a full belly, a warm beer buzz, the company of good friends, and the knowledge that I'd done battle with the forces of darkness and lived to tell about it. And right now, that was more than enough for me.

PART II

OPEN SEASON

1

The bloodsuckers were winning.

Not vampires. Vamps I could handle. A nice sharp machete to the neck, and the head goes rolling fast as you can say, "Drac's a dick."

Mosquitoes—now those suckers are evil incarnate.

Since I found myself in the middle of the Geneva Swamp hunting for a marsh monster, mosquitoes went with the territory. And no matter how much "Fuck Off" I sprayed, they seemed to find the spots I missed. Slapping at them would just end up tossing me out of my canoe, so they sang their high-pitched squeal around my ears, and I tried not to fantasize about eliminating their species.

Deep inside the Geneva Swamp, I found it hard to remember how close we were to civilization because the scrub plants and cattails blocked my view. If I listened carefully, I could hear the cars on the highway, but they were miles behind me as I paddled into the thick of the swamp.

Geneva Marsh stretches for about twelve miles in the upper corner of Northwestern Pennsylvania, the biggest marsh in the state. Everyone around here calls it "Geneva Swamp," regardless of its real name. No one knows for sure how deep it is. When the big bridges for I-79 were built, the pylons went down two hundred feet. Folks say they never hit bottom, just sank deep enough to be held up by the pressure of the muck around them. I've heard stories that construction equipment would vanish, sinking into the depths. People say that once, a whole train disappeared into the green waters.

In other words, a marsh monster couldn't ask for a better place to hide. And I was the sorry son of a bitch who had to go in after it.

I'm Mark Wojcik, auto mechanic and monster hunter. I've got no illusions about being some kind of hero; I just do the dirty work so other people can sleep at night, peacefully believing that supernatural shit isn't real. Like any public service, it's a thankless job with lousy pay. Then again, no one gets into hunting for fun and profit. We lose people we love, and it's all about vengeance. In my case, I lost my dad, brother, uncle, and cousin to a wendigo on a deer hunt up in the Big Woods. They died. I lived. Most days, I'm convinced they were the lucky ones.

In other circumstances, I could have enjoyed the beauty of the marsh. Green and lush, far removed from the noise and bustle of people, it sheltered bald eagles, ducks, geese, and herons. Cattails grew thick around the shore, along with pickerelweed and loosestrife. Duckweed gave the water a green cast, and lily pads tangled up the boating channels. Old trees verged on the marsh, some split from a recent lightning storm. In the more solid parts of the wetland, deer and fox and God knows what else thrived. Big-ass frogs harrumphed from the shallows in a bass chorus with a thousand voices.

And somewhere in the dark waters, hidden beneath the pretty plants, lay a killer.

Folks around these parts know that swamps are dangerous places. That goes double for bottomless swamps. You get snake-bit out here or half-drown yourself, and you'd better be able to haul your ass back for help, or they'll find your carcass when the vultures are done with it. Still, losing just one fisherman in a season would be cause for talk at the local watering hole. Losing three? That made people edgy and fueled rumors about snakeheads and the Creature from the Black Lagoon, and every other rubber-costume monster ever seen on the silver screen.

Before the fishermen went missing, no one thought much about the bad catch this season in the swamp. Or how there seemed to be fewer ducks than before.

My paddle dipped into the water, and the canoe tracked silently across the surface. Skimmer bugs tempted the bowfin and other fish that swam in the marsh's depths. Ducks and geese honked from their hiding places in the reeds. The swamp smelled like wet mud and rotting vegetation, with a little wild garlic and sulfur thrown in for good measure. I picked up a whiff of decomposition and wondered if a dead fish had floated to the surface.

Not with my luck. Up ahead, tangled in the spatterdocks, lay what was left of one of the missing fishermen. Just the bones remained, shreds of what might have been a flannel shirt and blue jeans clinging to the skeleton. I didn't figure he'd gotten there by himself. First off, no boat was in sight, not even an overturned canoe. Second, as I got closer, I could see that many of the bones were cracked as if the corpse had been squeezed.

Or digested and pooped out of a honkin' big marsh monster.

I didn't have much to go on when it came to hunting the damn creature. The guy I met in a Conneaut Lake bar who claimed to have seen it gave me a description that sounded like he'd watched re-runs of that sand worm movie with Kevin Bacon once too often, mixed with a liberal dose of Jack Daniels. The guy at the bait store said he'd heard the thing looked like a giant salamander with big teeth. I reminded him that we were too far north for either gators or crocs. The best look I got was from a kid who flew a drone with a camera over the swamp at dusk and got a photo of something that looked like a cross between a squid and a pile of wet leaves.

I watched the grainy footage from the action cam duct-taped to the drone and had to admit that no creature I'd ever seen moved like the thing in the video. On the muddy, not-quite-solid areas of the swamp, the creature schlumped along like a shabby octopus. In the water, it moved with frightening speed, and the shingle-like flaps that covered it blended in among the weeds and lily pads.

Everyone was talking about the "Geneva Marsh Monster," but no one knew what the damn thing was, let alone how to kill it.

So here I was, loaded up with more weapons than Elmer Fudd in duck season, looking for a carnivorous cryptid in a bottomless swamp. What could possibly go wrong?

Fuck-all, that's what.

I'd brought along a fish finder sonar that I'd borrowed from one of the guys at the auto repair shop I own—the job I do when I'm not hunting things that supposedly don't exist. It took a bit of fiddling to figure it out. Then I practiced for a while on the big goldfish tank at the pet store before they made me leave. It would have been nice to bring out my friend Louie's bass boat, but the swamp barely had enough clear water to let a canoe through.

So here I sat, with the fish finder clipped to the front of the canoe, trying to sort out a monster from old logs and whatever swamp junk and critters were down below. Do I know how to have a good time or what?

I like deer hunting, but I've never had the patience for fishing. Hunting just seems more active than floating around in a boat waiting for a fish to bite. Haven't gone deer hunting since everything went to shit, but I used to enjoy it. Good excuse to go for a walk in the woods on a snowy day and come back to a warm cabin to drink beer with my buddies. The kind of stuff I hunt now definitely makes for an "active" evening, if by "active" you mean "running for your life."

Sitting here, getting sucked dry by mosquitoes and watching a screen that looked like a bad hand-held video game from the nineties got on my last nerve. I tried for serenity and contemplation, listening to nature sounds and watching the birds. A duck came in for a landing a few yards from the bow of my canoe and floated, nice and peaceful.

Until a mat of "leaves" snapped up, something long and pink grabbed the duck, and it disappeared. Seconds later, nothing remained but ripples.

I pulled out a harpoon gun and held it up to my shoulder, sighting onto the camouflaged monster. Then I pulled the trigger and watched the spear dig into the flap that had lifted to suck in the Mallard. Instead of parting the vegetation and disappearing into the water, the point dug into flesh. A strange, warbling shriek filled the air, and something dark and slimy pooled on the surface of the water.

Then the damn thing took off like it had an Evinrude strapped to its ass. The harpoon had a long coil of rope threaded through a grommet on the front of the boat, and I grabbed the rope with my gloved left hand, holding on to the edge of the canoe with the other.

I've never water skied in a canoe before. I don't recommend it.

Without the glove, the rope would have stripped the skin from my palm in seconds. As it was, the damn thing practically wrenched my arm from the socket, and I had to plant my feet wide to remain in the back of the canoe and stay level. My right hand had a death grip on the canoe, so I didn't end up being pulled out and trying to ski in my Timberlands. I knew I couldn't hold on much longer, but I was also sure I couldn't paddle fast enough to keep up, and the little putt-putt engine on the back of the canoe wasn't going to do the job.

Worst of all, the harpoon just seemed to annoy the creature. It left a trail of black blood like an oil slick, so I'd hit it but hadn't done enough damage to slow it down.

Just as I reached for a new weapon, the slimy son of a bitch changed directions, dragging the canoe across the tops of the duckweed and water lilies, and jolting my ass so hard on the seat I was going to be bruised for a week. I'd have a hell of a time paddling out of the tangle of weeds.

The fish finder on the bow lost its little electronic mind as we zoomed over plants and swished by lots of things beneath the water that might or might not have had fins. I didn't have time to find out. My balls were taking a beating against the hard metal seat, and if I hadn't been pissed off before, that surely didn't improve my mood.

A large bird flew over, big enough to cast a shadow like a WWII bomber. It might have been a curious bald eagle, but with my luck, it was a vulture claiming first place in line for the pickings. I'd have flipped it off if I could have spared a hand.

A flock of frightened birds took wing, flapping away from the disturbance. I had a choice of having my arm pulled off or losing the thing in the weeds. Bad enough to be chasing a monster that looked like a combination octopus/trap spider, but at the speed it was towing me through the vegetation, the canoe kept smacking into the surface and soaking me with greenish goo. It looked like a soaking wet trash heap with eyes, and I decided to call it Marjory.

Then the creature turned back and headed straight for me.

I already knew Marjory was a man-eater, and I had no desire to follow the duck into its gullet. I let go of the rope and scrambled for a new weapon as it bore down on me.

Marjory rose higher in the water, and I could see thick tentacles beneath its bulbous body. The top of the creature had greenish-brown overlapping skin flaps that made it look leafy. Under the surface, the skin looked smooth. I didn't want to get close enough to find out.

Then the monster flipped up the top of its "head" and exposed a wide opening that looked more like a sphincter than a mouth; I got a lot more invested in fighting fate and telling destiny to go screw itself.

Damned if my bones were going to add fiber to Marjory's diet.

I grabbed for another weapon, my trusty grenade launcher pistol. In case the harpoon didn't work, I'd fitted the shell with an explosive charge and a sharp steel barb. I faced down that asshole and fired.

The barb hit the back of its...throat...and stuck. Marjory shuddered, her lid flopped back down, and she dove.

Shit. I saw Marjory in all her tentacled glory sinking faster than a politician's poll numbers, going straight down.

What went down was likely to come back up, explosively fast.

The paddles caught in the weeds when I tried to move the canoe away from the blast zone. Damned if I could remember how long the timer was on that charge, but it wasn't near long enough for me to skedaddle.

I'd come prepared for disaster this time, since it seems to follow me. I tethered the weapons bag to the canoe and kept it closed except for a Velcro flap I could use to grab stuff quick. If we flipped, my guns and knives stood a chance of not ending up in the depths. Much as I hated life vests, I wore one, cursing when it got in my way.

I resisted the urge to put my head between my knees and kiss my ass goodbye. Instead, I grabbed the other glove and reached down on both sides of the canoe, grabbing a fistful of spatterdocks in each hand and hung on for dear life.

A muffled boom sent the rest of the birds into the air, and my own personal tsunami lifted up the canoe as a rush of bubbles created a lump beneath the surface like a zit about to explode. A geyser of foul greenish water fountained up into the air, raining down on me and nearly swamping the canoe. I held on to the lily pads, white-knuckled, hoping they proved their reputation for hella long roots. I might end up with two dislocated shoulders instead of one, but damned if I was going to drown in a place that looked like a giant kale smoothie.

Dead fish started bobbing to the surface, killed by the concussion below. Columns of bubbles streamed from deep in the swamp, and it was like a herd of cows farting in unison. The air stank of rotten eggs and decaying muck.

Something big and solid blasted out of the water, tentacles thrashing, as Marjory rode the crest of the explosion. I might have overdone the charge since the top of her "head" was gone and bits of charred and still-burning monster flesh came raining down. It tore the spatterdocks out of my hands and hurled the canoe backward, rocking so hard I threw myself down to steady it and keep from capsizing.

I heard a hiss and a crackle, and the water caught on fire, a flaming streak that seared across the duckweed and flambéed the dead fish. I'd forgotten that swamp gas is flammable as fuck. The flames rose half a foot into the air and blossomed out from the center, flashing all around my canoe, and I wondered if my life insurance would consider spontaneous combustion to be an act of God.

The metal skin of the canoe warmed, but before I could react, the flames vanished as quickly as they had come. I sighed in relief and thanked my lucky stars, God, and every ancestor that went before me.

A sodden, ichor-spattered mass of charred tentacles landed with a wet thump in the bow of the canoe as Marjory crashed down to Earth. One slippery tentacle slapped my face harder than a roadhouse hussy, while another landed a solid hit to my beleaguered balls. The canoe flailed back and forth, and between the smell and the bits of creature-goop that now covered me, I thought I might be boat sick.

Nature recovers quickly. I still sat in shock with a lap full of monster guts amid blackened lily pads as the swamp came back to life. If the ducks noticed the carnage, they didn't show it as they flapped to a landing. A hawk circled, probably sizing up a free meal. Fish bobbed to the surface to grab monster gobbets and pulled their treats into the depths. The cow-fart smell was gone, replaced by something akin to the scent of burned spinach. And I still had what was left of Marjory sprawled in my lap like a drunk date.

Time to break up. I prodded the pale, flaccid meat sack that was left of Marjory with my paddle, flopping the blast-amputated tentacles and the black-streaked bulbous body into the water with an uneremonious *plop*. Fish churned the water, scrambling for the good bits, and I gave up, heaving my guts over the other side. Surprisingly, the upchuck was an improvement on the rotten egg and cow-fart taste it replaced.

The fish finder beeped, proudly telling me it found something in the water. "You're a day late and a dollar short, fucker," I muttered, turning it off.

It took me until almost dark to push-pull-paddle my way out, since the exploding swamp creature had sent the canoe into a tangle of weeds. By the time I hauled the boat and my gear bag out of the water, night had fallen, and one sketchy overhead light struggled to illuminate the gravel lot where I'd parked my truck. The bulb kept fritzing, and on TV, that would be the signal for demons or ghosts to ambush me.

With the mood I was in, I pitied the fool that crossed my path, corporeal or not.

The pullover sat just off the exit, across the street from a gas station and a concrete pad that had once been a shady bar. Two young men sat on the tailgate of a battered white pickup, and I couldn't tell whether they were having a beer or smoking weed. They paused to watch me, and I imagine my monster-splattered appearance looked like I'd been slaughtering innocents in the depths of the marsh.

My glare preempted anything they might have said, and whether they were high or drunk, they had enough self-preservation instinct not to piss off the guy covered in blood. I loaded the canoe and grabbed the tarp I kept to cover the driver's seat, since this kind of thing happened far too often. Still grumbling to myself, I started the truck and peeled out of the lot, taking perverse pride in being enough of a dick to spray gravel in the direction of the potheads.

The drive from Geneva to Atlantic was quiet, and I cranked up the radio, letting the Classic Vinyl channel occupy my thoughts. When I got back to my place, I hosed off the canoe, then washed out the back of my truck. If the water hadn't been so damn cold, I would have turned the nozzle on myself as well, but I'd built a little shower off the back to keep me from tracking blood and guts into the house. I might live alone, but I still have standards.

I left my boots on the porch after a quick rinse and peeled off my sodden but charnel-free clothing on the tile just inside the door. Demon met me at the door—my big, overly friendly Doberman who was way too interested in all the new smells in the gunk stuck to my body. I ruffled his ears, gave him a treat, and headed for the bathroom. A quick sprint got me into a hot shower, and I scrubbed down with Irish Spring until I couldn't smell the stink anymore.

All things considered, I'd made it back without injury, which was more than I could usually say. I ganked the ghoulie, didn't lose my guns in the swamp, and my tetanus shots were up-to-date, so for once, I didn't need the ER. I had my choice of a bottle of Jack or some cold beer in the fridge. Should have been a good night.

Except for the date.

Back when I was married, before Lara left me, I never could remember dates without setting my phone. Birthdays, anniversaries, and holidays just didn't stick in my head.

Then a damn wendigo wiped out four people I loved and sent my life into a tailspin. That's what it took to make me remember. And today was that day.

I sighed when I stopped by the photo over the mantle. We had taken it right before we suited up to go out. Five guys, grinning like fools, arms slung over each other's shoulders in easy camaraderie. No clue what was about to hit them.

Closing my eyes, I turned away. Fuck beer. Tonight belonged to JD.

Building a fire made sense. The night turned cold, and I wouldn't be getting any sleep. The remote clicked, and The History Channel came on TV, not that I planned to watch it, but it beat silence. Demon padded up and put his head on my lap as if he knew I needed a friend. I stroked his slick black fur absently, with my thoughts far away. After a moment, his ears pricked up, and he ran to the window, then barked.

"Shut up, Demon," I replied, wondering if he'd spotted a possum.

Just as I debated which frozen entree to sacrifice to the fires of Moloch—aka my finicky oven—I heard a knock at the door.

My cabin is down a dirt lane on the outskirts of Atlantic, which is to say, the middle of fucking nowhere. I don't get door-to-door salespeople. Hell, I'm lucky the mailman delivers. So I did what any self-respecting person in my position would do.

I pulled my Glock and edged along the wall to see who was on the porch.

"Put the gun down, Mark. We know you're there."

I turned on the porch light and saw Blair and Chiara Hamilton standing in front of my door with a hot pizza, a box of pastries, and a Cards Against Humanity deck.

Blair's ex-military, and though she's about six inches shorter than me, I'd bet on her in a fight. For one thing, she's not quite thirty, while I'm feeling every bit of thirty-five. Blair looks like she should be playing volleyball on some campus, with her dark hair back in a thick braid and that fresh-faced, no-pretense kind of tough pretty. Chiara only stood as tall as Blair's shoulder, with long dark hair, brown eyes, and olive skin. They'd been married for a couple of years now, though they'd been together since high school.

"We brought pizaaaaaaa," Chiara coaxed, drawing out the word and waving her hand to waft the scent closer.

"C'mon with the door already," Blair said. "If I had nuts, they'd be frozen by now."

I opened the door and ushered them in, still a little flummoxed at the sudden company. "Don't take this wrong, but why are you here?" I asked, although my eyes went straight to the pizza and the pastries. Chiara's family owns an Italian bakery, and their stuff is to die for.

Chiara looked at me as if I were a bit slow. "Because it's *that day*, and friends don't let friends drink all the JD by themselves," she added with a grin.

Bless their little gizzards. For a moment, my throat closed up. Then Blair delivered a clap to my shoulder that reminded me that she'd never lost her Army-strong fitness level.

"Can we eat the pizza before it congeals? I'm hungry," Blair said. Demon acted like any self-respecting guard dog and surveilled the food.

Chiara led the way to my kitchen table and pulled down plates and glasses. Blair set the pizza and pastries down, and I got the bottle of JD out of the cabinet, glad it was a new one. We helped ourselves to pizza, and Chiara poured the whiskey.

Blair took a seat next to her wife, sitting just close enough that their knees touched under the table. "How'd the job in the swamp go?" Chiara asked.

"It's done. But I've lost my taste for sushi," I replied, sliding two slices of pizza onto my plate and eyeing the pastries, which remained on the counter.

"You hate sushi," Blair countered.

"I hate it more now. But yeah, I ganked Marjory and sent her sky high."

Chiara raised a perfectly-groomed eyebrow. "Marjory?"

I shrugged. "No idea what the thing was, and that seemed like as good a name as any."

"It has to sound like fake Latin," Blair argued. "Like in those old cartoons. You know, maybe like 'Monsterus Marjorious.'"

Clair rolled her eyes. "You watch too much TV."

Blair elbowed her. "Those are classics!"

I filled them in on the hunt, and at one point, Blair nudged Chiara, who dug a five-dollar bill out of the pocket of her jeans. "What?" I asked.

Chiara laughed. "Blair bet me that you couldn't handle the swamp monster without explosives."

"And you bet against that? Have you met me?" I finished off my first piece of pizza.

"Yep. I send you a monthly bill. Higher than usual this month. I had to special-order that harpoon," Blair replied. Blair inherited Hamilton Hardware in downtown Conneaut Lake, a hometown institution for nearly a hundred years. Chiara runs the New Age/bookstore/coffee shop next door and runs a web development company out of their apartment over the store. In her spare time, Chiara runs Dark Web research for hunters like me, and Blair keeps an invitation-only back room to the hardware store stocked with our kind of hunting supplies.

"That harpoon saved my bacon," I replied. "But I'm gonna need a couple more spears for it. Marjory didn't give them back." I ran a hand over my chin and realized I hadn't shaved. My beard came in reddish, even though my hair was straw-colored blond to go with light blue eyes. Mom always said I had the "map of Poland" on my face, which I took to mean I strongly resembled my relatives back in the "Old Country" that my immigrant grandfather talked about.

"Yes, you're scruffy," Chiara confirmed, snickering. "Nerf-herder."

"You try herding nerfs and see how you like it," I shot back. "Worse than cats."

She pushed a glass of Jack toward me. "Drink. Are you due in the garage tomorrow?"

Wojcik Auto Body supplied most of my income, although Father Leo made sure the Occulatum, a secret branch of the Church that oversaw those who fought the supernatural, paid me a fair stipend. Of late, I'd been spending more time on monsters and less time on Mustangs. Pete Kennedy, my awesome shop manager, kept the place running while I was out saving the world. "Pete's covering for me tomorrow," I replied. "Like he does every year."

Blair and Chiara knew the story about the wendigo. They'd seen pictures of my dad, Uncle Christoph, my cousin Greg, and my brother Sean, and listened while I recounted our adventures until I was too wasted to talk anymore. Over the years, Blair had told me stories about missions gone bad during her stint in the Middle East, and how sometimes shit happened. Chiara told me food makes everything better, and she drank me under the table.

I'd been the only one to survive the hunt that day, but that wasn't really true. The guy who got carried out of the woods with half his blood gone wasn't the same one who went in. I didn't just lose my innocence about the kinds of creatures and things that stalked the shadows. I lost my sister-in-law, Amy, who couldn't forgive me for surviving when her husband and only son didn't. And two years later, I lost my wife Lara, who decided I'd had long enough to grieve and wasn't getting on with life fast enough, so she moved on without me. Fucking wendigo.

"Hey. Mark." Chiara must have picked up on my thousand-yard stare. "It's okay to miss them, but don't forget, you've got people here now who care about you."

"Or, as they told me before we shipped out, 'If you're lucky, you'll come back, but you won't ever be the same,'" Blair added.

I sighed and tossed off the whiskey. "I know. And...I feel like I should be past this. Sometimes I am. And then the date rolls around and—"

"That's why we're here," Chiara said. She put another piece of pizza on my plate, along with a couple of homemade pastries. "Eat."

They filled me in on what was going on with the hardware store and the bookstore, how the coven that met every week to "play Bunko" in the social room was doing, and the latest escapades of Chiara's multitude of brothers and large extended family. Every time my glass emptied, it mysteriously filled without my intervention. By the time Blair pulled out the Cards Against Humanity deck, I was a warm, boneless lump on the couch and Demon lay snoring at my feet.

"You still going to the dinner at the fire hall tomorrow night?" Blair asked.

"Shit. I forgot. Yeah. Should be done with my hangover by then."

Chiara rolled her eyes. "Glad to see you schedule these things."

"Louie Marino's looking for you," Blair continued. "Says he might have a case for you."

I snorted. "He owes me a case of Iron City."

"Not that kind of case. Haunting or something."

I downed another shot of the whiskey. "One thing at a time. We'll deal with his ghosts tomorrow. My ghosts tonight."

2

My cabin is in between Adamsville and Atlantic, Pennsylvania, two towns that have maybe four hundred people between them. A tornado damn near wiped Adamsville off the map a while back, and it never rebounded. Nice people, hard times. We don't have fancy coffee shops, and the nearest Walmart is in Conneaut Lake, but we do have a volunteer fire department, and its social hall is one of our community hubs.

Back before that deer hunt changed everything, I used to volunteer. Then I fell apart, and after that, monster hunting took up all my spare time. So I quit the department, but I'm still friends with the crew. Hell, I went to high school with half of them. Knew the rest from when I used to go to church, before I left my faith and most of my blood in the snow on that cold December evening.

The VFD put on a good monthly dinner. Most of the money went for upkeep on the trucks, but they always had another worthy local cause, like a school, library, or playground to support as well. The food was always good, and plenty of it, but most folks went because we knew we could get caught up on the local news and gossip.

Pete closed up the shop a little early to meet me and get over to the fire department before the line got too long. The social hall isn't fancy, just a cement block building with a coat of paint slapped on the walls and a tile floor, but it's a popular spot for wedding receptions, baby showers, funeral meals, and graduation parties. It's that or one of the church fellowship buildings, and the fire department lets you have beer.

"Smells good," Pete said as we walked in from the parking lot. Five o'clock, and the senior citizens had already beaten us to the line. A big plate of whatever was on the menu cost eight bucks, but seniors got it for six. That led to a septuagenarian stampede, and I knew better than to get in the way. Those old ladies had sharp elbows and heavy purses.

"Petey Kennedy! Is that you?" Mrs. McCarthy turned around and laid a wrinkled hand on Pete's arm. Pete's a couple of inches taller than I am, so he comes in at about six foot six, and built like a linebacker. He's only two years younger, but somehow, I managed to miss having Mrs. McCarthy in grade school—Pete wasn't so lucky.

"Yes, ma'am," Pete answered, dropping his head like he'd been caught playing hooky. I doubt anyone outside of his extended family had called him "Petey" since he shot up to basketball player height.

"You tell your mother that we missed her at the book club," Mrs. McCarthy chided. "We only had three ladies show up, and that left us with too much punch to drink."

Chiara's mother had gone to that book club for a while, and always came home tipsy, so I don't know what was in the punch, but it went beyond ginger ale and sherbet.

"I'll pass that along," Pete said, managing to blush. "She's been busy, what with Katie's wedding coming up and all."

Mrs. McCarthy shook her head. "You've all grown up way too fast! Where does the time go?" She patted my arm for good measure. "Good to see you too, Mark. I still miss your mother when the ladies play cards."

"I miss her, too." Mom had passed on many years before that hunt, so at least she'd been spared having to deal with the loss.

One of Mrs. McCarthy's friends drew her attention off as the line moved up, and Pete and I were left to ourselves again.

"Don't say it, Wojcik," he warned.

I'd tease him about "Petey," except that I'd had more than my share of "whoa-chick," as people often mangled my name. It's "voy-chick," but by now, I answer to anything close.

Tonight's dinner was roast chicken, mashed potatoes, green beans, a small salad, fresh yeast rolls, and a sliver of pumpkin pie. The firefighters didn't cook the meal—the auxiliary did that, made up of the wives, husbands, siblings, and friends of the crew—but they did show up to circulate and chew the fat. Pete and I took our plates over to an empty table and went to get some of their wicked-strong coffee, then sat down and waited for the rest of our gang to show.

I spotted Blair and Chiara, along with a couple of Chiara's brothers coming in the door. The place was starting to fill up. Children ran between the tables, babies cried, and the buzz of conversation rose to a dull roar. Before I'd gotten more than a few bites in, Louie Marino dropped into the chair beside me.

"Hey, Mark, I need to talk to you." Louie and I went to school together. He's a cop out in Linesville, which is just up the road. Louie knows the score about what I do in my "other" job, and so does Pete. I come back battered and bruised too often to hide the monster hunting from Pete, and Louie and I often run into each other in the wee hours of the morning in odd places, so cluing him in cut down on how much I spent on bail.

"Blair and Chiara told me you were looking for me." I kept shoveling food. I'd beaten down my hangover to a dull roar, and my abused stomach finally decided it needed solid fuel.

"You ever been to the fishing cabins on French Creek, around Cochranton?" he asked.

I nodded. "Long time ago. Fishing's not my thing, but I went with Sean and some of his buddies a couple of times. Somebody's parents had a place. Small, but nice." French Creek wound down from New York all the way to the Allegheny River. Along the way, it provided some mighty fine water for boating, kayaking, and fishing, and little two- or three-room cabins dotted the banks, places families returned every summer for generations. They weren't fancy, built and maintained on a factory income, but they were a working man's getaway.

"So I've got a friend," Louie said, leaning forward and resting his right arm on the table as he shifted his seat to face me. "Ronnie Danvers. You know him?" I shook my head. "Anyhow, he bought this place that had been on the market for a while, kinda run down, picked it up for a steal. He figured he'd make it his man cave, fix it up for poker nights, and get in some fishing time, too. Only no one told him it was haunted."

I raised an eyebrow. "What makes him think it's haunted?" There's plenty of scary shit out there, lurking in the shadows, but none of it works like in the TV shows. I can't count how many times I've gone in to investigate reports of ghosts, only to find it's actually squirrels in the ductwork, raccoons in the crawl space, or birds in the chimney.

"He saw Eli Wickers sitting on the dock, fishing."

I gave him a questioning look, prompting him to continue.

"Eli died of a heart attack last fall."

"Okay, that's a little strange. He's sure it was Eli?"

Louie nodded. "Yeah, except Ronnie says Eli looked solid—and really dead. Smelled bad, too."

"How sure are you that Eli actually died?"

"I went to his funeral."

"And he's back?" I asked.

Louie shrugged. "According to Ronnie. And before you ask, he's clean. He wasn't smoking anything that made him see dead people."

Pete snickered. I rolled my eyes. That line quit being funny a long time ago.

"All right. I'll look into it."

Louie slid a key across the table, and I pocketed it. "Thanks. If it were anyone but Ronnie, I'd think they were pulling my leg, but he's pretty freaked about it."

"You think someone is playing a gag on him? Prank wars?"

"If I didn't know what kind of stuff you run into, I'd say yes. That's the easier explanation. But Ronnie says there's no one who would be pranking him, and he just bought the place after it stood empty for a while. He wants to get in and clean it up. Right now, it's still the way Eli left it, and Ronnie says it's a mess."

"Still got Eli's stuff in it? That might be part of the problem right there," I mused. "Ghosts don't like to let go of things. I'll go over tomorrow," I added, stealing a glance at Pete, who nodded with a mouthful of chicken. "See if we can't evict the ghost so he can get the place in shape for spring."

"Thanks," Louie said and clapped me on the shoulder as he stood. "You still planning on helping with the Bingo game at Father Leo's on Saturday?"

I nodded. "Count me in as one of the bouncers. Last time, I had to break up a fight between two old ladies in their eighties because someone took someone else's lucky chair. Had to get a tetanus shot after one of them sank her fake choppers into my arm."

Pete snickered, and I smacked him backhanded across the chest. "Yeah, go ahead and laugh, but they're vicious, especially when it's double-or-nothing."

"I'll ask Father Leo for combat pay," Louie said with a laugh.

"Let me know how that works out."

Pete waited until Louie was gone. "You think it's really a ghost?"

I shrugged. "Could be, especially if the cabin was Eli's happy place and he didn't want to leave. If his stuff is there, something's probably anchoring him, so I'll find it, give it a salt and burn, and heave-ho the ghost." I made it sound easy. It rarely was.

The day got away from me, and by the time I headed for Ronnie's cabin, the sun already hung low in the sky. I had a couple of hours until dark, but given how late it was in the year, night fell early. I definitely wanted to have Eli out of commission before the sun went down.

Calling the place a "cabin" begged discussion. My house is a cabin, log walls and all, but it's a three bedroom with a full kitchen and basement, plus a loft. Ronnie's place was World War II vintage clapboard with a small porch, faded gray paint, and a roof that desperately needed new shingles. The place was the size of two small hotel rooms stuck together, with a minimal galley kitchen thrown in as an extra. It would have been tight for more than one person as a permanent residence, clearly designed for weekend or seasonal use. Out back, a garden shed that had seen better days looked like a stiff wind would knock it over.

Still, I guess I could see the charm, if I squinted. The gray boards of the dock were weathered and warped, but it looked solid. Although trees surrounded the cabin, giving it a secluded feel, the nearest cabin was close enough that I probably could throw a baseball and hit the side of it, if the ball could get through the branches. Town was less than two miles away, so supplies were easy to get. And the overhead wires and meter on the back of the building told me it had the hookups needed for modern life.

I unlocked the door and stepped inside, glad that the lights turned on when I flicked the switch. While the outside needed a coat of paint, a new roof, and some patches to the porch, the inside looked like what I'd expect from the bolt-hole of a crotchety old man. A brown film darkened the walls, and the stench of old cigarette smoke still hung in the air. I sniffed again and reminded myself to warn Ronnie about mold, and maybe a dead opossum somewhere.

The worn and stained furniture sagged, cushions flattened and upholstery threadbare. A faded throw rug showed a clear path where Eli most often walked. Fishing and hunting magazines covered every surface. A boxy TV with rabbit-ears sat on a table opposite the couch.

Taxidermied trophies of deer heads, prize antlers, and one or two big bass covered the walls. Little dangling oddments hung from some of the antlers, like a rustic substitute for a Christmas tree. Dreamcatchers, crystals, a saint's medallion, and a couple of other ornaments that looked handmade. They might have been decorations, or maybe lucky charms for good fishing. Sportsmen can be just as superstitious as athletes, especially when it came to beseeching the heavens for a good catch.

One glance into the kitchen and the tiny bedroom told me Eli had been living here full time before he kicked the bucket. Canned goods of questionable age lined a shelf on the wall, and a vintage refrigerator hummed in the corner, which I wasn't about to open. A back door squeezed in between the counter and the fridge. The bedroom held a twin bed, a rickety nightstand, and a small dresser. The bed was unmade, and a few articles of clothing lay on the floor. Apparently, Eli had run out of fucks to give.

Now I wished I'd have asked Louie where old Eli died. That might explain the haunting, although I was a little worried about Ronnie's claim that Eli looked solid. That usually meant a ghost powerful enough to cause trouble on the poltergeist level. Glancing around at the mess, I wondered what might hold enough emotional connection to keep Eli around.

A faded photograph in a frame with cracked glass sat on the nightstand next to the bed. From the clothing, I figured it was early 1970s. The couple smiling for the picture might have been in their mid-thirties, without a care in the world. I wondered what happened to her, whether she died or left, and how Eli ended up here. A look inside the nightstand drawer turned up nothing significant, and the dresser was mostly empty, with only a few changes of clothing. The bathroom was hardly bigger than an airplane restroom, too bare-bones to hide any secrets.

I walked into the living room as the shadows lengthened and looked out the window toward the creek to glimpse the sunset. An old man sat on the dock with a fishing pole in his hands.

Eli.

I'd brought my bag of gear in with me, and I grabbed an iron knife and the Parmesan cheese shaker I'd filled with salt because the larger openings in the lid let me spray more of Morton's finest faster. Then I headed out the door toward the wooden dock and my chance to lay this ghost to rest.

The smell hit me as soon as I cleared the front steps. I'd scraped a roadkill deer off the highway in front of my parents' house one summer, shoveling the bloated, maggot-ridden body into the woods on the other side of the asphalt. I'd thrown up afterward and couldn't get the smell out of my nose until I put menthol chest rub into both nostrils. This was worse.

"Eli?" I called out. I agreed with Ronnie—whoever sat on the old dock certainly looked solid. I could see a shock of straggly gray hair and a threadbare flannel shirt over stained work pants. His thin frame hunched forward, both hands on the fishing pole. Then he turned toward me, and I realized he only had half a face.

"Fuck, fuckety fuck *fuck*," I muttered, back-peddling quickly as zombie-Eli rose from the dock and threw his rod to one side. From the leer on the half of his mouth that still had skin, I guessed he thought I looked like a tastier catch than the pike in the creek.

Just like me to bring a salt-shaker to a zombie fight.

I didn't stick around to find out whether Eli was a shambler or a sprinter. I turned and ran, slamming the cabin door behind me.

"Fuck," I muttered for good measure and went to my gear bag. I threw the salt and short iron knife into the duffle, pulled out a steel machete, then looked for my Glock.

Machetes will take a head off real clean, but nothing beats a hollow-point bullet for once and done.

Before I could grab the gun, Eli plowed through the front window and knocked over the couch, trapping my gear bag—and gun—beneath it. I scrambled back, and Eli came over the couch like a cat, a decomposing cat with half its skin missing, eying me like I was the last can of tuna left in the world.

I swung the machete two-handed, aiming for Eli's neck, but he dodged and took the blow on his shoulder. It should have hacked his rotting arm clean off, but instead, the blade just stuck in the bone. I wrenched it free and ran for the kitchen and the back door. If I could get Eli to chase me, I could circle around, climb in the broken window, and get my gun.

All I could picture were the cartoon chases where the Scooby gang ran in and out of all the doors on a hallway chasing the guy in the mask. Only I was pretty damn sure Eli's rotting face was no mask.

I reached the back door, threw the bolt, and yanked it open, plunging down into the yard…and falling over nearly-invisible fishing line strung in an intricate web, a trip-wire trap. Either undead-Eli was smarter than the average shambler, or the old guy had been hella paranoid. I'd never know, and if I couldn't get free of my spider-wire tangle, it wouldn't matter, because I'd be zombie chow.

Eli reached the top of the steps as I began slashing around myself with the machete, slicing through the thin, strong lines that had me tied up like Gulliver. Eli sprang at me from the steps as I broke the last of the filament tethers, and I rolled to one side, letting him face plant with a squishy splat. He grabbed my ankle with a bony hand as I tried to get to my feet, and I slashed at his wrist. This time, my blade hit true, and I severed it at the joint, with the skeletal fingers still gripped tight around my leg.

I ran for the front of the house to get my gun, managing to get over the sill without impaling myself on any of the glass shards. My tumble over the couch wasn't nearly as fluid as Eli's, which says something when I can't move as well as a fucking zombie. Eli wasn't far behind me, and in a few seconds, he'd be through that window, and I'd be in big trouble. I kicked the couch to right it, and then grabbed my gear bag, dragging it back, away from the window to buy myself precious seconds. My hand closed on the grip, just as Eli pushed off from the window sill and launched himself at me like an undead zombie frog.

The Glock boomed in the small cabin and the bullet managed to hit Eli in the other shoulder, not the head.

Fuck. I had that shot. Just like I'd swung for his neck before. No one could be that lucky.

Lucky.

Shit.

I'd backed up under the antlers festooned with dreamcatchers and crystals. *What if one of these damned things actually sort-of worked?*

I grabbed the handful of trinkets down from the antlers, and Eli came to a sudden stop. He stared at me, his dead-fish gaze following the sway of the pendants that swung from their tethers. Seemed like confirmation of my theory, and I eyed the charms, trying to figure out which one might be the real thing.

So that left me with a zombie two steps in front of me, a machete in one hand, and the charms in the other, so how the hell was I supposed to burn the damn things? The long-unused fireplace behind me would be the perfect spot. I could salt and burn the charms without setting Ronnie's cabin on fire. But the minute I took my eyes off dead Eli, he'd have his zombie chompers on my neck. I had no desire to find out whether his kind of undead was contagious.

Our standoff couldn't last forever. So I did the only logical thing.

I attacked.

Eli's rotting brains hadn't expected me to go Rambo on his ass. I gave a full-throated battle cry and lunged forward, slamming the machete through Eli's chest and out the other side, taking him down to the floor with enough force to stick the tip of the knife deep into the boards.

I scrambled backward, covered with slime and goo, as Eli flailed like a gigged frog. The charms clinked in the fireplace when I hurled them, and after another couple of seconds, I'd retrieved the lighter fluid and salt from my bag. Eli flopped and wriggled, and he'd tear the hilt of the machete right through his ribs if I didn't hurry.

A douse of lighter fluid and a spray of salt, and then I flicked my Bic and threw the disposable lighter into the fireplace. The charms went up in a Butane flare, and a heartbeat later, so did what remained of Eli, crumbling into a pile of ashes around my soot-streaked knife.

Relief coursed through me, and I stumbled, catching myself on the mantle before I fell. The cabin looked like it had been hit by…a rampaging zombie. I pulled my machete free and reached for my phone. Ronnie was going to need to do something about that window.

3

"What makes you think this is my kind of job?" I asked when Louie caught me outside the body shop just as I was closing up.

"Because three kids are missing from a bus shelter, and the only thing we've got is a footprint in the mud that looks like Bigfoot," Louie replied. "We're running down everything we can through regular channels, but if this isn't a...normal...perp, then we're going to hit a wall. And if those kids might still be alive, we can't afford to waste time."

I pulled off my ball cap and wiped my sleeve over my forehead before I dug my key out of my pocket, opened the door, and motioned Louie toward my office.

The place smelled of grease and motor oil, with an undertone of burnt coffee. My desk, as usual, sat piled high with papers. Pete took care of everything he could, but when it came to official stuff, the buck stopped with me. I groaned inwardly, looking at a solid morning's worth of administrivia I'd need to sort through, and then pushed it aside and turned my attention back to Louie.

"A big footprint? That's all you've got?"

Louie shrugged. "Three middle-schoolers vanished. Their backpacks were still in the bus shelter. We found the footprint at the edge of the woods, but the rest of the ground was too hard to pick up anything else.

Searched the forest all the way down to the quarry, but came up with nothing."

"Hart's Quarry?"

"Yeah. They closed it a couple of years ago and just reopened a section back a few weeks, but the new dig is on the other side, and we didn't pick up anything near there."

I tried to remember what I knew about the quarry. When I was in high school, it was a favorite place to sneak off for some underage beer drinking. Been to more than a few parties in the quarry back in the day, until the cops got wise and started patrolling. Hart's Quarry sat back in the woods between half a dozen farms. It had been working its way through a large hill, hauling away gravel, for decades. Just a big pit with some construction equipment. I couldn't remember hearing about any gruesome deaths, which made it even less likely for the disappearances to have a supernatural cause.

"I'll check it out, but are you sure the kids didn't just run away?"

Louie gave me a look that said I was a dumbass. "And go where? Their parents saw them off at seven thirty in the morning. Mrs. McNamara waved at them at seven forty-five on her way to a doctor's appointment. The bus driver says that when he pulled up at eight oh-one, no one was in the shelter, but he saw their bags, and that's when he called the cops. They never showed up at school, and they haven't come home. I don't think they hailed a cab," he added sarcastically. Out here in the middle of farm country, cabs were a rarity, something we were more likely to see on TV than in real life.

"Okay," I agreed, rubbing the back of my neck. "I'll go take a look, but if I find anything, I'm betting it'll toss the ball back in your court."

Louie let out a long breath. "Frankly, if you just turned up a lead, I'd be happy. Right now, we've got three missing kids and no leads. Except one."

I looked up. "Yeah?"

"Carl Kinney lives at one of the farms that is assigned to that bus stop. He's in the same school as the missing kids, but he quit taking the bus last week. Said it was 'creepy.'"

"Huh." I slid a hand over my jaw and realized I needed a shave. "I know where the Kinney farm is. Think his folks would let him talk to me?"

"I'll call them. His cousin Jake is one of the ones who vanished. Pretty sure they'll do whatever they can to help."

Well, fuck. I hadn't planned to spend the next couple of days on a hunt, but I couldn't walk away from a case like this, not if I might be able to help. I still thought Louie was grasping at straws, but if he was desperate enough to risk the raised eyebrows of getting the local "ghost chaser" involved, the least I could do was sniff around.

I headed out to the Kinney farm an hour later, after I'd had a chance to shower, change clothes, and wolf down a sandwich. I tried to time my arrival to miss dinner and sighed when I got there and found the family still at the table. Mrs. Kinney hurried over to let me in. She was a comfortably plump woman with a short blond bob and a firm set to her jaw. I guessed that she was five or six years older than I was and pushed my mind away from dwelling on the fact that other people my age had families and tween children. I had a dog and a reputation as a crazy monster hunter.

"Mr. Wojcik. Come in. Officer Marino said to expect you. Have you eaten?"

"Thank you, but yes. Sorry to interrupt—"

"No interruption," she said firmly. "Coffee?"

I smiled, giving in gracefully, since I didn't think she'd stop until she'd supplied me with some kind of hospitality. "Please. Black with sugar." She hurried away, then returned with a generously-sized mug and motioned me toward the living room.

"Please, sit down. I'll get Carl."

She didn't return, but a young man who looked about fourteen shuffled in. Carl Kinney was all awkwardly long limbs, and he hadn't grown into his hands or feet. By the size of his sneakers, I figured he was due for a growth spurt that might put him on the basketball team.

Carl sat down opposite me but still didn't look up. Lank dark hair fell into his eyes, and even in the soft lighting of the side table lamp, I could see a sprinkling of acne. "I told the cops everything I know," he said quietly.

"I'm sorry to make you repeat," I said as gently as I could. I remembered being his age and how much it sucked, no longer a kid and not quite an adult. "But I look at things a little differently, and maybe I'll pick something up the cops didn't."

Carl looked at me then, and his pale blue eyes were troubled. "You'll just make fun of me, like everyone else."

"I promise that won't happen. Louie—Officer Marino—said something about you not wanting to wait at the bus shelter?"

Carl nodded and dropped his gaze again. "I didn't mind all of last year, or before that. We've always waited at that shelter. But lately, it just felt... strange. Like somebody was watching us. I tried to tell the others, but they just laughed it off, said I'd been watching too many horror movies. And then a couple times, I swear I saw something in the woods. But nobody else did, and they wouldn't believe me. That's when I asked Mom to drive me to school." He sagged against the couch cushions, braced for mockery.

"What did you see in the woods?" I asked. His head came up fast, searching my expression to see if I was pulling his leg. He must have found what he needed because he finally relaxed.

"I'm not sure," Carl said carefully. "It's not real sunny out at that time of day, you know? But it didn't move like a deer, and it looked bigger than a person. I couldn't shake the feeling that it was watching us."

"Did you ever go looking for it?"

Carl's eyes widened. "Hell—I mean heck—no. If it wasn't real, I didn't want the others to tease me about taking them on a wild goose chase. And if it was real, I didn't want to catch it."

"When did you first see it? How long ago?"

Carl was quiet, thinking for a moment. "About two weeks ago. When it didn't go away, that's when I asked Mom for a lift. The others wouldn't listen to me. I should have argued more—"

"Dude, you tried. It's not on you if they wouldn't listen. And we don't know what happened yet, so maybe they're all right. You're sure they didn't decide to go on some crazy road trip? Ditch school and run off to the big city?"

He snorted. "Where? Pittsburgh?" Carl shook his head. "Nah. And they wouldn't leave their stuff. Caitlin and Jay, they'd never go anywhere without their packs. Or their phones."

That, I could believe. "Anything else?"

Carl frowned. "Just...those times I thought I saw something? There was a strange smell. Like really bad B.O. Only not quite like in the locker room. It stank, but...different."

"Did anyone else smell it?"

Carl gave me a look like I was stupid. "You think I was going to ask? They'd blame me for ripping one."

I could tell he'd shared all he could. "All right," I said, rising and setting my empty cup aside. "Thanks for talking to me. And Carl—stay away from the bus shelter. Something's going on, and until we figure out what, you're safer in a car, no matter what anyone says."

Carl nodded without looking up. I clapped a hand on his shoulder and saw myself out.

W inter in these parts can be brutal, and it's damn cold early in the morning with the wind. Rural kids waiting for a bus could turn into icicles by the time their ride came, so little homemade plywood shelters sprang up to, at least, break the wind. They're not much, just a roof and three walls, open on one side. In some cases, they're hardly as big as a phone booth, while others have room for three or four people, huddled close. They dot the roadside, empty and a little forlorn. The challenge for their builders is to provide enough cover to protect kids from the winter wind and leave them open enough that they don't become make-out rooms.

I stood in front of the shelter where the kids vanished and slowly turned in a circle. The woods Carl mentioned began at the far side of narrow field that ran behind the little shack. I squinted against the cold breeze, straining to see beneath the treeline. In the mid-morning sun, the bare trees were a distant shadow. Even with the lone security light someone at a nearby farm had rigged up on the pole above the shelter, I questioned what Carl could have seen at oh-dark-thirty waiting for the bus.

From the trampled dead grass, I knew the cops had been here. They were looking for a human monster, and as I'd told Louie, my money still rode on that bet. Still, I'd promised I'd look for other possibilities, so here I was, freezing my ass off in the December cold. I rummaged in my bag and pulled out my EMF meter, moving it slowly through the plywood shelter, watching to see if the needle ticked up with a hint of electromagnetic frequencies that might indicate ghost activity. Nothing. I looked for traces of sulfur and came up empty.

The ground was frozen hard today, but when the teens vanished, we'd had a warm spell for a day or so, enough to allow for a footprint in a wet spot. I found the print Louie mentioned and put my own size twelve boot next to the giant impression. By comparison, my boot looked almost petite. I bent down. Not only was the print huge, but it wasn't quite right, even if an NBA all-star had decided to go barefoot in a Pennsylvania field in the middle of winter. Similar, but not quite human.

I walked toward the treeline, trying to figure out how far apart prints might be if the creature was tall enough to warrant such big feet. Just near the edge of the woods, I found another partial print, one the cops must have missed. The trees overhead were bare, and the scrub on the ground was leafless as well, just sharp, grasping twigs. I moved forward slowly and picked several long, straggly gray-black strands from one of the bushes. Another step brought me to some more hair, nothing that matched any animal I could think of in the Pennsylvania woods.

A few more feet in not only found another partial footprint but a tangle of blond hair that I bet matched one of the missing kids. Then a couple of threads that might have been part of a scarf. I looked up and found myself at the edge of the Hart Quarry.

A fence around the perimeter had been twisted and broken open. Odd, because the chain link didn't look snipped, it looked like it had been torn apart with bare hands. The bare dirt sloped steeply to the floor of the quarry. This section hadn't been worked in long enough that grass struggled to grow roots to start reclaiming the land. But right through the middle, the rocky ground had been disturbed, showing long, dragging strides.

I pulled out the binoculars from my pack and scanned the ragged ridges left by the backhoes and power shovels when they scored the ground for gravel. Plenty of crags and shallow caves could give cover to anything, from coyotes to...Bigfoot. Whatever took the kids could be down there, and there were too damn many hiding places. I needed backup, especially if I was right about what our teen-snatching cryptid might be.

"I think it's a troll."

Blair and Chiara looked at me like I had two heads. "Teenagers are missing, not billy goats on a bridge," Chiara replied.

"It fits. Trolls like caves and rocky places. They smell bad. They take captives and keep them for a while before eating them. And the coarse hair caught on the bushes, along with the big prints—"

"The quarry's been around for a long time," Blair protested. "Wouldn't someone have noticed a troll? They're kinda big."

I shrugged. "No idea where it came from. The more we build out into the wild places, the more creatures get grouchy and decide to go walkabout. Maybe it crawled out of an old coal mine and wandered here looking for food."

"Trolls can sleep for decades," Chiara said, looking up from her computer, where I was certain she had already cross-referenced and researched our cryptid. "So it might have gotten displaced from somewhere else, or it might have been buried in another section of the quarry, and the new activity woke it up."

"How do we stop it?" Blair asked. "Short of stuffing a wand up its nose."

"Pretty sure that only works in the movies," Chiara replied.

"If we could draw it off and see if the kids are still alive, we might not have to kill the troll," I mused. "That's why I need backup. I can't be the distraction and rescue the kids—if they're still alive."

"What are you planning to do with the troll after you distract it?" Blair asked.

"Nothing a little dynamite can't handle," I said with a grin.

"That's what I was afraid of," Chiara muttered.

"I thought if Blair and Louie went in with me and focused on the teens, I could take care of the troll."

Chiara and Blair shared a look. I remembered it from my married days. An entire conversation went on in those few shared seconds, one that included screaming, ranting, and a little begging, all unspoken. "I'm in," Blair replied.

Chiara put a hand on his forearm and squeezed, with a pointed glare that added a coda to their silent argument. I was pretty sure it boiled down to "don't let Mark get you killed or I'll haul your ass back from the afterlife and kill you myself." And I suspected more than a few threats to my wellbeing were included just for good measure.

"Good. The sooner we go after it, the more chance we've got that at least some of those kids are still alive. We're losing the light today, but first thing in the morning, once the sun's up, we can get in without having to navigate the woods in the dark," I said. "I need some supplies."

"Gonna make a stop at Explosives R Us?" Chiara joked.

"Nah. I've got dynamite. Father Leo and the Occulatum keep me supplied. I need to pick up lighter fluid and bacon," I said, flashing my best cocky grin.

"This is really out there, even for you—and that's saying something, Wojcik," Blair muttered as I set up for project Whack-A-Troll. Louie snickered but wisely kept his thoughts to himself.

"It's perfect," I countered. "Can you think of any universally appealing smell that carries better on the breeze than bacon?" I gestured toward the bank of charcoal briquettes I'd picked up at Walmart that glowed red as they worked up a good heat. Next to the open luau pit sat a case of bacon I wheeled out of a friend in the meat department at Giant Eagle.

"Pretty sure bacon isn't exactly universal," Blair replied. "Plenty of people don't eat it—"

"Doesn't mean the smell doesn't drive them wild, or that they don't have bacon-fueled dreams of forbidden crunchy pork goodness."

Blair cocked an eyebrow. "You're a strange man, Wojcik. Even stranger than I previously believed. Now that I know how much bacon presses your buttons, I might have to bleach my brain."

This time Louie did snicker, and I glared at him. I would have smacked him, but he's a cop. "Maybe it's a guy thing," I muttered.

"You sure you have the rest of the stuff ready?" Louie asked.

I nodded. While Louie and Blair covered me, I scoped out a shallow canyon in the quarry that appeared troll-free, but would do nicely for an impromptu, explosives-fueled landslide to send the creature back to sleep long enough to be someone else's problem.

"It's rigged. And I've got plenty of bacon to lure him in," I replied.

"All right," Blair replied, throwing her hands up. "I'd be hearing about this later, but now we had a job to do. "Let's go see if we can find where he's stashed the kids, and then you can kick off Operation Squeal-Like-A-Pig."

"Paddle faster, I hear banjos," I replied, punctuating my response with a gesture. Blair replied with an Italian hand signal she'd probably learned from Chiara.

They headed toward the old section of the quarry, and I started ripping into the case of bacon. While I waited for Blair and Louie to finish their recon, I readied some of the ammunition I needed to send the troll in the right direction without making him chase me. Since the goal was to blow up the quarry around him and bury him beneath tons of dirt and gravel, it would be really good for me not to be there when it happened.

Half an hour later, Blair and Louie came jogging back. "We found them," Louie reported. He pointed off to the left. "There's a narrow cleft back there, with some overhang, kind of a shallow cave. Blair spotted them. The troll—or whatever that thing is—looked like it was napping across the entrance. We saw at least three people behind it, but they weren't moving so no telling whether they're still alive."

Damn. "We need to bring them home, one way or the other," I replied. "Get into position. I'm going to throw some bacon on the grill."

A case of bacon is a hell of a lot of smoked pork awesomeness. I flung those beautiful fatty strips onto the banked coals. A pit like I'd made probably could have roasted a whole pig, but we were fresh out of banana leaves, and I didn't look good in a grass skirt.

Even with long tongs, the heat nearly scorched my arms as I laid out the meat on the hot coals. The aroma of cooking bacon filled the air, and I knew I drooled a little bit. Blair and Louie waited out of sight, near the cleft in the hillside where the kids were stashed, opposite where I hoped to lead the troll to buy them time.

If I'd have had an electric source, I would have brought fans to waft that powerfully salty-wonderful scent deeper into the quarry. There was enough bacon on the coal pit to make BLTs for all of Conneaut Lake, and have some left over. A troll might consider it a snack, but I just hoped he'd be hungry enough to come find those delicious smells.

The ground shook with a heavy footstep, and I figured the troll woke up. If he wanted coffee with his bacon, I was screwed.

Grabbing my bag of supplies, I made myself scarce, figuring it wouldn't be good if the big guy saw me by the food. Trolls weren't the sharpest tacks in the box, but even he might figure out a trap if he spotted me, since I had to reason to invite him for breakfast.

Each footstep sent a slight tremor through the ground. Here and there along the scraped sides of the quarry, little rivulets of rocks began trickling down. The troll had stomped his way out of the part of the dig where he'd left the kids, his whole attention focused on the bacon.

I finally got a good look at him. Carl was right: tall, muscular, vaguely human with feet and hands far too big for his body. But there, the resemblance ended. The troll's skin looked greenish-gray, and his bald, misshapen head and ugly, squashed-in features didn't resemble the big-nosed, funny-looking dolls I'd seen in gift shops. No friendly smile and mile-high shock of pink hair could turn this mofo cute. And when he opened his mouth, panting for the taste of the grilling meat, his sharp, filthy teeth suggested that his real preference ran more to long pig. He wore a ragged loincloth, for which I will be eternally grateful, and had a cow-horn that I guessed he used as some kind of trumpet on a strap around his neck.

My hand itched for a gun, but I fought down the urge. Although I had my Glock and my hollow-point bullets—as well as a shotgun—nothing short of an elephant gun or a cannon was going to punch a hole in the troll's thick hide. For that, I had dynamite and C4, but I had to get him into position. And I had to get myself out of his range, which meant scrabbling up to higher ground, on an outcropping that the gravel diggers had, for some reason, left behind. Now I stood above the bacon pit as if I were perched on my own rocky island. I could see Blair and Louie leading the kidnapped teens out the back way. And I had a clear shot at the troll.

First though, he intended to eat every strip of bacon on those coals. Then I watched in fascinated horror as the long gray cow-like tongue proceeded to lick the hot coals clean of every trace of pork drippings. Holy fatback, that was a sight I wish I could un-see.

When the troll was done choking down the bacon and sucking the briquettes clean, he looked around for more and gave a lonesome, anguished howl. I'd heard something like that when the all-you-can-eat Chinese buffet ran out of crab legs, but the troll managed to be even louder.

Time to play fetch.

"Hey, ugly!" I yelled. And I held up a tennis ball wrapped completely in bacon. I tossed it up in the air to waft the smell his way, and his dark little piggy eyes lit up. Then I threw it toward the canyon on the other side of the old section, where I had the explosives set. "Go get it!"

The tennis ball landed in the direction of the cleft where I wanted him to go, and he lumbered toward it. I thought he might pick off the bacon, but no, he just popped the whole ball into his mouth like a bouncy appetizer and swallowed it whole. By that point, I had my wrist-brace slingshot out, and I used it to shoot another bacon ball into the mouth of the canyon.

The troll followed, even as his heavy footsteps made the ground around me shake. I stepped back from the edge, not wanting to have it crumble beneath me. I shot more of the bacony lures to draw the troll farther into the deep, narrow "v" between excavated cliff sides, until he was far to the back, right where I wanted him.

Out of pity, I shot the last of my bacon balls, because even a troll deserves a good last meal. Then I pressed the button, and the hilltop and cliff walls exploded.

First, I fell flat on my ass as the whole quarry rumbled and the walls of the dig came tumbling down onto the troll, sending up a huge cloud of dust and dirt. I was just a little under an eighth of a mile from the target, within the range for my slingshot, but far enough away I thought I'd be safe from the blast.

I underestimated. The next thing I knew, I was tumbling, caught in a landslide of gravel and dirt, coughing and choking. When the earth stopped moving, I was buried alive, with no idea which way was up.

The waning oxygen limited my time for debate. I shifted, trying to figure out where there might be give around me. That wasn't a guarantee, but I hoped I had ended up toward the top of the cascade. I dug with my hands and felt heavy resistance. Then I kicked backward with my feet and felt the dirt shift.

Digging, wriggling, and kicking, I managed to turn over, only to get a face full of grit. I closed my eyes and clawed with my hands, as I felt myself begin to get lightheaded. Buried by an exploding troll and covered in bacon fat was not the way I wanted to meet my maker, but as my chest burned and I started to see sparks behind my eyelids, I feared I was running out of time.

As my strength failed, I thought I heard scratching and felt the dirt shift around my legs. Then voices, and the pungent smell of bacon. Either I was being rescued, or I was in Heaven, because I'm certain there's smoked pork in the afterlife.

"Got him!" Louie said, and I felt strong fingers dig into my arm. A moment later, Blair grabbed my other arm, and then hauled me free. I was covered with dirt, bruised from head to toe, and I smelled like a diner on a Saturday morning, but I could breathe again.

"You might have overdone the explosives," Blair noted. When I got my bearings, I followed her gaze. Where there had been a cleft between two cliffs each about four stories high, a bowl-shaped depression now lay. And underneath those tons of stone and dirt was the troll, if the charges hadn't blown him to smithereens.

"Damn," I muttered.

"Let's get out of here," Louie said, helping me stand. I waved off further assistance, and though everything hurt, I figured I could make it as far as the truck. I kicked at something in the dirt. The hollowed horn trumpet I'd seen on a strap around the troll's neck lay near the bank of charcoal, where it must have fallen when he was worshiping the buffet. I picked it up as a souvenir and put it in my pack.

"The kids?" I asked.

"Got them. They're traumatized, but not hurt," Blair replied. "Be interesting to see what kind of stories they come up with for their therapists because 'taken by a troll' probably isn't going to fly."

I shrugged. "They're smart. They'll lie, tell the shrink what she wants to hear. They'll be okay." I glanced back at the blast site. "Shit. I've got to make sure Father Leo gets the higher-ups to pay off the quarry and declare that section untouchable."

Louie loaded two of the kids in his truck. The third rode back with Blair. They could be the heroes and see the kids safely back to their families. Although my ears rang, my head throbbed, and I felt like I'd been tumbled inside a cement mixer, I ignored Blair's advice and drove home.

Demon greeted me at the door, tail wagging hard enough to sweep everything from the coffee table. I scratched him behind the ears, tossed him a cookie, and staggered into the bathroom. A hot shower did wonders, washing away the grit and bacon smell. Bruises bloomed all over the front of my body, and from the way my muscles ached, probably the back as well. I was sure I looked like I'd lost a cage fight. My lip was split, and a rock had clipped me hard on the back of my head as I'd been swept away with the falling gravel. Tonight seemed perfect for pizza delivery, a couple of beers, and whatever was on The History Channel.

Then my phone went off, with a reminder of the wedding reception at eight.

4

Ghosts didn't scare me. Neither did vampires or werewolves. I could salt and burn restless spirits, and shoot or slice the others. I'd even bagged a were-squonk, a zombie, and a troll, plus the marsh monster. All in a day's work.

Events that required dress slacks and a tie terrified me. Even more so if they required a jacket. Wedding receptions generally assumed civilized dress. Which meant I was shit out of luck.

I glanced in the mirror and figured I cleaned up well, although I still looked like I'd been in a bar fight. One eye had bruised into a not-quite shiner, my split lip had stopped bleeding but still looked puffy, and my hands looked like I'd dug myself out of a grave.

My friends wouldn't have cared. But they weren't going to be at the reception. My niece Nikki had gotten married earlier today, and tonight was the party.

Sean's daughter. My dead brother. With the wife who hated my guts for living when her husband died. Like I didn't have enough survivor guilt as it was. Amy refused to have me at the ceremony, but Nikki put her foot down about the reception. Which meant she was every inch my brother's girl.

So, for the second time today, I headed into battle. I grabbed the present I'd left by the door to remind me to go. The store wrapped it much better than I could have managed. Blair and Chiara picked it out and assured me Nikki would love it. Right now, I couldn't even remember what the gift was. That didn't matter. Nikki wanted her Uncle Mark to share her special day, and so I would, and the devil take the hindmost.

I even ran the truck through the car wash. Amy would find a million reasons to fault my continued existence, and I didn't want to give her any ammunition. Hell, I didn't want to fight over who missed Sean more, although I'd been his brother longer than she'd been his wife. I heard him scream when the wendigo tore him apart, after the creature had tossed me into a tree and knocked me senseless. And after I'd lit the monster up with my flare gun, too little too late, I'd held Sean while he died, right next to the cooling corpses of my dad, uncle, and cousin. I loved him, and I mourned him, and I'd miss him forever. And if there was ever a competition I didn't want to win, it was this one.

The parking lot at the Polish Club in Sharon was already mostly full when I eased the truck into a space. I adjusted my tie, checked myself in the rear-view mirror, and then grabbed my jacket and gift. My stomach clenched like it always did when I went to face my worst nightmares, and I felt naked without my gun. But my weapons wouldn't do me any good here, so I'd just have to rely on my natural wit and charm.

In other words, I was totally fucked.

The party had already started, and I slipped in the back, handing off my gift to a waiting attendant and giving her my name so I could get the right "hello, my name is" tag. I lingered in the back, not quite sure where to go.

After Sean and the others died, people who had been part of our friend group for years drifted away and never came back, as if they could catch death cooties from me. Some stayed, but many others didn't come around anymore. When Lara left me, that peeled away still more of my social circle. Now, I'd settled in with a core pack of people I could trust to have my back and take me for all I was worth at poker. But for a few years, when I needed my family, it had been rough.

"Uncle Mark!" Nikki's squeal sounded just the way I remembered from tickle-fests and bedtime stories. She made a beautiful bride, all grown up, no longer the sullen, grieving schoolgirl who had to bury her father. Sean had been seventeen when he'd married Amy. Nikki had just turned seventeen herself. I felt ancient.

I grinned from ear to ear and swept her up into my arms, ignoring my protesting ribs that might have been cracked from the landslide. "You look fantastic, Pumpkin," I said, kissing her on the cheek. She took my hand and led me into the fray, straight toward a young man in a tuxedo with a gobsmacked look on his face.

"Uncle Mark, this is Trey. Trey, this is my Uncle Mark."

Trey had a deer-in-the-headlights look I remembered from my own wedding. I took his hand and shook it for both of us. "Nice to meet you, Trey. You've got a real special girl here, hope you know that."

Trey managed a slightly incoherent answer, which I took to be affirmative. Before I had to make conversation, Nikki dragged me across the dance floor to greet a few elderly great-aunts whom I barely remembered. My mom had passed on by the time we went on the hunt, and Uncle Christoph was divorced. Greg, my cousin, had been dating someone, but they hadn't gotten engaged yet. I'd still been with Lara. And Sean had Amy and Nikki. Since Dad didn't have any other siblings and Mom was an only child, there wasn't much-extended family. Greg's sister had never stayed close. I'd just had Amy and Lara, and then even that went to hell.

"I'm so glad you came, Uncle Mark," Nikki said, tugging me in yet another direction. "I miss you. And I'm sorry about Mom. She's...Mom."

"I understand."

"I wish Dad could have been here," Nikki said, and her smile looked a little watery.

I hugged her close and kissed the top of her head. "Me, too, kiddo. Me, too."

Nikki pointed me to my assigned table for dinner, with a group of people I didn't know but which was fortunately out of Amy's blast zone. I'd glimpsed her a couple of times in the crowd and wondered if Nikki's sudden need to play tour guide had been an attempt to forestall an ugly showdown. I'd already resigned myself to taking whatever Amy dished out so as not to spoil Nikki's special day, and I hoped like hell Amy could put her grief aside long enough to do the same.

Over on the far side of the reception area, a DJ started setting up for dancing after dinner. I really hoped I didn't have to do the Chicken Dance, but I'm pretty sure you can't get issued a marriage license in Northwestern PA without it.

"Are you the guy who owns the auto body garage out near Atlantic?" My tablemate was an older gentleman with gray hair who looked wealthy and distinguished in a dark suit and power tie. His place card said "Ted Collins."

"That's me."

"The ghost hunter?"

I resisted the urge to tug at my tie. People's opinions tended to split into two camps when my other profession came up. Either they wanted to talk all about the shows they'd seen on TV or the ghost tour they'd done on their vacation, or they launched into a rant about how there was no such thing as ghosts. And in both cases, it left me struggling not to be a total asshole. So I smiled and hoped my eye didn't twitch.

"Yes."

To my surprise, Ted slid a business card to me. "I run an auction business out on Route 19, and we have a problem that I think is in your wheelhouse."

"Tell me about it." Talking shop meant I didn't have to strain for chit-chat.

The other people at our table were engaged in their own conversations, including Ted's wife. He leaned a little closer and dropped his voice. "We got in a new shipment for a big estate sale. Some doctor up in Meadville. Most of the stuff is pretty normal, but there's a painting that has me freaked out."

I raised an eyebrow. "What's the painting of?"

Ted shook his head. "The painting shows people sitting in the lobby of a grand hotel. It's nicely done in oils, although I've never heard of the artist. But I swear the painting is alive."

That got my attention. "Alive?"

"An object from one of the other collections will go missing—something distinctive, one of a kind—and the next time I look at the lobby painting, the missing item is somewhere in the picture, and it wasn't beforehand. Twice now, my staff has sworn they've seen a stranger milling about one of the rooms where no one should be, but when we go to look, there's no one there. Both times, they recognized someone in the painting as being the person they'd seen."

"Maybe they need more time off," I suggested.

"Then just yesterday, I noticed a new person in the scene. Someone who wasn't there before. It's the old man who owned the painting, the one who died. Now he's in the picture."

Okay, shit just got real. "That's...very interesting." My mind raced. "Can you tell me the name of the painter?"

"Thomas Arhawk. My staff researched his work, for the auction catalog and the appraisal. He isn't well known. The painting is nicely done, but hardly a Rembrandt." Ted wrote the artist's name on the back of his business card. "Maybe you'll see something if you look into him that we didn't."

If Arhawk was a dark witch or had made a deal with the devil, it wasn't likely to be on his web page, but I'd turn it over to Chiara and see what her online ninja tricks could come up with. "I'm very interested."

"Please, call me," Ted said. "I need your help, and I can pay your fee."

I pocketed the card, surprised and intrigued. Ted looked more like a banker than an auctioneer, and not the kind to believe in ghosts or ask for help. "I'll call you tomorrow," I promised. "How do you know Nikki?"

Ted smiled, and all of a sudden looked much friendlier. "She worked at the auction over the summers. One of the best employees I ever had. Happy she's going on to bigger things, but sorry to lose her." He glanced at my name card. "Family?"

"Her uncle." I could almost see the wheels turning in his mind and figured he remembered the news stories about the hunt. To my eternal gratitude, he didn't bring it up.

I found myself wishing I'd brought Sara with me. We weren't really a couple. Not yet, maybe never. But for the first time since Lara walked out, I'd found someone I enjoyed spending time with. She ran a bed and breakfast out near Kane, but my work took me through those parts fairly often, and I'll admit to taking a few detours to provide excuses to stop in. She was widowed, I was divorced, and we both were cautious. Six months had passed, and we were still going out. Right now, I missed her like crazy.

We made it through dinner and were heading up to the dessert buffet before Amy cornered me.

"I thought you'd have the good sense not to come," she hissed.

"Nikki wanted me here. So I'm here."

"Nikki wouldn't have asked you if she knew the truth. Sean's dead because of you."

I glanced around, hoping no one else was listening, and tried to nudge Amy away from the cake. "Sean's dead because a wild creature killed him. I wish I'd been faster with the flare gun, but I'd just had my head cracked open against a tree. God, Amy, I'd give anything for a do-over. But it doesn't work like that."

"People talk about you," she spat. "They say you're crazy, hunting 'monsters.'" She didn't need to put the word in air quotes. Her scathing tone did the job quite well. "Maybe you did something with all your mumbo-jumbo that called that thing, that creature that killed them. You brought this down on them."

I took a deep breath and willed my fists to unclench at my sides. Pointing out to Amy that I didn't start hunting monsters until after the tragedy wasn't likely to break through the story she'd told herself. She needed a bad guy, someone to blame, and since the wendigo had gone up in flames and I survived, I got to be the whipping boy. "Please Amy, not here. Not today. For Nikki."

"You probably made some kind of deal with the devil." Amy's expression showed her contempt. "All that occult stuff you're into, witchcraft, satanic cults—"

"None of that's true." I didn't mention that one of my monster hunting partners was a priest. Nothing at this point was going to change her mind.

"Oh, God. Did you come to put some kind of hex on Nikki? Are you going to take her away from me like you took Sean?"

Amy's voice rose, and I saw Nikki give me a look from the head table, trying to figure out what was going on.

"No hex, Amy. I'd never harm Nikki, or you—or Sean. Please, don't spoil Nikki's party. I'll go."

"Damn you to hell, Mark Wojcik. I hope you burn for what you've done."

I kept on walking. Everyone heard Amy's last salvo, and I knew they'd turned to look. I kept my face blank and made a beeline to the door. Nikki actually ran to intercept me, hiking her big skirt up to her knees.

"Uncle Mark—"

I cupped her face gently and leaned down to kiss her forehead. "It's okay, kiddo. Your mom's just tense with all the wedding stuff. Thanks for the invite. Hope you like the present. And call me sometime. I'll drive over, and we can do lunch."

Nikki stretched on tiptoe to kiss my cheek. "Whatever she said, I don't believe it," she whispered. "Love you."

"Love you, too, Nikki," I said. "Now go dance with your husband." And with that, I headed out the door and got in my truck, with a long quiet drive in front of me.

I spent some extra time scratching Demon's ears when I got home and took him for a bit of a walk around the yard, as I tried to let go of Amy's words. Back in the day, back *before*, she and Sean and Lara and I had been tight. We got together every few weeks, babysat Nikki so Sean and Amy could go out, and went on vacations together. Then it all went to hell, just another casualty of that damn wendigo.

Once I fed Demon, I texted Chiara with the info about the artist, poured myself a couple of fingers of JD and pulled out my laptop. Demon napped on my feet while I dug around on the internet. I'd do the easy Google stuff and let Chiara dig through the seedy virtual alleys of the Dark Web.

Ted was right: Thomas Arhawk was a man of mystery. I couldn't find much of a social media trail, which in itself seemed remarkable, especially for someone trying to promote their work. He'd had a few gallery showings in Pennsylvania and Ohio, and some museum acquisitions. His webpage didn't even have a digital showcase, and none of his work was featured on any of the popular online art sites.

But what I did find intrigued me. Three of his larger works sold at auctions throughout the country, for five-figure prices. Not too shabby for someone who only seemed to have a history going back two or three years. An article about one of those sales portrayed Arhawk as a troubled, reclusive genius who had burst on the art scene out of nowhere.

That worried me. Nothing says crossroads deal with a demon like someone who goes from zero to sixty almost overnight. If Arhawk didn't sell his soul, some of that black magic Amy was so sure I practiced might have been to blame.

I sipped my glass of Jack and tried not to dwell on the reception clusterfuck. Instead, I grabbed a pen and pad and jotted down the names of the galleries and museums—and any individuals—who had acquired an Arhawk original. A quick online search gave me the identity of the local doctor whose estate sale was being handled by Ted's auction house. Then I looked to see what became of them.

"Well, lookie here," I murmured. The list read like a disaster report.

Within a year of acquiring an Arhawk painting, two of the galleries filed for bankruptcy, something that came as a surprise to the business news sites. One of the museums had a major fire, while another had a very destructive water main break. The rest of the galleries and museums fared equally badly, including a few that were the site of random shootings. Individual collectors had just as bad luck, and as best as I could piece together, most of them died within twelve to eighteen months of purchasing one of his pieces of art. The causes varied, but all were sudden, and many violent. I did my best to find photos of the unlucky purchasers, to see if they had mysteriously appeared in the hotel lobby painting.

What little "art" I owned was either blown-up snapshots I'd taken myself from hikes in the woods or prints I'd picked up cheap from roadside vendors. Right now, I felt pretty lucky that I couldn't afford the "good" stuff.

I closed the laptop and knocked back the rest of my drink. The whiskey still hadn't taken the sting out of Amy's accusations, just like ten years didn't take the pain out of my grief. As much as I had wanted to see Nikki and make her happy by attending the reception, I had been afraid doing so would slice open barely healed-over wounds. Father Leo cautioned me on more than one occasion that "death by monster" can be a form of hunter suicide, and if I were honest with myself, I'd straddled that line too many times for comfort. I would have gladly traded places with any of the people I'd lost that day. If I couldn't, then hunting down creatures like the thing that killed them would be my penance for surviving.

Before I could think better of the impulse, I speed dialed Sara. She answered on the second ring. "Mark?"

"Hey," I said. I was smooth with conversation like that. "Just...thinking about you."

She chuckled. "Did you drunk dial me?"

"No. Maybe. More like buzzed-dialed. Thinking I need to come up and take you out to dinner."

"That would be nice," she said. I heard affection and a hint of amusement in her voice, as if she wondered whether I'd remember our conversation tomorrow. "Anytime soon?"

"Next weekend? And if I'm not hunting anything, you won't have to sew me back together first."

"A true romantic," she chuckled. "Sounds good."

"Miss you," I sighed. "But I'll see you soon."

"Miss you, too," she replied. "Now go sleep off your drink. Night, Mark." I echoed her good-bye and ended the call, suddenly feeling lonelier than before I dialed.

"Come on, Demon," I said, rousing the slumbering dog. "Let's turn in. I've got a haunted painting to hunt down tomorrow."

I didn't know what to expect from Ted's auction house. What I found was a combination of art gallery and a big cinder block building like the fairground has for its craft displays. Ted met me in the office. He looked a little more relaxed than he had at the reception, with a collared shirt—no tie—tucked into dark, pressed jeans over expensive cowboy boots.

"I'm glad you came," Ted said, shaking my hand with a firm grip. "We've had another incident."

He kept talking as I followed him back to the storage area behind the showroom. We walked through a modern all-white gallery that looked like something out of a museum, with paintings on the walls and breakable things in Plexiglas cases.

"What happened?"

He ushered me into the back room. Several workers looked up from where they were busy cataloging or photographing items. "Something went missing—and damned it if didn't show up in the painting. We all swear it wasn't in the picture before. But it is now."

I stood in front of the Arhawk picture. It gave me the creeps, and I don't have a magical bone in my body. No ESP, no spidey sense, mundane through and through. And still, it made my skin crawl. I was amazed the people in the room could stand to work around it, and I didn't even want to think about having it in my house.

The painting showed a group gathered in a well-appointed lobby. Some sat, some stood. Others leaned against the frame of a large window, looking out at the grounds beyond. Children played on the floor, and a dog curled at its master's feet.

"There," Ted said, pointing to an ornate timepiece on the mantle in the painting. "The empire clock." He pointed to a frou-frou decoration that looked like it should be in some French palace. "And this is the guy who owned the painting last," he added, directing my attention to an elderly bald man slouched in an armchair.

"How long did the doctor own the painting?"

"Four years. His daughter said that he bought it when he was at a low point in his life, and things turned around for him after that, until his death."

So another sell-your-soul reversal of fortune. Doc must have been a bad negotiator. Four years is a pittance. Then again, given his age, maybe it was four more than he would have had otherwise.

"Did he buy it from the artist? Or were there previous owners?" I circled the painting, careful not to touch it. I'm no art critic; my taste tends toward landscapes and wildlife photos. Maybe a sunset over the water to mix things up. But even I could appreciate that the artist had talent. The detail looked almost photographic, and the details were impressive.

"We know very little about Thomas Arhawk," Ted conceded. "His paintings came on the market for the first time about five years ago. He guards his privacy intensely, even when doing interviews might boost the value of his work. Some professionals are wary about that level of secrecy. All kinds of rumors went around."

"Like what?"

Ted shrugged. "Everything from Arhawk being a team of painters instead of an individual, to being the alias of another famous artist who wanted a fresh start, to questions about the authenticity of his technique, since it's very photo-realistic. He hasn't had new work out for a while, so of course, there's talk about him being dead."

"And what did the critics conclude?"

Ted chuckled. "They're critics. They never 'conclude' anything. But the market ignored them and liked what it liked. So the paintings sell well."

"Except that bad things happen to the people who buy them. And sometimes, to the places that show them," I added.

The look on Ted's face told me he knew about the rumors. "You don't really believe that kind of thing."

"Kinda goes with my business."

Ted paused long enough to send the two staffers from the room. "Yes, I've heard the rumors. But all kinds of crazy things get said on those forum boards. If I believed half of what I read, I'd think that there were haunted objects all over the place—"

"Which wouldn't be completely wrong," I interjected.

He looked a bit shaken by that. "We don't often get high profile pieces of art, given where we're located. I don't know why the family didn't decide to send this to Sotheby's or Christie's—"

"Or maybe they tried and were turned down."

Ted nodded. "Maybe, if the acquisitions people were superstitious. But this could be a big windfall for us—"

"Are you willing to let people get hurt for that? Because whatever forces Arhawk was playing with, they're real, and they're dark, and they feed on blood."

That's when I noticed that the painting had changed. Where before, the people in the scene were looking at each other, or out the window, or at the children playing on the floor, now all of them faced outward, right toward us.

Shit. The painting was sentient.

I turned my back and tried to play it cool, although my heart thudded. "Can we talk in your office?"

Ted glanced around the empty room. "There's no one..." I knew the minute when he realized the painting no longer looked the same. "All right," he said, clearing his throat. "I'll put on a fresh pot of coffee." From his voice, I figured he'd be tempted to dump in some whiskey, just because.

Ted's office had a practical, stripped-down look to it, despite him being a well-to-do businessman. "I don't want to talk in front of the painting," I said when he closed the door. "I think that somehow, it...listens."

"The people had turned around."

I nodded. "Yeah. I saw that, too." I paused trying to figure out the right way to ask my next question. "How much trouble would you be in if something happened to the painting?"

He frowned as if the question hadn't been entirely unanticipated. He licked his lips, struggling to answer. "There would be an inquiry. Insurance investigations. The estate would be unhappy, since the painting is likely to fetch a good price."

"Here's the thing: I don't think we can neuter the danger and keep the painting intact," I said. "I don't know how or why, but power like that is fed into an object throughout the creation process. Arhawk paints dark magic into his works, and they hurt people. If you sell that, it's going to hurt—probably kill—the next owner. If you keep it here, it'll likely ruin you, the way it's been a curse to others. So, I believe that I can solve your problem, but the only way to do that is to destroy the painting —carefully."

"That possibility occurred to me when I asked you to investigate," Ted replied with a sigh. "I can't in good conscience sell it, but we'd never be able to convince the estate of the danger." He looked up at the ceiling, beseeching the fates. "I feel like I'm talking to the Mob. Can you...can you make it look like an accident?"

I raised an eyebrow. "Yeah. We can do that." It wouldn't be the first time I'd faked a robbery to get rid of a cursed object. I had no intention of telling him that my partner in crime would be Father Leo. *Forgive me, Father, for I have sinned. Again.*

Ted gave a sharp nod. "Yes. Do it. I'll...deal with the consequences. Just please, stop it from hurting other people."

"Go about your usual routine for the rest of the day. Don't do anything that's going to look unusual. Just make sure nobody has a reason to come back here after hours."

B y the time I got home, Chiara had left a message to call her back. I suspected that the kind of intel she had for me shouldn't be left on a voicemail.

"Whatcha got?" I asked when I pulled into the drive and returned her call.

"Arhawk seems to have tangled up *Picture of Dorian Gray* and the collected work of Aleister Crowley," she replied. "He got into trouble in college for making terroristic threats toward other classmates and vandalizing a dorm room with pig's blood."

Sean used to complain about his roommate leaving dirty laundry on the floor. Arhawk was out of their league.

"What else?"

"Galleries shunned some of his early work for being too violent," she continued. "He had a thing for painting dismembered bodies. It didn't sell."

"I'm amazed. Didn't people buy paintings done by that clown serial killer?"

"Gacy. Yes. But I guess there's still a limit. At least this week." She shuffled papers for a second. "I wasn't kidding about Aleister Crowley. He was a painter, too, in addition to all his magic and occult writing. Arhawk became obsessed with him in college, which sealed the deal about getting him thrown out."

"I've seen Crowley's paintings. They're a lot more...symbolic...than the one at the auction house."

"Yeah, Arhawk apparently wised up," Chiara replied. "His crazy shit didn't sell, and he needed money. So, he started painting normal scenes and doing rituals to work the magic in with the paint. Most were curses that somehow worked to his benefit. He either gave them to people he wanted to be rid of or used them to influence buyers to hand over their money, their investments, even their wives."

"That's quite a racket."

"It worked—until he tried it on someone with more magic than he had," Chiara said. "Arhawk died of a mysterious wasting disease. His agent kept the death quiet. Arhawk's condition didn't match anything in the medical books. He believed he had been cursed and said so to anyone who would listen. But the doctors wouldn't believe him, and he'd made so many enemies in the supernatural community that I'm guessing they were all celebrating the fact that someone figured out how to get rid of him. He died young, but the source I found said he looked like an old man."

"You think he went into one of his paintings?"

"Could be," she allowed. "Maybe one of his curses backfired. Or maybe he thought he could be immortal if he transferred his essence into the art. But I think someone just didn't like him and whacked him."

"Good to know. Any ideas about how to get rid of the painting?"

"You could ship it down to those people you know in South Carolina who deal with that kind of thing. They could make it disappear."

"Yeah, I thought about that, but getting it there is the problem. That's a long way from here, and it'll have been reported stolen."

"Shit. I couldn't find anything specific about neutralizing the magic. Arhawk seemed pretty omnivorous in the kinds of power he studied, and so did Crowley, so I doubt he used spells from a single tradition."

"Just keeps getting better and better," I mumbled under my breath. "So we just try everything until something works?"

"Salt and fire are tradition-agnostic," Chiara pointed out. "Father Leo might be able to dampen the magic and give you an edge. Just be careful—Arhawk might not have actually been the big deal warlock he thought he was, but everything I've found says he did have power and knew how to craft a nasty curse. You'd be cute as a toad, Wojcik, but I don't have a terrarium big enough."

"Funny. Not. Okay, thanks for the info. How about you and Blair come over, and we eat popcorn and mock ghost hunting shows? We can turn out the lights and admire their night-vision goggles."

"And keep yelling, 'did you see that' every five minutes," she added. "Tell you what—why don't we go to your place before you get back and we'll be your alibi?"

"Works for me. Just don't eat all the popcorn." Good friends help you hide the bodies. Best friends not only help you dig the grave, they bring snacks.

For a priest, Father Leo made a damn good lookout. I picked the lock on the auction house's back door and silenced the alarm with a handy magical item a witch who owed me a favor made for me. The warehouse had alarms on the doors but no cameras, Ted assured me. And no motion sensors. Maybe in a big city, those would have been common. Not so much out here in the boonies.

We crept into the storage room and found it just the way it had been that afternoon. A security light gave us enough illumination to move without tripping over crates and chairs. Next to the wall, a workbench lay littered with jewelers' tools, specialty cleaning brushes, and an array of bottles that looked to my untrained eye to range from paint thinner to degreaser and Lysol.

My simple plan involved stealing the painting, hiking a mile behind the auction house into the woods to an old abandoned dump, and setting the artwork on fire, with Father Leo mumbling some Latin. I didn't really think it would be quite that easy, but life had taught me that complicated plans just made fate more determined to fuck me over.

Movement at the edge of my vision made me turn my head, only to find nothing but shadows. Another almost-there motion and my head whipped back the other direction, but saw nobody.

"Did you—"

Father Leo nodded. "Yes. There are entities present. Something not quite human and very unpleasant." I didn't ask how he knew that, but I'd always suspected that the padre had some clairvoyance of his own going on.

"Cover me while I snatch it," I murmured.

I moved forward while Father Leo began to chant. It wasn't the exorcism from the *Rituale Romanum*, which is the extent of my Latin, and I didn't recognize the words, but Chiara thought he could tamp down on Arhawk's curse, and any help was welcome. I had my eye on the big painting and tried to figure out how I was going to need to tilt it to get it out the door.

A woman in an evening dress body slammed me into the wall. I went to grab her, and when she turned sideways, she became nothing but a line. As if she were a drawing come to life.

I pulled a knife from my belt and slashed, cutting the figure in two. She vanished and left a slick of oil paint on my blade, along with droplets of pigment-like blood on the floor. Before I could move toward the painting again, a man in a dark suit came at me, hands outstretched to wring my neck. He dodged my blade, and I feinted to the right, trying to get around him. I wondered what would happen if I dug my knife down the center of the canvas. Would it destroy the sentience, or let it escape?

A knife flew through the air and hit the man in the center of his back, point protruding from his chest. Father Leo's no slouch: his chant never wavered, although I did catch a hint of a self-satisfied smirk. The man from the painting vanished, but in the next breath, two more of the figures from the canvas closed on me.

Father Leo apparently decided that faith without works would get us dead, so while he kept up the chant, he moved in with an iron bar he had brought from my truck. Ghosts hate iron, and it stood to reason other spirits didn't much like getting a beat down. He swung for the person on the right, a woman in a cocktail dress, while I went at the man in a polo shirt on my left.

The iron bar made the woman's spirit vanish. I swung and missed with my knife, and the painting creature grabbed at me. His ice-cold hands pulled at something deep inside me as they connected, and I swore my heart stuttered as I gasped for breath. Then Father Leo brought the iron bar down through the apparition with both hands, and I staggered.

"Don't let them touch you!" I warned as he kept up his chant. I dove for the painting, grabbing it and wrestling it off the tripod.

Arms reached out from the surface of the canvas, and I dropped the artwork, scrambling backward. It had felt for all the world as if the creature who had grabbed me wanted to pull me into that infernal portrait, sucking out my life and soul in the process.

The painting lay face-up on the concrete floor, and as I watched, a man began to emerge as if he were climbing out of a door to a basement. I stumbled backward and collided with the workbench. I threw the first thing I grabbed, a pair of pliers. They went right through the man, ripping a hole in his shirt, but this time, the creature did not just vanish.

I reached behind me, and my hand closed on a can. I meant to lob it, but hesitated long enough to read the label. Paint thinner. As Flat Man eased his way out of the painting, freeing first one leg and then the other, I wrenched off the lid and sent a spray of solvent splashing over both our 2-D menace and the painting beneath his polished oxfords.

Green melting witches had nothing on this guy. His face *smeared*, features blurring into a flesh-colored nothing, and his body began to *dissolve* from the middle out. I couldn't see what the liquid did to the actual painting, but angry shrieks echoed through the storage room: women, men, a child, even a dog frantically snarling as if he, too, wanted to rip out my guts.

Melted Man wobbled toward me, and though I couldn't see his expression, there was no mistaking the malice in the way he blindly reached for me.

I sloshed the rest of the solvent at him and watched his whole shape *run* like sidewalk chalk in the rain. The puddle that had been Melted Man inched its way toward my boots, still intent on dragging me into the painting, and I sidestepped, but it followed me. I'd never heard of possessed *paint*, but there's a first time for everything.

Father Leo ran to grab one side of the damaged painting, taking care to avoid any of the leaking pigment. I took hold of the other side, and together we navigated toward the door. The air smelled of acetone and the shrieking grew louder and more frantic. The canvas bubbled and rippled as the creatures trapped inside tried to escape. On the floor, rivulets of multi-colored haunted paint ran unerringly toward us like beads of mercury.

The image of people in a parlor was lost in a runny mess of colors and bare canvas. I kept my fingers well back on the edge of the picture. As if the presence inside the painting knew we were winning, the liquefying paint on the canvas started splashing, spitting pigment at us like a cobra aiming for the eyes. Trying to keep clear of the encroaching swirls of killer paint nearly made me fall down the steps, but I managed to make it out the door. I didn't think we could get the damned thing all the way out in the woods, not without being splattered either by the canvas or the runoff.

I wondered what the use was of Father Leo continuing to chant, until I realized that his words made the encroaching pigment shrink back. His raspy voice was giving out, and he was fading fast.

"Here," I said, indicating a bare patch of ground with a jerk of my head. "It'll have to do."

The painting bucked and rattled on the dry dirt, spraying droplets of paint like a contagious convict trying to infect his captors. I pulled on gloves and grabbed a welder's mask out of the back of my truck. Then I took a KA-BAR and stabbed the painting right in the center, and drew the tip down, cutting a slice in the canvas.

"Get back!" Father Leo warned, right before he tossed a match at the acetone-soaked artwork. It went up with a roar, sending a kaleidoscope of color into the flames, but thank God, the shrieking stopped. Images of the people from the painting writhed in the flames, burning and melting, and I wondered where their trapped souls would go. I grabbed a canister of salt from my bag and flung a thick spray of it into the fire. The colors vanished with a *whoosh* as the flames leapt high, nearly to the roof. The painting began to splinter its frame and crumble in on itself, cracking like bones as it drew up into a charred ball. The flames disappeared as quickly as they came, and in what must have been a trick of the light, a shadow engulfed the burned remains, blotting it out like a mini black hole and then suddenly, all traces of the painting were gone.

"Run," I said to Father Leo. We grabbed our tools and my bag and piled into my truck. A rough lane led away from the main highway. I'd scouted it earlier and knew it brought us out on a farm road that eventually connected to the back roads we could use to get home. I didn't let go of my white-knuckled grip on the wheel until I pulled up behind Father Leo's church in Geneva.

"You know how to show a man of God a good time, Mark," Father Leo said, clapping me on the shoulder.

"I'm going to ignore how that sounded, Padre, and just say thanks for the back-up."

Father Leo's eyes twinkled, and I think he actually enjoyed the evening. "Any time, Mark. Beats hell out of proofreading the parish newsletter."

I promised him I'd help with the next Bingo night and drove home. To my surprise, a black truck identical to mine sat in the drive. I parked in the garage and closed the door, then headed into the house. Demon met me at the door, smelling of popcorn. I went to the kitchen and grabbed a beer, then headed toward the living room.

From the quick gasp and shuffle, I suspected I'd interrupted something, but by the time I got to the living room, Blair and Chiara sat upright on the couch, with the popcorn bowl on Chiara's lap. They were too suspiciously posed, and Chiara's hair looked hastily smoothed.

"Whose truck?"

Blair grinned. "One of Chiara's brothers parked it right after you left and caught a ride back with another brother. So as far as anyone knows, you've been here all night."

"Tell him thanks, and I owe him a case of beer," I said, plunking down in my recliner. I glanced at the TV. In the greenish glow of night-vision lighting, anxious-looking ghost hunters with perfect teeth and fashionably mussed hair debated whether or not they heard strange noises in oddly loud stage whispers.

"It's a marathon," Chiara said, grinning. "And they're going into a haunted hospital next."

"Sounds good to me," I replied, cracking open the beer. "Anything but an art gallery. Pass the popcorn."

5

"Three hunters every year for six years?" I asked, pushing aside my empty coffee cup. My piece of apple pie sat untouched, a clear sign my thoughts were elsewhere. The Original Best Lakeview Diner lived up to its reputation for good pie.

Father Leo nodded. "At least."

I ran a hand back through my hair. "Deer hunters?" I clarified. Not "our" kind, the ones who went looking for creatures the Fish and Wildlife Commission didn't issue permits to kill.

"Yep."

"Ever find the bodies?"

Father Leo gave me the priestly stink eye. "No. That's why they're 'missing' and not 'dead.'"

Okay, I deserved that. "Do they have any connections to each other—family, friends, work buddies, neighbors?"

Father Leo shrugged. "They came from small towns all over the area, so that's hard to say, but nothing stood out to the cops."

I snorted. When it came to the supernatural sorts of things we hunted, even good cops tended to overlook the details that mattered. "Were they together when they disappeared?" I did my best not to think of my own hunt-gone-wrong, but I didn't fool myself or Father Leo.

"No. Each one, individually, over a period of weeks in December."

I frowned. "Weeks? There's not that long a season—"

"There is if you factor in archery as well as rifle and flintlock, and antler as well as antlerless," Father Leo countered. I must have looked askance at his unexpected knowledge because he frowned. "I used to go with my brother. Before I went to seminary. Now, I'm much more comfortable blessing the meal than blessing the hunt."

"Did the families get any kind of benefit out of the disappearances?" I asked. The human heart is dark, often darker than the things we call "monsters." I learned that a long time ago. "Insurance? Inheritance? Ending troublesome marriages?"

He shook his head. "Nothing that set off the cops' radar. Not saying there wasn't, but it didn't raise red flags."

Sandy, one of the owners of the diner, came by and filled our coffee cups. "I'm honored," I joked. "Getting the boss herself." I'd gone to high school with Sandy and her husband, Vince. We went way back.

"One of the servers called in sick," Sandy said with a shrug. "Something wrong with the pie?"

I grinned. "Nah. We just got busy talking."

She cuffed me up the side of the head. "Eat first, talk later. You don't disrespect a good piece of pie."

We both chuckled. "Yes, ma'am," I replied, which just got me a playful slug to the shoulder.

"I'm the same age you are. Don't ma'am me," she warned.

"Wouldn't dream of it," I replied with my best fake innocent smile.

Father Leo motioned toward the pie when Sandy headed off. "Better eat that. I wouldn't want to be the cause of bloodshed."

"You ain't just whistlin' Dixie," I muttered, but I dug into the pie with gusto. Minutes later, when I pushed aside a scraped-clean plate, I sat back, sighed, and washed it down with coffee.

"Now, speaking of bloodshed... These hunters in the Big Woods?"

"The Occulatum wants someone to go check it out. That many years in a row sounds ritualistic."

"And I'm the poor SOB who drew the short straw?"

Father Leo rolled his eyes. "You're the poor SOB who handles the territory. Plus, it's an excuse to see Sara."

I slid him a sideways glance. "Are you matchmaking? Because I'm past the 'be fruitful and multiply' age, just sayin'."

"You're thirty-five, so that's not true. And it wouldn't hurt for you to socialize more, Mark," Father Leo said. "And I'm saying that as a friend, not a priest. Whatever 'multiplying' you do is your business, but don't quote me to the bishop."

As a rule, Father Leo didn't stick his nose into other people's business. And he wouldn't be the first of my small circle of friends who tried to nudge me toward at least dipping a toe back in the dating pool. Lara and I divorced years ago, and she'd already remarried. I just hadn't found the guts to try again, although I began to reconsider after meeting Sara during my last visit to the Big Woods to bag a were-squonk.

"So...the missing hunters," I said, trying to steer the conversation in a safer direction.

"We've got no way of knowing where they were when they vanished, but here's a map marked with where they said they were going to enter the woods," Father Leo said, and slid the folded paper across to me. "From where their trucks were found, it's a good bet they did what they said they were going to do."

"No break-ins on the trucks?"

He shook his head. "Nothing missing except the men, their wallets, and their guns. The wallets and guns were recovered in the woods, but no sign of the men. No blood. Although in each case, the underbrush had been trampled."

"Footprints?"

"Nope. But I also marked where the wallets and guns were found. There's only one other thing—"

My eyebrows rose, and I waited for the other shoe to fall. "Yeah?"

"The area they hunted in had been off-limits for a hundred years, and it just opened up six years ago."

"Sacred to the Native Americans?" I asked, trying to remember which tribes had been in that area.

"No. Cursed."

I drove up to Kane with music blaring, first thing on Friday morning. For once it wasn't snowing, but weather in December up in these parts can change in an hour, so I came ready for a blizzard. The truck already had snow tires, and I threw chains and sand in the back, plus all the requisite lock de-icer, anti-freeze windshield fluid, and a full tank of gas that promised to avoid fuel line freeze-up. I had heavy enough clothes and outerwear to storm the arctic. And I had a date with Sara that night.

Even more importantly, Father Leo had finagled a hunting license for me, so I was somewhat less likely to get arrested.

The steel gray sky threatened snow, and the wind just made the cold worse. I parked the truck, patted myself down to assure weapons were appropriately sheathed and holstered, double checked that I had my phone and the map, and headed for the trail.

Just as a patrol car pulled in next to me. I took a deep breath and tried to relax. I recognized the guy behind the mirrored sunglasses. Sheriff J. Kranmer, aka Sheriff Sumbitch.

"Wojcik," he hailed, slaughtering the pronunciation. "What brings you here?"

I forced a reasonably believable smile. "Nice day for a walk in the woods."

We'd already established a mutual dislike when I came up to hunt the were-squonk. Sheriff Sumbitch was the kind of guy who needed to mark his territory, scrape antlers on trees, and whip out a ruler to measure who was bigger. I didn't have a lot of patience for that kind of thing, but I had to put up with it—and let him win—in order to not end up in handcuffs.

"The last time you came through these parts, a park bathroom blew up."

"Huh. Go figure." I happened to know that Father Leo arranged for the Occulatum to provide an anonymous grant to the state park service to replace the facility.

"You're carrying a weapon. Got a license?"

I smiled. "Hunting or concealed carry?"

"Both."

"The carry license is in the glove compartment. And the hunting license is on my hat on the front seat."

Sumbitch took his time confirming both, just because he could. "Looks in order," he muttered, sounding mighty disappointed.

"Like I said, just came up for a walk in the woods. Not even sure I'd shoot if I saw a deer," I replied. "Hate to get blood on my truck hauling it home. Just washed it."

Sumbitch gave me a condescending look, as if I'd just confessed to being a hipster, and snorted. If he made a crack about "city types," I might not be able to contain my laughter. Even Kane was more urban than Atlantic. "Stay out of trouble," he warned.

"Planning on it," I replied.

I watched him drive away and sighed, then snagged a six-pack and headed into the woods. The snow crunched beneath my boots, four inches deep where the wind scoured it, deeper in drifts. Despite my run-in with Sumbitch, I still felt a sense of peace descend as I moved away from the noise of the road and deeper into the silence of the forest. Still, I carried a rifle, handgun, and big knife for a reason, and I couldn't afford to forget that hunters had gone missing. I didn't want to be one of them.

After I'd walked about a mile, I got my bearings and headed over to a tree I'd notched on my last trip, so I would know I'd found the right one. I set the six-pack down at the base. "Hey, Gus," I called to thin air. "Thanks again for having my back. Brought you some beer. Hope you can find a way to drink it."

"Gus" haunted the forest where he had fallen from a tree stand and died half a century or so ago. Sara knew his real name, but I'd nicknamed him Gus. He'd done me a solid in the epic battle against the were-squonk, and one good turn deserves another.

Even as bitter as the day was, I felt it grow colder still as a figure took form a little ways off. Gus looked to be in his sixties, with a fringe of gray hair beneath his gimme cap and a graying beard. He smiled when he saw me, and I imagine that it got lonely up here. From the way Gus helped me hunt the were-squonk, I figured he had spent his afterlife helping other hunters get in a good shot.

"You know anything about hunters going missing?" I asked.

He turned and walked away. I followed. He could obviously hear me, although I couldn't hear him. I wasn't a ghost whisperer, but I certainly ran into enough of them in my line of work, although usually my job was to stop restless spirits that were causing problems. Gus didn't seem to be bothering anyone, and he wasn't in a hurry to move on, so we had left things status quo.

We tramped through the underbrush for a little ways, and then Gus paused and pointed toward a massive old oak. I frowned, trying to figure out what he meant me to see, until I realized a man's body lay beneath the tree.

I approached slowly, afraid the hunter had fallen asleep, and unwilling to get shot for surprising him. Then I grimaced, both from the smell and the details that became clearer as I got closer. The man sprawled against the trunk, missing half of his skull. The rifle in his frozen fingers took the mystery out of what happened. Nothing supernatural, which made it all the more tragic. He'd been dead long enough for the body to freeze, but still pretty recent.

"Shit," I muttered. I pulled out my phone, hoped I could get a signal, and dialed Steve Louden, a local cop who'd helped me out a couple of times. I figured out the coordinates and gave the location, then hung up. No sense hanging around. It was too damn cold, and Steve knew where to find me if he needed to.

I looked to Gus, who stood to one side, a sorrowful expression on his face. "Thanks for making sure he gets home," I said. Given that Gus had haunted these woods for half a century, I guessed that no one had ever found his body.

"Have you seen anything else spooky?" I asked. "Because hunters are going missing about the same time each year, and I need to figure out why."

Gus's eyes went wide, and he shook his head, raising his hands in a gesture that warned: "back off."

I frowned. "So you know what I mean, but you're telling me it's dangerous?"

He nodded, still looking like he'd seen, well, a ghost.

"I know it's dangerous. That's what I do. I don't think it happened this close to other people. Maybe in the backcountry, that area that didn't use to be open for hunting."

Gus looked torn. He knew I hunted bad things, creatures that weren't supposed to exist. But if he knew what took the other men, then he had a sense for the risk that I didn't understand. Gus looked like he was debating something with himself, and then he finally turned and started walking again.

I followed. The sun hung high overhead, though with the clouds, that did nothing to brighten the cold, gray light. We walked for a while, and I marked the coordinates as we went so I could find my way without Gus if

I needed to. After an hour, we came to what remained of an old fence, the now-obsolete demarcation that showed where the once-forbidden section of forest began.

"Out there?" I pointed.

Gus nodded. Any tracks or physical evidence left behind by whatever took the hunters last year was long gone, but at least Gus had led me to the hotspot, ground zero for the manifestation.

"Can you tell me anything else?" I asked.

Gus looked perplexed, and I knew he was probably trying to figure out how to say something complicated without using words. He began making swoopy gestures, and I found myself playing charades with a ghost.

"Something that flies?"

Gus nodded. He held up both hands, fingers splayed.

"Ten of them?"

Gus shook his head. "A lot?" I guessed. This time, he nodded. So the hunters got carried off by a flock of flying monsters. So not good.

"Wings?" No. "Eaten?" He shrugged. Taken away, but not killed immediately. Did the creatures have a nest? I didn't like what Gus managed to communicate, but then no news about a monster is good news.

I needed to do some thinking before I tried to confront whatever-it-was, and I also had to get back to civilization and get cleaned up for my date with Sara. I thanked Gus, and then we walked back to the spot where I'd left the beer.

"Hope you've got a way to enjoy that," I said, nodding toward the cans. "I'll be back tomorrow."

Gus stayed behind as I made my way back to the truck. The cops had arrived, and I saw them bringing the dead man's body out to an ambulance that was far too late to make any difference. Steve spotted me and moved to catch me.

"Thanks for calling that in," he said. "Guy's been missing for a couple of days."

"Like the others?" I asked.

He looked at me sharply, then shook his head. "No. We never found bodies for those. That why you're here?"

"Yeah, that and other things."

He smiled. "Oh, really?"

"Just dinner," I said, but I could feel my cheeks flush.

"Good," Steve said. "Sara's been alone too long. Don't fuck it up."

I'd been telling myself that same thing, so Steve's comment didn't boost my confidence. Then he clapped me on the shoulder. "Go have dinner. I'll need you to stop by the station and answer a few questions, but it can wait until tomorrow morning."

"Thanks," I replied, already trying to figure out a convincing story about happening upon the body since I could hardly say I'd been led there by a ghost. "I'll be in first thing."

I'd get the cops out of the way in the morning, so I could hunt a pack of flying monsters come afternoon. My kind of day.

Since Bell's Retreat, the bed and breakfast where I stayed in Kane, belonged to Sara, picking her up to go to dinner wasn't a challenge. The white clapboard Victorian home didn't fit my usual Motel 6 digs while on a job, but I could forego my aversion to doilies and chintz on account of its owner.

"You clean up well," Sara said with a grin when I offered her my arm as we went out to the truck. I'd brought decent slacks and a shirt with a collar—no tie—and a blazer, and my quick run through the bathroom got me a shower and shave.

"Thanks, I think," I replied with a chuckle. "You look pretty sharp yourself." Sara always dressed in a nice sweater and slacks, but she had added more sparkle, and her black lace top looked more "date night" than "business."

She blushed. Both of us were out of practice giving and receiving compliments. Her husband had inherited the B&B, and she continued it in his memory after he died in a car wreck. She had made me for a monster hunter almost as soon as we met. That made it unlikely I'd be ditched for being delusional, although I'd probably be able to fuck up something else. Handy also that Sara had been a nurse before taking up inn-keeping, and she'd stitched me back together again more than once.

Did I have a way with women, or what?

"Where to?" I asked as I backed out of the driveway. Since she knew the area, I let her pick the restaurant, with a plea not to go to Patterson's

Diner. I liked that place just fine for breakfast and lunch, but my hopes were for something a little quieter and more romantic tonight.

She gave directions, and I found myself parking in front of a mom-and-pop Italian place. It reminded me of the restaurant Chiara's parents ran, which was one of my favorites, and I felt a little like I was cheating by eating somewhere else. "Looks nice," I said, reaching up to straighten a tie I wasn't wearing. If she noticed the nervous movement, she didn't mention it.

When we walked in, Sara greeted the owners like old friends. Kane isn't that big a town, and I figured Sara probably did the Chamber of Commerce thing and rocked being a community booster. She knew everyone, and they all seemed to love her. Back home, I was used to a more mixed reaction.

Sara's connections paid off. We ended up with a table with a candle, tucked into a quiet corner. I'd hung out with Chiara and Blair long enough to know my way around a wine list and ordered a bottle. The candles played up her blue eyes and caught the highlights in her short dark hair.

For a while, we chatted about the weather, how the Steelers and Nittany Lions were doing in the season, and the latest action movies we both loved. Dinner gave my favorite restaurant a run for its money, although I'd never tell Chiara that. Not only would it be rude, but her *nonno* had Mob connections, and I didn't want to sleep with the fishes.

Finally, after we'd shared a fantastic piece of homemade cheesecake, Sara leaned back in her chair. "So...what are you hunting this time?" she asked, toying with her wineglass so that it caught the candlelight.

I slumped. "I'm sorry. I know I said I'd come up when I wasn't on the job. And then Father Leo called, and it kinda fell into my lap."

She reached out to cover my hand with hers. "I'm not complaining. You're always welcome. It would just be fun not to need to worry."

Damn. I'd gotten so used to flying solo, it hadn't occurred to me that someone would worry. One more reason I wasn't good boyfriend material. Then she gave my hand a squeeze and met my gaze when I looked up. "That wasn't meant as a dig," she said quietly. "I care. So I worry."

My heart did a funny little flutter that made me feel like I was back in high school, stealing a kiss from the girl I liked in tenth grade. "I'm glad," I said. Then rolled my eyes. "I mean, I'm not glad that you worry, I meant—"

She chuckled. "I know what you meant, Mark. It's okay."

Apparently, her requirements for male companionship didn't require coherence. I felt my cheeks flush and took a sip of my wine to allow more time between saying one stupid thing and the next.

"What are you after?" she asked, putting me out of my misery.

"Don't know yet," I replied, grateful for the save. "Just that we think it's behind the deer hunters who've gone missing each year. And maybe it flies and travels in a pack."

I could see the concern in her eyes. "I knew some of those men. The police tried to say, at first, that maybe they'd run off. Like they took a wrong turn and went to Vegas and never came back. But...that wasn't true. Those guys were solid. They had wives and kids and lovers they thought hung the moon and jobs and businesses—they weren't the kind to cut and run."

"It seems to be connected to that new part of the forest they opened up for hunting," I said, savoring the last of my wine. "Do you know if anyone's seen anything? It can't swallow up everyone's who's hunted there."

Sara frowned. "People talk. I've heard stories about strange lights in the skies and dogs barking when there shouldn't have been any dogs nearby. A couple of guys claimed to have been out on the nights when the others vanished, and they said they felt something rush by like a freight train and ran the other direction." She shrugged. "No way to know whether it's just a good story, but that's what's out there."

I didn't like the sound of that. I wondered whether I should have brought Father Leo along. Buzzkill for the date, but maybe this was too big for a one-man job.

"Promise you'll be careful." Sara's hand was warm, and the look in her eyes made me happy and a little scared all at once.

"I promise," I replied. And for the first time in a long while, I truly cared about making it back from the hunt in one piece.

We held hands in the truck on the way back. I'd have to remember that restaurant; in nice weather, it would have been a pleasant walk. When we reached the B&B, I leaned in for a kiss. Sara stretched up to reach me, and for just a few moments, we lingered in the foyer, trading kisses that held a promise for more.

By unspoken agreement, we were taking things slow. We'd both been hurt, and maybe neither of us knew what we wanted out of...whatever this thing between us turned out to be. I had my shop and my life back in Atlantic. She had the B&B and her life here. People had worked through worse odds. Hell, my parents courted long-distance when he was in 'Nam. If we wanted to figure it out, we would. But, it was too soon for those worries. Too soon for more than warm kisses and the way she felt so good pressed up against me. And then we were stepping back, and she brushed her lips across my cheek.

"Go get 'em," she said. "But be sure you come back."

6

"Fuck. It's the Wild Hunt." I stared at the laptop and ran my hand back through my hair.

It made sense. A once a year reaping, in an area the original inhabitants considered to be cursed, with strange lights and monsters that hunted in a pack and "swooped" down from the sky.

I re-read the lore around the Wild Hunt. People all over Europe had told stories for hundreds of years about a frightening cavalcade of spirits that rode the night skies during winter and harvested unlucky souls who would be doomed to ride with them forever. The baying of ghostly hounds and the clatter of spectral hoof beats went right along with the legend.

Some of the stories blamed the fey, while others said Odin himself led the hunt. Still more named the Erlking or Perchta as the leaders, frightening creatures known for a taste for blood. No matter who was in charge, the Hunt looked like an invincible foe.

I'd need to think about how to defeat the Wild Hunt, and no good ideas came to mind. So, in the meantime, I figured it might help to learn a little more about the men who vanished.

"Hey Steve," I said, calling up my cop friend. "I need a favor."

Two hours later, Steve Louden and I had holed up in the back booth at Patterson's Diner with a slew of folders spread across the table plus my laptop and two bottomless cups of coffee. Unlike Sheriff Sumbitch, I trusted Steve, who had been one of the guys who hauled my ass out of the woods when the wendigo attacked. Lucky for me, he also knew about the kind of creatures I hunted.

"Thirty guys vanished, one at a time, over five years, and no one blinks?" I asked.

Steve looked a little offended. "We investigated," he replied tartly. "We just didn't find anything to go on. Look at the reports."

I sighed. "Didn't mean it the way it sounded," I said, trying to smooth things over. "One at a time, it probably didn't seem connected."

"Oh, we tried to find connections," Steve corrected me. "We looked at serial killer profiles, tried to see if there were aggressive bears, or maybe a cougar. Nothing."

"And you're sure the men actually were out hunting when they vanished?" I had to ask. "They didn't just pull a runner?"

Steve passed a hand over his face. "We thought of that, too. Believe me, we would have preferred to find out that they were alive and living with a stripper in Vegas than just gone—poof—off the face of the Earth. But nothing." He took a swig of coffee and smiled as the server came by with a refill.

"And here's the thing—most people who decide to chuck it all and disappear slip up sooner or later. They use a credit card or access an ATM or get pulled over for speeding. Something from their past trips them up, and they show up on the radar. But these guys? Nada."

I flipped the nearest folder open. Marvin Keller had been forty-five years old. Divorced. No kids. Lost his job when a local factory shut down and ended up working as a janitor. Huh. I reached for the next folder. Rick Vernon had a similar story. Lost a nasty enough custody battle with his ex-wife that the cops thought she might have offed him. On probation at work for coming in late and hungover. The third file told the sad tale of Burt Walker, recently widowed, retired, with no close family and few friends. One of the notes said that witnesses claimed he took long walks at all hours and had seemed depressed.

"What?" Steve asked. "You've got that look."

I smirked. "Who, me?" I put down the file and looked at the rest of the folders. "Can you tell me if all of the men who vanished could have been considered depressed, maybe even suicidal?"

Steve frowned. "You think they killed themselves? We would have found bodies."

I shook my head. "No. But some supernatural entities are attracted to negative emotions. The three files I read had the blues written all over them. You said the victims were all different ages, incomes, professions, hell, even ethnicity. So there has to be something in common because other guys went hunting around the same time and walked back out."

It only took us a few minutes to comb through the rest of the files and confirm my theory. Steve slid down into his seat and drained his coffee. "Shit. You're right. They all had good reasons to be depressed." He looked up at me, confusion clear on his face. "But still, there are probably hundreds of people around here who are having a rough time of it. They don't disappear into thin air. Why these guys?"

I shrugged. "Wrong place at the wrong time. They didn't vanish walking down the sidewalk. They were out in the ass end of nowhere in an area that scared the crap out of the tribes that used to live here. That stretch of forest has probably belonged to the Wild Hunt for a lot longer than there's been a town."

"What did it do for victims before then?" Steve challenged. "Or when the area was closed to hunting for about a hundred years. Long time to go without a meal."

I nursed my coffee, thinking. "The Wild Hunt doesn't eat the people it takes. At least, not according to most legends. It kinda shanghais them to ride along forever. But maybe some people are more willing than others."

"So you think maybe even when the forest was off limits, it, what, called people to the hunt?"

"Maybe. There are cliffs with a reputation for enticing suicidal people to their deaths," I replied. "All those lovers' leap places."

Steve straightened as a thought hit him. "How are you going to stop it?"

"Haven't figured it out yet, but I'll come up with something."

"Can you shoot them? You know, silver bullets and all?"

"No idea, but probably not. And if there's a whole group plus a pack of hounds, I'd need an AK."

"We tend to discourage those for deer hunting," Steve remarked.

"At least, if you want anything left of the deer."

"Do you need backup?" he offered. "I have a couple of friends who are retired from the force, and they'd come out with us, no questions asked."

I shook my head. "Thanks, but I don't want to put anyone else in danger since it's not like we can ambush them. I'm going to go back and look over the lore again. There's got to be a way around this without going in full metal jacket."

"If we don't close the area off, it'll keep happening."

"Yeah. Can't tell the Park Service the truth, but maybe there's something dangerous to blame the disappearances on that gets that area blocked as a hazard."

"I'll work on it," Steve promised, finishing the last of his coffee. "I've got some friends who might be able to pull some strings. Just, be careful."

"Don't worry," I said with a laugh. "Sara has already warned me that she'll haul my sorry soul back from Purgatory and rip me a new one if I let anything happen."

Steve grinned. "Good. She's a fearsome woman, and a damned good catch if you can hang onto her," he added.

"I intend to do my best," I replied. And to my surprise, I realized that I meant it.

The afternoon passed quickly as I poured over all the information I could find about the Wild Hunt, not just on the regular internet, but on the Occulatum's Dark Web hunter information sites and some other, more dodgy sources that catered to customers working both sides of the supernatural street.

Now and again, I heard Sara singing to herself as she and the housekeeper made up the rooms, cleaned, and went through their daily routine. I hadn't really thought about what it took to keep the place running. Sara seemed to enjoy the work, as well as the constant stream of new people and returning guests who came through the inn and who became instant friends.

Doubt stabbed at me again. Sara and I were tiptoeing into...something. We had barely gotten past a kiss goodnight, but I felt a stronger attraction to her than I'd felt to anyone since Lara and I broke up. I wondered if she felt the same, and what that would eventually lead to. We both had baggage, but mine seemed heavier, and whether or not I was much of a catch seemed highly debatable. Still, she hadn't kicked me to the curb, so maybe all wasn't lost quite yet.

Reluctantly, I turned back to my research. Depending on the version of the story I read, there were a few loopholes for dealing with the Wild Hunt. Running away and covering your ears was the most popular. I couldn't blame anyone for that, but it wasn't going to accomplish my goal.

A few of the legends involved tricking the leader of the Hunt with a riddle. I sucked at knock-knock jokes and was worse at riddles, even the ones that came in fortune cookies and inside gum wrappers.

Some stories said that the leader gave each man a choice before conscripting him into his ghostly posse, while others made it sound more like a raid for hostages. But one or two tales involved a bargain, either a promise to be kept or some kind of barter. That sounded more promising than anything else I'd read, but I had no idea what to get for a dead guy who had everything.

As I debated the possibilities, I heard a knock at the door. "Come in," I called.

Sara poked her head inside. "Is coffee too much of an interruption?"

I smiled. "Never. Especially not if you brought two cups."

She returned the smile. "Just one cup, but there's a whole pot so you can have refills." She set the tray with the coffee on the other side of the table and perched on the edge of the second chair. "Find anything useful?"

I didn't want to worry her more than necessary, so I withheld the insights gained from going over the missing men's files. "I think I've got a lead or two. Still trying to come up with a plan."

"Is that how it works for you? Run in first, make it up as you go?"

I couldn't quite get a fix on her tone, but I figured it for a mix of worry and warning.

"Problem is, you can make all the pretty plans you want, and it all goes to hell once you're in the thick of things," I said, pouring a cup of coffee and taking a gulp that burned the whole way down. "I try to be prepared," I nodded toward the laptop, "and have a couple of game plans in mind. But when it all comes down to the wire, that's when you've got to improvise." I paused. "And it's not just me. I've heard it from all the hunters I know."

Sara sighed. "I understand. Truly. My brother was in the army, and he said the same thing about battles. Lots of nice plans and maps, and then it all goes ass-side upwards when the shooting starts."

"Steve's going to see if he can get the wheels turning to put that part of the forest out of bounds again."

"In case you can't kill whatever it is?"

I sucked down the rest of the coffee and poured more. "I'm pretty sure I can't kill it. But I might be able to make some kind of deal with it."

She frowned. "Don't sell your soul. I kinda like you the way you are."

Despite her joking tone, I felt a strange warmth in my chest at her words. "Thanks. Me too—I mean, I like you—"

"I know," she chuckled and patted my knee. "But seriously, don't put yourself in a corner. Aren't supernatural creatures supposed to be greedy? Maybe there's a way to bribe it—"

My eyes widened. I leaned forward and gave her a big kiss. "That's it! You're a genius!"

She kissed me back, and the warmth over my heart went south quickly. I shifted, hoping she didn't notice, but kind of happy that apparently, the rest of my body liked her just fine, too.

"Don't tell me now. I'll just worry. But *when* you come back," she added, "I want to hear all about it. Maybe we can celebrate." Her eyes promised mischief, and perhaps more.

"That sounds like the kind of plan I can stick to."

E very hunt feels different. Sometimes, the adrenaline buzz is like good whiskey, only it doesn't dull the senses, it sharpens them until it feels like I could see like a hawk, hear like a wolf, react like a cheetah. Other times, there's ice in my belly, and time seems to slow down like in one of those movies where people hover in midair when they kick someone. That doesn't actually happen, but it feels like it could.

Tonight, I thought I might throw up.

I had my gear bag over my shoulder and my shotgun in hand, for all the good it would do me. I couldn't fire salt rounds fast enough to take on an entire hunting party of ghosts, and I didn't figure that just shooting the leader would make the rest of them leave. Ditto for the iron crowbar and the silver knives—they worked great one-on-one, but I was wading into one of those big fox hunts like on TV, only everybody but me was dead. Well, me and any foxes that might be dumb enough to get close.

Sara hadn't been around when I left, and I figured it spared both of us an awkward parting. I planned to come back, more or less in one piece, but no hunt is a sure thing, and this one certainly wasn't going to be a milk run. Slipping out had been easier, and we could save the talking for later. If there was a later.

Stars shone brightly in a clear night sky. The lack of clouds contributed to the bitter cold, although Kane had a reputation for being the "ice box" of Pennsylvania, and in my experience, the nickname was well-deserved. We weren't far from the New York border, and the higher elevation meant colder temperatures and more snow. My heavy parka, scarf, and gloves kept the worst of the chill away, but nobody in his right mind went deep into the woods at night alone in this kind of weather.

I'd always been just a little crazy.

Gus materialized near where I'd left the six pack, and when I passed his tree, I noticed that the cans were open and crushed. That made me happy, thinking the guy could still enjoy a brewski on the other side of the Veil. Next time, I vowed to bring him a bottle of Jack to refill the flask I'd seen him pull from his jacket.

Gus fell into step beside me, and I knew what he meant by the quizzical tilt of his head. "Yeah, I think I've got something figured out," I said, watching as my breath froze and trying not to breathe in too quickly and make my lungs seize up from the cold. "Don't know if it'll work or not."

He made a gesture that I took to mean he was coming with me, and I shook my head. "No," I said.

Gus looked at me in exasperation, and his hand swept from his head to his feet. I guessed that he meant he was already dead, so what the hell was my problem.

"I don't know if they could make you come with them," I said. "These Wild Hunt ghosts are badass. Ancient. They might not give you a choice." I paused. "Unless...you're tired of being here."

Gus shrugged. I knew he helped out deer hunters and guys like me when we came through, and he'd probably saved more than a couple lost kids and hikers over the years. But the woods could be awfully quiet and empty, and maybe that got lonely. He looked like he considered the options. Then he frowned and shook his head.

"Yeah, I didn't think so. Because it's not just the hunting. I mean, that could be fun, swooping around on ghost horses, with ghost dogs baying at the moon. Kinda cool, huh? But not the taking people part," I said, sobering. "That's not right."

Gus nodded. Then he pointed to his eyes and back to me. We were back to charades with the dead. "You're watching me? You're going to keep an eye on me?"

He looked disgusted. Great. I could even annoy the dead.

"Oh—you'll keep a lookout?"

He touched his finger to the tip of his nose. "Okay. Thanks. I could use a good lookout."

A full moon reflected off the snow, making the woods surprisingly bright. A few more inches had fallen since my last trek this way, wiping out my footprints. Gus led the way, although I had the coordinates. If tonight went rough, I'd be glad for his help getting back to the car. I hoped to have that problem, given all the ways this could go south.

Gus stopped at the old fence. I knew from the look on his face he didn't want to, but I couldn't risk having him get shanghaied, and I didn't want the distraction of worrying about him.

I felt a change when I crossed over the boundary into the forbidden lands. A cold settled in my bones that had nothing to do with the frosty night. The moonlight made everything sharper, from the silhouettes of the trees to the crunch of the snow beneath my boots. I could feel my heart thudding in my chest, reassuring me that despite the cold, my blood still ran warm in my veins, reaffirming life.

The woods opened onto a clearing. I hadn't come this far before, but now I felt drawn to the open stretch of untouched snow that glowed blue in the cold light. This was the place. I knew it in my hindbrain, in the place where collective memory lives and dreams reveal old truths.

The farther I walked from the fence, the more the shadows wound around my heart. I cared about Sara, but what could she possibly see in someone like me? I'd failed at my first marriage, and I'd let down the people who counted on me to have their back—my dad, Uncle Christoph, Greg, and Sean. If it weren't for Pete covering for me at the garage, I'd have run that business into the ground with my obsession for vengeance.

And even as a monster hunter went, I was a fuck-up, managing to get the creature only after it handed me my ass. Comedy relief, not the hero.

Despite my heavy jacket, the cold seeped into my blood, slowing my heart, stealing my breath. I'd go back to a dog and an empty cabin, back to the nightmares and the guilt, back to the whiskey that kept me company more nights than I admitted to anyone, even myself. My own sister-in-law hated my guts, for good reason. She blamed me for Sean's death. And she was right. I had no business living when they died. No right to make it out and leave them behind. I should have ended it, right then. And instead, I'd fucked up my marriage and nearly dragged Lara down with me. God, I was pathetic.

But I could make it right. I could do what I should have done long ago. No more nightmares, no more loneliness, no more emptiness.

I set my gear bag down on the snow, worked the frozen zipper, and pulled out the troll's horn-trumpet. It crossed my mind that the mouthpiece was probably covered in troll spit, so I picked up a handful of snow and ground it over the mouthpiece until it was clean enough. Then I put the horn to my lips and blew with all my might.

I expected a god-awful sound, like the one and only time I tried to play a saxophone and it sounded like a cow giving birth. Instead, a pure, clear note rang out over the still forest, carrying across the cold air along with the wind.

From afar, dogs bayed, a chilling, hollow sound. Deep inside, we're all prey, and we know it. The hounds howled again, closer now.

I looked up into the clear sky and saw a dark streak across the stars. If I'd been a kid, I might have thought Santa and his reindeer flew early, but there'd be nothing jolly or generous about the riders who came to answer my summons.

As they drew nearer, the heavy thunder of galloping horses echoed from the rocks and trees. I'd heard that kind of pounding beat at the race track, but this time, I knew they were heading right for me, hard hooves shod in sharp iron that could cut me to ribbons and trample me to a pulp.

I squared my shoulders and stood up tall. A glance behind me assured that Gus stayed at his post. Whatever was coming my way, I'd face it alone.

The dark blur in the sky gained definition as it drew closer, and I could see wild black stallions, their manes and tails whipped by the wind.

Not racing steeds. These were war horses, huge and powerful. Ghastly riders urged them on, the withered remains of what had once been men, the hunters snatched from this very field.

And at the fore of the Hunt rode its terrible leader. I had wondered who would lead the way, whether one-eyed Father Odin on his eight-legged horse with a raven flying ahead of him or one of the other tarnished warriors of the past said to lead the cavalcade. But the figure in front wore a black cloak and hunched over his dark steed like the Reaper himself, and my heart shuddered beneath my ribs.

The noise roared like a freight train, like the whole Kentucky Derby rode me down, but I stood my ground, gripping the troll horn until I feared it would splinter around my fingers.

The riders circled me, never touching the ground, yet I saw the steam of their mounts' breath and felt the air stir as they rode past. Black dogs, their ribs showing through their fur, skin drawn tight over their skulls, watched me with baleful red eyes and lips drawn back to reveal sharp white teeth.

Then the master of the Hunt dismounted and glided toward me, lowering his hood. I stifled a gasp.

Perchta loomed over me, horns twisting up from a face that resembled a goat's skull with a fang-filled mouth. I'd read about him, a dark forest spirit from ancient days, before Christ, before the Romans, maybe even before the Druids. He had the body of a man and the feet of a goat. Six horns sprouted from his skull, some curving backward, others curling around and forward. An obscenely long tongue swept over blackened lips as he regarded me.

"Why have you called to us? Would you join the Hunt?"

"I want to offer you a trade," I managed to stammer. "To stop the deaths this year."

His withered skin drew back in a rictus grin. "And what would you offer, mortal? Your soul?" Perchta sniffed the air, scenting me. "You stink of fear and guilt—and grief. Come with us and leave that behind. Ride the winds with us, join the Hunt, and you will be like the gods."

"I don't think I'd make a very good god." Fuck, even facing down the Grim Reaper, I managed to be a smart ass.

"You haven't been a very good man," Perchta replied. "A failure. You cower in your bed at night, drinking yourself blind so that you don't wake weeping from your dreams. Who would miss you if you vanished? You're nobody. Nothing important. But in the Hunt, there is no pain, no sorrow, no regret. We are the thunder and the night wind. Immortal. Invincible."

Who would miss me? For a moment, Perchta's words hit deep. All my failures crowded my memory, accusing and remorseless. One of the dogs howled, and in that instant, I saw Demon's goofy grin, my Doberman watchdog who loved belly rubs and pizza, and played with squirrels instead of chasing them.

Demon would miss me. Chiara and Blair, too. Pete at the garage, and Father Leo. Nikki, despite what her mother thought of me. Other friends, like Louie, Steve, Dave Ellison with his tow truck, and the guys at the Drunk Monk. My poker buddies. Sandy and Vince at the diner. And Sara. I might be a failure in a lot of ways, but they were still my friends. They liked me anyhow. They cared. And if I couldn't hold out for my own sake, I owed it to them to hold out for theirs.

I lifted my chin and faced the monster. "I bring you a great treasure," I said and held up the troll horn.

Here's where I hoped to hell the internet had its shit together, because what little I could find out online said that troll-worked artifacts were rare and in the right hands, might even have magic. I didn't have a plan B, so if they were wrong and it was just an old cow horn, I'd be saddled up before you could say "yippie-ki-yay, motherfucker."

"How did you get that?" Perchta's raspy voice sent shivers down my spine, but I gritted my teeth, damned if he'd see my fear.

"I killed the troll that made it and took it for my own," I said. "You won't find another like this."

Perchta stretched out a skeletal hand, and I drew back. Terror made me a cocky bastard. "I want your word," I said, uncomfortably aware that I was small and mortal facing down a force of nature. "Your word that you will take no hunters from here this season. And that I can leave these woods alive."

The ghostly horses nickered and chuffed, stamping their hooves in the air, steam rising from their flanks and clouding from their breath. The dogs slunk in and around the huge hooves, eyeing me and growling low in their throats. Perchta regarded me in icy silence, and I knew the truth of being weighed in the balance. I prepared myself to be found wanting.

"You amuse me, hunter," the gravely voice said after an interminable pause. "You would make this bargain, even if I told you that the men who joined my hunt did so freely, to leave behind their pain?"

"Yes. Because they can never leave. Pain fades, eventually."

Perchta nodded. "True, though time alone heals nothing. I should know." He held out his bony hand once more. "You have my word, mortal. And I am bound to keep it. No more men taken here this season and safe passage for you from these woods. I swear it."

Resisting the urge to spit in my palm and shake on it, I handed over the horn. Perchta looked it over with a collector's eye. "A good trade. Now go, and do not try my patience a second time."

With that, he turned to the restless huntsmen and their massive steeds. Perchta raised the horn to his lips and sounded its otherworldly note.

I grabbed my bag and ran.

Gus caught up with me at the fence, but my feet didn't stop until we were back by the truck in the parking lot. The ghost stayed close to me, staring worriedly as I bent over and heaved for breath, my lungs nearly frozen from running through the frigid air.

"It's done," I wheezed, righting myself with effort and leaning hard on the truck, hoping my skin didn't stick to the metal. "No more missing hunters this year. Thanks for your help."

Gus grinned, doffed his gimme cap as if cheering my success, and then disappeared.

The ride back to the B&B gave me too much time to think, even as my numb fingers struggled to grip the steering wheel. I'd felt the pull of the Hunt, and the utter desolation that had settled over me when I crossed into the cursed forest hadn't been anything new, just the same old shit pegging the meter. For a few seconds, Perchta's offer sounded good, better than I wanted to admit. No more pain. No more guilt. Freedom to ride the wind forever. Even now, part of me longed to go. But more of me wanted to stay.

Sara waited for me in the parlor, although it was well after midnight. She pulled me inside and shut the door, then pushed back my hood and kissed me soundly. "I was worried," she murmured. "I was afraid maybe something had gone wrong."

I held her close so I didn't have to meet her eyes. "Worked like a charm," I said. "Never doubted it for a moment."

PART III

DEEP TROUBLE

1

G nomes suck.

Gnomes running amok in a cemetery? Even worse. And since the pointy-capped little creatures had taken a shine to pranking those who came to pay their respects to the dead, I'd been called in to put an end to the malicious hijinks.

Which explained how a grown-ass man like me ended up squatting down behind a cemetery angel in the middle of the night, looking for a two-foot-tall prankster with a helium-high giggle.

The fact that this wasn't the worst way I'd ever spent a Saturday night speaks volumes about my life.

I heard that high-pitched giggle and tried to get a fix on it. When I'd been called in to solve the cemetery's gnome problem, the only limitation was that I couldn't shoot up the headstones in the process. Even I know better than to do that. If the living don't sue you, the dead will haunt your ass.

Fortunately, I had plenty of tricks up my flannel sleeves that didn't involve damaging historic grave markers.

I'm Mark Wojcik, mechanic and monster hunter. I got into the monster hunting business after a wendigo killed my father, brother, uncle, and cousin—and made me wish I'd died with them. Since I didn't, I spend a lot of nights just like this, going after the things that go bump in the night. On good nights, I know that I've done my best to make the world a safer place. You don't want to know what I think about on the bad nights.

Greendale Cemetery has a gnome problem. That's a shame because it really is a beautiful place to be dead. There's a big stone arch over the front entrance and a creepy concrete "keeping vault" to store bodies when it's too damn cold to bury them. Everyone who was anyone in Meadville, PA, got planted here when they died—Revolutionary War soldiers, Civil War vets, and all the people who have streets named after them down-town, as well as the guy who invented Talon zippers. In almost two hundred years, the trees have gotten huge, the azaleas and rhododendron have grown to be enormous, and the ghosts have mellowed out.

I'd have said it was a perfect place for a long walk to appreciate nature if it weren't for the damn gnome.

That creepy, high-pitched laugh sounded again, and I knew the game was on. I shifted to get a better view. Dusk had fallen, so the cemetery gates were closed, which meant I didn't have to worry about bystanders. Just me and the gnome, which already made it an unfair fight.

Unfortunately, unfair for *me*.

I knew the pesky little bugger was trying to lure me into a trap, but I couldn't sit around all night waiting for a good shot. I dodged from the cover of the weeping stone angel, heading across a short open space for the shelter of a large granite obelisk.

My foot caught on a trip wire of spun gossamer—strong and almost impossible to see—and I went down, face first on a freshly dug grave. I came up sputtering with a mouthful of dirt and wilted carnations, picking greenery off my sweatshirt. The gnome laughed harder, and I felt my temper rise. This was exactly the kind of mean-spirited tomfoolery the gnome had been playing on visitors, and needless to say, bereaved family members didn't take kindly to being pranked.

I made it to the obelisk, still shaking off dirt and flower petals. In the distance, I heard the faint sound of drumming and smiled. I glanced to my right, and the ghost of Norbert Jones shot me the peace sign from where he sat on a tree stump with his bongo. Norbert had been a college student back in the seventies, when sneaking into the cemetery for keggers had been all the rage, and the local cops mainly turned a blind eye so long as no one did any damage. Norbert must have been one toke over the line the night he died because he managed to fall into the ravine behind the cemetery along with his bongo and the keg. The keg hit Norbert in the head, and that sent his future up in smoke faster than a cheap blunt.

I signaled Norbert, trying to get eyes on the gnome. When I put both hands on the top of my head, pressing my fingers together to mimic the gnome's pointy red hat, Norbert looked perplexed, then grinned and gave me a thumbs-up. He jumped onto the stump and put his hand above his eyes like a scout, then pointed off to my left. I waved my thanks and moved as stealthily as I could toward where I caught just a brief glimpse of a red tip.

I moved the stick I'd grabbed from beneath one of the big trees back and forth in front of me like a blind man's cane and managed to avoid setting off the next tripwire. At least I thought I had until I moved to go around the trap, only to walk into another wire at waist height that brought several precariously-perched flower pots down onto my head and shoulders from where the gnome had set them high up on two tall monuments.

I growled under my breath as I brushed away potting soil and bits of broken clay pots. I'd been lucky that the pots only clipped the side of my head, landing mostly on my back and shoulders. They were heavy enough to have given me a real goose egg, maybe even a mild concussion, if they'd have hit me square on.

I'd set a trap of my own, back at the big mausoleum by the front gate, but herding gnomes was harder than it looked. I slipped among the monuments to get a better shot, raised my wrist-brace slingshot, and fired a plastic Pokémon ball full of iron shavings aimed right for the back of the gnome's red-capped head.

The ball cracked open on impact, spraying the gnome with powdered iron, and he screamed, jumped into the air, and took off like I'd dropped fire ants down his pants. Iron burns fey creatures, and I was just fine with giving the gnome a rash he wouldn't forget. Unfortunately, he headed in the opposite direction of the front gate, so I had to chase after him, and this time when I fired, I intentionally hit off to one side—close enough to shower him with iron but steering his escape back in the direction I wanted him to go.

When I moved to follow him, all of a sudden the sprinklers came to life, dousing me with cold water and—not coincidentally—washing the iron filings off the gnome, who squealed and jumped up and down in the water, glaring at me and gnashing his teeth.

I noticed that Norbert followed me, still drumming on his bongo, with an expression of bemused curiosity I chalked up to all the weed he'd smoked before he went to the Great Beyond. His long blond hair was caught back in a ponytail, and his tie-dye shirt and bell bottoms made me think that all he was missing was a big dog and a psychedelic van.

A sopping wet, pissed off gnome headed right for me at full speed. Everybody sees those resin statues and thinks that with stubby little legs, gnomes would be slow. Hell, no. This gnome moved faster than Aunt Trudy's dachshund snatching a hot dog at the neighborhood barbecue. The next thing I knew, the gnome leaped into the air and caught me full in the chest. I felt like I'd gotten hit with a bowling ball, and the surprisingly dense gnome toppled me over, right into a pile of leaves and compost near the edge of the ravine.

We went down with a thud, with the gnome pummeling me with his tiny fists and pointy boots. Then the son of a bitch bit me, sinking his sharp teeth into the meat of my forearm. I swung a left hook and clocked that little asshole right in the side of the head, but he hung on like a pit bull, and I wondered if gnomes carried rabies.

We slid and slipped in the rotting compost like wrestlers in a vat of slimy green Jell-O. I needed to get him to let go with his jaw, but no matter how I tried to pry him loose, he held on, keeping him close enough to kick and punch my chest and gut. His fists and feet felt like stone, and I knew I'd be bruised and sore as hell tomorrow, not to mention having a bite on my arm like a Rottweiler used me for a chew toy.

The gnome kicked me again, and out of sheer fury, I moved my arm to pull the little biter over my knee and smacked him hard on his droopy little ass. That must have surprised him because he opened his mouth in shock, and I snatched my arm back out of reach. Then he launched himself right at my waist, and I knew there was no way in hell he was going to latch on to the family jewels.

I brought both fists down on top his red hat, knocking the gnome to the ground, and the damn thing went for my ankles. A kick with my steel-toed shitkickers usually ended this kind of misunderstanding, but gnomes are made out of enchanted stone, and it hurt me more than it hurt him.

The next time the gnome tackled me, we went down in the mud, rolling around like the Glorious Ladies of Wrestling, with me scratching for a hold on his baggy shirt and him snapping his teeth for another good bite of any meaty bit he could reach. We were both covered in mud and leaf muck, dripping wet, and before I knew it, we either rolled right over the edge of the ravine, or the soggy earth dropped away beneath us. Either way, I fell, and the bottom was a long way down.

I grabbed at the gnome and caught him by the waist of his pants because I wasn't going to let him get away, even if they had to pry my cold dead fingers from around him. That's when something icy and unnaturally strong grabbed my arm and flipped me into the air, sending me sprawling back onto solid ground.

Norbert Jones wiped the mud from his ghostly hands and gave me a thumbs-up, looking extremely satisfied that he'd saved me from the fall that had killed him. Before I had a chance to thank him, I realized that instead of still having a hold on the gnome, all I held were his baggy pants and that the bare-assed little bastard was running away from me, streaking through the cemetery.

"Thanks," I yelled over my shoulder, as I took off after the gnome.

"Come back here!" I shouted, but all he did was turn the other cheek. I did not need the mental image of the gnome with his teeny-weeny wiener dodging around and over the tombstones like a naked track and field event. I went right after him and managed to miss two of the traps he tried to lead me into, so I felt mighty proud of myself. But as we neared the front of the graveyard, I swung around a tall pillar monument and felt my feet go out from under me on a slick patch of soggy lawn clippings.

That damn gnome giggled when I started to go down. But instead of falling backward onto my ass, I dove forward, using the stretch of decomposing vegetation like a slimy Slip'N Slide. I grabbed the gnome by its hips, tried not to think about what was at eye level, and held on for dear life. When I ran out of slime, I kept a hold of him and rolled until we reached the door of the mausoleum where I'd set my trap.

I hurled that gnome into the mausoleum like I was throwing a pass on the Steeler fifty-yard line, shrugged out of the pack I wore, and grabbed for my secret weapon. While the gnome lay upside-down and stunned, I leveled a grenade launcher right at his naked ass.

"Say hello to my little friend," I muttered. "Meet Big Bertha." I pulled the trigger, firing a shell filled with holy water, salt, and iron filings. The break-away shell shattered on impact, flooding the inside of the mausoleum. I knew the mixture would weaken the gnome, and so I hauled myself onto my feet and grabbed the stunned ankle biter before he could collect his wits. I clamped cold iron manacles around his wrists and legs, keeping well back from his sharp teeth.

Then I lifted him by the chain between his feet, trying to ignore his dinky ding-dong flapping in the breeze. I didn't like doing it, but I still had to read him his rights.

"According to the Feral Fey Accords of 2011, you will be moved to a sanctuary location approved under the Gnome Relocation Act. If you are caught causing more trouble, the Accords and the Act permit us to report you to bounty hunters, who are licensed to turn your stone ass into gravel. Have I made myself clear?" I gave him a shake just to let him know I was pissed, in case he had somehow missed that.

I'd take his grunt as a "yes."

Dripping with mud, covered in leaf muck and slimy grass clippings, I picked up my pack and slung it over my back. The gnome, I carried upside-down and tried not to let his head bump into too many things on the way back to my truck. I tossed him into the iron cage I kept for just such occasions and glared at him as he swore at me.

"It's your own damn fault," I said, tossing his pants between the bars and reaching for the tarp I used to cover the contents of the cage from curious onlookers. "If you had left the visitors alone, I wouldn't have gotten called in." He kicked at the cage and gave me a murderous look.

"Give me a break," I muttered as I slung the tarp over the cage. "You'll like Saskatchewan. I hear it's nice this time of year." The Feral Fey Relocation Center was up in the far reaches of the province that even Canadians think is cold. The gnome banged at the cage again. I banged back.

"Quit yer bitchin'," I grumbled, as I got into the truck. "I gave you back your damn pants."

I speed dialed Father Leo. "I've got him," I said as soon as I heard him pick up.

"How much damage do we need to clean up?" Father Leo asked. He's a damn fine priest, a good poker buddy, and my contact to the Occulatum, the secret arm of the Vatican that oversees and supplies guys like me.

"Surprisingly little to the cemetery," I replied. The cage rattled around in the back of the truck, and I figured the gnome was throwing himself against the bars. I spiked the brakes, which slammed the cage and its temperamental stone prisoner into the back of the cab. *That might have rattled his rocks,* I thought. "As for me, nothing worse than a bite and some bruises." I wasn't going to admit that the short little fucker threw me off a cliff.

"Good," Father Leo replied, although the humor in his voice told me he might suspect the night didn't go smoothly. "Bring him in. I'll let the Feral Fey folks know, and they can come to pick him up."

"Can you say that five times fast? Feral Fey folks?" I asked. I swear I heard him roll his eyes. "Aren't they all shifters? Don't they have problems coming through Customs? Aunt Trudy couldn't get her dachshund across the border, but the wolf guys can come and go as they please?"

"If your aunt's dachshund could change into a person to cross over, he'd have probably gotten right through security," Father Leo said with belabored patience. "The FFRC agents don't travel in their wolf form. And they're the best equipped to deal with low-level fairy repeat offenders, like your gnome."

"He's not *my* gnome," I grumbled, hitting the brakes again to silence my unwilling passenger. "I'm driving straight to your place. Can't be rid of him soon enough."

"Nice work, Mark," Father Leo said, and I knew that he understood all the shit that went with the job. I might not be happy about having mud down my shirt or grass slime in my skivvies, but the job was done, and people could go plant marigolds around relatives' headstones in peace. As hunts go, I wasn't too much worse for the wear. And I had ESPN and some cold beer waiting for me when I got home. I knew when to count my blessings.

B y the time I made it to St. Gemma Galgani, Father Leo's church out in Geneva, I'd spiked the brakes more often than a nervous teenager taking his driving test. Father Leo was sitting on the back steps waiting for me. Leonardo Morelli, aka Father Leo, was the older brother of my friend Tom. Just shy of forty with wavy dark hair and big brown eyes, he probably broke a lot of hearts when he went into the priesthood.

"Sure is a spitfire," Father Leo said when I pulled off the tarp. The gnome threw himself against the bars like he was in a cage match, but at least he'd put his pants back on.

"That's one way of putting it," I replied. "I might have used some other terms."

Father Leo gave me a sidelong look that was more indulgent than judgmental. For a priest, he's a pretty okay guy. "They say there are no atheists in foxholes," he replied. "That may or may not be true. But I do believe the good Lord understands and gives dispensation to words said in the heat of battle."

I sincerely hoped so, or I was screwed six ways to Sunday.

Our contact showed up faster than I expected. "That was pretty quick to get here from Saskatchewan," I said. The FFRC agent might have been in human form, but he moved like a predator. If I hadn't known he was a wolf shifter, I would have bet Special Ops or Navy SEAL. His dark brown hair had flecks of gray, although I wouldn't have put his age much past mid-thirties, like me. Blue eyes tracked every motion, wary and watchful. And while I do my best to stay in shape, given the job, this guy looked like he bench pressed VW Beetles. Being a wolf apparently was a good workout.

"Fortunately, I was in the area," the Feral Fey guy said. "Had a couple of other pick-ups down in Pittsburgh." He shook his head. "No offense, but your neck of the woods sure seems to draw the crazies."

I couldn't argue that. "Keeps things interesting," I replied. "What happens to him now?"

The gnome glared at us with his hands on his hips. His red hat sat askew, and he looked like he wanted to chew me into little bitty pieces, but at least he had his damn pants on.

"We have a high-ensorcelled-security compound a long way from everywhere," he replied. "Iron fencing, plants that repel the fey, magical wardings. Guards are shifters and witches. Maybe a vamp or two on the night rotation. Whole place is filled with iron. If there are individuals who might be rehabilitated, we'll work with them, but most are too dangerous to ever release."

"And the fey let you get away with that?" I did my best to steer clear of the Old Ones, but everything I'd heard told me that they held grudges and had very long memories.

"We're doing them a favor," the shifter replied. "The kind that come to us are outcast. Saves the rest of the fey from having to do the dirty work."

Now that, I could believe.

It took all three of us to get the gnome's cage situated in the guy's truck. "The good news is, we've got a cargo plane coming in tonight. Saves me from a long drive and skips the awkward questions at the border." He climbed into his truck. "Thanks for the call, Father. Nice to meet you, Wojcik."

As usual, he mangled my last name. It's "voy-chick," but it's easier to answer to "woj-sick" than correct everyone. With that last indignity, the FFRC guy headed out, taking our problem gnome off our hands.

I turned back to Father Leo. "Now, what about this new job?"

He motioned for me to take a seat on the steps beside him. "Got a call from a friend of mine up in Waterford. Ever been up that way?"

I nodded. It's a little town on a back road up to Erie, and it gets more than its share of snow in the winter. "Yeah, I've been there. Not for a while."

"There's a historic old building up there, the Eagle Hotel. Been around since Revolutionary times. Got turned into a museum and a restaurant a while back, and now and then they do special events there."

"Sounds pretty tame to me."

He shrugged. "It usually is. Except now, it's not. And that's where you come in."

"What's the problem?"

"The hotel has always been haunted," Father Leo said. "Until now, it's been harmless—items get moved around, people report hearing a woman's voice or a baby crying."

"And now?" I knew he was working up to something. I don't get called in for nuisance ghosts.

He took a deep breath. "Now we've got a Revolutionary War soldier and a French and Indian War soldier who square off and fire their muskets at each other. A ghost of a housekeeper goes shrieking through the main hallway, and people hear a child's voice and breaking glass, but when they go into the room, there's no child and no broken glass."

I gave him a look. "Still, not my kind of thing. What's the real problem?"

"Three people have been attacked in the past two weeks, but there are no footprints, no fingerprints, and nobody showed up on the security cameras," he replied. "The ghost sneaks up behind them and chokes them until they pass out, military style, but doesn't kill them."

"That's bad for business," I replied. "Do we know who it is and why the ghosts suddenly went into overdrive?"

Father Leo shook his head. "If I knew that, we wouldn't have to pay you the big bucks."

"Har-de-har-har," I replied. I get a stipend from the Occulatum, but most of it goes to cover my co-pay at the doctor's, getting patched up from doing the work.

"One of the docents thought he caught a glimpse of a tricorn hat," Father Leo replied. "And a man he swore was Mad Anthony Wayne."

The name sounded vaguely familiar. "Who?"

"A Revolutionary War general known for his temper, hence the nick-name," Father Leo replied. "Spent a lot of time up around Waterford during the war, and on a visit years later, died near Erie and was buried up there. A few years after that, Mad Anthony's son came to claim the body. Dug it up, boiled off the flesh, and packed the bones into saddlebags for the trip down to his home in Georgia. The flesh is buried near Erie. Legend has it that not all of the bones made it down south."

"And you think Mad Anthony is looking for his missing bones?"

"Maybe."

I frowned. "Doesn't explain why he came back now."

Father Leo grinned. "That's where you come in. Just—be careful. Mad Anthony was known as a cunning warrior and a fearsome fighter. It sounds like he's still dangerous. Don't take chances."

"I'm sorry, have you met me?"

Father Leo rolled his eyes. "Don't take more chances than usual then, Mark. You still owe the parish charity fund money from our last poker game."

2

The Eagle Hotel, a three-story stone hotel in downtown Waterford, looked peaceful enough. With its red, white, and blue bunting around the window boxes and the painted sign proclaiming its name above the door, it looked charming and lousy with history. It had stopped being an inn long ago, and now, while a restaurant claimed the downstairs, the top two floors were part of a local museum. I might have gone to the museum on a field trip as a kid, back before I knew ghosts were real.

I parked my truck a few blocks away and walked past the hotel and around the block to get a feel for the place. The small lawn had been neatly trimmed, and electric candles glimmered in the windows, shimmering more than usual with the old, wavy glass. Father Leo's contact had given me a key, both to the restaurant and to the museum, but I wanted to scope out the whole setting before going inside.

The back gate wasn't locked, and I let myself inside, crossing the yard for a good look at the rear of the old hotel. I'm not a medium, and I'm sure as hell not a ghost whisperer—I tend to yell loudly at ghosts when I encounter them. But I *felt* a shift in the air all around me when I got close to the stone building, and it sent a warning prickle down my spine.

Right before a gun blasted behind me, and I nearly lost the hearing in my left ear.

I dropped to the ground and rolled toward the bushes, trying to get out of the line of fire. Someone returned fire, and I kept my head down.

It took a few seconds to realize that one person was firing a musket, and the other a breechloader rifle. I know my guns, even the old-fashioned ones. I have a few friends who are die-hard re-enactors. And the volley of gunshots that had me pinned down shouldn't have happened in the same century, let alone in *this* century.

I chanced a look over the bushes, long enough to rest assured that I was not about to die in a hail of bullets. Just as I gathered the courage to get to my feet, the gunfire stopped. I dusted off my pants and stepped into the yard, and that's when someone tackled me from behind.

The weight of a man's body knocked me forward as a strong arm came around my neck and pressed against my throat. Fortunately, Father Leo had warned me about Mad Anthony's little trick, and I was ready for him. I grabbed the iron knife from my belt sheath and plunged the point backward, right into what should have been my attacker's midsection.

The ghost let go immediately and stepped back. When I turned around, no one was in sight. I rubbed my throat, sure that if I hadn't been prepared, I would have ended up unconscious in the middle of the yard and with a hell of a headache when I woke up.

So why, after all these years, was Mad Anthony Wayne so...mad? What pisses off a two-hundred-year-old Revolutionary War general? I didn't know, but I needed to find out. Neither the restaurant nor the museum were going to do much business if the general's ghost kept choking out their customers.

I headed for the back door, braced this time for phantom gunfire. Just as I put the key in the lock, I heard someone moving behind me.

"Halt! Police! Put your hands in the air."

I had a split second to decide whether or not the cop was real or just a ghost. I erred on the side of caution and lifted my hands open and out to my sides.

"Turn around," the cop ordered. I complied, still holding the key to the door.

"I have permission to be here," I replied. "Father Leo sent me. I've got a key."

The man's eyes narrowed. "Is there a reason you're here after the place is closed?"

I shrugged. "The owners wanted me to see if I could figure out why there've been some strange things going on. People have gotten hurt. I'm going to try to fix that."

My answer seemed to satisfy him because he holstered his gun. His nametag read "*C. Dougherty.*"

"All right," he said, eyeing the key in my hand. "But how about if I wait down here until you're done, just to watch your back."

It was a statement more than a question, and I didn't think I got a vote in the matter. "Be careful," I warned. "There's a restless ghost who's been hurting people."

He nodded. "I heard about that. Don't worry. He won't get me."

"Suit yourself," I muttered, and opened the back door. The building manager had left the security system off, and the decorative candles in the windows gave me enough light that I didn't need a flashlight.

I left Officer Dougherty outside and slipped through the restaurant's kitchen and into the dining area. Everyone had gone home, but the faint scent of beef pot roast lingered, and my stomach growled. I made my way to the center of the room and then stopped. I didn't sense any cold spots or see any orbs, but I couldn't shake the feeling of being watched. In the distance, I thought I heard a baby cry, but the sound was faint enough it might have come from outside.

A second key got me into the museum upstairs. Where the electric candles' glow had given the restaurant a comfortable hominess, here in the museum, they seemed to accentuate the shadows. The two upper floors housed both museum exhibits and offices. The staff areas weren't high on my list since I figured they were unlikely to have any heirlooms or relics that might have triggered the haunting. The museum itself, however, was another matter.

Before my hunting days, I wasn't all that interested in history. Now, researching legends and lore helps me get a jump on the ghosts and bad nasties that I put to rest. Along the way, I've become a bit of a history buff because you can't make stuff that weird up. Who the hell boils his father's bones and then takes the skeleton on a road trip, leaving bits and pieces along the way?

The small museum covered Waterford's long history. George Washington actually did sleep here, in this very hotel, more than once. Several of the displays were dedicated to the French and Indian War, which—interestingly enough—did not involve the French fighting Native Americans. Instead, both the French and the native tribes fought the British—and since this was before the Revolution, that put Washington and his buddies on the side of the Redcoats. See? How weird is that?

The restaurant didn't have any noticeable cold spots, but upstairs in the museum—where the heat rising should have made the rooms warmer —I felt cold all over. The sense of being watched was even stronger, and the sound of that baby crying grew louder, though it seemed to be coming from downstairs.

The display cases showed the history of the area from the original native tribes to the French fur traders who collaborated with them and then to the influx of the English with their forts and settlements. Although the Civil War didn't range up this far north, Waterford's sons signed up and headed to battle, earning them a commemorative display of guns, uniforms, medals, and tattered journals. A number of the Revolutionary War and French and Indian items came from archeological digs by nearby Edinboro University around the remains of Fort LeBeouf, and I wondered as I looked at the lead bullet fragments and other relics how much ghostly energy the pieces carried with them.

I turned and found myself staring straight down the barrel of a flintlock rifle. I heard the bang, saw smoke rise, and staggered as my brain insisted I must have taken a direct, close-range hit. The man in the British Red Coat uniform vanished before my heart stopped thudding.

A rifle shot behind me sent my pulse hammering again. My hand flew to my chest, certain it would find a bloody exit wound, but my shirt and jacket remained intact. I kept enough of my wits about me to swivel, facing my attacker, and found only empty space.

"That's enough!" I yelled although the two ghosts had vanished. "The war is over, goddammit!"

That's when I saw a hatchet fly right past my left ear, and I heard its steel blade sink deep into the wooden post behind me. I looked up to see a dark-haired, bearded French fur trapper, complete with a Davy Crockett-style coonskin cap, giving me a murderous glare. I don't speak a lick of French, but from the stream of vitriol, I figured he was cursing his aim.

"You too!" I yelled, pointing at him. "Enough already! You're dead! You don't have to go home, but you can't stay here!"

He straightened up and squared his shoulders, surprised and offended. In the next heartbeat, he was gone.

My nerves might never be the same, since I had no idea when I'd get another ghost drive-by. The sound of shattering glass made me flinch, throwing up my arms to protect my face and head. After a second, I realized that none of the cases around me had broken, and the windows were still intact. I uncoiled warily. A woman shrieked, so close behind me I could have sworn I felt her breath on the back of my neck. I have faced down swamp monsters and wendigos, killer trolls and were-squonks with reasonable courage, but that scream in my ear nearly made me piss myself.

"What is your problem?" I yelled, turning to face empty air. "Geez." I don't know if shouting at ghosts actually does anything to them, but it makes me feel better.

The ghosts inside had been an annoyance, and they might give someone a heart attack, but otherwise, none of them posed a danger. Mad Anthony, on the other hand, might pull his cute little fainting trick on the wrong person and do some real damage.

I went back to searching the display cases, hoping that I would know what I needed when I saw it. The decorative candle didn't light up the room enough, so I played my flashlight over the tagged items, looking for something that might give me a clue on how to send our troublesome ghosts packing.

Museums always make me a little sad. All the things in the cases used to be just what people used in their everyday lives, part of their daily routine. I felt certain that when they went about their business with their personal possessions, they never expected strangers to be gawking at the flotsam and jetsam of their lives, neatly displayed and tagged. I was certain that the rough trappers and beleaguered soldiers would be astounded, and probably dismayed. I tried to imagine myself coming back in two hundred years as a ghost and seeing my dishes or my DVD collection enshrined in a glass case and decided to put a note in my will to burn everything my friends didn't want.

Brigadier General Mad Anthony Wayne had a whole display case of his own. A mannequin wore a reproduction of one of his uniforms, including the tricorn hat. Paintings and sketches pieced together his life, from his early days to the Revolution, and then sullying his legacy by battling the Native Americans. An odd assortment of his belongings was on display, but none of them looked like the kind of thing that would pull a man's spirit back from the grave. On closer look, some of the items weren't even really his—just period pieces like the kind he might have used. I sighed, having turned up a big, fat "zero" when it came to busting his ghost.

What was I missing? Mad Anthony hadn't been hanging around the Eagle Hotel for the whole two hundred years since he died, so something must have changed. But the obvious answer—that one of his missing bones had been put on display—hadn't panned out.

I wandered into the next room and found a history of Waterford after its colonial past. Sepia-toned photographs accompanied memorabilia from long-gone local companies, restaurants, and stores. A time capsule from 1968 that looked like a rusted metal box sat next to old milk bottles from a home-town dairy, cans from a now-defunct brewery, and framed pictures of Waterford-born men and women who had made good.

When I reached the end of the display, I slumped against the wall, out of ideas. I figured the ghosts were about due to show up and shoot me again, but this time, I was ready for them. With my back to a period cast-iron stove, they weren't going to sneak up on me, and I waited for them to reappear.

Trapper Jacques was the first to show up, and when he pulled his arm back to throw his ax at me again, I hurled a handful of rock salt in his face. Poof! One down.

Musket Guy appeared to my left. Lucky for me, those old guns are a bitch to fire. Before he could get his shot off, I salted him, and he vanished. The Civil War soldier almost got the drop on me, but I had enough salt to take him out, too.

Downstairs, the baby wailed, and an invisible woman screamed. I had no idea what to do about ghosts I could hear but not see, and fortunately, they weren't who I'd been hired to hunt. Which made me wonder how Officer Dougherty was holding up downstairs. I glanced out the back window and didn't see him, but I figured he had probably decided to sneak off for a smoke.

Strong arms gripped me from behind. One arm went around my throat, and the other hand knocked my iron knife from my belt. I could feel a large, muscular body pressed up against me, and instinctively, I rammed my elbow backward, but instead of sinking into his gut, it met thin air.

Unfortunately, Mad Anthony's arm around my neck felt entirely solid. I kicked back for his knee, but got nothing, and trying to stomp down on his instep did zilch. He held me, pinned, and no matter how I wriggled, I couldn't get free.

Shit. I tried to pull his arm clear of my throat, but my hands couldn't get purchase, although a force kept them from reaching all the way to my neck. Mad Anthony squeezed harder, and my vision began to blur, coloring my view with dancing spots.

Desperate to break his hold, I tried going limp. I almost slipped free, and then Mad Anthony had to compensate because if he was going to support my whole not-insubstantial weight, he needed to be more than a floating arm.

His body grew more solid, and that was my cue. I grabbed for the force around my throat with both hands, hoping I could keep from hanging myself, and lifted my feet from the floor, then pushed off with all my strength, shoving myself back against him.

We fell together, crashing into the display case. This time, real glass fell all around me, slicing into my scalp and hands, cutting my face. I was glad I'd worn a heavy coat and hoped that I didn't manage to impale myself since the ghost's body wasn't going to take the brunt of our fall.

Mad Anthony's hold loosened just enough for me to gasp in air, and then he tightened again. I tore at the energy with my right hand while my left grabbed for the iron knife I had glimpsed on the floor when we fell. All I got for my trouble were a bunch of glass splinters in my palm since the blade remained maddeningly out of reach.

Now would be a good time for Jacques the Trapper and Musket Guy to show up again, especially if their ghostly ax and bullets worked on another spirit. Just my luck, they didn't show. Mad Anthony, on the other hand, felt more solid than ever before.

I struggled to breathe and knew I couldn't take much more. No matter how I kicked and bucked, I couldn't dislodge my Revolutionary assailant. Black edged my vision, and I wondered if I'd been the lucky one to push Mad Anthony over the edge into murder. I tried grabbing for the ghostly arm with my left hand and slapped out with my right to steady myself.

My hand came down on something solid and metal, and I realized it was the old time capsule. Mad Anthony felt more real than ever, and that's when I knew I'd managed to find what I was looking for.

One of his missing bones was in that time capsule.

All I had to do was live long enough to open it up and give the damn thing back.

I grabbed the time capsule by the handle, swinging it at Mad Anthony. The box must have had some iron content because the ghost vanished, and I could breathe again.

I remembered a sign in the entranceway saying something about "new additions" to the exhibits. The display case sign, still standing amid the broken glass, said that the time capsule was part of a new "Twentieth Century" update. I stared at the box still held in a death grip and decided that I really needed to see what was inside.

The bang of a musket shot sounded close enough to make my ears ring, and if the bullet had been real, it would have either parted my hair or gotten me between the eyes. "Quit that!" I yelled. I knew the phantom ax was coming next, but to my surprise, instead of sounding like it hit the wooden support posts, I heard the *thunk* of metal on metal, and the lid of the time capsule sprang open.

Maybe the other ghosts were tired of Mad Anthony, too.

Trying to navigate around the broken glass, I lifted the open box and set it on one of the waist-high display cases in the middle of the room. I brushed the glass fragments out of my palms as best I could and tried not to bleed on anything historic. My flashlight revealed the contents of the capsule, and I had a little thrill of excitement, my very own Indiana Jones moment.

It's funny what people think will be important in the future. The box held newspapers and a telephone book, along with political campaign buttons, a Sears catalog, and a list of predictions about what the world would look like when the capsule was finally opened. I was pretty confident that no one had predicted that the newspapers, phone book, and Sears catalog would be extinct, or that most people would spend all day walking around staring at the phone in their hand.

I shook the box, and it rattled, so I kept on digging. Beneath all the paper, I found a yellowed finger bone with a note wrapped around it and tied with twine. The note read, *"found during the widening of Rt. 322, a bone believed to belong to General Anthony Wayne."*

Shit. This was it, the new arrival that prompted the spook-a-palooza. Now all I had to do was figure out what to do with the bone to make Mad Anthony go away.

The spirits downstairs had gotten quiet, and I could feel the presence of the ghosts around me, watching. Maybe Musket Guy and Frenchie had been roused from their long sleep by Mad Anthony's ghost and just wanted to be rid of him so they could rest. Could it be that the Revolutionary War general had such a turbulent personality that he managed to even piss off his fellow ghosts? Then again, since Mad Anthony hadn't perpetually haunted the museum, maybe unearthing the time capsule from wherever it had been buried had jerked him back from the afterlife and he was just trying to get home.

"Hold your horses," I yelled at the empty room. "I've gotta come up with a plan." For all I knew, Mad Anthony and the other spirits also had ghostly horses, and I envisioned them grabbing the reins and waiting for orders. I pulled out my phone and did a little research. In this case, hitting "pay dirt" was real.

"Hey, Mad Anthony," I called out. "If you quit choking me, I can get your finger bone back to where your flesh is buried. Can we have a truce? Because if you strangle me, they're going to put your bone back in the iron case and you'll have to wait for another sorry bastard to figure the whole thing out."

Nothing stirred, which I took to be a good sign. I looked around at the ruined display and the broken glass and figured that my bosses were going to get a bill from the museum. Still, if this solved their ghost problem, they might not mind, and I'd admit that this was probably the most unusual way I've ever been given the finger.

I tucked the bone into my pocket and headed downstairs. Officer Dougherty was still on watch, and I figured he'd headed off any unwanted police attention my noisy nocturnal foray might have attracted. I thanked him, and he gave me a snappy salute, then walked away.

Reburying Mad Anthony could pose a problem since his son had him dug up hired a doctor who boiled the corpse, scraped the flesh off the bones, and then reburied the squishy parts. The water and the tools used to do the deed were still in Erie, while his son took the bones back to Georgia, losing some—like his finger—along the way.

I was not in the mood to drive that far south, so the Erie site would have to do. A little time on Google revealed that while Mad Anthony's bones had been reburied on the site of an old Revolutionary War blockhouse fort, the original fort burned down long ago. But a reconstructed blockhouse held the general's tombstone. I figured that was my best bet. I pocketed the bone and headed back to my truck.

Fortunately, the Wayne Blockhouse wasn't all that far from the Eagle Hotel, so it was still the middle of the night when I arrived. I slipped onto the grounds and grabbed a shovel and my hoodie out of the toolbox in the back of the truck. Once I got to the door, I hesitated, debating whether to break in and somehow return the bone to the tombstone inside or put it back into the ground in which Mad Anthony's body had first been interred. It was three in the morning, and I was cold and tired. I opted for the easy choice, found a spot near the blockhouse wall, and started to dig.

I wondered what Mad Anthony had made of being dug up, boiled, and reburied. The stories about his ghost focused on the missing bones along what's now Route 322, so I guess he was more attached to them than the rest, but still, it didn't seem like the most reverent way to treat a hero of the Revolutionary War. Then again, he'd been part of the genocide against Native Americans, so maybe Mad Anthony got what he deserved. His choking kink made me wonder even more about just what sort of guy the general really had been.

I dug a suitably deep hole, about a foot deep and as wide as a shoebox, and bent down to put the bone inside. Maybe Father Leo would want to stop by and bless the spot, for good measure. All I cared about was that ghosts had stopped trying to kill me and that after a few more shovelfuls of dirt, I could head back to my comfy bed.

"Freeze and put your hands in the air."

Fuck. I was busted, and there was no good way to explain why I was burying human remains. I dropped the shovel and raised my hands.

Just then, I heard the cop begin to sputter and gasp. I turned, keeping my hood up to shield my face, and saw the cop caught in the grip of an invisible madman. Before I could warn Mad Anthony to take it easy, the cop sank to the ground, still breathing but out cold.

"Thanks, but you've got to quit doing that," I muttered, filling in the last dirt and smacking it down with the back of the shovel. "Go back to sleep. We're done here."

For a few seconds, the ghost materialized, looking like he did in his portrait at the museum, still wearing his Revolutionary War uniform and tricorn hat. Mad Anthony saluted me, then vanished. I grabbed my shovel and vamoosed before the cop woke up.

Once I headed back to my cabin in Atlantic, I called Father Leo, feeling not a bit sorry about the ungodly hour.

"It's done," I said and filled him in on the basics. "The part at the museum went a lot smoother with Officer Dougherty watching my back," I added.

"Charles Dougherty?" Leo asked, but I couldn't figure out why he sounded amused.

"Maybe. The nametag had a 'C' for the first name."

Leo described the man.

"That's him."

"His daughter runs the restaurant at the Eagle Hotel. She's the one who called us in on this. But Charles Dougherty's been dead for a couple of years now. It's really been your night, Mark, hasn't it?" Leo replied.

3

"Let me get this straight. Your son was using an ancient grimoire to raise the dead, and you thought it was part of a role-playing game?" I stared at the woman who sat at her kitchen table, twisting a dish towel between her hands.

"It looked hokey, and I figured it was fake, all right?" Veronica Ellerbee replied, looking up at me with red-rimmed eyes. "I mean, it had a fake eyeball in the middle of a leather cover, and a bunch of weird drawings and mumbo jumbo. I thought he'd gotten one of those *Caves and Cryptids* games and was putting together a campaign." She knocked back a slug of the whiskey I had poured for her. "I thought if he had friends over to play the game, he'd get a social life."

I wasn't even sure where to begin. Telling her that the eyeball wasn't fake and that the leather was human skin probably wouldn't make her feel any better. If he'd tried to use that particular book for an RPG, we were lucky not to be up to our armpits in wraiths and werewolves.

"Do you know where he got the book?" I asked. Father Leo had already picked up the grimoire for safekeeping, and a consulting witch-psychologist was debriefing Taylor to assess whether his soul had been permanently tainted or whether he could be rehabilitated. Spell books like the one he was using for his "game" are nasty business, and if they don't drive the user mad, they can eat away the soul and send the would-be witch on a spree of murder and mayhem.

"There's a used bookstore he likes—goes there a lot to play tabletop games with his friends, and he gets the books he needs to run his adventures," Mrs. Ellerbee said. "Taylor's a good kid. He does his homework, finishes his chores, keeps his grades up. He saves up his allowance and mows lawns to get money to buy stuff for his games." She sniffed and wiped her nose.

"I thought he was safe since I knew where he was and the kids he played those games with," she went on. "I remember years ago, people said that playing games like that would turn you into a Satanist, but I never thought..."

I shook my head. "It's not the games," I replied. "Trust me. I play *Caves and Cryptids* with a Roman Catholic priest every couple of weeks. It was the spell book, not the game itself." I didn't mention that having an actual exorcist in your quest party comes in handy for the rare occasions when it turns out someone used a real incantation in the game master manual.

"Why would they sell things like that to a minor?" she wailed. "I buy my romance novels there, and they make kids show ID if they want to buy any of the racy books."

I scrubbed a hand over my face, feeling like I'd been awake far too long already. "My guess is that the shop got the book by mistake and thought it was fake, like you did."

"Will Taylor be all right?" Mrs. Ellerbee looked up at me like I had answers, but all I could do was shrug.

"I'm not the one to ask," I said gently. "In most cases, the damage is minor and reversible." I didn't want to tell her that in the worst case, the witch-psychiatrist would wipe parts of Taylor's memory, which might or might not affect the rest of his personality if the soul-stain from the grimoire didn't kill him outright.

"Then what good are you?" she demanded.

It was a question I asked myself all too often, usually in the wee hours in the morning in front of a mirror, when a hunt didn't go right. "I'm just the clean-up guy," I said, with a pained smile. "I leave the other stuff to the experts."

"Get out," Mrs. Ellerbee ordered. "If you can't help my Taylor and you can't punish the person who sold him that awful book, get out." She picked up her box of tissues and pitched it at my head, nicking me in the face. "Get out!"

I muttered an apology and left. Part of me wanted to tell her not to shoot the messenger, but the rest of me couldn't blame her for needing to take out her fear and anger on someone, and I happened to be handy. Since we needed to contain whatever Taylor had unleashed before it caused havoc, I needed to retrace his steps. That started with a visit to The Lair.

Both the Ellerbee home and the shop where Taylor got the grimoire were in Grove City, a town about an hour south of my cabin in Atlantic. I'm the Occulatum's designated monster hunter for Northwestern Pennsylvania, from Lake Erie down to Pittsburgh, and from the Ohio state line over to the middle of PA. It's a big territory, full of all kinds of supernatural dangers, but it's home, and knowing that I'm helping keep my friends and neighbors safe makes up, a little, for the time I failed miserably.

"Welcome to The Lair. Abandon hope, all ye who enter here," a clerk dressed in wizard's robes greeted me as I walked into the used book and game store.

I had to give them props for atmosphere and standing out from the crowd. Outside, The Lair was just another storefront in a strip mall. Inside, it seemed like a different world. The gaming section had fake rock walls with LED glowing runes and lava, and the scarred wooden gaming tables looked like they belonged in a medieval tavern.

One area of the book section resembled a castle, with an elaborate mural on the wall, papier-mâché stone battlements and a fancy "gold" throne. The other area had a spaceship vibe, with blinking lights, a wall-sized vista of the galaxy, and futuristic reading chairs. Over in one corner, Dickens Coffee sold java and snacks. Fake candles glowed throughout the store, and the smell of incense hung heavy in the air.

My inner teenage self would have loved this place. I made a slow circuit, checking out The Lair before I talked to the owner. The shelves were full of recent books, movies, and games, all in nearly-new condition, sold at a good discount. Behind the counter, clerks dressed in fanciful costumes offered new and expensive dice, gaming miniatures, scoresheets, and other RPG essentials. Whoever thought this place up was a damn genius.

Unless he was a shill being used by dark powers to get dangerous magical objects into the hands of unsuspecting kids.

That thought threw cold water on my nerd-gasm, and I got back to business. An inquiry about the owner or manager got me directed back to the guy in the wizard's robes. He didn't look a day over twenty-five, fresh-faced and upbeat, and not exactly what I pictured as an evil warlock enticing innocent gamers to their doom.

"How can I help you? I'm Joey, part-owner and general manager."

"I'm Mark," I replied. "And I'm trying to track down where one of your used books came from."

Joey shook his head. "That's gonna be hard, man. We get stuff from all over—garage sales, store closings, clearances, and that's not counting the regulars who bring in their stuff to trade for store credit."

I pulled up a picture of Taylor's grimoire on my phone that I'd snapped before Father Leo took it to hand off to a friend of his from Charleston who gets rid of dark magical relics. "Recognize this?"

Joey studied the photo, then nodded. "Yeah, sure. Figured it was a movie prop or something. I thought about keeping it myself, to add to the atmosphere in the shop, you know? But one of my regulars came in the day we unboxed everything and went gaga over it."

"Did anything about the book strike you as odd?" I asked.

Joey frowned. "You mean like it was stolen or something?" He shook his head. "No way, man. I bought it at an estate sale. I go to all kinds of yard sales, flea markets, and that kind of thing to find stuff to resell and decorations for the store." He leaned forward confidentially. "I have another business on eBay where I sell off things that don't work for the store." Joey took a card from his pocket and slid it across the counter. "I don't advertise the online stuff here at the shop, but that's got the web address," he said, as I took the card.

"So, this sale," I said, "do you remember where it was?"

Joey thought for a moment. "Yeah, it was at the Hoffman house. I guess the old man who died had done a lot of traveling and was quite a collector. He had some great stuff, but not to everyone's taste, you know? They were selling things off by the boxful, and I liked enough of what I saw to bid on some of the lots. The cool book was at the bottom of one of the boxes."

He grinned. "Sometimes, you get a hunch about things. I remember bidding on that box. It was like it was calling my name."

I sighed and figured Joey was more right than he knew. Malicious items like that grimoire often could sense a willing victim like Taylor, or an easy accomplice, like Joey. I made a note to check out whatever I could find about Old Man Hoffman once I took care of the immediate problem.

"Do you have anything else from that box left for sale?" I put on my best "aw shucks" smile and hoped it worked.

"Nothing as cool as that book," Joey replied. "Let me see if anyone unpacked it." He ducked into a storage room for a minute and came back with an old cardboard box. "I don't usually let people go through new stuff that hasn't been tagged, but if you're a friend of Taylor's, I'll make an exception."

I don't have any magical ability. So, as I pawed through a box that smelled like it had been in someone's attic since the Carter administration, I had to rely on intuition rather than getting a spooky tingle from touching objects that had mojo. The thought crossed my mind to just buy the whole box, but as I dug down through the odds and ends, I just couldn't imagine any self-respecting dark witch cursing a set of touristy shot glasses or a bottle opener made from an alligator tail.

"Someone I talked to at the sale said the old man bought whatever caught his eye," Joey pattered on. "I mean, he also had a whole set of kitchen jars that all looked like owls. But I saw some cool tankards and a couple of candlesticks and figured I'd make enough off them to pay for the lot."

I bought the candlesticks, just in case, even though they didn't strike me as particularly unusual or especially attractive. Nothing in the other two boxes looked even remotely magical, and I figured I'd alert Father Leo, and he could send in a specialist if he thought the risk warranted.

My phone rang as I got into my car, and I recognized Father Leo's number. "The shop was a bust," I told him. "But I found out the name of the guy who owned the book. Sounds like he liked to buy whatever struck his fancy, and the book probably caught his eye."

"I'll see what I can find out about Hoffman," Father Leo promised. "But we've got a more immediate problem. I managed to work out the spell Taylor cast, and I read through the rest of the materials we took along with the book. He was playing a gaming campaign—I don't think he realized that the grimoire was real, or maybe the book deceived him. The first challenge for his party of adventurers was to fight an army of the undead raised from a sunken cemetery."

"That's what the spell was for?" I echoed. "Then we're fine, right? Because we're a long way from the coast, so there's no Atlantis to raise the dead from."

"Never said the graves sank in the ocean, Mark," Father Leo reproved me gently. "They flooded hundreds of acres of farmland to make that lake. Farms with small, private cemeteries from long enough ago nobody bothered to relocate them, if they could have even found them all."

"Shit." Lake Wilhelm is a man-made flood control lake made from damming up natural springs and creeks just a few miles up the highway in a little burg called Sandy Lake. I'd been out on Lake Wilhelm fishing a time or two. It's a pretty place, with boat launches and hiking trails, but a bunch of zombies would ruin the vibe.

"From what we can gather, Taylor based the idea on his grandfather's old farm, which is now mostly underneath the lake. There was a small cemetery that probably didn't get moved when they flooded the land. That's where the zombies are coming from each night."

"It's been happening since the last game?"

"Yeah, Taylor played with his gaming group on Saturday nights, at a cabin on what's left of the old farm," Father Leo replied. "So, yes, since then."

Aw, fuck. That meant that for three nights running, a bunch of sopping wet, long-dead reanimated corpses had been giving the good people of Sandy Lake one hell of a surprise. "There's a lot of shoreline and several boat launches. I can't cover them all myself, and if we bring in that many shooters, we'll have the civilians in a panic faster than you can say 'Jade Helm.'"

Father Leo chuckled. "Meet me at Chiara's coffee shop in an hour. I've got the topographical maps, and I know where his grandfather's farm was. I'm sure that you and Blair can come up with a plan."

I muttered some things under my breath that most people probably wouldn't say in front of a priest and hung up. I hadn't thought it was possible, but this might be a new low for a weekend, even for me.

"I made your coffee special, just the way you like it," Chiara Hamilton greeted me, and I caught a whiff of Jameson when she set the cup down. "It's from my private stock," she added with a wink, and I figured she spiked my cup from her flask since the shop doesn't have a liquor license.

"Blair's a lucky woman to be married to you," I grumbled, not able to completely hide my appreciative grin as I breathed in the soothing smell of coffee and whiskey.

"Damn right," Blair replied, plunking down next to me and giving me a good-natured punch in the shoulder that stung, just a little.

Blair Hamilton inherited Hamilton Hardware in downtown Conneaut Lake when her parents passed away, and after a couple of tours of duty in the army, Blair was ready to come home and settle down. She and Chiara had been head over heels for each other since high school, and despite Conneaut Lake being a small town and Chiara's very Italian family, their marriage didn't create much of a stir. Blair keeps a special back room at the hardware store for specialized "hunting supplies" for those of us who aren't going out loaded for deer. They bought the building next to the hardware store, knocked out a doorway, and Chiara opened a coffee shop and bookstore that's become a popular hangout. I can personally attest that Chrystal Dreams has the best coffee in a four-township radius.

"Are you bribing me or providing a consolation prize?" I asked Chiara.

"Maybe a little of both," she replied with a grin.

We grabbed our coffees, and then Blair, Chiara, Father Leo, and I regrouped around a table in the coffee shop's back room, since the store was closed. Usually, the the room is home to all kinds of gatherings, but tonight, the shop was oddly quiet.

"The group that usually plays Cards Against Humanity tonight went to a concert fundraiser instead," Chiara said, answering my unspoken question. "All of the concert's proceeds benefit LGBTQA charities," she added. The CAH group is open to everyone, but it's also known to be a local safe place for teens who, for whatever reason, don't fit into the local flannel shirt and pick-up truck culture.

Father Leo spread a map across the table, and we anchored it with coffee mugs. I sat next to him, while Blair and Chiara settled in across from us. "This is a map of the area before they built the lake," he said. "And the red outline is the flooded area. Most of what's down there was forest and pasture land, but if you go back to even older maps, you can see some family graveyards. By the time the land was purchased for the dam, no one had been buried in those old cemeteries for generations. Some of the farms had been sold several times, so I'm betting that people had forgotten all about the graves, and none of the bodies were moved."

"So, do you think Taylor's spell will reanimate all of them or just the graves on his family farm?" I asked. "And are the zombies going to swim for shore, or walk out on the bottom of the lake, like in that pirate movie?"

Father Leo shrugged. "Taylor meant to only target his grandfather's farm. Let's not borrow trouble. We just need to be ready for them."

"Setting up a sniper's roost with a high-powered rifle on parkland is a federal offense."

Father Leo grinned at me. "That's why you're not going to be on parkland," he replied. "And we've got back-up to drive any wayward zombies in your direction."

"Back-up?"

Chiara raised her flask in a mock toast. "Yep. I called in the cavalry. The coven is ready and willing." The Tuesday night women's group that met for "Bunko" in the bookstore's community room was, in reality, a coven of local witches.

"Are you sure that's a good idea?" I asked. We didn't usually involve civilians, although witches, at least, weren't going to be surprised about the supernatural aspects.

"Relax. It'll be fine," Chiara replied. "They'll use their magic to herd the zombies toward you. Then you pick them off, and bye-bye shamblers."

"How do we explain the dead bodies with their heads blown open?"

Blair grinned. "I've got a plan—and the supplies you're going to need. Leave it to me."

Who the hell thought it would be a good idea to flood an old graveyard to make a dam?

Apparently, the Pennsylvania Department of Wildlife, or Parks and Recreation, or whatever state agency gets to be in charge of lakes. I stood on a hill overlooking Lake Wilhelm, just outside of Sandy Lake, and waited for the zombies.

I'd found a sheltered spot with a good view in an old scout camp on a ridge above an abandoned gravel pit with a perfect vantage point to the lakeshore nearest the old graveyard on the sunken Ellerbee farm. The night wind rustled through the trees, reminding me that early spring in these parts is really still winter. I'd dressed for the weather, but since I wasn't moving around, I shivered.

Zombies were one of my least favorite things to kill. They could be wicked fast, and they stank. Any injuries they caused were guaranteed to get infected and blowing them up made a mess. Since leaving body parts strewn around tended to raise inconvenient questions, that meant I didn't just have to shoot the damn things; I also had to clean up the mess afterward.

On the plus side, zombies weren't clever, just driven by hunger and a reflex to attack. But since they couldn't feel pain and they were already dead, just shooting them or hacking them apart didn't stop them. That took a bullet to the brain or cutting off the head. Since I didn't want to get close enough for decapitation, here I was, freezing my ass off in a drafty, vandalized scout cabin the size of a school bus that I had repurposed as a hunting blind.

Father Leo had figured out a lot about Taylor's spell, but the timing had been tougher to pin down. That meant the witches and I were stuck keeping vigil for a couple of hours, which was the best the good padre could do to narrow down the timeframe.

"We've got a visual." Blair's voice came over my headset. Just to be safe, we had agreed to send her as a second sharpshooter to back up the coven, although if a bunch of witches couldn't handle a zombie invasion, then the odds were against me stopping them singlehandedly.

"Copy that. What do you see?" I replied quietly.

"Movement under the water that's too big to be fish," Blair responded. "So the 'sisters' are steering them your way."

Old records on the drowned cemeteries were non-existent, so we had no way to know how many shambling dead were likely to be answering the grimoire's summons. When I'd questioned Taylor, he'd been vague about what the zombies were supposed to do after they rose from their graves. I had the distinct impression that he intended to make that part of his gaming campaign up as he went or roll the dice to determine the next moves. But since Taylor was locked up for his own safety, and the grimoire had been spirited away by the Occulatum, nobody was controlling the zombies, who had no further directions other than "rise."

I guess that beat having a bunch of zombies programmed to eat the townspeople and wreak havoc, and in my business, I've learned to take whatever breaks I can get since there aren't many. I settled into my perch and swept the lakefront with my night scope.

And there they were. I saw the water ripple a few yards out, where the lake was deeper, and then half a dozen forms broke the surface. Even with my night vision scope, I couldn't see their faces, and given how long they'd been dead, buried and submerged, I thanked Heaven for small favors. I took in a long breath and let it out, stilled my mind, and aimed.

One shot rang out, then four more in quick succession. Even at this distance, I hit my targets, and I could see their skulls explode like ripe melons. It helped that they weren't running or even trying to dodge. The sixth zombie stumbled and fell back into the water before I could shoot him, but I figured I'd get my chance.

Rifle shots in the woods around these parts aren't remarkable since most people hunt. Gunshots this late at night, on the other hand, couldn't be easily explained away. Father Leo said he'd come up with a diversion to lead the local cops away from the lake and keep them busy for a while, but I didn't want to have to explain myself if they called for back-up.

Seven, eight, nine. More zombies, more bullets. I hoped the lake wasn't also a reservoir because no matter what we did to hide the bodies, there were going to be bloody bits floating around.

Ten through fifteen went down easy, walking right out of the water and into my sights. I kept firing and reloading, getting occasional updates from Blair to let me know more shamblers were on the way.

"Can you hurry them up?" I muttered to Blair. "The longer I'm up here shooting, the more likely that the local boys in blue are going to come around to see what's going on."

"Got you covered," Blair replied. "One of our ladies put a deflection spell on you, and she's distorting the sound to make it difficult to pinpoint. Should last long enough to get the work done."

"I don't like 'should,'" I grumbled. "I like definite words like 'will.'

'Should' might mean you and your wife need to come visit and bring me a cake with a file in it."

"If she bakes it, you know it'll be the best damn jail-break cake ever," Blair replied. Chiara's parents own a restaurant and bakery with drool-worthy Italian pastries.

"I'd rather not find out for myself," I answered. "But tell the 'sisters' thanks."

Bang, splat. Bang, splat. By my count, we'd edged upward of thirty, and I wondered how many people had been buried in that old plot. I'd been to a few small farm cemeteries in my line of work, and most had about a dozen tombstones, tops. Then again, this area's been consistently inhab-ited for a long, long time, so for all I knew, Taylor hadn't just raised the dead from that old graveyard, but the occasional unlucky trapper or explorer from before the Revolutionary War, perhaps even older bones buried by the Native American tribes that had once settled near the family farm. There are a whole lot more dead people than we like to think about, and we don't come close to knowing where they've all been buried.

I picked off another six zombies, but I couldn't shake the feeling that something was wrong. That's when I heard the scrape of footsteps on gravel and caught a glimpse of motion outside my hiding place.

Shit. Just as I turned to get out of the small bunkhouse, two dripping forms blocked the exit. The wind carried the smell of rotting flesh and fishy water, and I choked back a reasonable gag reflex.

I got off one shot before the zombies rushed me, but the second one charged as his companion crumpled. Up close, the stench was even worse, making my eyes water. I pivoted and smashed at his rotted face with the butt of my rifle. Brittle bones crumbled with a snap, but the thing kept right on coming. I backed up, enough to get the muzzle of my rifle jammed right up beneath the zombie's chin, and pulled the trigger.

The shambler's head exploded, all over me and all over the back wall of the bunkhouse. That did it. Everyone's got limits, and I'd hit mine. I puked all over his zombie gobbets, and if I'd thought that the bunkhouse couldn't smell any worse than it did, I was wrong.

I staggered, heaving, from the small cabin, only to find three more zombies scrambling up the hillside, leaving bits of themselves behind on all the bramble bushes and the barbed wire fence at the edge of the gravel pit.

"Aw, shit," I muttered, trying not to get light headed from the smell. My favorite rifle had been besmirched by zombie guts, both on the stock and on the muzzle, and somehow that made the whole thing even worse.

One of the creatures rushed me, and my first shot blew his chest apart. He dropped onto his back, but the legs kept dragging him forward as his hands pushed against the moist soil. I didn't have time to take the head-shot to put him down since the other two decided to come at me together.

I got one of the zombies right between the eyes, and he fell like a bag of bones. The other tackled me, and we went down in a heap. I used my weight to roll us since although zombies are crazy strong, they aren't heavy. The jelly-like squishiness of his rotten and water-soaked dead flesh made me dry heave, and I'll hear the squelch that accompanied every motion in my dreams.

If I'd had a handgun, I might have gotten it between us to put a bullet through his midsection. But my rifle wouldn't do the trick, and I didn't fancy using it to bludgeon him since I was too damn close in case it accidentally went off. The skull loomed over my face, with dangling tendrils of matted hair and tattered skin, jaws wide and teeth bared.

So, I did what I would have done in any bar fight and clocked the sucker right in the mouth.

The zombie reeled back, but his bony hands still gripped my shoulders. I brought my feet up and kicked, which ripped him apart above the hips and sent his lower half flying. It landed near the zombie I shot that was still dragging himself across the ground, and they got tangled up.

I didn't have time to worry about it because the top half of the zombie —the half with teeth—still had a hold of me. Water and other fluids I didn't want to think about dripped down on me. I rolled us again, coming up on top, and when the vise-grip the zombie had on my right arm faltered, I delivered an uppercut that went full Rock-em, Sock-em on his head and popped it clean across the clearing.

Under other circumstances, I might have felt more charitable toward the dead, somberly reflecting on their humanity or feeling sad that their eternal rest had been disturbed. Screw that. Tonight, I was pissed, especially since I now had a headless zombie's upper body still holding on to my left arm, and the shambler with a see-through chest hadn't stopped inching his way on his ass toward me.

I pried the half-zombie off my arm and shot him because he had it coming. Then I turned and got a headshot on the zombie with the hole in his chest and an extra pair of legs tangled around his torso. That was just all kinds of wrong, and I didn't want to think about it.

"That's all of them," Blair said through the headset. "At least, I don't see any more coming out of the water. Time to clean up."

Easier said than done, especially when I got stuck doing the mop-up. Grumbling under my breath, I grabbed the shovel and tarp I'd left in the corner of the bunk cabin. With the tarp spread out on the ground, I scooped up zombie bits and put them onto the plastic. When I'd collected all the big chunks, I tied off the tarp and hooked it to the ATV I'd left parked in the woods, then dragged the whole thing down to the lake.

Fortunately, I brought my rifle. Blair had the brilliant idea to spread a roll of chicken wire across the boat launch entrance below the gravel pit. Zombies aren't very agile, so having to navigate a path covered with fencing wire was designed to slow them down. Most of them managed to get across the obstacle, but several remained stuck, either because they had slipped through the holes or their rotted clothing caught on the sharp wire.

Five more shamblers flopped on the rolled-out fencing like fish out of water. Taking the kill shots was easy, and a little sad. The zombies hadn't asked to be disturbed from their final slumber, and no personal grudge of theirs made them rise. They had been pawns—no, puppets—of a teenager who hadn't realized that magic was real or ever dreamed that his actions had real-life consequences. And as much as I thought Taylor Ellerbee deserved a punch to the jaw for causing this mess, the truth was, he never thought the book would actually work. Just one big dumb clusterfuck, all the way around.

I rolled up the chicken wire with the zombies inside like a metal-and-rotted-corpse burrito. Then I pushed a small utility boat out of the weeds on the edge of the lake and tied a rope to the wire bundle. I fastened it to the back of the boat and pushed off, waiting until I got into deep enough water to start the engine. High-powered motors aren't permitted on Lake Wilhelm—it's too shallow—but neither is shooting your dead ancestors, so in for a penny, in for a pound as my granny used to say.

I put-putted out from shore, hauling the zombies behind me. All I needed to do was get them far enough out that they wouldn't show up if we had a drought and the water levels fell, exposing the lake bottom near the water's edge.

When I was far enough out that I thought it was safe, I lifted the engine and started to saw through the rope with my knife. Just as the rope parted, a decaying arm broke the surface of the water, and one last straggler started to pull himself on board.

"Oh hell, no!" I said, and swung my knife, slicing through the zombie's rotted neck. His head fell back into the water with a plop, but the body held on to the back of the boat, immobile. I sat down on the boat's seat and kicked with both feet, knocking the headless body free. Just for good measure, I dropped the engine and revved it until I saw chum in the water. If the Game Commission still stocked the lake with walleye and muskie, there would be some prize winning fish once the season opened.

I just wouldn't be eating any.

4

I used to think "tulpa" was a city in Oklahoma. It's not.

Tulpas are dream-creatures, or at least, they take form from people's dreams and nightmares, and from the stories we tell each other. They get their power from our beliefs and fears, and once they're real, they hunt.

And just my fuckin' luck, we had an honest-to-God tulpa, right here in River City. Or rather, Conneaut Lake.

I parked my car at the end of an overgrown gravel lane, just over a rise from busy Route 322. If I walked to the top of the hill and looked across the highway, I'd see my favorite soft custard stand. Unfortunately, I didn't come for ice cream tonight.

After I had pulled my gear bag out of the truck, grabbed my shotgun, and stuck my Glock in the waistband of my jeans, I stood by the front of my truck and got my bearings. Off to the right lay a crumbling castle, while to the left, I saw a giant lace-up shoe the size of a minivan. Straight ahead, a dilapidated pirate ship listed in a brackish pond. Beyond them, I knew, lay a Minotaur maze, a wall with a huge cracked egg, and a pumpkin prison. And somewhere among the ruins, a monster lurked.

My phone buzzed in my pocket, and I pulled it out and answered. "Whatcha got?"

"I hacked a satellite feed," Chiara replied. "Not showing people or large wildlife in the target area. So, whatever you encounter, it's the tulpa."

"Good to know. What else?"

"If you don't check in with us in two hours, Blair's coming after you."

"If I don't check in, stay the fuck away," I warned. "I mean it. Or send in an army. But don't send her after me."

"Sorry," Chiara replied, and I could almost hear her shrug. "Nobody tells Blair what to do. Have you met her?" She snorted. "Not even my 'feminine wiles' dissuade that girl when she makes up her mind."

I doubted that, but sometimes even I know when to keep my mouth shut. "Just be smart about it," I grumbled, knowing when I was beat. "I'm going in."

"Remember what I told you," she warned.

"Gonna do my best," I said. "See you on the other side."

I slipped my phone back into a secure pocket in my gear vest and loaded some rock-salt-filled shells into the shotgun. I'd never seen myself as Prince Charming, but here I was, about to storm the castle and kill the monster.

I headed out, stepping over the remains of a big faux-stone archway that had once proudly proclaimed the entrance to Wonderama.

As amusement parks went, Wonderama had been unlucky from the start. I don't know what gave its founder the notion that competing with the venerable Conneaut Lake Park and Fairyland Forest was a smart idea, not when those parks had been thriving for half a century, and Wonderama was less than twenty miles away.

Bad luck dogged the place. One of the workers died in a freak accident when the park was being built. An attendant was mortally injured when one of the ride cars tipped off the rails. A small boy drowned in Pirate Lake. Rumors started to circulate that it was built on an ancient Native American burial ground, or a potters' field, or the graveyard of a deconsecrated church. A few gossips suggested that the owners had made a deal with the devil, but if they did, they were damn poor negotiators because they sure didn't get much out of it.

Still, Wonderama might have survived on account of being something new and having a prime location by the ice cream stand, if it hadn't been for the highway construction. That first crucial summer, before the tourist season had begun, the cones and barriers went up, rerouting traffic and making the trek not worth the bother. The ice cream stand survived. Wonderama didn't.

In the decades since Wonderama closed its gates for good, the park sat empty, tied up in legal wrangling. Every now and then a rumor surfaced about a potential buyer, but it always fell through. The original owner had financial difficulties, and one personal tragedy after another befell the subsequent administrators, leading to whispers about a curse. Locals told stories about strange things going on, as thrill-seekers and vandals explored the grounds, which had been left to decay.

I'd heard those stories, about mysterious "fairy lights" and glowing orbs, scary shadow creatures and unearthly noises, and carousel music playing in the middle of the night. Lots of stuff around here is haunted, but it doesn't become my problem until people start getting hurt. Then a couple of people went missing, and a few bodies turned up with really unusual fatal wounds, and the whole steaming mess landed squarely in my lap.

Chiara and I had managed to find an old map of the doomed fairytale park and squared it up against Google Earth. That gave me the lay of the land, so I knew where I was when navigating from Mother Goose World to Fairy Woodland to Enchanted Forest and Gumdrop Dreams Kingdom. We had also pieced together the stories told by the frightened trespassers who survived their adventure, as well as the police reports of where the bodies had been found to give me a fair idea of where the tulpa would show up.

That didn't mean I really had any idea of what I was going up against. Just a guesstimate of where it might be lurking.

Moonlight gave me enough light to see, although I had flashlights and a lantern in my bag. Even after all this time, the main landmarks were recognizable despite the effects of weather and neglect. I decided to save the castle for last since it was the largest building, maybe the size of a ranch house. That also worked well since the castle was at the back of the park, and I'd have to pass the other attractions on my way in.

In daylight, if the grounds were tidy and happy music played through the overhead speakers, Wonderama could have been charming. In the dark, overgrown and fallen into disrepair, it was scary as all hell. I don't know who got the bright idea of reading fairy tales to children because those stories are dark as fuck, full of monsters and wicked queens and hungry wolves that eat people. And now, thanks to all the negative energy in the park's troubled past, those monsters were coming to life.

I headed for the huge shoe. The colorful old map showed the old woman's shoe as an orange lace-up boot. To me, it looked more like a high-top sneaker, but maybe the builder did the best he could. Windows opened on the sides of the shoe to let light in, and I could imagine cheery gingham curtains fluttering in the breeze. Once upon a time, the inside had probably looked like a Smurf cottage, with cutesy miniature furniture. Now, the windows and door were dark sockets, the brightly colored walls were peeling and streaked with mold, and dead leaves stirred in the cold wind, coming to a halt against the transom.

"Come out, come out, wherever you are," I murmured, raising my shotgun and pointing it at the empty doorway. I sensed more than saw movement as a shadow grew solid. But the creature that stepped into the moonlight was a hag, not a grandma, more Baba Yaga than *bubbe*. Filthy, matted gray hair hung in dreads around a wizened face. The hunched figure wore a stained apron over a tattered dress, and her bony arms and long-fingered, gnarled hands were dark with blood as if she'd just come from slaughtering dinner. Cunning eyes sized me up, and her thin lips curled into a malicious smile, baring sharp teeth.

There was an old woman who lived in a shoe. She had so many children; she didn't know what to do.

So she ate them.

The old woman snarled, then sprang for me, clawed hands outstretched. I fired, right for granny's head. The shot hit, dead on, and the figure vanished as the shell impacted with the concrete wall of the old shoe and scattered rock salt all over. The tulpa wasn't gone—my luck wasn't that good—but I'd sent it packing for a little while. I kept the shotgun handy as I reached for a jug of holy water from my bag as well as a bundle of sage and a lighter.

I splashed the threshold with holy water, then lit the sage and tossed it inside, where its cleansing smoke would fill the structure. Just in case, I recited the banishment litany Father Leo made me memorize. Nothing around me stirred. I took that as a good sign, grabbed my gear, and headed deeper into the ruins of a once-magical kingdom.

The rusted remains of a Tilt-A-Whirl hunkered beneath trees that had grown up through its railings. A little farther and I could see the undulating track of a caterpillar coaster poking up through tall brush like the spine of a dragon. The cars waited at the ride entrance for visitors that would never come again. Despite the years of neglect, I could still make out the smiling face on the lead car, although now it looked maniacal instead of friendly.

I paused at the Tilt-A-Whirl since it was the ride that had a documented fatality. Billy Kester, age ten. If other people had gotten hurt at the park, it hadn't been reported. Given that Wonderama didn't stay open for very long, I doubted it had the time or enough attendance to rack up a body count, at least, before the tulpa came into being.

I don't do magic, and I don't have any special talent for seeing ghosts. Whether that's a good thing or a bad thing in my line of work is up for debate. But Father Leo has shown me a trick or two about sending on spirits that are confused about being dead or just not sure how to move on. Vengeful ghosts or ones who are sticking around for a purpose are a whole different kettle of fish, and I leave those to the professionals.

The old ride's shell-shaped cars were rusted in place, no longer crazily swinging in circles. Despite the situation, I smiled at memories of throwing myself from side to side to make the cart spin when my brother and I rode rides like it at the fair long ago. Maybe if the ghost hadn't moved on, he or she just wasn't ready to go home yet after a day at the park.

"It's okay to let go," I said to empty air, keeping my shotgun handy in case the tulpa showed up again. If there were ghosts here, then they helped strengthen and anchor the tulpa, so getting the spirits to leave should weaken the tulpa's hold.

"The park is closed now," I said, feeling a little silly since no one was in sight. "It won't ever open. The fun is over. It's time for you to rest."

I was about to give up and just lay down some salt, holy water, and sage when a shimmer in the air caught my attention. As I watched, the figure of a boy who looked to be about ten years old gradually became clearer. He wore shorts, a striped shirt, and a pair of Keds, and I wondered why he had stayed here for so long, all by himself. Then a thought came to me, and I ran with it.

"Did your mom tell you to stay right here?" I asked gently. Billy hesitated—he'd probably been told not to talk to strangers—and then nodded shyly.

"Your mom went on ahead," I went on, wincing at the euphemism. Given how long the park had been out of business, his mother was more likely to be waiting in the Great Beyond than back home. "She said it's okay for you to catch up. She's waiting for you there."

Billy's ghost frowned, and I figured he was deciding whether or not to trust me.

"I bet she's been looking for you. She'll be really happy to see you. Just think about your mom real hard, and you'll know where to go."

I'm not expert on the afterlife, but I know what mothers are like, and since Billy looked well cared-for and had a family that shelled out for park tickets, I figured he'd have the kind of mom who didn't stop looking for him, even on the Other Side.

"Do you see her?" I asked, and held my breath.

Billy turned around, and I wondered whether he saw Wonderama as it had been on that fatal day, or whether he glimpsed beyond the Veil itself. But just as I thought maybe the whole thing had been a bad idea, he broke into a broad smile and began to wave his arms, jumping up and down to attract the attention of someone only he could see.

I blinked, and Billy was gone.

Just in case, I cast handfuls of salt over the old ride, sprayed the landing with holy water, and left a sage smudge burning on the metal deck. Deep in my heart, I knew the precautionary measures didn't matter. Billy finally went home.

I didn't have long to celebrate a minor win. In the distance, I heard the song of a carousel, and a few seconds later, the howl of a wolf.

That scumbag tulpa was trying to play with my head. I couldn't stop the shiver that ran through me, since the hindbrain doesn't listen to reason, but I sure as hell wasn't going to let that mofo run me off, not until I'd bagged its ass and banished it from the park.

Next up was a big pumpkin that looked like a Halloween reject. The oversized squash was large enough that I probably could have crawled inside on my hands and knees, plenty roomy enough for small children. The weathered mannequin of a wide-eyed woman gripped the rusted bars over the window.

Peter, Peter, pumpkin eater. Had a wife and couldn't feed her. So he put her in a shell and there he kept her very well.

Yeah, nothing creepy about that. The pumpkin looked empty, except for the bedraggled mannequin. But my spidey sense told me I wasn't alone, so I raised my shotgun and turned in a slow circle.

There. I saw a shadow flow from one place to another, where there shouldn't have been movement. Tulpas feed on fear. I hoped they choked on anger because this monster was getting on my last nerve.

"What kind of a lame-ass man locks his wife up in a jack-o-lantern?" I shouted to the darkness. "Seriously? That's the best you could do?"

Taunting monsters might not be a smart thing to do, but I never claimed to be a genius. Still, I've found that men and monsters get sloppy when they got pissed off, and so my sort-of plan involved annoying the tulpa into slipping up.

As plans went, it sucked, but it was the best I'd come up with since tulpas weren't as easy to kill as a lot of other creatures. I'd have to wing it, which is what all my "plans" came down to, anyhow.

Instinct made me wheel just as the monster rushed me from behind. He had a skeletally-thin body and unnaturally long arms, with fingers like sickles and a head like a pumpkin. Red hellfire burned behind the carved-out features. The leering face had a mouth filled with serrated teeth, and when it directed its fiery gaze at me, I couldn't help the fear that fluttered in my belly.

"Suck it up, summer squash," I growled, leveling my shotgun and hitting that pumpkin center mass.

Seeds and stringy pulp showered me in a slimy rain of pumpkin guts, but the tulpa vanished. I repeated the cleansing on the cement house, preventing the spirit from returning, and moved on, once I'd reloaded. My hunts never went this well, and at the risk of jinxing myself, I wondered when the tulpa was going to get serious. I had the feeling it wanted to lure me deeper into the defunct park, where its power was strongest.

Chiara hadn't been able to get details about the other deaths at the park, so I had no way to know which ride had turned deadly, or which of the cheerful structures had killed its builder. Having blood spilled during construction didn't bode well, since that was like catnip to a lot of super-natural creatures. The park was a kingdom of broken dreams, so it made sense that the tulpa attached itself, feeding on the misery of the owner and then on the fear and death of the urban explorers and curious teenagers who were unlucky enough to venture into its lair.

The carousel music seemed to come from everywhere, louder now. I remembered the cute map, done in 1960s-style illustrations, that put the carousel right on the other side of Mother Goose Land, in between the Fairy Forest and the Enchanted Woods, past Pirate Lake and before I got to Gumdrop Dreams Castle.

The skeleton of a Ferris wheel rose, silhouetted against the stars. A car dangled from one hinge, and I wondered whether that happened long after the park closed, or whether it was another nail in the unlucky park's coffin. Wonderama hadn't offered big thrill rides, but it provided the basics that younger kids and their slightly older siblings loved.

I skirted Pirate Lake, keeping an eye on the ominous wreck of a ship in the center of the algae-thick water. A swan boat sat mired in the muck near the lake's edge. Back in the day, a merry band of pirates entertained visitors with silly songs and dances, funny pranks, and a three p.m. plank walking. I looked at the fetid water and shuddered, hoping that the lake had been healthier back then than it was now if some poor bastard had to cannonball into it off the side of the ship.

The boom of a cannon made me flinch. I heard a wet, sucking sound, and saw the drenched figure of a drowned man rising from the murky water. I doubted Wonderama's pirates looked like the horror crawling out of the lake. This wasn't a sexy rogue or a dashing brigand. He looked more like a Hell's Angel meth addict, dressed in a ragged shirt and torn pants. Long, filthy hair hung around a bloated face. He either had the pox, or the lake's fish had been nibbling. Madness lit his eyes, and he fixed his attention on me with an unpleasant grin.

He carried a musket in one hand, and we both aimed and fired at once. I swore as a piece of lead shot grazed my left shoulder, sending warm blood trickling down my arm. My aim fared better, blowing away the pirate's hat and most of his head. Damn tulpa was taking different shapes, matching its appearance to the theme of whatever was nearby. The tulpa vanished, but he made his point.

He'd drawn blood. This was real.

It's all fun and games until somebody dies.

"Quit running!" I shouted at the darkness. "Some big, scary monster you are! Nothing but a scum-sucking coward. You don't scare me!"

Famous last words.

The wolf's howl was louder, closer. I turned slowly, looking for the source. If it were a real wolf, my Glock would serve me better than the shotgun, since a hollow point does more damage than rock salt. But there hadn't been real wolves in these parts for a long, long time. I kept my shotgun ready, betting my life that the tulpa and the wolf were one and the same.

The last buildings in Mother Goose Land were a tidy cottage on my right and three small houses on my left. Since the left-hand structures had been decorated to look like they were made of sticks, straw, and bricks, and the right-hand cottage was decked out in red, I figured the wolf fit right in.

"Come on, you bastard. Show yourself!" I had better things to do than tromp through high grass in a defunct theme park looking for a monster that wanted to play coy.

He was out there, watching. I could feel it, that primal prickle at the back of the neck that warned of danger. The hindbrain memory of long ago when humans weren't the top predator.

A dark form came at me from the shadows, hitting me on my wounded left side. The weight of it took us both to the ground, slamming me onto my back hard enough to knock the wind out of me. A black wolf that probably weighed as much as I did pinned me to the ground, its muzzle snapping dangerously close to my throat.

I had forgotten the first rule of tulpas. They're as real as they want to be.

My knee came up, hitting the wolf hard in the belly, distracting it long enough for my left hand to grab the iron knife from my belt sheath and stab between its ribs. The wolf's body jerked, and the head came down again, mouth open, lips drawn, teeth bared. I slammed the stock of the shotgun into its nose, and it reared back. Not enough for me to have room to fire the shotgun, but plenty to change how much leverage I needed to throw it clear.

I scrambled to a crouch, drew my Glock, and fired.

The shot hit the tulpa in the shoulder, but that didn't slow it down. It leaped, and as I rolled to get out of the way of its snapping teeth and sharp claws, my second shot went wild. I felt claws rake across my chest, barely missing my throat. Before I could fire again, the tulpa vanished.

Shit. I sat up, breathing hard as my heart hammered. My shirt and jacket were tattered and bloodied, between the musket shot and the wolf's attack. I was wounded and stank of blood, which was an "Eat at Joe's" sign pointing right at my head for predators. A sane person would have retreated and called for backup.

My ex-wife always said I was crazy.

My gear bag includes a med-kit. I sprinkled salt and holy water in a circle around myself and lit a bundle of sage to protect me while I patched myself up. The alcohol wipes stung like hell, and I knew I'd need some of the healing poultice the bookstore coven made for me, effective against supernatural contamination. But as I daubed away the blood, I realized that the musket ball wound wasn't serious, and the shallow grooves dug by the wolf's claws probably wouldn't require stitches.

The tulpa was toying with me, playing with its food. That just made me even more set on destroying it.

While tulpas might begin as a thought form, they grow more real, solid, and sentient as others believe in them. We had proof that this tulpa could kill. I couldn't unthink it or choose not to believe in it, not without ending up dead. If it was as easy as magicking it away, the coven would have done so. And since the whole abandoned park was steeped in disappointment and despair, waiting for the tulpa to starve to death wasn't going to happen.

I had a theory about how I might destroy the tulpa. Father Leo had already ruled out exorcism, since it wasn't hell spawn. That meant I had to get creative. Sending Billy's ghost on was part of the plan. I'd cleansed the pumpkin where I sensed bad juju. I didn't know if the spirits of the trespassers who got killed had hung around, but if they had, sending them on could help loosen the tulpa's hold. I headed for the building I figured was the heart of the problem: Gumdrop Dreams Castle.

I grabbed my stuff and walked deeper into the park, grateful that I hadn't found a pressing reason to visit the Fairy Woodland. The Fey were real, and real trouble. I had no intention of messing with them, especially after all the trouble they caused a friend of mine. And the Minotaur Maze? Hell, no.

That didn't mean I was thrilled crossing the Enchanted Forest. This didn't look like the woods in cartoons filled with happy bunnies and singing squirrels. The trees of the forest weren't real; they had been fabricated from the same wire, wood, and concrete as the rest of the park's attractions, and these trees weren't friendly. The gnarled trunks and long branches loomed over the walkway, ready to snag anyone who stepped off the path. Some of the trees had eyes painted onto them, while others had full faces twisted in expressions of hunger.

A parent would have to be nuts to bring their kids through here, but I could just imagine the older kids, like Billy, daring each other to run through. During the day, the ominous overhanging limbs and hulking trunks would have been intimidating enough, but at night, they took on a whole different level of freaky.

I've always figured that a good offense is the best defense, and I decided to start offending. I brought out the biggest, brightest, blindingly bright flashlight in my bag and snapped it on. It lit up a ten-foot circle like high noon and cut through the shadows at least twice that far. In the cold light, the spooky trees were just sad-looking props, badly weathered and slowly crumbling into dust.

Just to be obnoxious, and to buck up my spirits, I started reciting the Lord's Prayer at the top of my lungs, then moved on to the Hail Mary. I'm not very religious, so when I ran out of prayers before I ran out of forest, I started on Christmas carols.

The black wolf appeared in the middle of the path, head lowered, red eyes glaring. *My, what big teeth you have.*

I shot; he dodged. But by taking physical form, the tulpa was hemmed in by the terrifying trees, just like I was. Whoever designed the forest made sure that the branches and trunks formed a barrier that kept visitors on the path. It really wasn't possible to wander away. That meant the wolf and I had to square off like gunslingers at the OK Corral.

I never really liked Westerns.

The wolf leaped at me, and I dropped and rolled. I knew I'd never be able to hit him with a shotgun blast while he was moving, so I shot at the tree behind him and dove forward out of the way. Normally, rock salt shouldn't have done a lot of damage, not like buckshot would have, but the old concrete was damaged enough to be brittle, and a huge, heavy branch collapsed, right on top of the wolf. The twisted limbs trapped the wolf like a cage, and I racked another shell, aimed, and fired. He vanished with a snarl that boded trouble if he ever caught up to me.

I might have bought myself some time since the tulpa seemed to need to recharge after being dispelled, but I had a feeling I was running straight toward the monster's true lair, where odds were good he'd be at his strongest. I didn't count on having as much of a break between attacks as I'd had toward the edges of the abandoned park and stayed on alert as I picked up my pace to a jog eager to get through the nightmare forest.

On the far side of the grasping trees was the carousel. The music must have been a trick of the tulpa's because the once-beautiful ride didn't look like it had played its calliope for decades. Seeing the old merry-go-round looking so decrepit made me sad. If the owners of the park had been hard-pressed for money, surely they could have sold off the carved horses and beautifully painted friezes to collectors for cash. Now, the wooden horses, giraffes, and other exotic animals were weathered, their wood splitting, faded paint peeling. If I had to pick one image to sum up Wonderama with all its squandered promise and broken dreams, this would be it.

Hearing carousel music playing when it couldn't possibly come from the ride was creepy as fuck.

If the tulpa was messing with my head again, it bounced back quicker than before. Then again, I'd almost reached my target, the Gumdrop Dreams Castle.

Compared to the big-name theme parks with castles, Wonderama was definitely low-budget. Its Gumdrop castle didn't soar high into the sky with flag-tipped spires or boast mosaics of Italian glass in its entrance hall. Instead, it looked like a two-story house with delusions of grandeur. The boxy shape had what looked like a silo on each end, but with a pointy top instead of rounded. Its stucco finish had faux stonework painted onto it, but the thin material had weathered badly, cracking and mildewing, and in many places, chunks had fallen away exposing the plywood beneath. A "moat" beneath a rickety drawbridge was no more than a shallow ditch, filled with mud and high grass, more likely to harbor ticks than a sea serpent.

All of the dead bodies had been found in and around the castle. Of course explorers would make their way here; any video game player could tell you the castle was the ultimate destination. All of Wonderama's banners and pennants had featured Gumdrop Dreams Castle, with its turrets topped with plaster candy and a fence row of brightly colored lollipops. Now, the giant faded treats looked more like an enticement to the witch's house from Hansel and Gretel.

I was going to have fun storming the castle. What fed a dream monster? Hopes and wishes, and childhood fantasies of princesses, knights, and dragons. Gumdrop Dreams Castle encouraged all of that, with a Wishing Well in the center of its courtyard that begged children to drop in coins for charity and think their dearest desires. In its heyday, the castle had come alive with kids living out their daydreams, battling inflatable dragons, braiding daisy chain crowns, and sitting on the rock candy throne. All of that energy should have been happy and positive, but the park's bad luck darkened and twisted those dreams, and the tulpa rose from the shadows of those grim fairy tales like a secret Id.

Time to burn the fucker down.

I grabbed a few essentials from my pack, but I'd already put the most important pieces in my tactical vest. If the police caught me, I was totally screwed, unless my cop buddy Louie Marino could call in a big favor. Since I was supposed to have a date with Sara tomorrow night, I had no intention of standing her up for a stint in the county pokey.

An ear-splitting roar, loud enough to make the ground tremble beneath my feet, froze me in my tracks. Standing guard at the entrance to Gumdrop Dreams Castle was a huge, bat-winged dragon. Not the cute cotton candy-colored flying reptile from the Wonderama map, but a fire-breathing, dwarf-eating, treasure-hoarding monster whose smoke and brimstone breath could cause plenty of smog. Of course, the tulpa would be a dragon. Fan-fucking-tastic.

And me without my shining armor.

A blast of fire singed past me as I threw myself out of the way, unwilling to get incinerated trying to prove it was all an illusion. A slew of dead men and missing-presumed-dead explorers proved the tulpa was real enough to kill.

I didn't have a magic ring to turn me invisible, and the dragon kept me in its sights, giving me the slit-eye as it moved with disturbing speed to roast me again. I had the ammunition I needed to take out the wishing well and the castle, but I didn't want to fire through the dragon, in case it could foul my aim or neutralize the payload, and I didn't have unlimited rounds. That meant I had to fight him. Yippie-ki-yay, muther of dragons.

The beast had a long, sleek body with bat-like wings and a head with a narrow snout. Its scales were dark red, and its slit eyes were bright yellow. The tulpa eyed me like dinner, probably figuring it was just a matter of time before it added me to its list of victims. I swallowed hard, wishing for a magic sword. The overgrown lizard filled the castle entrance, putting itself between me and the targets that might make it vulnerable. I had to get inside the castle to be able to kill the tulpa, but I had to get past the dragon to do that.

A round of rock salt bounced off the red scales without even making an impact. The rumble from the creature almost sounded like a laugh, daring me to do better, confident that it already knew who would win. I hadn't brought armor-piercing bullets with me, or a Howitzer to take out a monster bigger than a tank. None of my knives would even scratch that tough hide, and I bet that even my Glock's hollow-points would be useless.

So I was going to need to play dirty.

The next time I fired my shotgun, I aimed for the dragon's eyes. Salt hurts, and while the dragon tried to blink away the sting, I sent my next shot right through the crumbling castle wall, blowing through it in a cloud of plaster dust and splinters.

I dove through the hole as the tulpa roared, barely evading the long talons on the end of its front foot. I wasn't as lucky dodging the powerful tail, which knocked me halfway across the courtyard with one swipe. Still, I'd gotten inside, and the dragon's bulk wouldn't allow it to turn around in the entranceway, so it either had to go out or back up. Maybe the tulpa hadn't thought out is new form very well because while it was fearsome, it had the maneuverability of a gunboat, at least on land.

Shit. If it went forward, it could get lift off, then circle around and fry me to a crackly crunch. New strategy. I reloaded with buckshot, rolled, and came up shooting, aiming for the wings instead of the tough hide. Iron pellets might not have penetrated the scales, but it tore through the thinner skin of the dragon's wing. The creature's tail lashed, but I scrambled out of range before shooting at the other wing and managing to put a hole in it.

The dragon roared, shimmying forward, but it needed a few minutes for its bulk and length to get out of the narrow castle entrance before it could turn around and charge back to kill me. My best bet lay in doing what I came to do and worrying about the dragon afterward—as stupid as that sounded.

Inside Gumdrop Dream Castle, Wonderama's faded glory had its last hurrah. The candy cane throne had aged badly, revealing it as a weathered chair backed by warped, splintering boards. I could barely make out what had once been colorful murals, as the mold and decay destroyed the stucco and the paint faded in the sun. In the center of the courtyard, the wishing well was a ruin. Most of the shingles were gone from the roof, and the bucket hung askew.

I reached into my bag and grabbed my grenade launcher, already loaded with a shell holding my special concoction of salted holy water and iron filings. The dragon had slithered its wide hips out of the castle entrance like shedding a too-tight pair of pants, and its lumbering steps thundered in the quiet night. If it made it back here before I finished, or if my hare-brained plan didn't work, I was toast.

The bang of the grenade launcher reverberated from the castle walls as I fired straight down into the depths of the well. Maybe the cash-starved owners had gathered up all the dimes and quarters thrown in by hopeful children, but I figured that they'd left those wish-coins down there, not realizing those thwarted dreams would spawn a monster.

The shell detonated when it hit bottom. I heard the dragon roar, but this time, it sounded more like pain instead of belligerence. Tulpas were thought-forms, created from belief and dreams. The wishing well was the heart of the Gumdrop Dreams Castle, where thousands of children had visualized their most cherished fantasies, as sacred as prayers. That bastard tulpa twisted that innocence into something monstrous, and it was time that came to an end.

The next part of my plan was trickier. The whole castle had to go. It was, after all, about Gumdrop *Dreams*, and the fact that this was where the tulpa brought its victims told me that it felt most powerful here.

That meant I needed to commit a little arson, for the good of humanity.

The tricky part would be getting out after I set the castle on fire and before the tulpa fried me or ate me. While I felt sure I'd wounded it by destroying the wishing well, I couldn't be sure that torching the castle would get rid of the tulpa for good. It wouldn't be the first plan I'd hatched that didn't turn out as planned, but it might be the last.

The tulpa-dragon roared, and I knew it would come thundering through the castle gate any minute. I fired a shotgun blast to give myself a back door through the ruined rear wall, then chucked my shotgun and grenade launcher back in my bag and picked up my rifle.

Incendiary bullets are a beautiful thing. I squeezed the trigger and laid down a line of fire across the front wall of the castle, then turned to continue shooting until I ran out of ammo. The rounds pierced the stucco façade, and the old plywood and timber went up like tissue paper, lighting up the night. I took my chance while I had it and dove out of the hole in the back wall, with my arms over my head to protect me from the splintered wood. The walls caught fire with alarming speed, and I knew that I'd have to dodge the local VFD as well as the tulpa to get back to my car.

I landed wrong and went down with a curse as my knee folded under me. When I tried to get back on my feet, my knee had other plans, and I almost fell again, but I managed to put some limping steps between me and the flaming walls.

That's when the dragon burst through the fire, coming straight at me.

I stumbled backward, knowing that I'd never be able to outrun the monster, not with a bum knee. Of all the ways I thought I might die, getting eaten by a dragon had never crossed my mind. I had a lifetime of regrets, too many to flash before my eyes, but one, in particular, stood out. If I died here, turned into lizard-chow, I'd never find out whether Sara and I really had a chance. And that would be a damn shame.

I staggered until I fell, then crab-walked backward, wracking my brain for anything in my bag of tricks that might buy me time. Fire didn't harm the creature, and none of my puny guns would make a mark on its tough hide. It roared again, and my head snapped up at the change in the sound, desperate hope leaping in my jaded, cynical heart.

The dragon was transforming as the castle behind it burned.

When I'd first glimpsed the monster, it had been straight out of a Peter Jackson blockbuster, fearsome and menacing. That was the tulpa, taking its form from the way the energy of the park had grown dark and twisted through its failure. But as I watched, the outline of the dragon shifted, growing shorter and rounder, its blood-red hue fading, damaged wings disappearing altogether, long legs and powerful tail turning stumpy.

It roared again, this time in frustration as much as menace, as if it realized what had happened. Gone was the terrifying creature of legend. In its place was a light pink, goofy looking cartoon dragon with innocent, wide eyes. The tulpa had been robbed of the well of dreams that fed its energy, and what remained was its original form, the silly caricature from the Wonderama map.

Before the tulpa could get used to its new form, I lobbed a grenade in front of the dragon and threw myself down on the ground, arms protecting my head. I didn't figure that the grenade would hurt the tulpa, but it made a nice hole in the ground, giving me a moat of my own for the shell-shocked monster to navigate around and providing me with at least a little head start.

I glanced behind me as I dragged myself to my feet, forcing myself into a gimpy run as my knee protested. The castle had nearly burned to the ground, going up even faster than I expected. I circled around, giving the carousel a wide berth, though I realized its music had gone silent. With the flames behind me, I navigated the Enchanted Forest much more quickly, and this time, the creepy trees were only constructs of chicken wire and plaster, nothing more. I heard the dragon lumbering in pursuit, and I quickened my pace as fast as I dared, afraid that any moment I would feel its breath on the back of my neck.

Mother Goose Land loomed ahead, and this path took me past Humpty Dumpty on his wall and the Billy Goats Gruff bridge, but I paid the broken and faded figures no attention, too afraid of the monster closing the gap behind me. In the distance, I heard sirens. I had no intention of being caught by the fire department, but I didn't want to lead them into an ambush by the tulpa.

Time to turn around and face my fears. I turned around, leveled my rifle, and fired my last incendiary bullet. And as I did, I focused on my own hopes and fears, visualizing the dragon's heart and wishing it real.

Tulpas are thought-creatures, and robbed of its dream-well and its hoarded wishes in the cindered castle, it took direction from the next strongest source—me. My bullet tore through hide the color of cotton candy, burrowing through flesh and sinew, and bursting into flame inside the heart of the dragon.

For an instant, its cartoonish eyes widened in shock, and then an age-old knowing overtook them, an instant before the pink dragon vanished in a puff of smoke.

I limped the rest of the way to my truck, slung my bag into the back, and took off, hoping the old road still came out at the park's back entrance, since I didn't want to explain myself to any arriving firefighters. The asphalt had long ago crumbled to gravel and potholes, giving me a rough ride as I navigated the park's perimeter. I kept my headlights off, but that meant trading off speed for stealth, and I almost ran into the wooden barricade that blocked off the far end of the exit road. It was meant to keep traffic on the main road from turning into the abandoned park, not to keep anyone in. I nudged it with the grill of my truck, and the old boards fell apart, as rickety as the rest of the park.

With the glow of the flames in my rearview mirror, I turned onto the road and flipped my headlights on. The gashes from the big bad wolf still bled across my arm and chest, my knee hurt like a son of a bitch, and I couldn't get the smell of smoke and mold out of my nose. I headed for home, deciding that dragon slaying was highly overrated.

5

My favorite *Star Trek* quote is, "Social occasions are only warfare concealed."

I found myself thinking about that quote as Sara adjusted my tie before we walked into the dinner for her hotelier conference at the historic Hotel Conneaut. "Relax," Sara said, smoothing down my collar, and giving my cheek a pat. "It's just a bunch of people who run B&Bs. You face down scarier things for breakfast."

Sara knows I'm a hunter more often than I'm a mechanic. We met when I was up in the Big Woods hunting a were-squonk, and I ended up staying at the B&B she runs up in Kane. She's smart, practical, and not into drama; plus it's a relief being with someone who knows the truth about what I spend my nights and weekends doing. She's widowed, I'm divorced, and we've both been hurt, so we've been taking it slowly. This was the first time I'd been her plus-one for any kind of gathering. To say I was out of practice being someone's arm candy would be a powerful understatement.

"They're your colleagues," I grumbled. "I don't want to embarrass you."

She smiled. "Don't exorcise the hotel's famous ghosts, don't throw holy water on the speaker, and it'll be fine." I think she was joking, but maybe not.

"Okay," I said, feeling far more nervous about the reception and dinner than I did hunting things that could kill me and suck out my soul. "Just don't expect much small talk."

She stretched up to kiss me, and I felt some of the knots in my gut loosen. "I'm glad you're here." Sara laced her fingers through mine. "Don't give the others another thought."

I made it up to Kane every few weeks, mostly on monster business, but sometimes just to see Sara. My job gave me more flexibility than hers did, since running a B&B is a 24-7 kind of thing. That was another reason for moving slowly. We knew we liked each other, a lot. But neither of us were the casual relationship sort, and if we got serious, we still didn't know where that might end up. Would I relocate my mechanic business to the Big Woods when my friends and support crew were here in Atlantic? But unless Sara sold her B&B and bought something near me, then what would she do?

We weren't ready to answer those questions yet, so we took things one day at a time, trying not to go too far too fast, and maybe both scared about getting our hearts broken if we mucked this up.

Which is why the conference gave Sara both a reason to see me closer to my home and an excuse not to spend the night. She'd invited me to the reception and dinner, but with the caveat that she had a late-night business session afterward and an early breakfast. I can take a hint. That didn't mean I wouldn't be taking a cold shower when I got home, but I was on board with the going slow thing, except when she pressed up against me, and I could smell her shampoo and kissing her sent my downstairs brain into overdrive.

I really hoped I did the same for her. From the flush in her cheeks and the naughty smile she gave me, I thought maybe so, but it was hard for me to feel confident. Give me a gun and a round of silver bullets, and I'm a scary SOB. Ask me to win over a beautiful woman with my charm and sparkling personality, and I'm SOL.

She kissed me again, this time lingering a little longer. "I'm glad you're here, Mark," she repeated. "Really glad." The way she brushed against me almost made me believe it. My ex-wife Lara took my self-confidence along with my DVD collection and half the cash in my bank account when she left me, and while I've replaced the movies and the money, the confidence is still missing-in-action.

We walked in hand-in-hand, and I tried not to hyperventilate. Hotel

Conneaut is a beautiful Victorian resort on Conneaut Lake, with wide porches, lovely period details, and several documented ghosts. Since the ghosts have never hurt anyone and the hotel plays them up as a feature, I figure they don't fall into my job description. And with a ballroom full of people, spirits from the other side were highly unlikely to make an appearance. They are almost as uncomfortable around the living as I am.

A big banner that read *"Welcome NW PA B&B"* hung across the far wall, a jumble of letters that actually did make sense. I took a deep breath and did my best not to freeze in my tracks as several people turned to watch us enter. Friends of Sara's, regarding me with interest. If I was lucky, I wouldn't recognize anyone here, and no one would have heard about me, or at least, about my side job. Oddly enough, many people are dubious about the whole "monster hunter" gig.

Sara pulled me forward, and I let her lead me into the crowd. I guessed that about a hundred people filled the ballroom, which was set up with round dinner tables. Not a huge crowd, and maybe half of them were just like me, smiling with deer-in-the-headlights eyes, doing their best to make nice as spouses and significant others. I squared my shoulders and told myself to man up. Surely I could get through a cocktail party and dinner without causing a catastrophe.

"You must be Mark." My head whipped up as a red-haired woman in a tailored pantsuit sidled up to us. Sara and I were the same age, thirty-five, and I judged the woman to be perhaps a decade older. She had the perfectly put-together look that usually screamed "real estate agent," and her gaze made me suspect I had lint on the lapel of my sports jacket that she wanted to flick away, but she resisted, and I tried not to tense up.

"Mark, this is Joanna Wright," Sara said, and I knew from her body language Joanna wasn't someone Sara completely trusted. I shook the woman's hand, and her thin fingers were ice cold.

"We've heard just enough to be intrigued, Mr. Wojcik," Joanna said. As usual, she mangled my last name, but I was used to it.

"Voy-chick," Sara corrected reflexively, sparing me.

"So are you also in the hotel business?" Joanna probed, letting the mispronunciation slide.

"I'm a mechanic," I replied. "I own an auto body shop out in Atlantic."

"Then I'm guessing you don't mind getting your hands dirty." There was nothing wrong with what Joanna said, but something about her inflection added an innuendo I didn't like.

"I like cars," I replied, finding that much safer than saying that I liked "working with my hands." "Always have. Fixing them, keeping them tuned, refurbishing a classic now and then—it's satisfying."

"Sounds like fun," Joanna replied in a tone that told me she thought it was anything but. "Maybe Sara can tempt you into the inn-keeping business," she said with a broad wink. "It would be good for her to have a man around the house, up there in the frozen north," she added, with a side glance at Sara as if she expected collusion. When Sara didn't play along, Joanna looked a little flustered.

"Well, glad to finally meet you," she said. "Pardon me—I see the bar just opened." She hurried away, and Sara gave a quiet sigh.

"Sorry about that."

I shrugged. "There's one in every crowd. But...how did she know my name?"

Sara blushed. "I've mentioned you, more than a few times. Some of my friends kept trying to fix me up and, well, I wanted to let them know I wasn't in the market."

My heart beat a little faster at that, and I hoped I didn't have a dopey smile, but that was likely asking too much. I'm not smooth, or good at playing hard to get. I'm a WYSIWYG kind of guy, and that's a blessing and a curse.

Sara led me in the opposite direction, toward the bar on the other side of the room from where Joanna headed. I had to drive back, so I just got a Coke, but Sara chose a white wine, and then we headed back into the fray. She introduced me to a dozen people, and I knew I'd never remember their names. I smiled and nodded and tried to look manly but harmless.

"You work on cars? Sweet." Jon, a dark-haired man with green eyes, looked genuinely interested, and I tried to relax. "There's a garage near the inn we own in Brookville—specializes in classics and imports. I like to stroll by now and again and look at what they're working on."

Jon and I discussed cars for a while, saving both of us from having to mingle while our partners worked the room and talked shop with colleagues. I felt like I'd dodged a bullet, and Jon looked equally relieved until his partner, Pete, returned to claim him when the emcee asked people to head to their tables.

"Hope to see you around," Jon said, as Pete led him off toward their assigned table. Sara showed up a few seconds later.

"We're over here," she said, steering me to the left. I'd enjoyed the chat with Jon, and from the way several other adrift significant others had joined into the conversation, I knew I wasn't the only one who felt out of my element.

Our table for eight included six total strangers to me. It didn't seem as if Sara knew them either, except to recognize that they were with the group. One of the guys, Chip, looked familiar, and he kept glancing in my direction as if trying to place me.

"This hotel is beautiful." Carly, a woman in her middle years with a bright red bob haircut, gestured with a sweeping motion to encompass the old Victorian. "So well maintained, and a great lake view."

"It reminds me of some of the grand old hotels in Cape May, or up in the Adirondacks," Simon added. He and his partner, Chip, ran a B&B near Grove City.

"Ooh, I bet it's seen plenty of history," Shelly chimed in. She was married to Nate, and they ran a mid-century modern B&B outside of Greensburg.

"You think it's haunted?" Nate asked. From the look on his face, I couldn't tell whether he thought that was a plus or a minus.

"That's what the brochure says," Kendall replied, and I guessed he went with Carly. "I bet they charge more for the thrill of maybe seeing a spook."

"What I read says the hotel has a bunch of ghosts," Carly added. "There's a bride who was killed in a fire, a little girl on a tricycle who fell off a balcony, and a couple of other regular ghosts. It would be cool to see them."

"You're that ghost hunting guy." Chip hadn't said anything since we sat down, but his voice silenced everyone at the table. Nate's comment had probably made the connection for him of where he knew me from, although I didn't recognize him.

"Actually, I'm a mechanic," I replied. "Everything else is a hobby." Technically, that was true. Although my garage manager, Pete, could tell anyone who asked that I tended to spend more time away from the job than on it.

"But you're a ghost hunter, like on TV," Chip persisted. "Simon's friend

Maxine said somebody put you in touch with her when weird things happened out at her lake house, and you took care of it."

I remembered Maxine and her lake house. An antique leather trunk she'd bought at an estate sale ended up having a nasty poltergeist attached, and by the time Father Leo and I waded into the mess, the negative energy had attracted a bunch of dark entities and angry ghosts that were more than happy to come along for the ride.

"It's really not anything like what you see on TV," I replied, really wishing someone, anyone, would change the subject. Nate looked like he wanted to ask questions. Carly's gaze was cool and assessing. Simon crossed his arms over his chest.

"I call bullshit." Simon's gaze bored into me. "There's no such thing as ghosts. It's all just parlor tricks, like those fake mediums who con people out of their money and break their hearts. It's a scam."

"Maybe some of the time it's fake," Shelly agreed. "But my sister has had a bunch of experiences she can't explain, and that convinced her."

"It's all subjective," Simon replied. He wasn't just a skeptic; he was an evangelist for skepticism. My heart sank. I didn't want to be the focus of the conversation, and I definitely did not want to embarrass Sara in front of her fellow innkeepers. "How much do you charge people to get rid of their 'ghosts'?" He made air quotes.

"He doesn't charge," Sara spoke up. "And you can believe what you want to believe, but lay off him, Simon. Everyone's entitled to a hobby— don't you collect toys or something?"

Simon glared at her. "I collect vintage action figures. They have resale value."

I got the feeling that Simon and Sara had faced off before, and that I might just be collateral damage in an ongoing war. That didn't make me feel any better about being put on the spot, or about having Sara feel like she needed to defend me to her peers.

"I want to know more about the ghosts," Nate said. "Are you some kind of medium?"

I thought for a moment Nate was trolling me, but he looked sincere. Much as I wanted to the conversation to shift, I didn't want to be rude. "No. I'm not a medium. I only step in when ghosts get dangerous. Then I help them move on."

Honestly, ghosts aren't usually a big problem. Monsters and supernatural creatures were where the real danger lay, but I was not going to bring that up.

"So like the ghosts in this hotel, you wouldn't banish them?" Nate asked.

"Not as long as they aren't hurting anyone," I replied. I could feel the others staring at me and felt judged. Sara's hand gripped mine under the table.

"Ghosts aren't real," Simon lectured. "How can you take this seriously? Ghosts are just a figment of people's overactive imagination. They're invisible friends made up by people who want attention. Most of this crap is all rooted in mental illness—"

Just then, the lights suddenly went out. I felt the temperature drop in the room, where it had been pleasantly warm only minutes before. People gasped as an orb of light zipped from one end of the ballroom to the other and vanished. The scent of jasmine filled the room, and off in the direction of the front porch, I heard the *brrring* of the bell on a child's tricycle. Only the tea light candles in the centerpieces lit the room, but we had just enough light to glimpse a bride in a white gown glide past the window and disappear.

The lights came on as quickly as they went out, blinding us. Instantly, the room was abuzz.

"Offhand, I'd say the ghosts don't like to be dissed," Sara said with a grin that dared Simon to disagree. Simon scowled at her, but no one else at the table paid him any attention; they were all busy comparing notes and speculating on what had just happened.

I kept my head down and focused on my meal, which was excellent. By the time the guests had finally finished talking about the unplanned "dinner show," dessert had been served. Much as I would be happily rid of our supper companions, I'm not one to ever pass up a good piece of pie with ice cream.

If Simon intended to say more, Chip's glare kept him quiet. I just wanted the evening to be over, and I wondered whether Sara would break up with me after dinner or wait until tomorrow. After all, I was at best a sham, and at worst a laughingstock in the eyes of her colleagues, and I'd known from the start that Sara could do much better than someone like me.

When we had all finished dessert, the emcee announced a twenty-minute intermission before the evening session. I figured that allowed for a smoke and a bathroom break and gave the plus-ones a chance to go back to their rooms or head to the bar.

Chip steered Simon away before his husband had the chance to make a parting shot. Nate seemed sincere when he said it was nice to meet me, but the rest of the farewells were banal pleasantries. Sara took my hand as we walked out to the parking lot.

I turned to face her when we reached my truck. "I'm sorry," I said, choosing to be the one to bring it up. "You didn't need that tonight. Blair always says that you can dress me up, but you can't take me out." I braced myself for the worst. This thing between Sara and me was new, and we were both gun shy. She certainly didn't need me making her lose face in front of her colleagues—and competitors.

"You've got nothing to be sorry about," Sara said, with a flash of anger in her eyes. "Simon Graham is an asshole. He's the one who brought up the whole subject, and he's the one who pissed off the ghosts. You did fine."

"I didn't mean to cause you any embarrassment," I replied.

"You didn't," Sara countered. "Simon managed to embarrass himself single-handedly. As for your hunting—what you do is hard and danger-ous, and important. Some people might not understand, but I do." She reached up to touch my cheek. "No harm, no foul, Mark. I'm still really glad you came for dinner. And I'm sorry I can't go home with you tonight, but..."

"I know. Evening session, then more mingling," I replied, and while I wished Sara could take the night off, I was equally glad not to be involved in the evening wind-down at the bar with Simon and the others.

"I'll call you when I get back to Kane tomorrow," she promised. "And we can plan your next trip up to visit. Okay?" That's when I realized she looked a little scared, too. Maybe she was afraid being put on the spot by Simon and Nate had made me ready to bolt.

"Definitely okay," I said and pulled her close for a kiss. It was just right —and not long enough. She looked a little flushed when she finally stepped away.

"I've got to go. Stay safe, and call me," she said, ducking in for another peck on the cheek.

"Have a nice evening," I said, reluctantly letting go of her hand. "And be careful driving back."

I watched her go into the hotel, then climbed into my truck. Much as I hated social events, it was worth it for some extra time together. I looked back up at the old hotel, silhouetted against the night sky, and thought I caught the scent of jasmine and the faint ring of a tricycle bell.

"Thank you," I said to the ghosts of Hotel Conneaut. "I think you got the last laugh."

I didn't go straight home. Since I knew I'd be kinda down after leaving Sara at the hotel, I headed over to meet my friend Louie Marino out at the Drunk Monk, our favorite watering hole on the east side of the lake.

The Drunk Monk has a picture of a tipsy friar on its sign. Inside, it's a cozy neighborhood bar with a pool table, some dart boards, good food, and cheap beer. Danny, the bartender, is a retired Marine, so there's never any trouble—at least, not for long.

Tonight, Louie already held down a table, and he'd brought a friend. I remembered the guy's name—Patrick Carmody—just before I sat down.

"How'd it go?" Louie asked. I signaled the server for a beer like they were drinking and slumped back in the booth.

"About as well as you might expect."

Louie snorted. "My expectations for you are pretty low, Mark."

My response was the one-finger salute. Louie and I go way back—all the way to grade school. He's a cop in Linesville, which is just up the road from the little burg of Atlantic where I live. And Patrick, if I recalled, was a police officer in Meadville.

"Haven't seen you for a while, Patrick," I said. "How are things in the big city?" Meadville was only "big" compared to how small all the other towns were.

"Mostly good," Patrick replied with a shrug. He was about the same age as Louie and me, with white-blond hair and blue eyes. "The wife and kids are fine, parents doing okay, nobody's sick. So—good."

"Patrick's having some trouble, and I think you can help him with it," Louie said, falling silent as the server brought me a beer.

"Oh, yeah?" I asked, taking a swing. "What's going on?"

Patrick looked around, checking to make sure no one around us was listening. "I got called up to Radio Tower Hill because of some property damage and a report that someone had seen a hairy naked man running around. So, I went up, and I found some odd footprints. I tapped into the security cameras around the broadcast tower, and I got this."

He held out his phone and brought up a grainy video. At first, it looked like a hunched over, very hairy shirtless man walking across the camera's range. But when Patrick zoomed in, there was no mistaking it. The creature had the body of a man—and the head of a pig.

"Shit. The pig people are back," Louie muttered.

Everyone around these parts knew about the pig people of Radio Tower Hill. The hill is one of the highest points around here, out off Kerrtown road. Since the road only goes up to the fenced-off broadcast tower, it's a popular make-out place for horny teenagers. But the isolation that makes the hill road a Lovers' Lane also attracts cryptids that would rather not have a lot of people around. Chief among those are the infamous pig people.

"Where the hell do they come from?" I wondered aloud. The pig people were Meadville's version of the Jersey Devil or the Mothman—creatures so strange you'd think they had to be fictional, reappearing generation after generation but never scientifically confirmed.

Lucky for us, the pig people just wanted to be left alone, but they protected their privacy by scaring off anyone who crossed their path and damaging property, like the radio tower fence. They were good at evading cameras and hunters. There were never more than one or two of the pig people at a time, and while they had the constitution of a wild boar, they had the intelligence of a human. But the pig-man hadn't hurt anyone, hadn't even threatened anyone. Killing him wouldn't be easy. Trapping him would be even harder.

"Did you call Animal Control?" I asked, even though I felt sure I knew what Patrick was going to say.

"I told them we had a wild boar up there," Patrick said. "They just laughed and asked if I was the 'new kid' and that it was a snipe hunt."

"Which is why I thought he ought to talk to you," Louie said. He didn't push me into explaining why, and I appreciated him letting me make that judgment.

"Can you help?" Patrick asked.

I ran a hand over my face, fighting the urge to rub my tired eyes. After the clusterfuck at the hotel reception, I had to get my head back in the game. "Yeah. Maybe. Do you know how many of them there are?"

"Just saw one on the cameras," he replied. "Pretty sure it's the same one because he's got a big scar on one shoulder."

"Okay, do you know anyone with a beater camper? One they don't want back."

"A camper?"

"Yeah. We're gonna do a catch and release."

That's how I ended up out on Radio Tower Hill with Louie and Patrick, ready to snare ourselves a pig-man. Louie and I had gone boar hunting once, so we knew how to set a snare. Patrick had called a large animal vet that worked with the Meadville PD and said he needed tranq darts for a really big wild hog.

I wasn't crazy about the tranqs. They're unpredictable, even with a vet involved. Boars also can get heat stroke easily, and while I didn't know how much a pig person had in common biology-wise with a boar, I didn't want to kill the guy if I didn't have to. If I had my druthers, we'd trap the pig man, knock him out, and take him way up into the Big Woods where he wouldn't bother anyone else.

This should have felt like an easy run. After all, no ghosts, demons, ghouls, zombies, or really scary monsters were involved. Just a guy who was more pig than man. Then again, I've seen things go south on an average deer hunt, so I try not to ever let my guard down. And something in my gut told me this wouldn't be as easy as it looked.

"You think this pig-man is bigger than the boar we got the last time?" Louie asked as we set the steel cables.

"Bigger maybe," I replied. I dug a few inches down into the dirt and buried the mix of fermented corn and grease that wild hogs love. I was betting Pig-Man had the same fine tastes as his porcine relatives, and that it would draw him into the snares, where Patrick could get off a clean shot with the tranq gun. "I don't think the boar we got weighed as much as a full-grown man."

Louie shrugged. "Maybe not a linebacker, but a little guy? Maybe."

"That's just it," I said, wrinkling my nose at the smell of the bait. "That's a big range. Make the dart too weak, and it won't take him down. He'll be groggy—maybe—but not for long. Too strong, and he's dead before we get him down the hill."

"I thought you were a monster hunter," Patrick said over his shoulder as he set up a rough blind to hide him from the pig man's view.

"When I have to be," I replied, finishing up the last snare while Louie spread leaves and dirt to camouflage the snares. "But this guy is just busting up fences, scaring the locals. If we can move him out where there aren't any fences or locals, he's happy as…well, a pig in slop."

Once we had everything set up, we pulled back to the blind to wait. Stakeouts were the boring part of monster hunting and being a police officer. We had to stay quiet and focused, but no one can stay at high alert for hours on end. The real challenge was not getting distracted because that was when everything was sure to go to shit.

After a few hours, we heard snuffling. Louie and I had checked out the whole top of Radio Tower Hill, looking for where the wildlife made their trails. Even this close to town, there were more deer, foxes, possums, coyotes, and other wild animals than most people think. The trick when trapping was to find a path that only your target animal used. I felt pretty sure that's what we snared, but it's not like we had any control over the rest of the furry creatures to tell them that route was off limits.

I listened, and I saw the others rouse as well. Patrick reached for the tranq rifle. I had a K-bar and a nice heavy sap, in case the dart didn't take and the pig person needed a little tap on the back of the head. Louie had a pole snare, the kind Animal Control uses on raccoons, only the industrial-sized version made for restraining unruly livestock without hurting them.

Shuffling, heavy footsteps sounded like they were in the right place. I didn't want to move, didn't want to breathe wrong and have the wind pick up my scent or snap a twig and ruin everything. I had no idea how well the creature could hear, but I knew that regular pigs could sniff out truffles and bombs, despite being immune to their own odor.

Closer. Closer. Then a loud, angry squeal as the snare caught.

"Go, go, go!" I ordered. Patrick already had the tranq gun ready. He fired once, then twice. We waited. For an animal that had been shot full of sedative, the pig-man thrashed and howled plenty.

"Shit," Patrick said. "I must have missed on one of those."

"How many does it take to bring him down?" Louie asked. I wondered the same thing, if we also had to worry about over-tranqing the creature.

"At least two good hits," Patrick said. He loaded another round and fired. "Shit. He's moving too much."

"Tranq him again, Patrick," I said. "I don't want to have to shoot him."

Patrick edged around the blind with the dart gun. Louie moved off the other side to cover him. I stayed where I was, ready to jump in if they needed me.

Patrick took a step closer to the pig-man for a clean shot. But he underestimated the creature's reach, and Piggy swiped out with one arm, slashing with sharp nails. Louie dove to push Patrick out of the monster's way. He and Patrick went down in a heap, out of Piggy's reach. When Louie rolled off, Patrick didn't move.

"Shit. I think he tranqed himself," Louie said. He felt for a pulse. "Yep. Out cold."

I swore creatively. "That's just great! Now we've got to carry two of them down the hill to the truck." I reached into my bag for my secret weapon that works on most carnivorous monsters. Bacon balls.

I realized that it would have been wrong to give Piggy regular bacon. Pig people might be monsters, but as far as I knew, they weren't cannibals. I'd altered my recipe. These were turkey bacon balls, for a more civilized trap.

"One little piggy went to market," I coaxed, edging closer with the bacon ball in front of me, letting it waft its hickory smoked goodness toward the snared pig man. "One little piggy stayed home." I had the bacon in my left hand and the heavy leather sap in my right. "And one little piggy went wee-wee-we—" I tossed him the bacon ball, and as he dove for it, I brought the sap down with a thud on the back of his head.

Piggy slumped. Louie pounced with heavy-duty zip ties and restrained his wrists. I rolled the pig-man over and kept a foot in the middle of his back while Louie released the creature's feet from the snares and zip tied his ankles.

"How long will that keep him out?" Louie asked.

"With luck, more than two hours," I repeated. "We need to get him to the Big Woods and out to the drop point." I straightened and looked at our two fallen comrades. "So…which one do you want to carry?"

A lot of grunting and straining later, Louie and I got Piggy and Patrick down the hill. Louie dumped Patrick into the back seat of the truck cab. I rolled Piggy off my shoulder with a *thunk* and into the beat-up camper. We stuck our gear bags next to Patrick and headed down Radio Tower Hill for the highway. Night had fallen by the time we headed east.

"I love this drive in the fall," Louie said. "The trees are beautiful."

"Yeah, but there's a whole lotta nothin' out there," I replied. "The middle and top of the freaking state is nothing but forest."

Patrick was still out, and after Louie checked in with the vet who gave us the darts, we knew that the hospital couldn't do more than let him sleep it off, but we'd be tied up with a bunch of hard-to-answer questions. We ignored Patrick's snoring and kept driving. Louie found one more dart in Patrick's bag that had gotten overlooked in the excitement, which we'd need if Piggy woke up before we made it to the drop point.

Kane was a little over two hours from Meadville, and I kept to the speed limit since I didn't want to get pulled over. An hour and a half into the drive, we heard irate squeals from the back, and belatedly realized we should have gagged Piggy. Not long after, the thud of him hurling himself from side to side made the whole camper shake.

"You're sure he's not going to get out the door?" Louie asked.

"That's why I put the steel bar on it."

"And we just hope passing motorists don't wonder who we kidnapped?"

"You're a cop. You just flash them, and they go away."

Louie rolled his eyes. "Flash my *badge*. Not flash *them*. God, you're a child sometimes."

I grinned. "And yet, you've known me all my life, and you're still here."

Louie groaned. "I blame it on being from a small town. Not many people to choose from." The grin on his face put the lie to his words.

From the sounds of it, Piggy trashed the inside of the camper like a rock star. I didn't know whether he'd gotten out of his zip ties or just managed to hurl himself from side to side trussed up. Since we had another dart, my brilliant plan was to get to the trailhead, knock out a window in the camper, and tranq Piggy again. He might have a hell of a hangover from the drugs, but it was better than having to shoot him.

Louie and I chatted about everything and nothing as we drove. Louie filled me in on what was new with his wife, Madison, and their kids. He asked about Sara; I told him about what an embarrassment I'd been at her dinner and how I figured she would never want to see me again.

"I doubt that," he assured me. "Not that you aren't an ass, or embarrassing, but Sara knew about the whole hunting thing the first time she met you. She knows that the stuff you hunt is real."

I shrugged, still feeling insecure. "Being able to deal with danger is one thing. Getting embarrassed in front of your colleagues is another."

"But the ghosts showed up," Louie protested. "That means the skeptics are the ones who should have been embarrassed, not you."

"Maybe."

Louie looked at me appraisingly for a moment, and the silence got uncomfortable. "Mark, she's not Lara."

My ex-wife Lara had gotten impatient with how long I grieved after the wendigo attack. I hadn't gotten the memo that said grief came with a deadline. She wanted to move on, and I couldn't, so she moved out. Other than a few disastrous blind dates set up by well-meaning friends, Sara was the first woman I'd dated. The fact that I cared for her made it even scarier.

"I know that," I snapped. "But be honest, Louie. I mean, I'm damaged goods."

Louie sighed and rolled his eyes. "You aren't the only guy to ever get a divorce. Or to be a little fucked in the head."

"Thanks," I muttered, giving him the side eye.

"You know what I mean," Louie replied. "I know plenty of cops and guys who came back from the military who saw shit that screwed them up a bit. It happens. Some of them have partners or find partners who can handle it; some don't. You are more than your scars."

"That's profound. Did you come up with that yourself?" The snark lightened the mood, just a little.

"Hell, no. That was in a book Madison made me read about cops and PTSD and marriage. She told me she's in it for the long haul, so I needed to keep my head on straight." He grinned. "She's one scary woman when she sets her mind on something." And I knew from the smile on his face that Madison had her mind set firmly on keeping Louie alive and well and with her. I found myself hoping Sara would feel the same for me.

"I'll think about it," I muttered. Then I turned the music up, the universal guy signal to indicate that the conversation was over.

We pulled into the trailhead parking lot around ten. To my relief, no other cars were nearby. Piggy had quieted down, no longer making the camper rock from side to side, and I hoped he had worn himself out. Since I didn't intend to take any chances, I waited until Louie loaded the dart gun, then I busted a window in the camper and let Louie take the shot. Piggy went down.

"Shit. Look at the mess," I muttered under my breath as we lifted the bar from the door and looked in. Piggy had managed to dent the walls, splinter cabinet doors, and destroy the overhead light. If the camper hadn't been on its way to the junkyard before, it was certainly headed there now.

"What about Patrick?" Louie asked as I hefted Piggy over my shoulder in a fireman's carry.

"Lock the doors. He'll be fine. We'll be back before he wakes up," I replied. Louie locked Patrick inside the cab and jogged over to me.

"Where are we taking pig man?"

"I've got just the spot," I promised.

"What's the beer for?" Louie had spotted the six pack in my left hand. I had the sap in my right hand, in case Piggy came around, and my gun in my holster, just in case.

The last time I'd been in the woods here, there'd been snow on the ground. Louie followed me as we moved through my familiar path through the forest. Up ahead was the tree I was looking for. I set the beer down at the base, grunting at doing a squat with Piggy's weight on me, and stood.

"You're leaving it out here?"

"It's for a friend," I said and smiled as the air shimmered nearby. "Hi, Gus," I greeted the ghost that materialized.

Gus grinned. He was an older man, still clad in the camo jacket and pants he'd been wearing when he'd fallen out of a tree stand and died sixty some years ago. His ghost haunted the forest, helping lost hunters and hanging out in the woods he loved so much. Gus had given me a hand on a couple of dicey cases. I always brought him beer; my way of saying "thank you."

"I'm not imagining this," Louie said, sounding a little breathless as he stared at Gus.

"Nope. This is Gus. Gus, meet my friend Louie."

Gus nodded, pointed to the beer, and nodded his thanks. Then he pointed to Piggy and frowned.

"He's causing a nuisance where he was," I explained to the ghost. "Didn't hurt anyone, but he couldn't stay. I didn't want to have to shoot him. I figured he'd have plenty of room out here, maybe on the forbidden land?"

Gus thought for a moment, then nodded. Part of the state forest was off-limits because it was sacred to the local Native American tribes. That land was closed to hunters, but I had a feeling that for a creature like Piggy, it would be just fine.

We headed off together, two men, Piggy, and a ghost, and before long, we reached the fence that marked the tribal preserve. Piggy had already slipped his zip ties. I leaned over the fence and lowered him down onto the ground on the far side. He snuffled, rolled over, and went back to sleep.

"Keep an eye on him, will ya?" I asked Gus. "Help him stay out of sight. There's got to be enough backcountry out here for him to be able to avoid trouble."

Gus nodded solemnly and made a motion to cross his heart, letting me know he'd do his best. Louie watched Gus in a mixture of fear and fascination, but Gus just seemed happy to see us. I chatted with the ghost on the way back to the beer tree, filling him in on this and that, just talking.

We stopped at the tree. "Hope you like the brewski. I'll bring some whiskey next time."

Gus laughed and nodded. "I'm sure I'll see you before long. Take care of yourself," I said, and realized that was an odd thing to say to a ghost. Gus just grinned and gestured at me, basically saying "you, too." I waved as Louie, and we headed back to the parking lot. Behind us, I heard a beer can collapsing. Don't know how Gus drinks it, but I'm happy to know there's alcohol in the afterlife.

Louie had all kinds of questions about Gus, which I answered on our way to the truck. My phone buzzed, and I glanced at it. I had a text from Sara.

Loved seeing you for dinner. Ghosts were a bonus. Call me. Missing you already. Sara.

Maybe she wasn't going to ditch me, after all.

Just as we reached the lot, I held up a hand, and Louie went quiet.

"Shit," I muttered. A local cop was shining a light in through the passenger window.

"You know him?"

"Yeah. Officer Sumbitch. He kinda hates me." The feeling was mutual. The cop had given me a hard time on my last couple of creature hunts out here. I couldn't remember his real name.

"Leave it to me."

Just that fast, Louie switched into cop mode. His posture, the swagger, the tilt of his chin, he was the same guy, but not. He already had his badge in hand as Officer Sumbitch looked up and pointed the flashlight at us.

"You're trespassing," Officer Sumbitch announced.

"Louie Marino, Linesville PD," Louie said like he hadn't heard the man. "That's Patrick Carmody, Meadville PD," he added with a nod toward the man sleeping in the truck. "Pat and Mark and I came up for dinner with my grandpa, Fred Houser."

The local cop's brows drew together. "Chief Houser?"

I forgot Louie's mom came from out here, and apparently, her dad was a big deal. "Yep. You know him?" He kept on talking as if it was assumed that everyone in these parts knew Chief Houser. "So Pat had a few beers too many, and we were just driving back, but Mark and I had to take a whiz, you know? So we just stopped long enough to take care of business, and we'll be on our way."

"What's wrong with your camper?" Officer Sumbitch growled. I could see he didn't like losing, and he was going to find something to fight about.

"Doing a favor for my grandpa," Louie lied. "He picked us up and drove us out here, and we promised to drive that beater back to the scrap-yard in Geneva, 'cause they'll give him the best price. Pretty awful, isn't it?"

Officer Sumbitch wasn't stupid. He knew we were up to something, but he had nothing to pin on us. It rankled, and he'd probably take it out on me when next we crossed paths, but invoking Chief Houser's name had convinced him to bide his time.

"Better get moving then," he grumbled. "And watch your speed."

"We're just leaving," I promised, getting a glare in return. The cop stood with his hands on his hips, glaring at us as we backed up and headed away.

"Another member of your fan club?" Louie needled as we got back on the road.

I sighed. "You know me. Mr. Popularity."

6

—————

"Thanks for coming, Father Leo. You too, Mark." Thomas Horvath leaned forward over the table in the back of Nemeth's Pub. A murmured comment to the man behind the counter had earned the padre and me a once-over, then a nod to Thomas confirmed we'd have our drinks refreshed, and food brought, but be otherwise left alone.

The crowd at the bar cheered the score as they watched the playoff on the huge screen. On the other side of the room, a pool game had the full attention of half a dozen guys and several women, while a dart board in the far corner drew other competitors. It looked like we'd found the hotspot in tiny little Cheswick.

Downtown Cheswick looked like a lot of former coal mining towns in these parts. With its heyday long past, the business district had a depressing number of defunct shops, and what remained looked like they were hanging on by a thread. The homes were well-kept but appeared as tired as their owners, and most of the younger people fled for greener pastures. Yet, on our way in, I'd spotted a surprising number of new apartment buildings.

"Who's doing all the construction?" I asked. "You getting a big new fulfillment center around here?"

Thomas shook his head. "I wish. It's the frackers. You know, natural gas extraction. The energy companies bring in their crews and put up their equipment, then once they're done, they they take the natural gas, and we're left with polluted groundwater and earthquakes. The crews come in, overrun the place, and leave when the drilling goes elsewhere." I couldn't miss the bitterness in his voice.

Fracking had turned a lot of Pennsylvanians militant. The process pumped liquid under high pressure into the layers of rock underground to push reserves of natural gas out, making deposits available that couldn't be extracted any other way. But doing that disturbed the bedrock, causing tremors, and many communities blamed fouled water supplies on the fracking. Tempers flared, the big corporations and communities lawyered up, and things got nasty, sometimes violent.

"What's this all about, Thomas?" Father Leo asked. He wore a black shirt with a clerical collar over jeans and a worn pair of Timberlands, but the canvas jacket hid the collar from prying eyes. On the rare occasions Father Leo was out of "uniform," he looked like a regular guy.

Thomas slid a manila folder toward us. "I've had four murders in the past month, and that's four more than Cheswick's had in a couple of years," he said. Even if Father Leo hadn't told me Thomas was a cop, I would have known from the no-nonsense voice and the eyes that looked like they'd seen far too much. I saw eyes like that whenever I looked in a mirror, and more than once, people had guessed wrong that I was either ex-military or police. The horrors I'd witnessed came in a different line of duty, but they all left a mark, regardless of the source.

"Mob? Serial killer?" I ventured. Father Leo winced at the sight of the pictures. I felt my stomach roll. The bodies had been mutilated, then burned. Whoever the killer was, he had a hell of a lot of rage.

"Those are some of the theories," Thomas said, in a tone that let me know he didn't believe them. "But there's no physical evidence at the scene. No footprints, DNA, hair, weapon, fingerprints, tire marks—nothing. Two of the dead men had security systems active at the time of the murders. The system doesn't even indicate that the door was opened, let alone forced. One of the men was on the phone when he was attacked, and in the five minutes it took the cops to arrive, he was cut to hell and burned. Doors locked from the inside, no blood anywhere but under the body."

"You think it's our kind of thing," Father Leo said, leveling a gaze at Thomas, who nodded.

"I can't bring you in officially. I'd lose my badge," Thomas admitted. "But standard operating procedure isn't going to catch this killer."

"You need us to poke around and figure out what might be doing the killing, or do you have a theory?" I asked.

Thomas reclaimed the folder and put it into his backpack. "You ever hear of the Harwick Mine Disaster?" At our shrugs, he continued. "Happened back in 1904. Killed 181 men and a mule. Actually, the mule killed two of those men."

"The mule?"

"The mule was going down in the shaft elevator when the explosion ripped through the mine. It shot the lift cage and the mule out of the shaft so hard the poor creature flew up in the air, right through the tipple building, killing two workers."

"Holy shit," I muttered, and Father Leo sighed. "Sorry."

"What does the Harwick disaster have to do with the murders, and us being here?" Father Leo asked.

"I'm getting to that," Thomas promised. "The four men who died didn't know each other, didn't have any business dealings with one another and had no enemies. No drugs, no funny financial stuff, no messy divorces. They all came from families that have been in Harwick for years, and they're all the oldest male in their family. Ages ranged from forty to seventy. They had very little in common except for the kinds of injuries that killed them. And the fact that all of them had traces of coal dust on their clothing, although none of them had any reason to be near coal."

"I don't understand," I said.

He lifted a hand for silence. "Pete Mihilov was the one who made the comment that got me thinking. He's almost retirement age, one of the oldest cops on the force. Grew up in a mining family and went down in the mines himself when he was a young man. Said that the only time he'd ever seen injuries like that was when a mine fire broke out."

"What did the dead men do for a living?" Father Leo asked.

"Accountant, car salesman, graphic designer, plumber," Thomas replied.

"Any of the mines around here still working?" I asked.

Thomas shook his head. "Haven't been for decades. But I did find one other thing the dead men had in common. Their ancestors were all mine management back when the disaster happened."

"It's a small town," I said, playing devil's advocate. "Isn't everyone in Cheswick related to someone who had a connection to the mine?"

"Not to the bosses," Thomas replied. "The Harwick disaster was a cluster…" He cut himself off with a guilty look at Father Leo, who just smiled. "The fire boss was supposed to make sure no machinery had been used for a specific amount of time before a new dynamite charge was set off and that the area was watered down to get the coal dust out of the air. That didn't happen. The ventilation system had ice in it that didn't get cleared away, and that meant the fresh air wasn't circulating and methane built up deep in the tunnels. The people who were supposed to check those things didn't. And when the charge went off, it ignited the very flammable dust and methane gas. The men close by were blown up and burned. The ones farther out died from asphyxiation from the methane. And flying mules not withstanding, it was a hell of a blast. Caused a cave-in and ripped apart the elevator, which made it all the harder to go looking for survivors."

"Were there any?" I asked.

"One," Thomas said. "A sixteen-year-old boy who was pretty badly injured. Of course, there was an inquiry, and lots of noises made about safety, and some low-level guys got scapegoated, but no charges were brought against the mine owners, or the foreman, general manager, superintendent, or fire boss."

"Figures," I muttered. I'd never been a miner myself, but I'd heard my grandfather tell stories about his father growing up around South Fork out in the middle of the state, in the coal mines back in the 1930s. Mining was hard, dangerous work, and if the hazards underground didn't kill you, odds were good you'd wheeze out your last breath from "black lung" when you were older.

"I think something happened when the frackers came in," Thomas said, dropping his voice to a near-whisper. "I don't understand how ghosts work, or any of that supernatural stuff, but how can it be that the frackers start up, and a few months later, something's killing people with ties to the old mine?"

I had to work at it to make the connection, but Thomas seemed to see the link clearly. "So you think the fracking disturbed something in the old Harwick mine, and it's come back for revenge?" I asked.

"Either the fracking process itself or the earthquakes it caused," Thomas replied. "No one had any reason to kill those men, except for them being descended from the overseers whose negligence caused those deaths."

"Is there an anniversary of some kind?" Father Leo probed. "Maybe it's some kind of vengeance from the miners' descendants?"

Thomas shook his head. "Locked rooms. Security systems and video cameras that didn't trip. No physical evidence. I'm telling you, ghosts did this. And I can't arrest a ghost."

Father Leo and I exchanged a glance. Thomas might be onto something, or he might just be desperate to find an answer, any answer. But his theory provided means, motive, and access, and Thomas deserved having us at least check it out.

"We'll see what we can find," Father Leo promised. "And if it's ghosts, we'll deal with it."

Thomas let out a long breath, relief clear on his face. "Thank you. I didn't know where else to turn. Everything else has been a dead end."

Father Leo and I got a room for the night, since Cheswick, the town where the Harwick mine was located, was over an hour's drive from home. We wanted to get an early start to see what remained of the old mine and get prepared if Thomas's hunch proved correct.

The motel was the park-in-front kind, unchanged since the 1970s, with gold shag carpet and cheap paintings of Italian landscapes. All the other hotels were full, and we were trying to save money.

Father Leo looked around the room. "I think my virtue is in peril just walking into the room. Are you sure this place doesn't rent by the hour?"

"It's not old...it's 'retro,'" I replied with a smirk. "And it's got a coffee maker. If the sheets are clean and the shower works, I'm good."

"Not exactly what I had in mind when I swore my vow of poverty, but we'll work with what we've got," he retorted with a grin. I'd had more than enough hunts where I'd slept in my truck. I wasn't going to be particular.

I'd stopped for pop and snacks on the way back from meeting with Thomas, so we were set for the night. I set up my laptop while Father Leo pulled out the copied files Thomas had shared with us. I knew the cop risked a lot to bring us in on the murders, and I felt certain that handing over the files to us was highly unorthodox. I hoped that after all that, we could come through for him.

As the padre studied the files, I read everything I could find online about the Harwick mine and the disaster. The old photos were grim: coffins lined up row on row, bleak-eyed families clutching their coats around them against the snow, officials at podiums making empty promises. Newspaper articles talked about how the disaster had claimed two or three generations of men in some families, and how more than fifty of the unfortunate miners had been members of the same church.

Cheswick wasn't a large town, so losing nearly two hundred men all at once would have been catastrophic. That kind of cataclysm leaves psychic scars and horrific energy resonance. I'm sure psychiatrists could talk for days about the sort of impact such widespread, traumatic loss had on the survivors and their children. But I was more interested in what kind of ripples that massive, sudden loss of life left behind in the spirit world. The miners had been wronged by negligent managers, and they'd had over a hundred years to stew about it. Some of the bodies had never been recovered, and all had died horribly.

"What are you finding?" Father Leo asked, closing a folder and scrubbing a hand down over his eyes as if to remove the horrific images.

"More about the disaster itself," I replied. "We can go out tomorrow morning and have a look at what's left of the site." I'd already been through the satellite feeds, but nothing compared to seeing it first-hand.

"Any ideas on how to stop the killing?" he asked, leaning back in his chair.

"For all we know, the ghosts might be done if they killed the descendants of the men responsible for the disaster," I replied.

"What if they aren't?"

I grimaced. "That's where you come in. Read the exorcism, say the blessing, rebuke the evil spirits. That kind of thing."

"Exorcisms only work on demons," Father Leo replied, popping open a can of cola. "Usually. Blessings never hurt, but rebuking isn't going to dispel them for long."

"If all else fails, a few rounds of salt and buckshot usually does the job." I paused. "What if it's not ghosts?" I asked. "There are other spirits that live underground. Maybe the fracking woke them, and they're angry."

"We'll find out, one way or the other," he replied. "But for now, let's get some sleep."

N ot much remained of the Harwick mine. Abandoned coal mines were common in Pennsylvania, and it wasn't unusual to see old, half-rotted tipples, rusted railroad spurs, and left-behind carts. But where the entrance to the Harwick mine had been, only forest remained.

"Someone must have been in a rush to erase what happened," Father Leo remarked. I had to agree. While the explosion itself might have destroyed the main shaft elevator and the unfortunate mule took out the tipple, effort was required to tear up railroad tracks and obliterate any sign of the big operation.

"Even if the mine owners didn't change their ways, I imagine the disaster was bad for public relations," I mused. "They probably were happy to tear everything down and pretend it never happened."

"Something the families didn't have the option to do," Father Leo said.

All that remained of the mine entrance was a ledge of rock and a slit of darkness beneath. All the rest had been filled with tons of gravel. As we walked around the site, we found rusted iron grates over what had been ventilation shafts hidden among the overgrowth. I stared into the darkness and felt a cold presence watching me.

"Doesn't look like anyone comes up here," I said, taking in the view. "Then again, maybe the families go to the disaster monument instead."

"Ghosts often cling to where they died, not where they're commemorated," Father Leo replied. "Especially when the death is violent."

"Thomas says there haven't been any reports of hauntings at the graveyard or the monument," I said. "At least, nothing new."

We poked around, and as we did, the haste with which the site had been abandoned became clear. My boots kicked up the rusted remains of tools, bolts, and twisted bits of metal. A closer look at the underbrush that had begun to reclaim the area revealed more left-behind equipment.

From the hilltop, we could see where the fracking equipment had been set up and the bustle of workers and vehicles at the project site. I guessed that their location was a couple of miles away, but that could easily intersect with the web of underground tunnels for a mine like the

Harwick. Even if the frackers had attempted due diligence, old mine maps were notoriously inaccurate. It wasn't a stretch to think their efforts might have bothered something long asleep in the Harwick tunnels.

I didn't run into any cold spots, and the EMF meter in my pocket didn't go off, but I couldn't shake the feeling that I was being watched. Father Leo didn't say anything, but from the way he kept looking around and over his shoulder, I was certain he felt it, too. Some presence lurked near the old mine, but whether it was ghosts or not remained to be seen.

Once we'd gotten a good look at the remains of the mine mouth and mapped out the area in our heads, we went back to town to eat and gather equipment. Father Leo seemed quiet as we drove back to Cheswick.

"Cat got your tongue?" I teased. I felt a bit melancholy after visiting the mine, and I wondered if that was also affecting the padre, or whether he had something more on his mind.

"It's a terrible business, mining," he said quietly, not looking at me. "I've heard a lot of stories over the years about men getting killed, and mine owners or supervisors who skimped on safety precautions, and miners who were too afraid of losing their livelihood to say anything."

As we drove through town, a storefront caught my eye. "Harwick Mine Disaster Museum and Memorial." Father Leo looked curious when I suddenly parked, then saw the sign and nodded.

"Looks like a good place to check out—after lunch," he said. My stomach growled in agreement.

Pauley's Diner was a greasy spoon, the kind of place that serves fantastic, no-frills burgers and homemade pie, with great coffee to wash it all down. No one gave Father Leo and me a second glance as we walked in and found a table.

While I studied the menu, I tuned in to the conversations all around me. Most of them had to do with sports scores, fishing season, and politics, pretty typical fare. A glance around suggested we were probably the only non-locals in the diner, a guess supported by the fact that the servers knew the other patrons' names and bantered with them like long-time friends.

The food came quickly, and we dove in like starving men. One of the conversations nearby caught my attention. A glance out of the corner of my eye found four middle-aged men, clad in canvas or camouflage coats with trucker hats. The din of conversation, dishes, and the TV made it hard to catch every word.

"...explain the dreams?" one of the men demanded.

"...one of those urban legends," his companion replied with a dismissive gesture, as if the comment wasn't worth their time.

"...why hasn't it happened before?"

"...letting their imagination get away with them."

"...fucking frackers."

A younger man with a receding hairline clad in a rumpled jacket hustled past the table on his way to pay at the register. "Hey, Newt! Surprised you're not gloating in the letters to the editor about how the miners finally got their justice." From the tone of the laughter, I figured Newt wasn't the most popular guy in town. He kept on walking, head down, although I could see the flush color his cheeks.

"What do you think that was about?" Father Leo asked. He glared at the mockers, and they silenced as if they felt the weight of his stare. No matter what Newt had done, neither of us could stomach bullies.

"No idea. Small towns and old grudges. But the comment about miners getting their justice—"

The priest nodded. "Yeah. The connection Thomas mentioned."

"Maybe the museum will have some answers," I replied. Just then, our server brought the pie. I knew we had work to do, but I wasn't going to hurry dessert. Hunting monsters was dangerous, and you never knew which meal might be your last, so I intended to savor each one.

The loud men were still lingering over their coffee by the time Father Leo and I paid our bill and left. We ducked into the mining museum, and the bell over the door jangled. No one was in sight. A glass counter held keychains, old postcards, and local history books, and a big wooden box sat on top marked *"Donations."* I pulled out a five and crammed it into the slot.

"They're not worried about thieves," Father Leo remarked, glancing around the empty room.

"I don't imagine they have a big staff," I said. "Someone probably just needed to use the bathroom." As if on cue, we heard the rush of water through old pipes.

"Hello," I called out, not wanting to startle the desk clerk.

Newt from the diner bustled out. "Sorry," he said, wiping wet hands on his jeans. "Just stepped away. Welcome to the museum." He squinted at us as if trying to place faces. "You're not from here."

I smiled. "Nope. Just passing through. I always heard about the Harwick disaster from my granddad, and we thought we'd just take a little road trip."

Newt looked from me to Father Leo. "With a priest?"

"It's my day off." Father Leo managed to look suitably pious.

Newt shrugged. "Sure. Whatever. Anyhow, welcome. The museum is this room and the back room, plus we have some archives for journalists. Everything in the museum was collected from families of the miners who worked the Harwick, plus some materials from the mine's owner, the Allegheny Coal Company."

He gestured toward the walls, which were full of sepia-toned photographs, and to the crowded glass cases with their treasures. "We have photographs of the miners and their families, Bibles, newspaper clippings, anything we could find."

"That's comprehensive," I said, thinking *that's a fucking ghost magnet.*

"Do you get many tourists?" I asked, making my way around the room a few steps behind Father Leo. The yellowed papers and faded photographs documented a local tragedy, and I doubted people from Cheswick stopped in more than once.

"School kids, for history class," Newt replied. "People who are into family history, and believe-it-or-not, coal mining junkies, who for whatever reason track down old mines."

I wondered how many of those "junkies" were also urban explorers, thrill-seekers, and photographers who liked to go into forbidden and abandoned places. "You ever hear about ghosts from the disaster?" I tried to make my tone off-handed, but out of the corner of my eye, I saw Newt flinch.

"Why d'ya ask?"

"Just curious. I mean, I watch TV. They always say ghosts from tragedies don't rest easy."

Newt crossed himself, a reaction that looked more reflexive than dramatic. "Some. If you believe in that sort of thing. It's not something people like to talk about."

"I do believe," I replied. "And I'm curious."

"Why?" Newt looked suspicious.

"I collect ghost stories." It wasn't exactly a lie. "Always looking for some I haven't heard."

"You can't quote me," he hedged.

I held a hand to my heart. "Of course not."

Newt glanced toward the front window as if someone might see us talking, but none of the scant passers-by paid any attention. "There've been stories about miners appearing to their kin since the first night after the explosion," he confided. "It's all hearsay, but the stories get passed down. People who saw a dead husband, father, brother, son, standing in the parlor, waving good-bye. Widows who say their husbands' ghosts came to tell them how to find missing keys or money. Children who say they saw the ghost of a dead relative that protected them from harm. There are some who swear they saw their ghost for years, as a warning before a tragedy."

"What do you think?" I saw Father Leo slip into the back room and figured I'd keep Newt talking.

"People around these parts don't lie much," he said. "Except the mine bosses," he added, curling his lip. "To this day, the priest up at the Hungarian church mentions 'and all our lost sons and fathers' in his prayer each week, meaning the mine dead. That explosion changed everything for this town. The mine never recovered. The jobs never came back. The men who didn't die in the mine moved away to find work. Families lost every man they had." Newt's expression grew far away. "It might have been a hundred years ago, but wounds like that don't heal with time."

"How about the murders," I prompted. "Do you think they have to do with the mine?"

"All you have to know are the last names of the victims, and you know it had something to do with the Harwick," Newt replied. "But who did it, and why now? No idea."

"After all this time, did people still hate the descendants of those mine managers?" I couldn't quite fathom blaming grandchildren and great-grandchildren for their ancestors' misdeeds, but I knew how small-town grudges went.

"At first," Newt replied. "Not lately. It wasn't forgotten, but most people did realize that the men responsible for the disaster died a long time ago. Over the years, the descendants tried to make it up with good deeds—penance, I guess. Folks had to allow how the younger ones might be related, but weren't that kind of men."

"So why kill them?"

Newt looked away, and I knew he was hiding something. "You've got a theory?" I probed.

Before he could answer, Father Leo called out from the back room. "Mark, you need to see this."

I hurried back to join him and found myself facing a strange wax mannequin of a hunched old man in a fur robe. The figure had very pale skin, and a mouth with blood-red lips stretched open across sharp teeth. The sign read "*Shubin*."

"You ever run across a *shubin* before?" I asked Father Leo.

He shook his head. "Nope. I've heard of kobolds, *skarbniks*, tommy-knockers—all things that live in mines and cause trouble. But this is a new one."

"They're Ukrainian mine monsters," Newt said from the doorway where he'd followed me. "Folks in these parts came from all over Eastern Europe. Hungary, Romania, Ukraine. There's been talk about *shubin* in the Harwick since the first shafts were opened. Some people think they're what caused the explosion. Maybe the murders, too."

"Where did the statue come from?" I asked, examining the figure. It looked handmade, not mass-produced.

"Illya Vann made that," Newt replied. "Said he kept seeing it in his dreams and he thought maybe if he made the statue, it would go away."

"Did it?" Father Leo asked.

"Don't know. Illya shot himself a couple of days after he sold it to me."

That didn't bode well. "Anyone else see the *shubin*?"

Newt bit his lip, a nervous habit, and I wondered if he was worried about saying too much. Then again, I got the feeling not many people stopped by, and from his reception at the diner, he probably didn't have a busy social calendar. "Yeah. At least, that's what a bunch of old diaries say. The ghosts that showed up never hurt anybody. But the *shubin*, that's a different story. The men in the mine, they believed. They used to take down food and whiskey as offerings, leave it for the *shubin*, so he didn't cause cave-ins or send afterdamp—bad air. Had all kinds of superstitions about what not to do to keep on its good side."

"Obviously, that went badly," I replied.

"Real badly," Newt agreed. "But after the disaster, nobody saw the *shubin* again. Until recently."

"What changed?" Father Leo asked.

"People don't want to say it out loud, because of the money that's coming in, but me, I think it's the frackers. They're disturbing the ground down deep, where the tunnels are. I think they pissed the *shubin* off."

I didn't know if Newt had come to his theory independently, or if he and Thomas had talked, but I thought their guess was probably right. Creatures like the *shubin* don't like to be disturbed, which is why they played malicious pranks—sometimes deadly ones—on miners who troubled their slumber. Drilling of any kind into the depths wasn't likely to go over well.

"We ate at the diner," Father Leo said. "People mentioned bad dreams. And we couldn't help hearing what that man said to you."

Newt rolled his eyes. "Don't mind Keith. He and his buddies are full of hot air. It's a funny thing—people in coal mining towns hate the mine companies and the bosses, but at the same time, they've been whipped so many times they're scared to say anything. The mining companies are always threatening that if miners complain about bad conditions, skimping on safety, even breaking the law, that the mines will get shut down and the town will die."

His voice grew angry. "Even now, what have we got to lose by telling the truth? The mines have been gone for decades. They aren't coming back. It's been long enough; there aren't even people alive who could lose their pensions."

"So those editorials Keith was talking about, you decided to name names?" Father Leo asked, raising an eyebrow.

Newt nodded vigorously. "Yes. Why not? The miners deserved better. And so did the underlings who got left holding the bag. The managers and the fire boss screwed up—or didn't care—and they blamed it all on Joe Bohdan, the junior mining engineer. He denied it, but no one would listen. People needed a scapegoat, and they took out their hate on Joe. He couldn't move away; no one would hire him. Hanged himself out in his barn."

I exchanged a glance with Father Leo. Two suicides connected to the disaster, ghost sightings, and a mine monster. What had looked like a simple salt and burn had gotten complicated.

"But I'm going to clear Joe," Newt continued, oblivious to our silent conversation. "I found papers to prove the mine bosses knew the vents weren't working right, and that the foreman was told to not wait the whole hour after running machines to let the dust settle. Cutting those corners, it was just a matter of time before the Harwick blew."

"What are you going to do about it?" I asked. On one hand, Newt seemed a little too wrapped up in a long-ago clusterfuck. And yet, his crusading spirit had an idealism that touched my jaded old soul.

"I'm working on an article for a history magazine," Newt said with a conspiratorial smile. "They want to know the whole truth. And I'm going to be the one who tells it." He sighed. "It won't bring anyone back or get reparations for the families, or even an apology. But there's something to be said for just having the real story known."

"Sounds personal."

Newt gave a sheepish grin. "My great-grandmother told me stories about the disaster, about the night her father didn't come home. Even as a kid, I could see how much it still hurt her. I guess I've been a little obsessed with it ever since."

The wistfulness in his voice made me picture a chubby-cheeked kid consoling an old lady, and it drove home how deep the scars of the disaster went that the pain remained a century later. I understood why he wanted justice, for the miners and the scapegoats, and why even the fruitless act of speaking out mattered. My "truth" about the supernatural had cost me my marriage and some friendships, plus the customers who didn't want a "wacko" working on their car. Truth might set you free, but it didn't come cheap.

"Good for you," I said. "Don't let anyone talk you out of it." Father Leo and I headed for the door. We'd gotten much more than I expected from the visit. "Thanks for the tour."

When we were back in the car headed for the motel, Father Leo turned to me. "What did you make of that?"

"I think the ghosts are the least of our worries," I replied, parking in front of our room.

As Father Leo selected the best weapons and materials for the fight, I searched online and in our lore books for anything about how to fight a *shubin*. "There's next to nothing," I growled, utterly frustrated.

Father Leo chuckled. "I didn't expect there to be. But if it's like a kobold, then it can be dispelled. We can't destroy it—those creatures are forces of nature—but they can be sent back to their caverns and trapped there."

"To be let out by the next dumbass who drills nearby, like that singing frog in the cartoon?"

He shrugged. "Maybe. And if that happens, we'll send him back again. I don't make the rules."

We headed out after dusk. I wasn't afraid of running into anyone at the old mine site, but I didn't want our car to attract attention, parked on the overgrown access road. We hiked in, carrying our gear, shielding our flashlights to avoid notice.

When we reached the place where the Harwick's main shaft had been, I could sense the change in the air as soon as we arrived.

"You feel that?" Father Leo asked.

I nodded. "It knows we're here."

"I think it always knew. It just wasn't sure whether we were the enemy."

Moving quickly, I made a circle of salt and iron filings around Father Leo so he could work his exorcism undisturbed. It's not that he can't hold his own in a fight—the Occulatum is a bad-ass monster fighting organization, after all—but I'm more of the brawn in our duo. That's why I got ready to watch his back and give him all the time he needed to send the *shubin* down where he belonged.

The temperature plummeted, although the night had been mild when we headed out. Orbs appeared, faint at first, then glowing brighter. They danced and zipped like fireflies, then slowed and gradually took form. A baleful line of dead miners faced us. Coal dust darkened their pale skin, along with the soot of the fires that killed them. Strips of charred skin and rough clothing hung in tatters, stained by blood. They stared at me as if daring us to settle the long grievance keeping their spirits tethered to the place that claimed their lives.

"Shit," I muttered. Father Leo ignored me, pulled out his rosary and prayer book, and began to chant. Maybe I've been at this too long, but I find the *Rituale Romanum* familiar and comforting.

"*Exorcizamos te, omnis immundus spiritus…*" Father Leo began.

The ghosts shimmered, closer now than they had been seconds before, and I readied both my shotgun and iron knife to keep them away from the priest. The spirits' faces held no emotion, and I found that more frightening than malice or rage. They advanced, slowly but remorselessly, drawing into a circle surrounding us.

"Stay back!" I warned, gesturing with the shotgun. "I don't want to hurt you, but I will if you attack him."

They revenants stopped, shoulder to shoulder, all around us. At least fifty of the miners' bodies had never been recovered, and the Harwick had become their tomb. These were their ghosts. If they rushed forward at once, I couldn't hold them all off, not even with my grenade launcher of salted holy water. I backed up a step, closer to Father Leo, ready to do whatever it took to protect him. Leo's chant never faltered, and when I glanced his way, I saw his face raised skyward, eyes closed, with an expression of trust and serenity.

The ghosts surrounded us, and I wondered what they intended. They couldn't get to Father Leo inside the circle, and I had a glass bulb filled with salt I could smash and then step into the scattered grains in an emergency, but we couldn't hold the ghosts off forever like that.

"What do you want?" I yelled to the ghosts. "Vengeance? The men who took advantage of you are long dead, and now you've killed their descendants. There's no one left to punish. You want vindication? The truth will be published. Everyone will know."

The ghosts circled us in silence, dead-eyed and somber, just inches away. I shivered with the cold of the grave, under the judgment of their remorseless stare. Then the energy shifted, I felt a gut-deep, primal terror, and beyond the semi-solid ring of ghosts, I saw the *shubin* materialize.

The figure at the museum resembled the mine spirit, but no model could convey the creature's true appearance. The *shubin's* corpse-pale skin had a sheen like the sightless lizards found inside caves: a creature never meant to see the light. It stood hunched over, accustomed to the tight conditions in the mine tunnels. Unlike the mannequin in the museum, the real monster was naked and hairless, but heavily muscled. Its powerful arms and hands were built for rending, and its sinewed legs could run and lift. Most of all, I noticed the *shubin's* red glowing eyes and its sharp, pointed teeth.

The monster appeared right in front of Father Leo and gave an earsplitting shriek. It moved toward the priest, and I shot it, point blank in the chest, with a salt round. That made it stagger backward, but when the creature's head came up, it fixed its baleful glare on me.

I shot it again, right in the face.

The rock salt ripped into its fish-belly white skin but did not draw blood. Maybe *shubin* don't bleed. It hissed and looked like it wanted to come after me, but then Father Leo started on a new line in the exorcism, and the *shubin* flinched like the words were weapons.

I reloaded, this time with iron pellets, and blasted the creature with both barrels.

The iron hurt the *shubin*. Where the pellets hit, the skin shriveled like cracked leather, opening deep gashes. Between the pain of the buckshot and the discomfort of the exorcism chant, the *shubin* looked like it was on the edge of madness. It flung itself toward Father Leo, only to bounce back from the circle of iron and salt, repelled by the invisible barrier.

With an enraged shriek, the monster lurched at me before I could reload and knocked the shotgun from my grip as we fell onto the hard dirt. Its hands held my arms so tightly I thought it might break bone, but all I could focus on were the pointed teeth that snapped close to my throat.

I couldn't break its hold, so I rolled us, figuring that we weighed about the same. Pinning the *shubin* with my legs, I twisted enough to draw my iron knife. Gripping the hilt in both hands, I fell forward with my full weight, driving the blade deep into the *shubin's* chest.

The *shubin* screamed and flung me away with enough force to send me rolling. I smacked into the side of an old coal car and wondered whether my tetanus shots were up to date. Then the *shubin* lunged at me, and I decided lockjaw was the least of my worries.

Father Leo said the *shubin* couldn't die. I just needed to distract it—without getting myself killed—just long enough for him to finish the ritual.

"Chant faster!" I yelled, and threw myself out of the way. The *shubin* landed face-down in the dirt, and I dove on top of it, driving my knee into the small of its back and using my weight to keep it from getting leverage.

The *shubin* gnashed its teeth and bucked beneath me, trying to break my hold. I dug my fingers into its upper arms and shifted to increase the pressure on its back and pelvis. Its angry screams made my head throb, and the malice in its red eyes made me certain it looked forward to tearing out my throat.

Father Leo was in the home stretch of the litany. I really hoped the main Latin ritual would be effective because if he had to start over with another chant, I knew I wouldn't survive. As Father Leo came to the end of the exorcism rite, his voice grew louder, filled with the authority of Heaven and Hell.

With a mighty lurch, the *shubin* mustered all its strength and twisted us once more. I brought my knees up, desperate to keep those teeth away from my neck. The iron had taken a toll—the *shubin's* skin had split and tightened where the buckshot penetrated, and a gray shadow radiated from the hole my knife had made. The legends that said iron could make such a creature turn away were wrong. It might have weakened the *shubin*, but not nearly enough. The teeth skimmed my throat, and I swore its fingers were going to dig all the way to the bone as it held me tightly.

I spat in its face and then brought my head up with all the strength I could muster, smashing against its skull and nearly knocking myself out. Blood dripped down my forehead and into my eyes, but the move won me a second's reprieve, enough to knee the creature in the nuts and push it away from my chest.

The *shubin* flung itself down at me, eyes wild, teeth bared. It had me pinned, and I knew that this time, I wouldn't be able to get away.

"*Sánctus, Sanctus, Sanctus Dóminus Déus Sábaoth.*" Father Leo's voice rose in a triumphant finale, just as the *shubin's* face hung inches above my own, poised to rip into my flesh. Instead, a fierce trembling seized the creature, and its head fell back, teeth bared, eyes wide and staring, as a guttural cry tore from its throat. Its whole body jerked as if it were being pulled at by unseen forces, and it screamed again in pain and frustration before it vanished into the night air.

I sagged back against the ground, utterly spent, in shock that I was still alive. I heard Father Leo drag his foot through the salt and iron circle; then he ran to where I lay and knelt beside me.

"Mark! Are you all right?"

"Peachy." Everything hurt, from my head to my toes. I'd have bruises on top of bruises tomorrow, plus a split lip and what felt like a black eye from the fight with the *shubin*. "Is it gone?"

"It's been sent back to the depths," Father Leo assured me, with a glance toward the old mine entrance just to be certain. "When we get back, I'll have the Occulatum reach out to the Hungarian church here and make sure someone comes up and does a blessing and banishing every few months."

"But if the fracking continues—"

"The Occulatum has agents everywhere," he assured me, offering a hand to help me up, and then getting under my shoulder when I staggered. "I dare say it can throw its weight around to have the fracking operation moved elsewhere."

"There are mines all over this part of the state," I reminded him. "No telling what's down in those tunnels. They could go somewhere new and wake up something even worse."

He patted me on the shoulder. "Then we have job security, you and I."

"Is that supposed to make me feel better?"

"No, but I brought a bottle of good whiskey—for medicinal purposes —and it's in the motel room. *That* will make you feel better. I'll join you in a nip. I think I feel a cold coming on," he added with a grin.

We hobbled back to my truck. When I moved to go for the driver's side, Father Leo cleared his throat and held out his hand for my keys. "I'll drive. We've tested the Lord's protection enough for one night," he said archly, opening the passenger door and gesturing for me to get in. I felt shitty enough to let him get away with it since, usually, no one drives my truck but me.

An hour later, after a hot bath, a few stitches, and a change of clothes, I sat propped up against the headboard of my bed. Father Leo poured a couple of fingers of whiskey into one of those flimsy plastic cups, which even I knew was a travesty. I could tell it was good stuff, just from the smell. He tipped a generous portion into his own cup and raised it in a salute.

"Nice work back there."

"You did some pretty fancy chanting yourself," I replied. A swallow of the whiskey burned down my throat, and I started to finally relax.

"The ghosts were there to protect us," he said, staring down at the amber liquid in his cup. "I think they've taken it as their mission to keep an eye on the *shubin*, since they're all down there together."

"Will you—should you—send them on?"

He frowned, thinking. "When the local priest says his blessing, those who want to will find it easier to let go. Some may not be ready. Maybe to them, they're still taking care of their families, warning them, keeping the monster at bay."

"Even after a century."

Father Leo shrugged. "Even so." He looked at me, studying me in that way he had of seeing right through me. "Those ghosts lost one purpose in life and found another. You're a good hunter, Mark, but that shouldn't be your main focus."

"It's not," I protested. "I've got the body shop, I play poker with you and the guys, Blair and Chiara come over for movie night, Louie and I meet up for drinks, and things are...evolving...with Sara. It's not like that."

He smiled. "Good. Glad to hear it. And speaking of poker—you still owe the Charitable Fund from the last game. Again."

I groaned. "I'll pay you when we play next week. Cross my heart."

I might hunt creatures few people believe are real, face down super-natural threats, and save the region from monsters and dark magic, but when it comes to poker, Father Leo is the real badass. Nice to know that crazy as my life can be, some things never change.

PART IV

CLOSE ENCOUNTERS

1

I think I'd know a mammoth if I saw one.

After all, I've seen the bones and tusks in a museum, so if I met one with its skin on, *alive*, I'm pretty sure I'd recognize it.

This was definitely *not* a mammoth, despite the excited blubberings of the kid at the convenience store, where I'd stopped to pick up lunch and gas. He told me all about the strange prehistoric creature that had been spotted near Lake Pleasant with the energy level only a true dinosaur geek could muster. I felt for the kid because I understood why he'd think having a real, live mammoth practically in his own backyard would be exciting. But, at the same time, when ancient monsters suddenly come back to life, I'm the sorry son of a bitch who has to go in and gank them.

I'm Mark Wojcik, mechanic and monster hunter. I'm not in it for the thrills, and I'm sure as fuck not in it for the money. No one *wants* to become a monster hunter. They want to avenge someone they loved and lost, and if they survive their first encounter, they discover that they're part of a small, mostly secret club of people who do the dirty work of cleaning up creatures and cryptids so that everyone else can sleep safe and sound at night. In my case, it was a deer hunt with my father, brother, uncle, and cousin that ended up with a wendigo hunting us. They died, I didn't, and monster hunting is my penance and atonement.

So I listened to the nice boy with the bad acne go on at length about the huge creature fishermen had glimpsed near the lake that must have started *eating* people, because why else had they *disappeared*? And, oh yeah, its hooves were on backward, wasn't that *cool*?

I sighed and counted down from ten for patience. Joey, the clerk, seemed so genuinely happy to have someone to talk to that I felt bad about encouraging him to get to the point.

"Do you know when people saw the…mammoth?" I prompted.

"Carson told me that his dad's friend said it was right around dusk," Joey supplied helpfully. "Are you going to go see for yourself?" He grabbed a piece of paper. "If you get a picture, can you text it to me? That would be awesome!"

I accepted the number because he meant well, but I don't generally do selfies—of me or the monsters. And in this case, I didn't intend to give Joey any photos he could show around because I felt certain someone who did know what a mammoth was supposed to look like would figure out that the cryptid in the shot wasn't a big hairy elephant with tusks.

"Depends on the light," I hedged. "It might be too dark to get a good shot."

Joey nodded. "Right. Like how those Loch Ness monster photos are always blurry?" He leaned across the counter. "My grandma gets *Fate Magazine*, you know, about all the weird stuff that happens? I've read all of them."

I managed to suppress a sigh. *Fate Magazine* is something of a legend in monster hunter circles because, while it sensationalizes the fuck out of stories to sell copies to mundanes and keep the authorities off our asses, it usually gets the details about the sightings right.

He rang up my items, and I paid. "Thanks for the tip," I said, glad to have found a local who would talk to me.

"Just remember to send me that picture!" Joey added with a laugh. Maybe I could figure out how to send him something out of focus or with my thumb covering part of it so he'd have bragging rights without giving him evidence the Feds were going to want to rendition him over. I grunted something noncommittal and headed back to my truck, wishing that a wooly mammoth really was what I expected to see.

Lake Pleasant is tucked off to one side in the woods between Erie and Waterford. It isn't as big as Lake Erie, or as commercialized as Conneaut Lake, so most people overlook it, except for the local anglers and people with nearby summer cabins. If anyone outside the area has heard of it, that's because a few years ago someone snagged an old skeleton and paleontologists practically peed themselves over finding mammoth bones. Those were the real deal, and I could see why locals thought this new sighting might be Manny from *Ice Age* come to life.

I was pretty damn sure it wasn't and that the real story was a lot scarier.

Lake Pleasant was formed by the glaciers from the real Ice Age, and it's a "kettle lake," where bits of the ancient ice flow broke off in a trench and melted to form a permanent body of water. That means it's really old, Pleistocene old, and no one actually knows what's buried in the muck under forty feet of water. Or what was sleeping, until recently.

Father Leo put me on to the job. He's the parish priest of a church near me and a good poker buddy. More importantly, he's the local point man for the Occulatum, a secret, monster-hunting branch of the Roman Catholic Church. So Father Leo is kind of the area dispatcher for cases, and I'm on his short list of who he's gonna call when there's something strange in the neighborhood.

See, a real wooly mammoth wasn't likely to eat people, even if it somehow had been kept in suspended animation at the bottom of a lake for a couple of million years. But there were other very nasty possibilities, none of which ought to be left to roam the countryside, munching on the neighbors. Which is why I was out here on a very nice Tuesday instead of fixing Mr. Zimmerman's brakes at my garage out in Atlantic.

I came prepared for a fight. I had a permit for the Glock in my glove compartment, and a shitload of other weapons that they don't issue permits for in a hidden compartment. I suspected what the creature might be, and the gear bag on the floor held some specialized items I'd need if I was right. But I wouldn't be sure until I saw the cryptid, and by then, there'd be no backing out.

My plan was simple: wander up to the lake and present myself as a tasty monster snack, then turn the tables and kill the critter before it polished off any more locals. I'm not much for nuance. Monster hunting requires a lot of lore, a little luck, and plenty of brute force. I had a lot of high caliber "persuasion" with me, but if we were right about the creature, it would take as much trickery as firepower to stop the killings.

I drove out to the lake and parked in an out of the way spot, in case I came back covered in blood—my own, or better yet, the monster's. I loaded the gear bag with some of the less conventional weapons, including a sawed-off shotgun with rock salt rounds and a couple of clips of silver bullets for my Glock. I strapped a silver-edged Ka-Bar in a sheath on my hip, just in case. Then I texted Father Leo to let him know I was in position and headed off to meet the creature for dinner.

Normally, a walk around a beautiful lake on a nice afternoon would be my idea of relaxation, but not today. I couldn't afford to let the scenery distract me because whatever had killed four people was out here, somewhere, and it would kill again unless I put a stop to it. But Lake Pleasant didn't look like Camp Crystal Lake, and no suitably ominous music warned of the creature's approach. Some cryptids had the ability to lull their would-be victims into a trance, an extrasensory roofie that dulled their self-preservation instinct until it was too late. I was hoping that the blessed silver Saint George medal—patron saint of monster hunters— would give me some protection. It wouldn't save my ass, but if it even bought me a few extra minutes of reaction time, that might be enough to save my life.

The sun glinted off the still water. My approach spooked ducks near the water's edge, and they took wing. I was intentionally not trying to be quiet, my way of ringing the dinner bell.

And suddenly, there it was, a beautiful black horse with an elaborate bridle and saddle, standing at the marge of the lake. It looked at me with uncanny sentience, sizing me up as a threat. Those ancient eyes regarded me warily, taking my measure.

I'd never seen a kelpie except in books. Even so, I couldn't imagine how anyone would mistake something the size of a huge draft horse for a mammoth. The mane and tail were wet, resembling seaweed more than hair, and the hooves pointed backward. Even so, it was a breathtakingly gorgeous animal, and I felt its siren call to come closer.

Although my silver medal and weapons did help me keep a clear mind, I allowed myself to move toward the creature, trying to act as if I were under its spell. I shrugged out of my gear bag. Now that I knew for certain what the monster was, I had everything I needed on me. The kelpie lifted its head, making eye contact, drawing me into those liquid brown eyes, promising me wonders. It snorted when I came within reach, sidestepping closer, offering me the ride of a lifetime. Or, more to the point, to my doom.

I reached behind me and drew my Glock, intending to put a silver bullet right through the blaze between the kelpie's eyes. Before I could aim, the kelpie swung its huge head, slamming into my hand, knocking the gun out of my grip. It flew through the air and landed several feet away, useless. But once your skin touches a kelpie, you can't let go. It dragged me until I had no choice except to climb up into the saddle, and then the kelpie ran full speed into the lake, with me unable to jump clear.

This wasn't how I wanted to fight Freaky Flicka, but I was going to need Plan B. As usual, that meant winging it and hoping for the best. The kelpie never broke speed as the water deepened to its withers. The lake was cool, and down in its depths, where the kelpie made its lair, I knew it would be even colder. The kelpie wasn't swimming; it walked out on the lake floor, and it would keep on walking as the water grew deeper and deeper until I drowned.

I'm not a horseman. The extent of my riding experience ended on the pony track on my fifth birthday. Watching Westerns didn't count. But the kelpie had me prisoner for the moment, so staying on wasn't my top priority. If the lore was right, I could get loose by closing my hand around the piece of steel in my pocket. Getting off before I drowned and killing the monster—that was what I had top of mind.

Later, if I survived, I could beat myself up for missing the shot. The nice, easy headshot. But the kelpie was running deeper, and the water was already covering my chest, so I had to get to work. I squeezed my knees into the kelpie's sides so that if he decided to try to buck me off, I could finish the job. Then I pulled my Ka-Bar and leaned forward, grabbing the reins and starting to saw through the bridle.

That was how you're supposed to kill a kelpie if you don't shoot the damn thing. But the bridle wasn't easy to cut, so the kelpie continued to gallop into the lake, backward hooves sinking into the deep muck. We were in the water up to my shoulders, and I was sawing away for all I was worth. The kelpie snorted and chuffed, not quite trying to buck me off, but giving me a rough ride to distract me long enough for him to drown me. I wondered whether kelpies rolled you in the deep water like alligators, and decided that I really didn't want to find out.

My silver-edged knife had a wicked sharp blade, but the bridle was enchanted, giving the kelpie some of his power. The lore hadn't said anything about magical saddles, and if I didn't drown sawing through the bridle, I'd worry about it later. The kelpie pranced and bucked like a show horse, which was funny considering he was the one who'd trapped me on his back.

That's one of the things that pissed me off with monsters. It's all fun and games when they're trying to kill you. But turn the tables and try to kill them back, and they get bitchy about it.

A regular knife wouldn't have made a dent on the bridle, but the silver edge sank into the hard leather, making slow progress. The deep saw teeth of the Ka-Bar ripped into the bridle, and for the first time, the kelpie seemed to realize its danger. It plunged farther into the lake, up past my chin, and when I ducked down to reach the bridle, I had to hold my breath.

I wondered why the kelpie didn't just release its hold on me. But maybe it couldn't. Perhaps it didn't fully control the magic, and that meant we were locked together, 'til death did us part. I also didn't know what cutting the bridle would do to the kelpie. Reports varied, and the lore is, by its nature, vague. Some said it would kill the kelpie; others said it would merely free me. But from the way the kelpie began to buck and sidestep, tossing its seaweed mane and frothing at the mouth, I figured it had started to see me as a threat more than a meal.

I broke the surface, got a deep breath, and then ducked under again, sawing as hard as I could. Each time I went up for air, it was harder to reach because the kelpie continued its trek back to the depths. Soon, I wouldn't be able to get a new lungful of air, and if I hadn't cut my way clear by then, Father Leo was going to need a new hunter.

The kelpie's next steps sank a couple of inches into the primordial ooze at the bottom of the lake, and we went under. I felt the bridle begin to give as I put my weight into the blade, ripping at the straps as my lungs burned and my vision began to darken. The kelpie lurched, and that was exactly what I needed, his weight and bulk pushing against the frayed leather. The bridle snapped, and I ripped it free.

When it came loose, the kelpie lost its hold on me. But I couldn't let the monster return to the depths and continue its killing spree. I tangled a hand in its mane and held on, kicking with my feet as I darted forward and sank my silver blade deep into the kelpie's neck.

Those huge eyes fixed on me, sparkling with flecks of red. Or maybe that was me, succumbing to oxygen deprivation. Silvery tendrils of fairy blood rose in the dark water of Lake Pleasant as I drove the blade in deeper. The kelpie tried to turn and snap at me. Regular horse teeth are terrifying, capable of biting off fingers. The kelpie's jagged, razor-sharp teeth looked more alligator than Appaloosa, and I figured it could bite through my arm if it caught me.

We were locked in a death dance, the kelpie and me. I sawed at the creature's neck, raking that sharp, serrated blade against the spine. Few creatures except ghouls, zombies, and cockroaches do well without their heads. With one final stroke, I severed the backbone, and the fire went out of the kelpie's eyes.

I'd won, but my overtaxed lungs couldn't hold out any longer. I let out the breath I'd been holding and fought the instinct to breathe in because I was below the surface. This was it. I couldn't fight reflex, and the water flooded into my nose and mouth. The kelpie's corpse dropped away below me, returning to the sludge. I stopped struggling, and as consciousness slipped away, realized I didn't have enough time left to think about all my many regrets.

On the rare occasions when I thought about the afterlife, I hadn't imagined being smacked around. Then again, my life's track record was spotty, to say the least, so maybe my eternal severance package came with extra pummeling.

"Come on," a voice muttered. "Breathe, dammit!" More smacking commenced, right between my shoulder blades, and the next thing I knew, I was horking up lake water and everything else in my stomach.

"Wow! That worked!" Joey, the kid from the convenience store, sounded utterly amazed. "Thank you, YouTube!"

I cleared my throat twice before I found my voice. "Joey?"

"I saw you floating, and I swam out to get you," he said, sounding proud and sheepish. "Then I dragged you back, but I failed my lifeguard exam, so I YouTube'd how to get you to breathe again. And it worked!"

I patted his arm, with all my waning strength. "You did good, kid." It took a few minutes for my brain to catch up. "How were you out here, anyhow?"

Joey reddened like I'd caught him doing something he shouldn't. "I followed you," he admitted. "I wanted to see the dinosaur. But I missed it, didn't I?"

He sounded so sad and so terribly sincere. And since he'd saved my life, I felt guilty. "It wasn't a real dinosaur," I said. "I think it was some kind of mutant alligator, and I killed it, but it rolled me. Whatever it was, it's down at the bottom of the lake now." It was a lie, but I was letting him down easy and keeping him safe because, in my business, a little knowledge can get you into a whole lot of trouble.

"Well, at least you're okay," Joey said, trying to find the bright spot.

"And I owe you one," I replied because the kid did save my life. "If I ever do see one of those alligators again, I'll make sure to get a photo for you." It was a hollow promise, but Joey looked so hopeful, I decided I had to find something, somewhere to send him that wouldn't make problems for him.

Joey headed back to town, and I walked back to my truck, dripping the whole way. That's when I realized I still had something clutched in my left hand, and when I opened my fingers, I found a shard of something that wasn't quite metal, not exactly ceramic, and definitely odd. The piece was a little smaller than the palm of my hand, just large enough for me to make out strange markings that I didn't recognize, and I wondered when I had found it. I didn't remember grabbing ahold of anything except the kelpie, but the moments after I killed the creature were a little hazy from lack of oxygen.

I regarded the shard suspiciously and opened up a lead box I keep in the back of the truck for just such occasions and tossed the piece in. When I had time, I'd ask Father Leo to take a look. But before that, I needed to get out of my soaking wet clothes. I grabbed a towel and wrung out my shirt as best I could, threw the towel over the upholstery, and got in. I couldn't leave Lake Pleasant in my rear-view mirror fast enough.

2

_____

Who thought it was a good idea to build a sanitarium on the grounds of an old orphanage? Color me surprised when restless and vengeful ghosts decide to wander.

Mercer Sanitarium, or more to the point, the Mercer Hospital for Nervous and Mental Disorders, did a booming business in the early half of the Twentieth Century. It had been built on the grounds of the Mercer Soldiers Orphans School, which took care of the children left behind by soldiers during the Civil War. Nothing remains of either building now, thanks to time and the purifying flames of arson, but the land on Sanitarium Drive remains abandoned, although the Sanitarium burned after it was closed down in the post-World War II era.

Father Leo drove down to Mercer with me, since laying ghosts to rest is more his gig than mine. I'm more about shooting things or blowing them up, so I went along as back up.

"Have you heard tell of ghost problems before now?" I asked as Father Leo came around the truck.

He had his black shirt and clerical collar on, along with blue jeans and steel toe boots. The stole for Last Rites was a nice added touch. I had the weapons bag full of salt, iron filings, several iron knives, a heavy piece of rebar, and a Super Soaker filled with holy water, along with a few other helpful items. I was going to go along with the good cop/bad cop routine for starters, but if the ghosts got pissy, I intended to do whatever was necessary to keep the padre and me safe.

"No, and that's odd," Father Leo replied. "It's been almost seventy years since the sanitarium closed, and over a hundred since the orphanage shut down. I'm sure we would have heard if there'd been problems all these years."

"D'ya think something woke the ghosts up?" I asked as we walked along the road. Not too long ago, all of the natural gas drilling—fracking—had disturbed ghosts in an old mine and caused a lot of problems. I wasn't looking forward to more of the same.

"That's the only reason I can come up with," Father Leo replied. "But no one's mining for gas around here, and I haven't heard tell of any local necromancers." Dabblers in the dark arts were a pain in the ass and often blundered their way into lethal consequences. "So something's annoyed the ghosts, and now we're the ones who have to set things right."

I looked across the large, empty field and tried to picture it as it had been. The Orphans School was a collection of tidy white clapboard buildings on a small farm designed to shelter and teach the children left dependent by the war. After it closed, the mental hospital reused some of the buildings and added others, expanding the farm for "therapeutic" reasons.

The large, empty lawn should have felt peaceful, but a chill ran down my spine. Odd that while much of the land that once belonged to the sanitarium had been sold off and put to other uses, this central area—where the buildings once stood—remained vacant after all this time.

"In its day, the sanitarium was considered cutting edge," Father Leo mused as we looked out over the grounds. "They pioneered the 'water cure,' which was supposed to help everything from 'nervous conditions' to depression to psychosis. Sometimes that meant a warm bath to soothe the nerves. But in other cases, it was overdone, and it was much more like torture than therapy." He sighed. "Great harm usually comes out of well-meaning efforts when the person on the receiving end has no say in their treatment."

I'd heard stories about patients who were wrapped up like mummies and doused with cold water, or restrained and then sprayed with fire hoses. How that was supposed to help someone whose nerves were already on edge was beyond me. No matter how noble the intentions of the treatment's inventor, I wondered whether, in practice, the more "creative" approaches weren't just the hospital staff taking out their frustration on unruly patients or providing a cautionary example to keep the hapless residents in line.

"I asked around, talked to some of my relatives in the area," I said as we ambled through the empty field. "No one remembers hearing about any scandals at either the school or the hospital."

Father Leo shrugged. "It was easier to hush things up back then," he replied. "And it's a small town. People could have had all kinds of reasons not to tell things they saw."

A small red car pulled up behind my truck, and Dixie James got out. Danielle—Dixie—James was a short, plump woman in her middle years with chin-length graying brown hair and bright blue eyes. For some reason, she just didn't fit my mental image of a ghost whisperer, but she was a damn fine medium, and we'd benefitted from her assistance on a number of prior cases.

"Hello, boys," she called out in greeting, and I couldn't help but grin, wondering how often Father Leo hears that kind of salutation. Then again, I get the feeling he appreciates the few people who treat him like a real person instead of an unapproachable cleric.

"Hey, Dixie," he replied. "You feeling ghosty today?"

Dixie is the most powerful medium I'd ever had the pleasure of working with, and I wouldn't want her gift for all the money in the world. I've met ghosts that deserved my sympathy, because of the circumstances that led to their deaths, but in general, if I get involved, it's because the spirits pose a threat to the living. I can't kill a ghost, because they're already dead, but I can dispel them with extreme prejudice, and Father Leo can force them to move on to the afterlife, or set their soul to rest.

"I've done my meditation and called down plenty of white light to ground myself," Dixie replied. "And I've got my silver and onyx charms. So nobody's going to outstay their welcome."

Sometimes, Dixie talks to ghosts or at least listens to them. But other times, she allows the ghost to possess her and speak through her body— the classic medium-at-a-séance scenario everyone's seen on TV and in the movies. That freaks me the fuck out because I don't let anyone else drive my truck, let alone hijack my body. But Dixie's been doing this all her life, and that means she's one of the bravest people I know.

"Are you picking up anything yet?" I asked. Even though I get creeped out watching Dixie work, I'm also intrigued, and I had a feeling there was more to the wandering ghosts of the orphanage/asylum than we'd been told. I also suspected that whatever secrets we ultimately uncovered wouldn't be pleasant.

Dixie got a far-off look in her eyes. "There's definitely energy here," she replied. She started walking, and Father Leo and I fell into step behind her, letting her lead the way but staying close in case of trouble. Dixie walked the perimeter of the field in silence. I wondered what she saw with her extra perception, but so far, nothing seemed to spook her.

Along the far end of the grounds, Dixie came to an abrupt halt. "I see four children," she said, looking toward a patch of lawn in front of her that, to my eyes, was entirely empty. "I'm guessing ages three to about ten. They won't answer me, but they're standing in a row." Dixie frowned. "Wait. There are more now. All lined up like they're mustered out for inspection, standing at attention, very straight posture, arms down at their sides."

She paused, and I couldn't tell whether she was listening or just sensing the emotional feedback from the ghosts. "They're sad. And some of them don't look well. I get the feeling they've been sick." Her frown deepened. "A few of them have bruises. I think they've been hurt."

I felt my gut twist. Nothing pisses me off more than bastards that hurt kids, and it's even worse when it's children who don't have parents to look out of them. "Do you think they were abused?" I asked, and saw the concern in Father Leo's eyes.

"Some of them, but not all, I don't think," Dixie replied, and her voice took on a sing-song quality that told me she was in a trance, relaying her impressions from the spirit world. "Not abuse, but maybe not good care."

"Did they have to line up for inspection?" I couldn't figure why they were all in a row, and in my mind's eye, I pictured them lined up like little soldiers, some sick fuck's idea of "discipline."

"No," Dixie said thoughtfully, and looked earnest as if she were straining to hear a distant voice. "Not...standing." She paled. "Not standing at all. Lying down." She turned to look at Father Leo and me. "In their coffins. This was a cemetery."

I looked around the land where we stood. Nothing indicated a grave-yard had ever been here. No broken stones, no periwinkle, no strange mounds or depressions. "Unmarked graves?" I asked.

Father Leo shrugged. "That wasn't uncommon back then, especially at public institutions. Without a family to mourn or care, sometimes there was just a common, pauper's grave."

These kids got the shitty end of the stick at every turn. It wouldn't have been unusual for them to have lost a mother in childbirth, and then they lost a father to war. Relatives didn't want them, or couldn't afford to take them in. Maybe the orphanage put a roof over their head and some food in their bellies, but it didn't look like anyone was looking out for them. Or maybe the place was overfilled and understaffed, and they fell between the cracks.

"Can you find out why they woke up?" I asked.

Dixie concentrated, staring intently at what appeared to be thin air. Finally, she shook her head. "They're old ghosts, and their energy is very faded. They wouldn't have been able to manifest on their own. I don't think these are the spirits causing problems. They're barely able to make themselves seen to me, so they're not wreaking havoc. I think these kids were collateral damage."

And wasn't that just their lot in life, I thought bitterly. Even after death, their final rest got disturbed—not because anyone was paying attention to them, but because they were in the way.

"Can you help them?" Father Leo asked. "They deserve better."

Dixie nodded. "Yes. Between you and me, we'll make sure they pass over. But we need to find the source, or they'll just get drawn back." She turned her attention back to where the ghosts stood beyond our mortal vision, and I assumed she was making a promise to the spirits that we would return to help them.

Finally, she looked up. "All right. They understand as well as they can. I don't think they have the energy to get involved, but I've asked them to wait here, and we'll take care of them. Let's go find the troublemakers."

Father Leo was contacted because of reports of glowing orbs and strange green lights in the empty field. If that were all, we probably wouldn't have gotten involved. But there had been several car accidents due to drivers being surprised by the orbs, and while no one was killed or even seriously injured, we didn't want it to get to that point. Some other odd happenings, originally chalked up to coincidence, now looked in hindsight to be malicious ghostly pranks. Tree limbs had fallen across the road without a windstorm. Power lines stopped working when diagnostics showed no problem. A nearby factory reported strange noises, odd lights, and disruptions to their electrical system.

The restless ghosts were getting stronger and testing their limits. We needed to shut them down before this got worse.

Dixie started walking again. Father Leo and I fell in behind her, giving a wide berth to where the children's ghosts had been. I tried to picture the grounds as I'd seen in old photographs, getting my bearings from where the building used to be and wondering what other secrets lay below the lawns or farm fields.

We made a circle of the perimeter, then began walking concentric rounds. As we headed down the back side of the property, the air grew cold, and I felt a breeze stir when the day had been mostly still. It didn't escape me that we were fairly close to the road, where most of the incidents had occurred.

I noticed that the road looked as if there'd been recent construction on the berm, either widening the street or doing some utility work along the side. I wondered if that had churned something up that had been long buried, and decided to take a closer look before we were through.

Suddenly, Dixie stumbled backward as if she had been pushed. Father Leo and I rushed forward, but she waved us off. She shifted her course a bit, but when she started forward again, the force lifted her off her feet and tossed her through the air. She landed hard on the ground.

"I'm fine," Dixie yelled, looking surprised but unhurt.

Father Leo and I rushed toward the spot where the energy had manifested. I had the rebar in hand, and I swung it through empty air, knowing how much ghosts hate iron. The iron bar met no resistance, but I heard a muted shriek and felt a change in pressure that made my ears pop.

Father Leo pulled out a fistful of salt from his jacket pocket, threw it down in a rough circle and stepped onto the protected area, then began to chant.

The wind picked up, although the sun shone bright and no clouds were in sight. I made sure I was between Dixie and where the energy had manifested, rebar still gripped in both hands. "Get between us," I said to Dixie, nodding to indicate a spot for her to my right and Father Leo's left. I shrugged out of my pack, grabbed a big salt container, and made a rough circle to protect her, and one for myself as well. Ghosts couldn't cross the salt line, but we could step over it if needed, or retreat to safety.

The wind howled around us. I put the salt back in my bag within the circle and grabbed the Super Soaker, so I had the rebar in one hand and the huge holy water rifle in the other. I recognized Father Leo's chant as one of protection, not yet banishment or exorcism. We just needed the ghosts to calm the fuck down so we could figure out what the hell was going on.

Dead people are so impatient.

"So many," Dixie murmured, scanning the empty field for the people only she could see.

"More kids?" I asked, hoping not.

Dixie shook her head. "No. Adults. Men, women, all ages. Pretty sure these are from the sanitarium."

It didn't take much, back in the day, to get committed to a mental institution. Being quirky, or odd, or defying gender norms could get you a one-way ticket, as could being an inconvenient spouse or parent if someone wanted to move on without you. And of course, the disenfranchised were most at risk: women, people of color, poor people, LGBTQA folks. Rich white men could be wildly "eccentric," but people with power rarely got involuntarily committed to a public institution unless it was a family coup.

Since I have more than my share of PTSD and depression, I felt a kinship of sorts with the long-ago dead of the Mercer Sanitarium. If my ex-wife Lara had her say, I'm sure she'd have shipped me off to the looney bin for not grieving fast enough after I'd lost nearly everyone I'd loved to that wendigo. My sister-in-law, Amy, hasn't forgiven me for surviving the hunt that killed her husband—my brother—and would have been first in line to suit me up in a straightjacket.

And yet, here I am, muddling through with a combination of good friends, a little therapy, some alcohol on the rough nights, and a purpose in life—if you count fixing cars and killing monsters to be of benefit to humanity. So it made me wonder how many of the poor souls who died here were sent away because they embarrassed their families, didn't fit in, or were just more trouble than anyone wanted to handle. I couldn't really blame them for being angry, but as they say, you don't have to go home, but you can't stay here. Dixie's job was to make last call, and Father Leo and I were the spiritual bouncers.

"Why are they angry? And why now?" I asked as Dixie lifted her face to the cold wind. The supernatural storm's vortex churned over the place we stood, and as the fog rose and the wind howled, I swore I could make out faces in the mist, even though I'm not psychically sensitive at all. That meant the ghosts were expending an awful lot of mojo to vent their fury, and usually, ghosts put on a show to send a message.

"They say that they were awakened, and 'it' won't let them rest," Dixie reported, in the dreamy voice that told me she was trancing. As if the ghosts were satisfied they were finally being heard, the wind quieted, and the fog rolled back, present but no longer swirling.

"What's 'it'?" Father Leo asked.

"They don't know, only that it screams so loud they can't sleep," Dixie replied.

Father Leo and I exchanged a glance. "Something at the factory?" he asked, looking toward the large manufacturing plant not far away.

"No. Near the road," she replied, frowning as she passed along the spectral insights. "They keep trying to make it stop."

That might explain all the incidents along the street, although the people getting hurt had nothing to do with the ghostly noise complaint.

"How did they die?" Father Leo asked, watching the mist with concern.

Dixie tilted her head, listening. I knew the ghosts were still nearby because the hair on my arms and the back of my neck was all standing up, and my gut was telling me to get the hell out of there.

"Some of the doctors tried new therapies that didn't go well," she replied quietly. "Experimental treatments, surgeries, drugs. Drilling holes, electroshock, the water cure, sedation…it often went wrong."

I bet it did. My anger flared, and I knew I needed to tamp down on it because we didn't want the ghosts getting riled up again. Even if the docs had the best of intentions, they'd caused harm, and that rankled. Like the orphans, these patients were the throwaways, with no one watching the watchmen, and it all got predictably fucked up.

"Can you guide me to wherever 'it' is?" I asked, looking to Dixie but really speaking to the spirits. "And if we find 'it' and take 'it' away, will they go quietly and stop hurting people?"

Again, Dixie conferred with her invisible crew, and after a moment of silent conversation, she looked to me with a nod. "They don't want to be here," Dixie said. "And they're sorry anyone got hurt. They just want the screaming to stop."

"Okay," I said. "I'm stepping out of the salt circle now. Don't throw me around." I took a chance that the ghosts could hear me, even if I couldn't hear them.

"They understand," Dixie confirmed. I exchanged a glance with Father Leo, since I'm skeptical about ghosts telling the truth, and his shrug didn't fill me with confidence. I knew what he meant: we were going to have to take our chances and see what happened.

Easy for him to say since I was the guy stepping out of the salt circle.

I laid the Super Soaker in easy reach of Father Leo, but kept the rebar with me, just in case. Then I took a deep breath and stepped carefully over the salt line, ready to bound backward if attacked. When nothing happened, I took a few hesitant steps toward the road. Even without Dixie's directions, I had a feeling the construction area was where the ghosts wanted me to go.

"You're moving the right way," she encouraged. I traveled a few more feet, not yet to the muddy area scraped clear by the big machines. The recent rains had probably chased the road crews away, although for Penn-DOT, anything seems like a good excuse to take a day off.

"How about now?" I asked, betting on a hunch. I might not have real clairvoyance, or Dixie's ability to summon spirits, but my gut instinct was right more often than not.

"Keep going. A little to the right," she urged. I adjusted my path and found myself glad I'd worn my hiking boots, since the soil beside the road was a wet mess, as were the mounded piles of dirt that had been scraped away.

"Marco," I called out, looking for guidance.

"Polo," Dixie responded, as I moved slowly forward. I really didn't want to try to dig through all that mud to find whatever had started all this. As I passed my truck, I paused to get a shovel out of the back. I always carry one—helpful for digging up hidden relics and troublesome graves, and in a pinch, the solid iron blade makes a helluva weapon.

"Marco," I yelled again, moving forward, toward the part of the project that looked the newest. My hunch said that since the disturbance hadn't been going on for as long as the road work, the problem occurred somewhere in the section dug up most recently.

"Polo," Dixie called back.

"Can they describe what it looks like?" I asked. I didn't know whether or not in her trance state Dixie could hear the "screaming," but neither Father Leo nor I could. That made it tough if the ghosts thought I'd stumble over whatever-it-was because it got louder.

"It isn't supposed to be here," Dixie answered. "It's a long way from home, and it's trying to find the way back."

"Animal, vegetable, or mineral?" I yelled. "Is it sentient?" I get the heebie-jeebies when inanimate objects start having thoughts and feelings. That's always cause for trouble, whether there's a haunting or a curse involved, or even just a human spirit that's so bound to the item they can't let go.

"The ghosts can't tell," Dixie replied, and I wondered how much translating she was doing between what the ghosts said and what she told me. "The newest ghosts here are from the Forties, so I've got to work with the understanding they have."

Which meant it could be some new-fangled piece of electronics being added to the roadway that was setting off a dog-whistle squeal. Although why anyone would need a self-driving car or even a detailed GPS image on Sanitarium Road was beyond me. We were nowhere many people ever needed to be, and I couldn't imagine a PennDOT project getting that fancy.

I kept moving, calling out to Dixie as I went and adjusting my progress accordingly. I'd definitely reached the newest part of the project, where nothing had been done except to clear away topsoil about two feet down from the level of the field. With a sigh, I started to scrape away at the muck on the right side of the road, intending to do the same on the left, before slogging through the sludge in the piles along the berm.

"You're cold," Dixie said, and I had to think for a moment because now that the wind and fog had died down, the temperature was kinda nice.

"You mean, I'm not close to it?" I hadn't played these kind of games since I was a kid, and even back then, they always annoyed the fuck out of me.

"Yeah," Dixie confirmed.

I walked forward, still on the right side. "Am I getting warmer?" I asked, feeling like a dweeby kid at summer camp.

"Not much."

I crossed to the other side.

"Freezing."

Well, that was something. "Now?" I asked, back on the right and a few feet ahead of where I'd been. I was in the last twenty yards of where dirt had been cleared, which meant I'd pretty damn well better get "hot" soon.

"You're warmer," Dixie replied. She looked puzzled, and I wondered if the ghosts were providing spectral charades to help us along. "Keep going."

I took a few steps, then a few more.

"You're burning up!"

The temperature in this spot seemed to dip a little, for no good reason. Maybe the trigger item had its own malicious ghost haunting it, and we were caught in the middle of an otherworldly neighborhood dispute. I looked down at the mud beneath my boots, and then to the nearest pile of dirt heaped along the side. With a sigh, I started to scrape away the soft ground around my feet, but found nothing, even after displacing several inches of sludge.

Reluctantly, I turned to the heaped dirt and started to dig. The mud flew with every shovelful, streaking my arms, spattering my chest, and soaking my shirt. I moved down the row, digging until I hit bottom and then starting on a new pile until my shovel clinked against something in the slurry.

"Red hot!" Dixie shouted.

I knelt in the mud—since it didn't seem like I could get any dirtier— and carefully dug with my hands. An oddly shaped, hand-sized chunk emerged, dark brown and carved with weird markings. Even before I'd completely cleaned it off, I realized it looked a lot like the smaller piece I had found in my hand after the battle with the kelpie.

"I've got it!" I yelled, and climbed to my feet, heading back to the truck. I unlocked the lead box and laid the fragment in beside the other piece, then closed the safe.

Dixie let out a whoop of joy. "You did it! You made the screaming stop!"

I couldn't help grinning since I'd apparently done the ghosts a real solid just by digging in the mud. "Did it help?"

Dixie's wide smile gave me my answer. "They say they can rest now, although they'd appreciate it if we could raise a marker to them—and to the children—instead of just paving over where their bones lie."

Father Leo stepped out of his salt circle and nodded. "Show us where the graves are, and we'll work with the county—or the church—to take care of it."

Dixie led us to a long rectangle toward the back of the land where the sanitarium had buried their dead. Father Leo gave them Last Rites, and Dixie told them it was all right to move on, whether or not they were Catholic. Then she led us back to where the orphans waited and had them show us exactly where their bodies lay. Once again, the combination of Last Rites and Dixie's farewell helped the unquiet spirits find their way.

"Think we can get the land reclassified, maybe made into a park?" I asked as we walked back to the truck.

"I'm pretty sure I know some people who can make that happen," Father Leo replied, and I knew he meant the Occulatum.

"I'm just glad they're at peace," Dixie said as we reached the truck. "What did you find, anyway?"

"I'm not sure," I replied, and it was the truth. "An old relic with strange marks. I need to figure out what it is, in case we ever come across something like that again."

"Well, nice working with both of you," Dixie said as if what we'd just done was the most normal thing in the world, and maybe for her, it was. "Call me the next time you need some ghosts whispered at!" With that, she got in her car and drove off.

I tossed my keys to Father Leo and went to get a tarp out of the back, then proceeded to wrap myself up like a burrito before I hitched up into the passenger seat. "You get to drive, Padre," I told him.

"You're letting me drive your truck?" he asked, with a look as if he wondered if maybe I'd gotten possessed when he wasn't looking.

"Christo," I said, just in case he decided to go full holy water on me. "Yeah, you can drive. This one time. Because I just cleaned the upholstery, and I want to wait at least a week before I have to do it again."

3

What smells like wet dog, sprays the tires on your truck, and humps your leg?

A drunk werewolf.

No, it's not a joke. Donny the defective werewolf was sitting on my front steps, shifted back to his human form but somehow still smelling like wet dog. I had a shotgun across my knees, just in case he got any ideas about my leg.

"One time, Mark." He sniffled. "I took your car through the wash, and I apologized about the leg thing."

"Good boundaries make good friendships, Donny," I told him, although to be honest, I'd always considered Donny more of a rescue pet than a human friend.

Donny had shaggy black hair and mismatched eyes—one blue and one gold—and when he shifted, he looked like a big-ass malamute or a husky instead of a wolf. Blew coat like a husky, too, and the time I let him ride in the truck—with his head hanging out and tongue lolling—it took months to get all the fur out. He's not exactly fearsome, and that's the problem.

He's too wolf-y for the humans and too person-y for the werewolves.

Father Leo got him a part-time job over at the slaughterhouse—decent pay and first pick of the trimmings and rejects—and Donny keeps an ear open for us about goings-on we might not otherwise know about.

"What's got your hackles up this time?" I sighed.

Donny let out a despairing sigh. He's a bit of a drama wolf, but then again, I know he's got it rough. The pack hasn't exactly thrown him out, but they don't make him feel welcome, either. He's conflicted about the whole wolf/human thing, so he isn't in a hurry to find a mate and have a litter of little shifter-pups if he can't feel comfortable in his own skin. Dating a human isn't really an option, no matter what you read in those sappy romance novels.

I could overlook the shedding and the peeing on my truck and the leg humping thing because who among us hasn't done some things we'd rather forget when we were drunk? And I liked Donny, in the same way I liked Mrs. Carmody's rescued Labrador Retriever. It's just that the guy really needed to find himself and get a girlfriend—preferably one who was just as much of a nerd-wolf as he was. Because coming home to find a drunk wolf puking on my back porch was getting old.

"I thought you had a date?" I asked, bringing him a cup of black coffee. I'd already pushed him into the outside shower and hosed him off, then found him a pair of jeans and an old shirt since shifters never have clothing with them when they change back, like they do on TV.

"Human…and she said she was allergic to dogs," he snuffled.

Ouch. "Have you tried a different shampoo?" I asked, at a loss for words. I care about my friends, and I'd do anything for them. And maybe Donny was more of a friend than I liked to let on. After all, I didn't have that many. But I'm not real good with words, and I'll never be Dr. Phil. So giving advice to a lovelorn werewolf was stretching my limited people skills.

"It's not the shampoo," Donny said miserably. "It's me. I don't like to hunt. I hate raw meat. It's not like I'm vegan or anything—I just think it tastes better cooked. With a baked potato and maybe sautéed mushrooms. Is that so unforgivable?"

"I agree with you on the steaks," I said. "But I'm the wrong person to ask for romantic advice."

"You've got a girlfriend," Donny sulked.

"After getting dumped by my ex-wife and a really long dry spell," I said, amazed to be having a heart-to-heart with a shit-faced shifter on my back porch. "And I'm still a little surprised about it myself."

I met Sara when I was up in the Big Woods hunting a were-squonk.

She owns a bed and breakfast up there, and she already knew about my kind of hunter. We hit it off, in the shy, awkward way two people who've been burned sidle around each other. But we'd been going out for about over six months now, and she hadn't ditched me yet, so I felt like the luckiest guy in the world.

"That's all I want," Donny moaned. "There's got to be a shifter girl who likes video games and Marvel movies and books where the monster lives happily ever after."

Donny was the sensitive soul born into a werewolf culture of jockstrap assholes. And while I'd gotten along just fine with my pack—er, family—losing four of the people I loved the most to that wendigo made me the outsider. My mother was already gone, and the attack took my father, brother, uncle, and cousin. My sister-in-law blamed me for surviving, and my aunt's family never wanted anything to do with me after that. And although I wasn't dumb enough to try to tell the cops we'd been jumped by a monster, there were plenty of people around these parts that gave me the side-eye ever since. So, I could relate, at least a little, to Donny's problems.

He blinked and made a face, and I wondered if he was getting a hangover. Without thinking, I handed him what was left of my Jack and Coke. "Here. Good for what ails you. Hair of the dog that bit ya."

Donny glared at me. "Is that supposed to be funny?" Still, he downed it in one gulp and set the glass aside.

"Is there a reason you picked my porch to sleep off a bender?" I asked. "Not that I mind, but you're a long way from home."

There weren't a lot of werewolves in these parts nowadays, not after some secret government agency came through in the 1890s and wiped out a whole pack of troublemakers. Those that survived either relocated or stayed real quiet, numbers dwindling almost to extinction. Father Leo and I almost never had to deal with a werewolf incident, and when we did, it was more to help cover up for some poor son of a bitch who accidentally shifted himself around witnesses.

"I don't like the new wolves," Donny said, pulling his legs up and resting his head on his knees. I knew for sure he was twenty-three, but at the moment, he looked like a tipsy thirteen-year-old.

"What new wolves?" I asked as I realized what he'd said.

"There's a half dozen new wolves that came in from Buffalo. They were supposed to be just visiting two of our guys. But then they decided they liked it here."

"And your Alpha is letting them stay?" This was news to me. Moe Carpelli was the local Alpha, and he was just as tough as his name and his tattoos suggested. I didn't have a beef with him—he'd always played it straight with me and Father Leo, and the pack stayed out of trouble. As swaggering jock types went, Moe wasn't too much of a dick, most of the time. But I couldn't imagine that getting a bunch of out-of-town hotshot young wolves would make him happy.

"Hell, no. But they're staying anyhow. And that's going to cause problems," Donny said.

"Which you aren't supposed to be telling me, are you? Because, hello? I'm a hunter."

"Nope. But I'm scared," Donny said. "I don't want to see my pack get hurt, even if they think I'm a mongrel. And one of them, Taylor, is pretty full of himself. Like he might even try to challenge Moe."

"Moe can handle himself, and you're not a mongrel," I replied. "And pedigrees are overrated. You don't want to get hip dysplasia, do you?"

Donny's expression was somewhere between mollified and offended, but he wasn't sniffling, so I'd done something right. "I don't think that the new wolves are going to go without a fight. Moe can't let them defy his orders. And the others don't want outsiders in our territory."

"Let me guess. Some of the women in the pack are interested in fresh meat."

Donny sighed. "Yeah. There've been some...incidents."

"What kind of incidents?" I asked because I had to know. It's my job. If it was just inside the pack, that was up to Moe. But if it involved humans —mundanes—I had to get involved.

"A couple of our guys and a couple of their guys got in a fight out at Woodcock Dam a few nights ago. Tore the place up pretty good. No one got killed, and no humans were around, but it left a mess," Donny said. "From what I heard, it was a real rumble."

Great. All I needed was *West Side Story* with werewolves.

"And it's not just the strangers coming," Donny continued. "Everyone's been on edge lately. Snappish. Like it's that time of the month, all the time." I knew he meant the full moon, when shifters went a little wild, but I had to wince at his wording.

"Why now?" I asked. "Things have been good between humans and the pack for over a hundred years. Your Alphas have kept everything locked down. Is Moe not up to the job?"

Donny shook his head. "Moe's a good guy. He's tough but fair, and people respect him—not only because he can rip your ear off. I just don't know what's gotten into everyone lately."

"Including you?" I nudged, starting to see a connection.

Donny gave a dramatic sigh. "They get feral; I get emo. Story of my life. They want to fight and tear up the town. I want to burrow under a blanket and eat ice cream and watch movies."

I'd had days like that myself, so I wasn't going to judge. I swore off all the bullshit that went with toxic masculinity when I spent months healing up from the wendigo. Not that I'm good at touchy-feely stuff, but I quit trying to pretend to be the Terminator when I'm not—and I realized that neither is anyone else. Still, if I thought I had the weight of family expectations on my shoulders, I guess I could count myself lucky I hadn't been a shifter. I would have found a whole new level of disappointing my relatives because I didn't want to eat someone.

"Okay, tell me about this feral shit," I said, pouring myself another drink from the bottle I'd brought out onto the porch.

Donny gave an uncomfortable shrug. "Just a lot more fights lately, over nothing. People seem more territorial, quicker to get pissed without a good reason. Like I said—edgy."

"Do you think Taylor or the new wolves might have done something to cause that—besides show up? You know, maybe magic of some kind?"

He frowned, thinking. "You know that I suck at being a wolf. My hearing isn't as good as the other wolves', or even most people's dogs. So I can't confirm from my own experience, but I've heard people say that lately, there's been this weird whistling sound that is driving them nuts. And I wonder if after a while, they just snap."

"Some kind of new security system gone wrong?" I speculated. "Is there new machinery at a plant somewhere?"

"Not that I heard. It seems to be worse a little north of Meadville. That's where the Buffalo wolves are holing up. But there's something else I need to tell you, Mark," Donny said. "There's talk that the new wolves want to raid the fairgrounds when the county fair starts next week. I mean, most of us keep our distance, even with good control. All those cows and pigs and horses in one place..." He started to drool and wiped his mouth with his sleeve.

"Donny, we can't let them turn the fair into an all-you-can-eat buffet," I said. This was shaping up to be my kind of thing, dammit. "People will get hurt. Pictures will be taken. A mob will come after you with torches and pitchforks—and silver bullets—and there'll be too many of them for Father Leo and me to stop."

"That's why I'm telling you," Donny repeated. "I just had to get drunk enough to get over being scared."

Shit. Donny had put himself in a bad position to do a good thing. Moe wouldn't be happy with him talking about pack business with an outsider, even if Moe had a truce with me and Father Leo. Donny's place in the pack was shaky at best, and so he couldn't trade on good will. And these new Buffalo wolves sounded like real trouble, maybe more than Moe could handle.

"Look, I've got an idea," I said. "My friends Blair and Chiara have a job opening, out here in Conneaut Lake. It pays room and board, not much money. But you'd be safe, you could cool things off with the pack while I look into the problem, and maybe Blair and Chiara could give you some good advice on finding a nice girl."

Donny's mismatched eyes widened with something like hero worship. "You'd do that?"

"I can hardly let you sleep on the porch," I replied. I knew I was going to regret my next words, but I said them anyhow. "Come around back. Get a real shower and sober up. I'll call Blair and make arrangements. You need to look decent to meet them."

"Thanks, Mark. You won't regret this. I'll do a good job. I promise." Poor guy would have been wagging his tail if he'd had one. Donny paused. "What about Demon?"

I could hear my Doberman, Demon, whining behind the door. If he'd thought Donny was a real threat, he'd have been snarling and barking like the guard dog he was in his dreams. The truth was, Demon was a pushover who just looked like a hellhound, and I was pretty sure he smelled dog on Donny and wanted to come out to play.

"He thinks you're here to romp with him," I said with a sigh. "Scratch him behind the ears, then duck into the bathroom, and I'll corral him.

Make sure you close the door, or he'll be in the tub with you. He likes baths."

I got Donny settled in the bathroom and warned him to clean the fur out of the drain when he was finished. I made sure Demon was happily distracted with a cow bone in the kitchen. Then I called Blair. "Hey, are you still thinking about getting a guard dog for the hardware store?"

"Why? Someone you know have puppies?" Blair asked. I could hear Chiara chuckle in the background. They make a ridiculously cute couple. Blair's ex-military, and she inherited the family business, Hamilton Hardware, in downtown Conneaut Lake. Chiara's her wife, and she runs the coffee shop/bookstore next door, plus doing some web design—and hunter research—on the side.

"Better than that. Can I bring him over to meet you?"

"You're taking in strays, Mark?"

Considering that she and Chiara had taken me in when I was in a bad place, who was I not to return the favor? "Something like that. He just got a bath, so he'll be nice and fluffy," I promised.

"Ohh, Chiara loves puppies," Blair teased. "She'll want to let him sleep on the bed."

"Um, you might want to hold off on that until you meet him," I said. "He's kinda big."

Donny was quiet as he drove with me to Conneaut Lake in the morning. I filled him in a bit about Blair and Chiara, omitting things he didn't need to know, like the secret back room at the hardware store that sells supplies for supernatural hunters, and the hacking help Chiara provides for the Occulatum. But there was plenty I could tell him, and I hoped they hit it off because I thought it would be good for both sides.

"So they need a night watchman?" Donny asked. "I'm not the most fearsome guy, Mark."

"They need a security guard, not a bouncer," I assured him. "Just being there will make it less likely anyone will break in. And if Chiara likes you, she'll save you the day-olds from the bakery."

"Her family runs that big Italian restaurant and bakery, right?" Donny was already salivating. "Oh my god. I love that place."

"You've been there?" I asked.

His cheeks colored. "I've raided their dumpster. It's the best in the area."

And that was Donny in a nutshell. He didn't want to go run down a deer in the forest with the pack and howl at the moon. He was happy with dumpster diving for primo manicotti and probably washed down his treasure with cheap red wine. Personally, I thought pasta sounded better than raw venison, but then again, I'm not supposed to be a fearsome werewolf.

"Um, maybe don't mention *how* you got the food when you meet Chiara," I suggested. "But she and Blair are cool. You'll like them. And the coffee shop and bookstore draw a pretty nice crowd."

"So why do they need extra security?" Donny asked. "Don't they have an electronic system?"

I sighed. "Yeah, but they've had a few problems lately. Blair and Chiara are *together*. As in, married. Now, most folks in town don't give a damn about them because they've grown up in Conneaut Lake and everyone knows the family. So even if they aren't open-minded about strangers, they make an exception." People are weird. They believe things unless they don't want to, and then they twist themselves into knots pretending to be logical.

"But someone does mind," Donny supplied, with a sadness in his tone that told me he had experience being bullied himself.

"Yeah. There've been hang-up calls, some vandalism, and other shit," I said, and just thinking about someone picking on my friends made me hot under the collar. "Cops haven't caught anyone—and they actually are trying." I knew this because I grew up with half of the force and had a few buddies who kept me informed behind the scenes. "But Blair and Chiara are taking it seriously, hence the extra security."

"Wouldn't they do better with some big bruiser who looks intimidating?" Donny asked.

I cleared my throat. "Um...they want a guard dog."

Donny stared at me. "They want a *dog*?"

"Room and board, Donny, plus pay. You can stay in town. It's a manly job, so Moe will stay off your back. And I am positive Blair and Chiara can help with your other...problem."

Donny sighed. "All right. Geez, this is embarrassing. But beggars can't be choosers." This from the wolf who puked on my porch last night.

We parked near the hardware store, and Donny followed me inside. Blair was finishing up with a customer and grinned when she saw me.

"Mark! Great to see you! Who's your friend?" Her eyes went big. "Oh, is he the guy with the puppy?" She looked behind us as if expecting to see a doggo on a leash.

"Um, it's complicated," I said quietly. "Do you think you could get someone to cover the register for a while, and have Chiara meet us in the bookstore back room?"

Blair gave me a look but nodded. She went to call someone up front, and I motioned for Donny to follow me through the doorway in the wall that led to the bookstore. Crystal Dreams had quickly become a local social hub, and between the excellent coffee, eclectic selection of books, and welcoming vibe, business was booming.

I led Donny to the back room, where all kinds of groups held meetings. The Tuesday night Bunko club was actually a local coven, and the Cards Against Humanities Friday and Saturday night gathering was open to all teens but drew a lot of LGBTQA kids, as well as anyone else who didn't fit the football-and-flannel mainstream.

We waited a few minutes in silence, and then Blair entered, followed by Chiara. Blair is tall and athletic. Chiara is pretty and petite, but don't let that fool you—she's a spitfire, and while Blair has military training, Chiara's family is mobbed up, and her grandma has the evil eye. They're a force to be reckoned with, and two of my very best friends.

"I don't get it. Where's the dog?" Chiara asked, looking like a disappointed little girl.

I cleared my throat. "About that. I brought you a twofer." Donny squirmed, and the two women looked at me like I'd lost my mind. "What if you could have a guard dog that could also work the security system and if necessary, call the authorities? Wouldn't that be awesome?"

"I'm a shifter," Donny blurted. "And I need a job."

Blair and Chiara exchanged a look. I could see they weren't quite sold yet. "Donny—how about showing them your other half?" I suggested. Donny blushed, but he got up and walked behind the screen that hides the little kitchenette. I heard a few grunts, and then a large sled dog trotted out, looking shy and adorable.

I knew the moment I saw Chiara's face this was a done deal. "Oh my god, you are so sweet!" she crooned, dropping to her knees and scratching Donny behind the ears. "Can he bark and scare off intruders?"

Donny howled, and then demonstrated a remarkably fearsome bark. He sat down, and I swear he smiled.

"Room and board, plus an hourly wage," I negotiated. "He just needs a nice dog bed. Donny works several days a week over at the slaughter-house, but he can be here every night, and you just leave him a burger and a bowl of water."

Chiara turned her own version of puppy dog eyes on Blair, who looked skyward. "Yes, you can keep him." She glared at me. "We don't have to get him neutered, do we?"

Donny yelped and backed away. "Um, that's not part of the deal," I said quickly. "In fact, I was hoping you might be able to help in the romance department."

Chiara stood up as Donny headed back to change. "You mean, 'Queer Eye for the Shifter Guy'?"

"Something like that," I said. "He's kinda non-traditional, and he needs someone who isn't all Team Jacob."

Blair and Chiara exchanged a look as Donny rejoined us, changed back to human form. "Oh yeah, I think we can help," Chiara said. "I've got just the girl in mind. Comes over from Linesville, so she's not part of the local pack. Can't stand all the posturing and peeing on trees. Drives in for the card game nights." She looked Donny over from head to toe, taking in his uninspired wardrobe. "Um, yeah. First, we go shopping." She sniffed. "And change your shampoo. You smell like you came from the groomer."

N ow that I'd taken care of Donny's pack problems and love life, and gotten Blair and Chiara's security issue handled, I needed to deal with rogue werewolves. I called my friend Simon Kincaide, a mythology and lore guy, to get caught up on wolf-y stuff, and then made arrange-ments to meet Father Leo for lunch. It occurred to me that today was pretty typical of my social life, and while I'm sure there's some kind of insight to take from that, I don't know what it might be.

I met the padre at the Original Best Lakeview Diner. It's a locals' place, with good food and decent prices as well as a view of the lake. Sandy, the owner's wife, brought out coffee. She and I went to school together, so she knows where all the bodies are buried, metaphorically speaking.

"Haven't seen you two in here for a while," Sandy said as she set down two steaming cups. "I hope you're staying out of trouble?"

"Always," Father Leo said, with an innocent look that wasn't fooling anyone.

Sandy smirked. "Yeah, I'm sure. Just don't get caught unless you've got enough donuts to pay off the cops," she added with a laugh. Little did she know how many times we'd greased the wheels of justice with pastries from Chiara's parents' shop.

She left, and Father Leo took a sip of his coffee before getting down to the issue at hand. "So...werewolves."

"Yep. We've got a problem we aren't supposed to know about, a touchy pack Alpha who needs help and also has to save face, and a county fair that's going to turn into wholesale slaughter if we don't do something about it." That summed it all up. We were fucked.

Father Leo drummed his fingers on the table. "I think I know how to approach this."

My head came up. "You do?" We needed to have someone on our side because I didn't like the odds of the two of us between two warring werewolf gangs.

"Moe Carpelli's grandmother, Isabella, goes to Mass at my church," Father Leo said with a smile. "Isabella is a very pious woman, and she rules the family with an iron fist. Moe's her favorite grandson. If she brings him to the table, he'll stay, and he'll listen."

"What are you going to propose? Moe can't look like he called us in because he can't handle the threat."

Father Leo shook his head. "I don't think Moe wants a war. And his pack has been in the area for a long time. They have a lot to lose if things go wrong at the fair. So, I'm going to suggest that he put his resources on security detail at the fairgrounds and let us take out the trash."

I nodded. "Okay. I can go for that. And Mama Isabella will like that it keeps Moe out of the fight while letting him save face."

"Exactly."

"Can we handle six rowdy weres? After all, we're coming between them and the feast of the century."

"We can if we cheat," Father Leo replied with a gleam in his eye. "And that's exactly what we're gonna do."

The Crawford County fairgrounds take up a large corner of a rural crossroads. It's a pretty big deal in these parts, with a midway, tractor pulls, drag races, a concert featuring famous country singers, the local beauty pageant, and plenty of displays, attractions, rides, 4-H exhibits and of course, blue-ribbon livestock. Just going to the fair makes me nostalgic for the grilled Italian sausage sandwiches, and the thirty-five flavors of homemade pies served up by the women's auxiliary. Fair Week might sound hokey, but it's much-anticipated in these parts, and I'll admit that my inner ten-year-old is front and center when I enter the gates.

Unfortunately, Father Leo and I weren't heading into the fair. We were across the street at an abandoned orchard where Moe let on the trouble-makers were holed up. The corner lot had a faded blue pole barn toward the front of the property and hundreds of long-neglected apple trees and a pond farther in. Behind that were acres of woods, plenty of room to hide and hunt despite houses and farms lining nearby roads. A well-behaved pack could run comfortably in that land for a long time if they were careful and didn't overhunt the deer or bother the neighbors. Hell, with the deer overpopulation Pennsylvania has, they'd be doing a public service.

Unfortunately, these wolves were assholes, and we needed to supply a little extreme dog training.

Hunting weres isn't like going after vengeful ghosts or other creatures. Werewolves are smart, and they had a real advantage, being able to change between their wolf and human forms. They also aren't restricted to a particular time of day or tied to a location, like other cryptids and spirits. If you pass them on the street, you'd probably never figure them for what they are. That complicates things for monster hunters because unless we catch them mid-shift, it's hard to prove we haven't just whacked a human. Cops get testy about those kinds of things.

Fortunately, I knew the property pretty well. I was friends with the owner's kid growing up, and we'd had plenty of hot dog roasts and sneaked lots of six packs down the lane. Not much had changed, although everything looked a bit sadder and unloved. The grass and weeds grew knee-high, many of the trees were blighted, and the pond was choked with cattails. But the old deer hunting tree stand was still in place, a rickety sniper's roost for Father Leo with a rifle full of tranquilizer darts. Just for good measure, I had a stun gun and a Glock full of silver bullets I hoped I didn't need to use.

As for the rest, I intended to improvise. We knew Taylor and the other Buffalo wolves were in the woods somewhere since the shabby squatters' camp of tents and gear was currently deserted. And we had no idea whether or not they were watching. That limited the set-up we could do, although I had some tricks they weren't going to be expecting.

I casually walked a line just inside Father Leo's range, dropping some homemade "surprise packages" into the tall grass as I went. When I finished, I turned toward the woods and decided it was time to play my role—bait.

"We know you're out there, Buffalo Wild Wolves," I yelled to the tree line. "And we know all about the plan to go full carnivore on the fairgrounds. Give yourselves up now, and you'll just be sent home with your tails between your legs. We don't want to have to do this the hard way."

I was several feet closer to the trees than where I'd dropped my surprises in the grass. The distance was carefully calculated, or at least I hoped it was. I'm no Usain Bolt. But I can put on a burst of speed when I have to, and I was betting on being able to get behind my defenses before the wolves could close the distance from the trees.

Then again, I'm terrible at betting, so I hoped I wasn't going to get chomped in the ass.

I looked back to the trees and saw six big biker-type guys all standing at the edge of the woods. "You're trespassing," I yelled at them. "The local pack disavows you. We're Animal Control, and we've come to relocate you."

I fully intended to poke the bear, or in this case, the wolf. From what we'd gathered, both Moe and Donny saw these rogues as short-fused and full of themselves, so the idea that a human thought he was going to take them out single-handedly was guaranteed to set them off. And as they all started running for me, still in their two-legged form, I knew we'd figured right.

Shit. I needed to run.

I wanted to get them into Father Leo's range, but not too far beyond my surprises. Since I needed to give them time to close the gap, I did my little end zone dance, shook my booty, and taunted them mercilessly.

"Is that all you've got? You're looking a bit mangy there," I yelled. "Talk about a bunch of obedience school dropouts!"

I backpedaled a bit more and made sure the remote control was in my pocket. Then I reached my left hand into the other pocket and gripped my stun gun, just in case.

Six pissed-off werewolves crossed the finish line, and I pressed the button. My customized IEDs popped open and sent their payload flying, probe darts that hit their targets and sent jolts of electricity surging through the wolves. Taylor screamed in anger, but he went down on his knees, jerking and twitching, just like the others.

I backed the hell up, out of range, and Father Leo took aim. Six shots, six tranq darts, and six wolves went nighty-night.

Father Leo scrambled down from the tree, reloading. I pulled out my stun gun, made sure my Glock was secure in my waistband and went to the bag I'd stashed by the tree, where twelve sets of silver coated handcuffs were waiting.

"Cover me," I said, as I started down the row of sedated wolves. I'd been tranqed in my life, and I'd been Tasered, and neither was fun to wake up from. The sedative in the darts would keep a human out for hours, but weres have a faster metabolism, and I didn't want anyone waking up while I was still in the process of restraining them.

I moved quickly, with Father Leo keeping a clear line of sight, rifle pointed. As I went, I pulled out the stun darts, but I had my Taser in case any of the rogue wolves started to stir. When they were all cuffed, I pulled out six black hoods, and once the prisoners were all Gitmo'd, I left Father Leo on guard while I got the truck.

"Shit, they're heavy," I muttered as we hefted the unconscious men into the bed of the truck. We laid them all in the back, closed the cover over them to keep the cops from getting nosy, and then drove off to the rendezvous point. That was going to get unpleasant very quickly in the sun, not only for warmth but because the stun guns had caused at least a couple of the men to piss themselves. From the smell of it, one of them lost his shit as well.

"Think they'll fall for it?" I asked as I drove.

"I don't get the feeling they're deep thinkers," Father Leo observed. "And maybe we'll get some answers while we're at it."

Father Leo had a key to an abandoned clapboard church out past

Blooming Valley. His contact from the Occulatum was going to meet us there and take Taylor and his wolves up to Buffalo, but we wanted to make sure they didn't come back, so the padre and I were going to put on a little performance, and possibly ferret out intel at the same time.

By this time, it was dusk and the streets around the old church were empty. The light by the back door had burned out long ago, so we could get the tranqed men inside without having the local cops in the way. Father Leo supplied our costumes, simple black cassocks, and sashes with eye holes cut out that wrapped around our faces, just in case they managed to see us. We also had his rifle and my stun gun close at hand, although the silver cuffs weren't going to let these puppies go anywhere.

They woke up cursing and grunting, and their language grew worse when they realized they were bound and hooded. The warm, closed-up church quickly took on a sour, bathroom smell of sweat, piss, and shit.

"You don't belong here," Father Leo said in a deep, authoritative tone invested with the full authority of the Holy Roman Catholic Church. "You came to this pack without permission and intended to cause panic. Your actions would have exposed the pack to humans and caused bodily harm to humans and shifters. You have already been judged and found guilty, and your punishment will be meted out."

I expected Taylor or the other wolves to lash out, throw a few "fuck yous" our way, or mouth off. Then I realized that two of the guys were shaking, one was outright sobbing, and Taylor, lead bad-ass, was sitting up on his knees rigidly, as if he expected us to cap him from behind.

"Why did you come here?" I asked, making my voice grave and rough.

They were silent at first, and then Taylor spoke up. "It's my fault," he said. "I ran into Moe at a pack conclave, and he was so full of himself, thought he was better than everyone. So we wanted to give him a bit of trouble, bring him down a few pegs. And when I found that thing, I thought we had the perfect way to do it."

Father Leo and I exchanged a glance. "Thing?" I asked.

Taylor managed to convey annoyance even hooded. "I don't know what it is. I found it in the woods. It looks like a broken piece off a thick old pot, and it's got weird marks on it. I brought it home with me. My hearing's for shit, so it didn't bother me, but everyone else said it sounded like one of those dog whistles, but worse. Really pissed people off. So we got this idea that maybe we'd come down here and yank Moe's chain, get his wolves riled up, make trouble and let it all get blamed on him, then bug out."

"Why didn't the shard affect your wolves?" I asked.

"We put wax in our ears, just like in that story they made us read in high school English class," he replied, disdainful even in his circumstances.

"Where is the shard now?" I hadn't liked Taylor from Donny's description, and now that the asshole had spilled his guts, I liked him even less.

"Back in the camp," Taylor replied. "Look, this was all my idea. I know I fucked up big-time. But don't hurt them. I'm the one you want. I started this, and I had the hard-on about teaching Moe a lesson. Let them go, and you can take me wherever I have to go."

Taylor's little speech surprised me. I had figured him for the type that would try to broker a deal for himself and fuck the others over. Maybe after our little rendition scare was over, he might straighten up and stay out of trouble, although I suspected that becoming a "respectable citizen" was asking a bit much.

The door opened, and a man I didn't know entered. I hoped he was Father Leo's Occulatum contact because otherwise, he'd walked in on a scene out of a bad horror movie. It creeped me out that he didn't seem fazed in the least.

"Take them," Father Leo said, with the weight of judge, jury, and executioner in his voice. "We've gotten all we can from them."

The cuffed wolves started to beg and plead, but we had what we needed. I figured that they'd never dare set foot in this area again. The Occulatum guy had a panel van waiting, and for a moment, I was afraid we really were turning Taylor and his screw-ups over to a black site.

Father Leo caught my eye and shook his head, then grinned, his way of telling me that it was all still security theater. When the six sorry wolves had been loaded into the back and the door locked behind them, the driver came up to greet us. "Leo," he said, shaking the priest's hand. "And you must be Mark. I've heard stories."

I shook his hand, but groaned internally, wondering what tales had carried. "I'm sure they weren't all true, regardless," I replied. I also noticed the contact didn't offer his name in return.

"What's the plan?" Leo asked, and I figured it was as much for my benefit as his since he tries to keep the Occulatum's dealings with us transparent. No small effort given the Church's vast experience with obfuscation.

"I'll drive them home the long way, let them sweat," he said with a shrug. "We've contacted Taylor's home Alpha, who is quite unhappy with their little road trip. They'll be delivered directly to him and subject to whatever discipline he decides to mete out. I don't think we'll see them back here, if that's what you're worried about."

We watched him drive away and took off our costumes. Other than a lingering potty odor, there was nothing in the old church to show we'd ever been there. I stared after the panel van, and my thoughts must have been clear in my expression because Father Leo laid a hand on my arm.

"What happens now is pack business, out of our hands," he reminded me. "It would have been far worse if they'd gone through with the plan at the fairgrounds. People would have died, the shifters would have been all over the news, and if you think the packs and the Church are tough, you really wouldn't want the Feds involved."

I sighed, knowing he was right. "Let's get out of here," I said. "I want to go back to the pond and check out their camp. Moe's group won't get any peace until we find that shard and lock it up."

We drove back, with Father Leo looking out the window. "What do you think it is? The shard, I mean."

"Don't know, but if it looks like the other two pieces I've turned up, whatever it is causes trouble." I told him about the strange item from the kelpie attack and how it matched the relic I'd found near the sanitarium. "I can't explain where they came from or what they do, but locking them up in lead seems to do the trick."

"Take pictures," Father Leo instructed as we got back in the truck. "See if Simon or Chiara can make anything of those symbols. There's got to be something behind this, and until we figure out who—or what—made those things, we're bound to keep running into trouble."

4

I knew it was bad, DEFCON ONE bad, apocalypse, world-ending bad, for Amy to call me.

Amy had been married to my brother, Sean. When Sean died in the wendigo attack, I wanted to die with him, but the Fate-bitch had other plans. Amy never forgave me for living when Sean died. She and I used to be close, but her affection turned to venom in her grief, and time had not blunted the intensity.

Only one thing could make Amy call me. Something had happened to Nikki, my niece, something the regular police couldn't handle. Shit.

"Hi, Amy," I greeted her, tensing for the claws to come out.

"Mark. It's Nikki. She's disappeared, and I think it's your kind of thing," Amy said in a strangled voice.

Considering Amy threw me out of Nikki's wedding not long ago, I hadn't expected to ever hear from her again, although Nikki never stopped loving her "Uncle Mark." Nikki had me around her little finger from the time she was born, and she and I kept in touch even after what happened in the Big Woods.

Amy not only didn't forgive me for surviving; she made it very clear that monster hunting was "nonsense" and "insane." So for her to swallow her pride and call me for help with a supernatural threat was huge, and only our shared love for Nikki could bridge that chasm.

"Tell me," I said, feeling my chest tighten at the thought of Nikki in harm's way.

"That's just it," Amy admitted. "I don't know what happened. But she's gone, and her friend says she vanished into thin air."

She sounded like her legendary control was slipping. I knew how much she adored Sean, how gutted she was over his death, but she hadn't shed a tear at the funeral even though I could see how grief tore her apart. Now, Amy's roughened voice and stuffy nose told me she'd been sobbing, and that terrified me like nothing else could.

"Where's her husband?" Nikki had invited me to the wedding reception in defiance of her mother, and I'd met Trey. He seemed nice, if a bit gobsmacked. But when a wife went missing, the logical first step was to look askance at the husband.

"His father's in the hospital," Amy said. "Trey went back to Albany to take care of his mom and sister and help out. Nikki had to work, but a friend up near Cambridge Springs invited her up for a girl's night out sort of thing. Nikki was going to stay over and drive back in for work since she had the morning off. But she didn't show up."

I don't have kids of my own. Lara and I didn't make it that far. I'm only thirty-six, and there's still time, I guess, to become a father, but I don't see it in the cards. So I take my duties as an uncle very seriously, and Nikki is very much my daughter-of-the-heart. Thinking about something happening to her simultaneously spiked my fury and froze my chest.

"When you say she 'disappeared,' do you mean that someone—or something—took her?"

Amy remained silent, and I figured she was biting her tongue. "Her friend Kerri said that Nikki walked into the Riverside Hotel and didn't come out."

Now it was my turn to find the right words. "That's not possible. The Riverside burned to the ground."

"Don't you think I know that?" Amy's voice grew shrill. She paused. "Sorry. Sorry. That's why I called you. Because it doesn't make any sense. I know the hotel is gone. But Kerri stuck to her story with the cops, with me, even with her friends. I thought maybe they had gotten drunk and done something stupid and she was afraid to tell anyone about it. But she insists she's telling the truth."

I rubbed a hand over my eyes. "Okay. Where's Kerri now?"

Amy gave me Kerri's phone number and street address. "Tell her I'm coming," I said. "Ask her to meet me in the parking lot for the Riverside in an hour." That would be enough time for me to get from my place up to Cambridge Springs and nose around a bit on my own.

"I'm coming, too."

"I think it would be best if you didn't," I said as nicely as I could, but as glad as I was that Amy had called me, having her on site would be a big problem.

"She's my daughter," Amy snapped.

"And that's why I need to give Kerri some distance so she can feel comfortable talking to me," I replied in the voice I use to talk down vicious creatures. "She might not talk freely in front of you."

I heard Amy huff, and I knew she'd be red in the face by this point. To my surprise, after a moment of silence, she conceded. "All right. But I want a full report. You're working for me."

"No, I'm working for Nikki," I corrected. "And I'm not 'working.' I'm doing this because I love her. So we do this my way." I couldn't threaten not to do it at all if Amy wouldn't back off, but I could vow to do it without her, and I would if Amy insisted on interfering.

"I hate you," Amy muttered. "But—I love Nikki. Get her back for me, Mark. Whatever it takes. You owe me." Her voice had turned cold and bitter, and once again, I was tried and found guilty for living through something I never wanted to survive.

I bit my tongue until I tasted blood, promising for Sean's sake not to retaliate. "Gotta go," I said. "I'll be in touch."

The drive from Atlantic to Cambridge Springs seemed to take forever. I couldn't help remembering a time when Sean and Amy and I were close, all the picnics and cookouts and holidays. Amy had been fun and lively, a dynamo for sure but not malicious. Sean's eyes lit up every time he saw her. And when Nikki came along, everything seemed perfect. I adored her from the first time I saw her in the hospital nursery, and it was mutual. Sean's death broke something in Amy that didn't heal, but that was as much choice as chance, and up to Amy to deal with.

Nikki was in trouble, and she'd be counting on me to come get her. I wasn't going to let her down.

Once upon a time, a hundred years or so ago, the Riverside Hotel was a big deal. The huge Victorian-era hotel was a favorite of the rich and famous from as far away as New York City, Pittsburgh, and Philadelphia for its famed mineral springs baths and lush golf courses, as well as fine cuisine.

Over the years, new resorts wooed away the glitterati, and the Riverside's fortunes declined. The huge boardwalk that led from the main building to the bathhouse fell into disrepair. Locals remembered it slowly disintegrating until nothing remained except the stone supports. The hotel itself went on about its business, offering high tea and evening dinner theater and hosting weddings and events until, like many of the Gilded Age resorts, fire claimed it.

The blaze had been all over local news. The huge old building had gone up like tinder and, when the smoke cleared, all that was left were the gardens—still remarkably untouched—and a blackened shell. Once the fire department and insurance investigators finished their work, the ruins were razed, leaving nothing but an empty lot and plenty of memories.

I got to Cambridge Springs with time to spare, so I stopped in a local diner not far from the old hotel site. From the hometown feel of the place, I knew the coffee would be good and the pie awesome, but it really wasn't about the food. When the server came back to refill my coffee, I saw my chance.

"Such a shame about the Riverside, isn't it?" I asked off-handedly.

Darcey, the server, made a noncommittal sound. "Maybe."

I tried to look surprised. "Not a fan?"

She shrugged and glanced over her shoulder. "It was haunted," she whispered. "I worked there in high school. Creepy place when everyone goes home."

"Did anyone ever get hurt by the ghosts?"

Darcey gave me a look like she wasn't quite sure whether or not I was making fun of her, then the desire to gossip won out. "Sometimes. They didn't want us to say anything because it would be bad for business. Overnight guests saw people who weren't really there, dressed up in old-fashioned clothing. Sometimes, the ghosts scared guests off, or pushed people on the stairs, or spilled tea."

"So it was a good thing when the place burned down?"

Darcey's expression told me there was more to the story. "Ever since the Riverside burned, once they cleared it all away, there've been people who said they saw it, big as life, under the full moon at midnight. Then it goes away until the next moon."

A chill went down my spine. "Has anyone tried to go into the hotel, when it reappears?"

"A few. But nobody came back out."

Shit.

Darcey got called away, leaving me with my cold cup of coffee and a half-eaten piece of pie. I glanced at the time and realized I was due to meet Kerri. But if Darcey's story was true, then I had a good idea of what happened to Nikki, but no plan—yet—for how to bring her back.

I walked back to the parking lot in front of the lawn that used to be the Riverside Hotel. I knew people who had their prom or wedding reception at the old Victorian, and I remembered my mom and my aunts going to the dinner theater for a night out. I vaguely recalled seeing the remnants of the old boardwalk when I was a kid, but even then, it had been blocked off and unsafe. At the end of the pylons, the boarded-up bathhouse was the last remnant of the hotel's former glory.

"Are you Mark?"

I turned and saw a woman I guessed to be Kerri. She had dark hair in a ponytail and a gymnast's build. Without makeup, she looked younger than her mid-twenties, which I knew she had to be since she and Nikki were the same age.

"Kerri?"

She nodded and looked like she was going to tear up again. "I'm so, so sorry," she said, lower lip quivering. "It was all supposed to be just a dumb prank."

"Tell me." I wanted her to trust me, so I was trying not to look threatening. At the same time, that "dumb prank" put my niece in danger, so I struggled to keep my temper in check. I settled for a wide-legged stance with my hands in my pockets.

Kerri sniffed back tears and squeezed her eyes shut. "So we were at my apartment, watching scary movies and drinking wine. Me and Nikki and Allison. The movies were kinda lame, so we started telling ghost stories, the kind you hear around a campfire." She ran a hand over her mouth nervously.

"You—or someone—told the story about the Riverside coming back, and it was a full moon," I said, already knowing where this was going.

Kerri nodded. "It was just a stupid story. But then Allison wanted to go and see if it was true. I live a couple of blocks away, so we walked over. And there it was."

Dammit, Nikki knew better. She didn't know much about my sort-of-hidden life hunting monsters, but whether her mother believed in it or not, she knew the story about how a wendigo killed her dad, uncle, cousin, and grandpa. She knows Amy thinks I'm nuts for believing in monsters. So whatever she did, she should have known better.

Famous last words.

"Then what happened?"

Kerri took a deep breath. "Allison wanted to go inside. She said she just wanted to grab something to bring out with her, a trophy, to prove it was real. Nikki told her not to. They argued. Allison went anyway."

"And Nikki went after her," I said, seeing now how it all played out. Nikki didn't go in because she didn't take the risk seriously; she went because Allison didn't. Nikki believed the threat was real. That sounded like my girl.

"So what were you doing while all this was going on?" I couldn't help asking.

"I was afraid someone would call the cops on us," Kerri admitted. "I was the lookout. I didn't think Allison would do it. But then she did, and we waited half an hour, but she didn't come out. She said she was just going inside the door to grab whatever was handy and come right back, but she didn't. So Nikki made me swear to stay outside, no matter what happened, so that if she wasn't back soon with Allison, someone would call you."

"Nikki wanted you to call me?"

Kerri nodded. "Except she didn't tell me your number, and so I called her mom. I didn't realize—"

"Yeah. I know." Nikki picked a helluva time to follow in dear old Uncle Mark's footsteps.

"Can you find them? Can you bring them back?" Kerri looked like she was going to cry again.

"Okay," I said, making up my mind. "Tell me the rest of the story. How long does the hotel stay visible?"

"It appears at midnight and vanishes by three in the morning," Kerri said. "I'm not sure everyone can see it because wouldn't there be reporters here if they could? And they say it only happens on the three nights of the full moon."

Fuck. Last night was the second night. I needed to get Nikki and her friend out tonight or wait a month for another chance.

"So we're going to come back here at midnight," I said. "And I'm going to go get Nikki and Allison." A thought occurred to me. "The Riverside didn't burn down long ago. When did the ghost hotel start showing up? Right away? Or a bit later?"

Kerri thought about it for a few moments. "Not right away, or at least, I didn't hear about it until recently, maybe two or three months."

"What happened around here in those two or three months?" I asked, feeling the prickle of suspicion in the back of my mind.

"Not much. Mostly, people fighting about what to do with the property," Kerri said. "I hear arguments about it all the time. They want to build a new hotel, or apartments, or a park. It seems like it's all anyone talks about."

"Has there been any construction on the grounds? Any roadwork? Hell, have they dug up the water main recently?"

Kerri gave me a funny look. "Yeah. It's summer. All that stuff goes on."

"Nearby? I mean, really close to where the hotel used to be?"

"One of the old water pipes that used to go to the Riverside broke a few months ago and flooded the road. I heard the pipe was iron, and it just rusted through. Made a big mess. They had to close the road for a while and dig everything up."

Bingo. By this point, I was pretty sure that somewhere around that busted pipe I'd find a shard with strange markings, but I didn't dare go looking until Nikki and Allison were safe. If I disturbed the shard, it might break the cycle, and then Nikki and Allison would be trapped. The hotel's reappearance just after the excavation of the old water main was too much of a coincidence, and I felt certain that the repair work had unearthed another piece of whatever-it-was and activated its power. Once the girls were safe, I'd make sure the hotel never lured anyone else inside, but for now, I needed it right where it was, for just one more night.

After securing Kerri's promise to be ready for me to pick her up at her apartment at eleven, I started making plans. My gear bag was in the back of the truck, and the less conventional weapons were secured in a hidden compartment. I tallied up what else I'd need and headed for the store. On my way, I called Dixie and Father Leo and told them what we were up against. Both of them promised to meet me by eleven thirty in the old hotel parking lot.

When the time came, I wondered whether Kerri would show, but she met me at the door, her mouth a grim, resolute line. She dressed all in black, a nice ninja touch, like a brunette Buffy. At the hotel parking lot, I turned off the headlights on my truck because we didn't need to have the cops interrupting us. I always assume that if anything can go wrong, it will.

We got to the parking lot at 11:45, and there was no sign of the Riverside. Father Leo and Dixie were waiting for us, so Kerri and I walked over. I could see Kerri trying to figure out why a priest and a lady who looked like she should be running a book club were part of a secret ghost hunter rendezvous.

"This is Kerri," I said, intentionally not introducing the others because the less Kerri knew, the less trouble she could get into. "She was here when the other two went missing, and I figured it would be best if she was here for what we do tonight."

"How does this work?" Father Leo asked, gesturing toward the empty lawn. I looked to Kerri, who shook her head.

"Beats me. It was already here when we came over from my apartment," she said.

The next few minutes seemed to last forever. I was puking terrified that the old hotel wouldn't materialize and that Nikki and Allison would be trapped inside it forever.

The timer on my phone went off, right at midnight.

Between one breath and the next, the Riverside Hotel came back from the dead.

I stared at the ghostly hotel, stretching up four stories with a mansard roof tower and a wide, covered porch, painted in shades of gray as it had been before the fire. The grand front steps welcomed travelers, and the main doors stood ajar. Gaslight flickered in the windows, not the cold electric light of recent times. Off to my left, the long-demolished boardwalk led off to the bathhouse. I wondered whether the hotel itself was the ghost or if there were spirits trapped inside from the century-plus of its existence, and I sincerely hoped that the apparitions didn't include two new residents.

"I spoke to a few friends," Father Leo said. "As long as we don't light a bonfire or set off fireworks, the local cops aren't going to come looking." He glared at me when he mentioned the fireworks, and I rolled my eyes. Geez, it wasn't like I did it all the time. Once. Okay, maybe twice, but it had all been part of the hunt.

"Good," I said, rubbing my hands together. "Very good." I knew what had to be done, and I was the guy to do it, but that didn't mean I wasn't afraid. I was afraid of being too late to save the girls, afraid of letting Amy down—yet again. And, yes, afraid of going in a hotel that didn't exist anymore.

I poured a big salt circle around Kerri, Dixie, and Father Leo, giving them plenty of elbow room. Then I handed Kerri a piece of iron pipe. "Ghosts don't like salt or iron," I explained. "Stay inside the circle, no matter what happens. You're safe inside the circle. If the circle gets broken and something comes after you, hit it with the pipe."

Kerri looked skeptical—like a sane person would—but she just nodded and said nothing.

I left the salt from my bag inside the circle, along with my knives and rebar. Father Leo gave me a look. "I'm not going to take the chance of dispelling it by trying to carry that stuff inside."

"Then how are you going to protect yourself?" he asked quietly.

I shrugged. "Dunno. Maybe I won't have to. We don't know if the hotel is luring people in or trying to keep them. I'll make it up as I go."

Father Leo clapped a hand on my shoulder. He's quietly accused me of attempting suicide-by-monster more than once. I know he worries, and that's one of the things that keeps me here.

"It's Nikki inside," I said to him. "We're all going to come back out, together."

I hefted my bag, with its specially-selected contents, and glared at the entrance. "It's showtime."

The ghostly gray hotel welcomed me with its open door and flickering gaslight, but the temperature dropped as I walked closer, and the air felt cool and clammy, like the inside of a tomb. When I lifted my foot to go up the steps, I braced myself to fall, but the stairs held, and I began to climb.

With every step, the Riverside grew more solid, its outline sharper and better defined. A glance over my shoulder showed me swirling mist that gradually hid the parking lot and the anxious figures waiting for my return. I'd spent some of the time between this morning and now reading up on legendary journeys to the underworld, enough to remind me to not eat any tasty treats and watch out for three-headed dogs.

But on the off chance that some of the stories had a glimmer of truth, I picked up a couple of packs of pomegranate seeds at the grocery store. Those suckers are expensive, so I figured they'd better be good for helping me find my way back from the realm of the dead because they were far too pricey to sprinkle on breakfast cereal. Every few steps, I dropped one of the seeds, leaving a trail like drops of blood between me and the way home.

By the time I reached the hotel's front doors, everything around me seemed solid and real, even if the temperature felt more like February than August. I shivered, some from the cold, and the rest from dread and fear. I wasn't afraid for myself. I'd been ready to die that day back in the Big Woods with the wendigo, and sometimes, it felt like everything since then had been a half-life of sorts. But I was frightened for Nikki and Allison, who had so much untarnished life still in front of them. Mostly, I was terrified I would fuck this up and prove Amy right in the worst possible way.

I couldn't think about that right now. All that mattered was finding the girls and getting us all out of here.

The entranceway looked as quaintly elegant as I recalled from photographs, a country Victorian style with ornate wood furnishings and lots of lace. I'd wondered if the hotel had its own revenant staff, but no one waited behind the check-in desk or by the bell stand.

I looked around, wondering if Nikki and Allison might just be stuck for some reason in the lobby, comfortably waiting in the overstuffed high-backed chairs. No such luck. I was going to have to go looking for them and hope that the Riverside wasn't going to go all *Hotel California* on us. Or worse, turn into Cambridge Spring's own version of The Overlook.

So I stood in a ghostly lobby of a hotel that didn't exist, trying to figure out where to go next. A grand staircase led to the guest suites. The dining room and event space stretched off to one side, and I knew that somewhere behind the kitchen or down a service corridor, there would be stairs into the basement and mechanical rooms.

Sweet baby Jesus, I hoped Nikki had the brains God gave a Chihuahua and didn't go into the cellar. For that matter, I also hoped she and Allison didn't head upstairs. But my gut told me Nikki would be smart about this. She already knew she was mounting a rescue. So, either Allison wasn't right inside the door, or they couldn't get out the way they came in. I went back to the entranceway. If Allison was trophy hunting, there was plenty of Victorian bric-a-brac for her to pocket.

In the distance, I heard piano music and the clink of glasses. The muted hum of conversation carried from elsewhere, along with the rustle of skirts and the sound of footsteps. The Riverside was waking up around me.

Although the hotel had survived for over one hundred years, maybe it wasn't ready to go just yet. Perhaps enough emotional resonance had seeped into its floors, draperies, carpets, and furniture to make it "real" despite reality. All I knew was, we were stuck in our own personal Brigadoon, and, Oz or not, I wanted to click my heels and go home—with Nikki and Allison.

I debated whether to call out. I might find the girls or attract unwanted attention to them or me. For now, I decided to poke around. The music grew louder, and I caught a faint whiff of roast beef and strong coffee. Out of the corner of my eye, I glimpsed motion, like the swish of satin or the edge of a man's great cloak. Near the front door, I could swear I heard the whinny of horses and the crunch of gravel.

The longer I stayed, the more "real" the Riverside became—and the more likely I was to become a permanent resident of *The Twilight Zone*. I checked my watch, but it had stopped the moment I walked inside. My phone was completely dead. Fuck. I had three hours before we all disappeared and no way to know how much time I had left.

I needed to pick up the pace. I glanced out the window, wondering whether the moon I saw was "my" moon or a ghost moon. If it was the real moon, then the position had shifted enough to let me know that I'd already lost about an hour. Dammit—it only felt like minutes. I'd need to be very careful. Legends told that time in other realms didn't pass the same way it did in the real world. If what seemed like only fifteen minutes was really an hour, then my chance to find the girls was waning fast.

Think! What would Nikki do? If Nikki couldn't get out the front door, she'd look for a different way out. I glanced around myself. The big porch wrapped all around the hotel, and I was certain other doors opened onto it, but I couldn't see Nikki voluntarily going deeper into the haunted building. Then I looked to my left and saw the boardwalk stretching on beyond double doors, toward the mineral spring's bathhouse.

Going outside meant a chance to be seen and heard, to go over the side—although I remembered it being a long way down—or maybe make it to the pools. Water grounded energy. Pools were thresholds in myths, a way to cross from one realm to another. Nikki loved the old stories. She'd head for the baths.

Everything around me felt more real than when I'd first entered. The carpet under my feet, the walls around me, the light of the gas lamps. Colors were more vivid, sounds and smells more sensual. Even the things I saw in my peripheral vision looked more solid than ghostly. If we didn't get out soon, we'd become the Riverside's newest residents.

I jogged for the French doors that led to the boardwalk. When I reached them, I wasn't sure whether I'd go right through them like an apparition, or whether they'd be solid. I didn't break stride and knew I'd find out one way or the other. They parted for me on their own. I didn't slow down to figure it out.

"Nikki! Allison!" I yelled, now that I was outside the building. My running steps should have echoed, but instead, the sound seemed muted, although the boards beneath my feet felt solid. Maybe I should have marveled at the sight of the magnificent old hotel restored to its former grandeur, but my heart thudded too hard in my chest to take in the scenery. I still hadn't found Nikki, and the clock was ticking.

"Nikki!" I hollered again. This time, I thought I heard a faint sound from the far end of the boardwalk and saw a twitch of motion next to the mineral bath doors. I sprinted toward the end of the elevated walkway, wondering whether it elongated as I ran.

Then I saw them, huddled against the stone wall of the bathhouse, arms wrapped around each other, looking cold and miserable.

"Nikki! Allison!" I called out, and this time, Nikki raised her head and gave me a weary smile.

"Uncle Mark. I knew you'd come."

"Are you hurt? We've got to get out of here." I gave them both a hand up, and they got to their feet, looking worse for the wear. They'd been here for a full day, but from their drawn features, I felt sure it had seemed like longer.

"We couldn't get the doors to open," Nikki explained.

I looked at Allison, who wasn't meeting my gaze. "Turn out your pockets," I said.

She shrugged moodily but didn't budge.

"We don't have time. Turn out your damn pockets, or so help me, I will pick you up by your ankles and shake you until your fillings fall out," I growled.

Allison gave me a surly glare and pulled out a silver sugar bowl.

"You're going to put that back where you found it, and that's going to happen *now*. Because Nikki and I are getting out of here, with or without you."

Nikki's eyes widened, unsure whether I'd leave Allison behind. I wouldn't be happy about doing it, but hell yes, if it came down to a stupid memento or getting out alive, I'd leave her ass here in the ghost hotel if she wasn't smart enough to drop her treasure and run.

Allison seemed to realize I wasn't bluffing because she nodded, even though she wasn't happy about it.

The wind around us shifted. My gut told me we had to go. "Run!" I yelled, grabbing Nikki's arm and leaving Allison to keep up with us on her own.

I had dropped pomegranate seeds all the way, and they glowed red against the gray of the boardwalk. That's when I realized that the hotel had started to lose color—and the bathhouse behind us didn't look as solid as it had just minutes ago.

"Faster!" I yelled as the boardwalk began to feel spongy under our feet. Fog closed in, hiding the hotel that I hoped was still in front of us. I tightened my grip on Nikki's arm and heard Allison right behind us.

We burst through the French doors. The piano had gone silent; I couldn't smell coffee. The dining room and foyer looked blurry, like chalk lines dissolving in the rain.

"Put down the damn sugar bowl!" I ordered and heard a muted *thunk* as something heavy dropped.

The front doors were only a few strides away, but already the gas lights had dimmed. Out of the corner of my eye, I saw that the parlor and the dining room were lost in shadow, and the grand front staircase seemed to lead up into the clouds.

"Go!" I shouted, reaching into my gear bag and grabbing my flare gun. I wagered that if the Riverside's ghost had any sentience, it wouldn't want to burn again. I fired the flare, and a red ball of fire streaked through the open doors with us close behind it.

I pushed the girls in front of me and followed hard on their heels. We rushed through the big wooden front doors...and fell. The wide porch vanished from around us before we ever reached the front steps. I landed hard in the wet grass, on the empty lawn. We'd dropped about six feet, enough to knock the wind out of me. As I lay on my back, staring up at the stars—real stars—I breathed in the cool night air and started to laugh.

Nikki threw an arm around me and buried her head in my chest. "You did it!"

I had the presence of mind to fold her into an embrace. "You okay, kiddo?"

She nodded, sniffling a bit. "I'm sorry, Uncle Mark. I knew we shouldn't go in. But—"

"You tried to do the right thing, and it went south. Happens to me all the time," I said. With a grunt, I pushed up to sit. Father Leo and Dixie were running our way. I saw Allison curled in a ball a few feet away, but I couldn't tell if she was in shock or just pissed off.

"Mark! Is everyone all right?" Father Leo called.

"Yeah, I think so," I replied. "What day is it?"

Father Leo chuckled. "Same as when you went in. Dixie did her best to slow things down for you, but the ghosts put up a fight. In the end, I think they were glad to see the back of you."

"Story of my life," I muttered as I stood up and pulled Nikki with me. I hugged her tight, then let go and stood back to see her face. She looked pale, but the grin she flashed was pure Wojcik. I pushed her bangs out of her eyes and kissed the top of her head. Kerri was cajoling Allison to get up and losing patience rapidly. I hoped Nikki reconsidered some of her friend choices after this.

"Let's get you both back to Kerri's place," I said. "Then I want you to call your mom and let her know you're okay." I winced at the thought. "Tell the truth, but maybe leave out some of the details, huh?"

Nikki's expression told me that she fully understood. "Will do, Uncle

Mark. And—thanks." She stretched up to kiss me on the cheek. "Love you."

"Love you too, kiddo," I murmured, wishing Sean could have seen what a great daughter he had. The flare gun I'd shot was the same one I'd used long ago to kill the wendigo, so maybe just this once, fate was smiling on me. I knew better than to get used to it.

We saw the girls to Kerri's apartment and then went back to the parking lot. The Riverside Hotel was gone, nothing more than a memory and an empty lawn. It didn't take long to find the utility construction nearby. With Dixie's help and a little ghostly "Marco Polo," I was once again shoulder deep in mud, but I knew what I was looking for and surfaced victorious with another mysterious shard in my hand.

"Got it!" I said, holding it aloft so Dixie and Father Leo could see.

Dixie kept her distance, and Father Leo eyed the relic skeptically. "Tomorrow, we put Chiara and Simon on the trail of those pieces. Someone somewhere must recognize them. We're way beyond coincidence at this point."

I wiped off with towels I put in the truck specifically for this purpose, and we all climbed in with me behind the wheel. "Roger that, Padre," I said. "But right now, there's nothing in the world I want more than a cold beer and a hot shower. The mysteries of the universe are gonna have to wait their turn."

5

"I've got an order of wings, two burgers, a salad, and nachos," the server called out as he came to our table. I hailed one of the burgers, Sara flagged down the salad, Louie Marino claimed the other burger, and his wife, Tania, reached out for the nachos.

All around us, Friday night at the Drunk Monk on the East side of Conneaut Lake was in full swing. TVs over the bar showed a couple of games plus a big race. Most of the tables were full, the beer was flowing, and for once, all seemed right with the world.

"So you've known Mark a long time," Sara said with a mischievous grin aimed at Louie.

"Sure have," my buddy, the Linesville cop, replied. "Long enough to know that he would, without question, willingly assault a sworn officer of the law if I tell you any of the things you probably want to know."

Tania snickered. Sara gave me an appraising look, and I tried—and failed—to look innocent.

I'd finally gotten Sara to take a couple of midweek days off to visit, and after getting the grand tour, she wanted to sample the area's so-called nightlife and meet my friends. Blair and Chiara had an event at the coffee shop, so Louie and his wife drew the short straw and here we were, double dating.

I squeezed Sara's hand under the table, and she bumped her knee against mine. Even though I told myself I was too old to feel twitterpated, I liked Sara, maybe more than was safe. After all, she'd been widowed, and I'd been kicked to the curb, so we were both okay with moving slowly and seeing where things went. I liked talking with her and spending time just snuggled on the couch watching a movie. We had a nice time, whether we stayed in or went out. Best of all, it just felt comfortable between us. I liked that best of all, because while it wasn't the dizzying, breathless infatuation movies consider to be romance, it seemed solid and workable, something for the long haul. I really, really hoped she felt the same way.

"To be honest, there aren't a lot of interesting stories anyhow," Louie went on. "I mean, Mark wasn't the most exciting guy growing up—"

"Now wait a minute!" I objected. I'd sworn Louie to secrecy about a couple of embarrassing moments in elementary school, like getting pantsed in gym class in fifth grade or showing up on the wrong baseball field in sixth grade and causing the team to forfeit the game, but that didn't mean I wanted to sound *boring*.

Louie just grinned, and I knew this was revenge for the time I told his junior prom date about how he got bus-sick on the way to summer camp and barfed all over the chaperones.

"I guess you'd call him a late bloomer," Louie went on with a devilish glint in his eye. "I mean, senior year, no one would have voted him 'most likely to save the world.'"

Inwardly, I groaned. Louie was right. In fact, I think I got voted "least likely to ever leave town" or something lame like that.

Sara smiled, and the warmth in her eyes made my heart stutter. "I think he bloomed just fine," she said, twining her fingers with mine.

After a couple of beers and some good food, everyone relaxed. Conversation flowed naturally, and I started to feel a little more comfortable. I wanted Sara to like Louie and Tania, and them to like her. It didn't escape me that, although part of me kept thinking "take it slow," another part kept envisioning Sara around for the long run. That scared me and excited me in equal amounts, so I just stayed quiet, but the part of me rooting for the future chalked up a win as the night went on.

After dinner, we took over the pool table in the back. Sara and Tania proved they had a hidden talent for the game, while Louie and I just tried not to get shown up too badly. The night was still young when we headed out, promising to get together again soon. Sara regarded me quietly as I settled behind the wheel and headed back to my cabin.

"I like them," she said. "They seem like good people."

That mattered to me more than I first thought, and I realized I'd been holding my breath, hoping everyone got along all evening. "They are. And I think they liked you, too."

We didn't have a long drive back to my place. "Cabin" sounds a little rustic for what is actually a log house on a nice piece of property in the woods. It's got all the important amenities and a few of the necessary comforts. Demon barked as the truck pulled up, and I knew that for as ferocious as he sounded, he was wagging his butt off, anxious to have Sara scratch him behind the ears.

"You've got a nice view of the stars out here," Sara said as we got out of the car. She walked a few paces to where she could see better between the tree branches. I followed and slipped an arm around her shoulder. For the moment, we ignored the frantically barking dog and focused on the Milky Way.

"Sometimes, when I get home late, I can see meteor showers," I said. Without the competition of city lights, the sky was dark and vast, littered with diamonds.

"Once in a while, if the conditions are right, we get a glimpse of the Northern Lights, up in Kane," Sara replied. "It's worth standing out in the cold to see it."

I pulled her into my arms and drew her close for a kiss. She kissed back and pressed against me, and I never wanted the moment to end, just me, Sara and the stars.

So of course, my phone rang. I'd have gladly ignored it, except that it was Louie's ringtone, and since he knew I was with Sara, he wouldn't have called if it wasn't important.

"Sorry," I sighed. "It's Louie." She stepped back, and the world felt colder. "This had better be good," I growled into the phone, as Sara chuckled.

"Apologies for interrupting, but we've got a situation," Louie replied. "Pat Carmody from Meadville PD just called me. Zombies at Greendale Cemetery."

Fuck. Pat and Louie know about my "side gig" hunting monsters. Most of the cops wouldn't believe me if we told them, but Pat and Louie had seen things they knew weren't normal, and we'd handled a few problems together. Unfortunately, there wasn't anyone else to call.

"What'cha got?" I asked.

"The groundskeeper for the cemetery called Meadville PD with a complaint about rowdy visitors after hours. Fortunately, Pat was on the call. Six women, all in their early twenties, all dressed like it was a hundred years ago—and all dead but active."

"Shit. What'd he do?"

Louie gave a tired sigh. "He called me, swore his partner to secrecy, and retreated. Since the cemetery's closed, the situation is under control for the moment, but we've got to put the zombies down—"

"And figure out why they rose," I supplied. "How many total are there?"

"That's the thing," Louie replied. "As far as Pat can tell, the six women are the only zombies in the whole freaking place."

"Count your blessings," I replied. Greendale Cemetery is old and beautiful, with Victorian monuments, huge azaleas, and rhododendrons as large as trees. It's also packed to the gills with dead people, so if they all decided to wake up and roam around, "bad" wouldn't begin to cover it.

"Is Sara there?" At least Louie had the decency to sound sorry about ruining my evening.

"Yeah. I can explain—"

Sara was suddenly next to me, folding her hand around my phone. "Come on," she said. "You've got a job to do."

"Hold on, Louie," I muttered, then turned back to Sara. "I know it sucks, but you can be comfortable here in the cabin, and I'll be back as soon as I can—"

"I'm coming with you," she said, lifting her chin. "Zombies are nothing to fool around with. I'm pretty good with first-aid if you or the others get hurt."

"It's dangerous."

"I'm an expert shot." The look in Sara's eyes told me she wasn't going to back down. Hell, I wasn't sure I wanted her to. After all, if we were going to go forward with our relationship, this sort of situation would keep coming up. And armed with a gun with high-caliber bullets and locked in the truck, Sara should be safe.

"All right," I conceded. "But you stay in the truck."

Sara made a noise that might have meant any number of things. I lifted the phone once more. "Okay. We're on our way."

"We?"

"Sara's coming with me. Long story. It'll be all right." It had better be. I'd already lost four people I cared about to a monster. I wouldn't survive losing anyone else, especially not Sara.

The drive to Meadville didn't take long, and the gates to the cemetery stood ajar when we arrived. Usually, the entrance locked at dusk, but I could see two cop cars inside waiting for us.

I looked over at Sara. "All right—I'm going to get out to open the gate the rest of the way. You slide over and drive through; then I'll get in the passenger side after I close the gate again. Just stay in the driver's seat. And keep the gun handy."

Sara kissed me on the cheek. "You're cute. I've got this. Go."

I jumped out of the car, she moved over, and the truck rumbled through the gate. Louie and Pat jogged up to greet us. "Fill me in," I ordered. Sara remained in the truck, but she put the window down to hear, and I moved us closer to make sure she wasn't left out.

"We left the zombies some cheap drive-thru hamburgers to keep them occupied," Louie said. "They're up around the curve, but they'll go looking for more meat soon."

"Lovely. Who are they?"

"Six young women, identical markers, different birthdates, and last names, but the same death date," Pat recounted. "Back in 1918."

"House fire? Apartment? Brothel?" I asked, trying to come up with a set of circumstances that would account for the odd details.

"I think there was a fire at the college about that time," Pat said. "Could have been a dormitory or a rooming house."

"So why are they back?" Louie asked.

I sighed, getting a bad feeling about the answer. "Is the college doing any construction projects? Utility work? Tearing down an old building? Anything that disturbs the ground?"

Pat frowned, thinking. "I don't go up there much. Campus Security handles the routine calls. But yeah, I think I saw some equipment around. Why?"

"My bet is that the construction dug up a strange shard like Father Leo and I found at other places where there've been…incidents…lately." Pat knew a little about what I did, but I didn't want to drag him any deeper into the Occulatum's secrets if I could help it. Louie already knew far too much.

"Okay," Louie said, in that tone that told me he guessed there was a whole lot I was leaving out. "So, now what?"

The zombies would be shambling their way down toward the front gate very soon, but I knew the missing shard held the key. "These are the ones we've found so far," I said, opening the back of the truck and unlocking the lead box. I tilted it so Sara could see. "They're like really hard pottery, except not. And the markings don't look like anything else I've seen. Got a couple of people working on it; no answers yet. But... lock the shard in the lead box, and whatever it's powering up gets unplugged."

I drew a deep breath, sure I was going to get push-back from all three of my companions. "So here's what I think—Pat and Sara go to the college and look for the shard. It's probably fairly near the top. Check the mud piles. Find it and throw it in the lead box. Then come back and get us. If that alone doesn't shut the zombies down, it should take a lot of the mojo out of them." I hoped.

"I don't like it," Pat said. "That leaves you and Louie against six zombies."

"Six co-ed zombies in long skirts," I replied, because I'm a smartass, and I was trying desperately to get Pat and Sara out of harm's way now that I had a good excuse.

"You need us here," Sara argued.

"We'll have a shorter fight if you go find the shard," I countered. "For all we know, as long as the shard is out there, we won't be able to put the zombies down. We'll get exhausted—and they'll just get hungrier."

"How about we all go, and we'll find it faster," Sara suggested.

Louie shook his head. "We need to keep the zombies from leaving the cemetery. There are neighborhoods all around. We'll just stay here and play 'whack a mole' until you get back."

Pat and Sara exchanged a glance. They hadn't met before, but they're both smart and stubborn—and insanely loyal. I knew I was asking a lot for them to leave us here, but I didn't want either of them in the line of fire. And I hadn't been kidding about the shard—I had the awful feeling that this case was connected to all the others.

Reluctantly, Pat and Sara finally nodded. "Okay," Sara said. "But we'll come right back here, to back you up."

I wanted them anywhere but here, but I knew not to push my luck. "Just, be careful," I replied. "Be safe."

Sara gave me a look. "You're the ones staying here with the zombies. So it goes double for the both of you." With that, Pat got into the truck, Sara turned around, and they headed down the hill. The college wasn't far, but finding the shard in a construction mess was certain to take longer than I wanted to battle the zombie hoards.

Even if the legion of the undead were more like a decomposing sorority.

I'd grabbed my gear bag out of the truck, so I had a shotgun and plenty of shells, plus a very sharp machete and a few other surprises. Louie had his service handgun, and a backup tucked into his waistband.

"Ready to go deal with Shauna of the Dead?" I asked as staggering shadows appeared on the horizon in the pale glow of the cemetery's few security lights.

"Shouldn't they call them the Shambling Dead?" Louie asked, eyeing the zombies. "They really don't walk." Both of us were talking smack because we were scared shitless, an old habit from middle school gym class and dodgeball against the jocks.

"We gonna do this loud or quiet?" I asked, realizing that Louie also had a Ka-Bar with him.

"Pat's not the whole Meadville PD," Louie said. "We're pretty close to houses to do a lot of shooting."

That's when we realized that only four zombies approached from the direction we expected. Two of the rotting co-eds had broken off to flank us. That meant these weren't the usual dead walkers, because most zombies have the brains of one of those windup toys that keep bumping into the wall.

I heard a growl from behind me and started to turn as something foul and strong landed on my back. Louie yelped as the other missing zombie lunged at him from behind.

My zombie attacker smelled worse than a dumpster left in the sun on a hot summer day, and the cold, rotting skin left a trail of slime wherever it touched. But the bones and sinew were strong, and so, apparently, were the teeth, which snapped and clicked far too close to my jugular.

"Fuck it all," I muttered, ineffectively spinning as if centrifugal force itself might throw the creature off me. Louie was equally unsuccessful at jabbing his elbows back and trying to buck the zombie off. In the meantime, their four dead BFFs had closed in.

I spun and slammed the dead girl into an obelisk, hearing a satisfying crunch of bone and squelch of bursting membranes. Her bony arms unlocked from around my neck. I wheeled and slashed with my machete, taking her head off.

Louie copied my move, and he was currently trying to scrape his attacker off him against one of the other monuments, using the wing of a weeping angel to try to pry off the zombie attempting to rip out his throat.

I squared my shoulders and faced the incoming hoard. It was the first time I'd ever rushed a sorority.

"Let's get this party started," I muttered. I went left. Louie went right. He'd offed the shambler who'd grabbed him from behind, and who now lay in a headless heap beneath a scary-looking angel. We had bigger problems. Four of them.

I let out my best battle roar. Louie responded in kind. This was just like when we'd gone toe-to-toe with Sammy Hogan after the creep stole my favorite lunch box in fifth grade. Except that Sammy wasn't undead, and we just gave him a bloody nose, instead of sending his severed head bouncing from bloody shoulders.

Still, Louie and I waded into battle shoulder to shoulder, whether it was bullies, Bigfoot, or badass zombies. I stabbed one zombie through the heart. Didn't do a damn thing except piss her off, so I freed my blade by giving her a kick to the gut. That sent her reeling backward to land on a rusty iron fence surrounding an old grave. The spiked posts impaled the zombie, keeping her pinned while not letting her pull free.

Fuck-it-all, these were fast zombies, and even the ones we decapitated didn't completely stop moving, which told me the shard was behind this. Despite the three we'd downed, there were three more in good shape and ready to rumble.

I blasted two of them with my shotgun at close range, removing most of their heads. Louie gave up on his Ka-Bar and shot the third. Normally, that would have taken care of regular zombies, but these fuckers kept on grabbing and crawling, and I was afraid we were going to have to hack them into bits to stop them.

One of the sorority sisters got back to her feet, even more monstrous with half a skull, glaring at me with her remaining eye. I hadn't had time to reload, so I swung the empty shotgun like a baseball bat, giving vent to my inner Negan.

"Picked a fine time to leave me, Lucille!" I belted, off-key, as the heavy gun stock connected with her skull like a Tee-ball on a stand. It flew far enough I might have been able to run to second base if this were a game instead of a desperate fight for our lives.

We had squirming zombie pieces strewn around us, so now instead of being menaced by six shamblers, we had skulls and severed hands trying to get a piece of us. Louie and I shot, stabbed and hacked, but it just seemed to piss them off more.

"Cover me!" I yelled, digging in my bag. I pulled out a can of hairspray and a lighter. I sprayed and prayed, and my cheap-ass flamethrower roared to life, barbecuing the zombie bits. The cemetery smelled like cooked, rotted meat—no surprise there, I guess. But the fire drove the zombies back—even the severed limbs retreated—so we had a temporary stalemate, at least until I ran out of Aquanet.

"Now what?" Louie asked. We stood back to back, each armed with hairspray and a Zippo, sending a fiery blast any time the zombies tried to encroach. "I'm almost out of hairspray." He winced. "Now there's something I never thought I'd say."

"If we're lucky, Sara and Pat find the shard, and they come back and rescue us," I replied. I didn't have to spell out what happened if our luck ran its usual shitty course.

"Unless you've got a whole salon in there, we can't keep this up all night," Louie warned.

The zombies didn't look much like people anymore. One of them was still stuck on the iron fence, impaled by an arrow-shaped support. She was the only one of the six still intact. The others were missing limbs or heads, but still doing their gruesome best to attack. We covered for each other so we could reload, but blasting these zombies apart didn't stop them; it just made more of them. We were at an impasse.

"Come morning, someone's bound to notice," Louie observed. "We might even make the evening news."

"If the zombies don't eat the reporter."

I heard the dying hiss of one of the cans of hairspray. We were running out of time.

All of a sudden, the zombies stilled. The ones still standing fell, and the bits stopped moving. Even the one thrashing on the iron fence stopped flopping like a gigged fish.

"They did it," I breathed, still watching the zombies warily in case it was a trick. "They found the shard."

We looked around us at the carnage. "How are we ever going to clean this up?" Louie moaned, back to practical matters now that death was no longer imminent.

"Watch my back. I've got another idea." I handed off my can, shoved the lighter in my pocket, and grabbed a huge container of powdered coffee creamer. I'd only seen this work on YouTube, but I hoped like hell it wasn't fake news.

"What the fuck?" Louie asked as I kicked a heap of zombie pieces into a pile. As I shook out a thick curtain of powdered creamer over the bits, I lit the dust, and the whole thing went up in a fireball.

"Holy shit! That's the last time I put that in my coffee!" Louie shouted, jumping back reflexively.

"You play soccer," I muttered. "Kick the pieces together, and I'll light 'em up." I might never get the gore off my boots, but we sent up some damn fine flames, reaching high into the night. In the distance, sirens wailed.

"Fuck." I didn't see a way in hell we'd talk our way out of this.

That's when I heard the roar of an engine and saw my truck heading right for us, with Sara behind the wheel.

Pat jumped out almost before the truck stopped. "Nice job," he said, taking in the burning zombies. "Thanks—now get out of here before the fire department arrives. I'll stay and cover it. Gas leak," he said, with a credibly serious look on his face.

I slapped him on the shoulder. "Good luck with that," I said, glad that the clean-up wasn't my problem. I jumped into the passenger seat as Louie got into his squad car, and we all took off, taking the old road that ran alongside the cemetery's edge, going out the back way as the fire engines and cops came in through the front.

"Your timing is amazing," I said, collapsing against the seat. "You found the shard?"

Sara grinned. She was splattered with mud. Dirt streaked her face and clumped in her hair, but she looked triumphant. "Hell, yes! Took some digging, but we found it. Put the damn thing in with the others. How many more of them are there, do you suppose?"

I couldn't help grinning back. Our date had been ruined, we'd been cockblocked by zombies, and now, we were running from a crime scene, but Sara looked like she was having the time of her life.

"No idea. Not many, I hope," I replied. "But you've got to admit, I know how to show a girl a good time."

6

_____

"It doesn't match anything," Chiara told me. "I'm sorry, Mark. But those symbols aren't a match for any language, current or historic."

Simon Kincaide had told me the same thing just an hour earlier. "It's got to mean something. Did you look at alchemy?"

"Alchemy. Enochian. Atlantean. Mystical and arcane languages. Hidden codes. They don't match up."

"Someone made them. I don't think the marks are for decoration." I plopped onto the couch, holding my phone. "Where do we go from here? The shards are dangerous. And until we can figure out what they are—and who made them—I don't know how to stop what they do. Or what they'll cause next."

All things considered, Sara had taken the zombie BBQ pretty much in stride, which just further convinced me this was the woman for me. Pat must have sold his fellow cops on his gas leak story because no one came after us, and the local papers didn't say anything about the dead rising. Father Leo stopped by Greendale to say a blessing and Last Rites, just in case. In fact, we'd gone a whole week without a catastrophe, which told me I was pushing my luck, and everything was about to go to shit.

I stared at the whiteboard that was still where we'd left it last night when Blair, Chiara, Father Leo, and Louie all came over for pizza and to help sort through what we knew. I had the points where we'd found the shards plotted on a map, but all I saw was a rough arc, curving down from the New York border, past Cambridge Springs, Meadville, and Mercer. The arc didn't lead anywhere in particular, and we had no idea if there were other shards out there, waiting to be dug up and activated.

I shuffled the pictures of the shards that I'd taken with my phone and printed out for a closer look. Handling the shards seemed like a bad idea because I didn't want them to juice up anything else. Keeping them locked away seemed the wisest thing to do, for now.

"We don't even know what they're made of," I complained, although I wasn't telling Chiara anything she didn't know.

"Hard to analyze it if you don't dare take them out of the lead box," she agreed. "I've got friends who can run spectral analysis and a bunch more tests—figure out the age, material composition, etc.—but you'd have to risk not keeping them wrapped in lead."

"Would *you* want to take them home with you?" I challenged. "Because I wouldn't. And I don't want to send it to some poor son of a bitch to run tests on it and find out he's been chewed on by werewolves or attacked by zombies or ravaged by rampaging revenants."

Chiara snorted. "Can you say that five times fast? Ravaged by rampaging revenants?"

"Gobbled by galloping ghosts," I replied. "Bite me."

"Sounds like I'd have to stand in line," she joked. I heard her sigh. "Seriously, Mark. I don't know what to try next."

"Could it be a hoax?" I asked although I doubted that as I said it, especially after what happened with the zombies. "Did you look at fictional languages?"

"You mean, like Elvish?" I could hear the skepticism in Chiara's voice. "Doesn't seem likely to me, not from what you've said."

I was grasping at straws. "Humor me. Sometimes the people who make up things for movies and books base it on some weird thing they've found in real life, the more obscure, the better. Think of it kind of like a back door." Maybe someone made a cool movie prop, and it somehow got juiced with dark magic. I guess it could happen.

"I'll give it a go," Chiara replied. "And I'll dig a little deeper on magical languages—real magic, Theosophists, Spiritualism, and stage magic. Maybe I'll get lucky."

"I'm sure Blair can arrange that," I said with a smirk.

"Perv," she retorted, but I could hear her smile. "By the way, Donny is working out great."

"Oh?" I had wondered how their new were-watchdog was doing.

"He helps out in human form sometimes during the day when he isn't at the slaughterhouse," Chiara said. "Follows Blair around like a puppy. And since we've had him working nights, we haven't had any more problems with vandalism."

"Awesome," I replied, so happy the situation was good for them and Donny. "He's not a bad guy, if you don't mind the shedding."

"He's adorkable," Chiara replied. "And don't tell Blair I ratted on her, but she totally slips him dog biscuits and people cookies. He's going to get fat."

"No chocolate," I warned. "I don't know if it's bad for werewolves, but I'd hate to have to find an emergency cryptid-vet in the middle of the night."

"Noted," she said with a laugh. "Seriously, it's all good. And we'll figure out the shards. Just give me a little more time."

"Thanks," I said. I was exhausted, and we'd all been going full-tilt combating the problems the shards stirred up. I wanted nothing more than to put this in my rear view, spend a normal week at the garage, and take Sara to a nice, uninterrupted dinner on the weekend. Saving the world sounds cool, but the pay sucks.

We ended the call, and I sank deeper into the couch cushions, too exhausted to move. Demon nudged my hand with his wet nose, probably checking to see whether I was dead. Not that I thought he'd grieve; he'd go jump on the bed once he was sure I wouldn't yell at him for it.

I scratched his ears, and he plopped his huge head right in my lap, looking up at me longingly. "You've already been fed," I chided. "Your Jedi mind tricks won't work on me. That *was* the kibble you were looking for."

My beer was empty, and my bladder was full. I dislodged Demon, took my glass to the kitchen, used the bathroom, and returned to get myself a refill. When I came back to the couch, Demon had curled up next to where my feet had been, and I found myself staring at the shard pictures, which were scattered across the coffee table.

"Wait a second," I murmured, setting my beer aside. I leaned forward and frowned as I studied the shards more closely. I'd been so busy focusing on what was written on those damn pieces, I hadn't really looked at the shards themselves.

"What if..." My voice trailed off. I went to get scissors and tape, then cut the shards out and started to tape the pieces together, feeling like the guy in that movie who turned his mashed potatoes into Devil's Tower.

When I was done, I felt breathless although I didn't know whether that was excitement or fear—or compulsion. I'd fit the shard photos together like a jigsaw puzzle, and they formed a rectangular tablet of some sort. Even better, it looked like we had all the pieces.

Now if we just knew what the hell it was for.

I took a picture of the composite and texted it to Chiara and Simon, begging for help. Then I sat back and thought about the other aspect of the shards we hadn't explored—what they were made of.

I'd handled them all, except for the one Sara and Pat found, which looked just like the others. They weren't metal, fabric, stone, or wood. Nothing about them seemed organic—not flesh, bone, or plant material. They reminded me of pottery—freaky strong, heavy, weird pottery. So, I grabbed my laptop and started searching.

Not pottery, maybe. Ceramics. Ceramic engineering was a thing—and it didn't have any connection with throwing pots on a wheel. Instead, it was all about materials that could withstand high heat and strong forces, to be used in engines and planes and...spaceships.

Holy fucking shit. Maybe the shards weren't magic. Maybe they weren't from our world at all.

I sat back, stunned. Demon gave me a questioning look, decided everything was all right, then stretched out so I had no room for my feet and farted.

What now? I plotted the path of the shards on a map. The "tablet" I had put together from the photos looked complete, but then again, I had no idea what it was supposed to look like. Maybe there were more missing pieces out there or other tablets like this one. Hell, for all I knew, maybe E.T. dropped them off like an other-worldly newspaper boy, hoping to make First Contact.

There was too much I didn't know, and not enough that I did.

Story of my fuckin' life.

I sat down at the table with my laptop, looking for reports of strange activity in the swath of PA that seemed to fit the trajectory of whatever left the tablet. On a good day, this state is mighty weird, so that took a lot of combing through all the back channels that the monster hunter and cryptid researcher community use to share information. But after I had done some digging, I needed to talk over what I'd discovered.

"Have you found anything?" Father Leo sounded a little sleepy, and I realized that it was after eleven.

"I've eliminated a bunch of Bigfoot reports that might or might not be true but don't have anything to do with this case," I told him, "and I've made notes on some low-level cryptid issues we can come back to later. Oh, and I sent you the Elvis sightings. I thought your folks were supposed to keep better track of him?"

Father Leo sighed. "They try. He's good at sneaking out."

"Have you tried taking away his blue suede shoes?"

"Yes. It doesn't help. Did you have a point to make?"

"Amazingly enough, yes. After I sorted through everything, I've got about a dozen incidents that map to a shaky arc. It might continue the flight path of whatever dropped off the shards—if they were, in fact, dropped out of the sky."

"So then the real question is: when did the shards fall?" Father Leo mused, sounding more awake. "Nothing we handled had been a problem for long. They all started up after the ground was disturbed."

"I'm not an archeologist, but most of the places didn't look like they'd dug down more than a few feet," I said. "So this isn't some Ancient Astronauts thing from back when the pyramids were built. Maybe a hundred years?"

"Possibly less," Father Leo theorized. "A lot of those areas were farmland a century ago, so anything that fell would have been brought up pretty quickly."

I rubbed my eyes, but I wasn't really tired. In fact, batting ideas around with the padre had made me curious to see what else I could find. "What's on your agenda tomorrow?" I asked. "Up for taking a drive?"

"I figured that's what you had in mind," he replied. "I'll bring the leftover cookies from the parish committee meeting."

We agreed on a time for me to pick him up, and I ended the call. Demon shifted, paws twitching, and I wondered how he'd get along with Donny if they spent time together. With my luck, they'd be great pals, and Donny would teach him to dumpster dive.

I got myself another beer and started to track UFO sightings in Pennsylvania. There were more reports than I'd expected, going way back. Some were the usual Area 51 bullshit. (Everyone knows that the real Area 51 is jointly run by the CIA and the Occulatum, with the occasional territorial pissing match between them.) But other incidents looked much more likely to be real, and I jotted notes on the ones that fit with the trajectory and our estimated timeline.

When I finally shut down my laptop, I had a list of a dozen likely spots. I sent my notes to my phone, finished my beer, and closed down for the night. Tomorrow, I vowed to get up early enough to pick up a dozen donuts, pack a cooler full of ice and pop, and throw a bag of snacks in the car. I knew the road we'd travel well enough to have a few favorite lunch and dinner spots along the way, something to break up the drive.

Road tripping with a priest. Do I know how to live it up or what?

The next morning, Father Leo showed up with two huge Thermos containers of hot coffee to go with the donuts, and we headed out right after daybreak. The donuts didn't make it past the county line before they were gone, washed down by coffee as strong as sin.

"Damn, that coffee could peel paint," I said, sputtering a bit even as I got him to pour me a refill.

"Amateur," he teased. "How do you think novitiates manage all-night vigils?"

"I don't know. Speed? Cocaine?"

Father Leo shook his head. "Seminary coffee ranks right up there with hospital java and police station joe."

"Rank is the word," I said, as my eyebrows crept up toward my hairline. Then again, I definitely wasn't sleepy anymore, although I'd be twitchy as fuck if I kept drinking the stuff.

"Where are we going?"

"We're chasing E.T.," I said. "Checking out sightings and looking into places people say strange objects fell out of the sky." I made copies of the photos I'd taken of the pieced-together shard tablet, as well as the individual pieces, to see if they would jog anyone's memories.

"Did you know Pennsylvania is one of the states with the most reports of Bigfoot and UFOs?" I continued, feeling the sugary donuts mingling with the strong, acidic coffee to form something akin to rocket fuel in my stomach.

"Does that surprise you?" Father Leo sipped his coffee and leaned back in his seat.

"Not really. There's plenty of pretty remote forest, and the area's been settled continuously for a very long time."

"And some of those reports are ancient," the priest said. "There are notes in the journals of the first clergy to come to the New World not only reporting their own sightings but also mentioning the stories the Native Americans told about people who came from the heavens."

I was silent for a while. "Do you think it's real?"

"We've certainly seen that the shard—or the tablet—has very powerful energy, and an ability to influence creatures that aren't human."

"I mean, UFOs? And if there is life out there," I said, waving vaguely at the sky, "what does that mean for folks in your profession?"

"It means that we will all have to become more open-minded," he answered. "Which is why there's a branch of the Occulatum that's been working on protocols for First Contact for quite a while."

"Um, you're going to handle it better than the last time, right? No offense." Much as I adored Father Leo, we all knew the Church had a tarnished record when it came to indigenous peoples.

"We have attempted to put better measures in place, and I sincerely hope we have learned from history," Father Leo replied. "No offense taken."

Our route meandered down state highways, passing plenty of barns and fields, and going through small towns I could barely find on my map. By lunch, we'd made four stops, with little to show for it.

"I would have thought folks might have more to say on the subject," I said as Father Leo and I took our lunch from the pick-up window to a weathered picnic table. I was a sucker for the independent, mom-and-pop "dairy isles" that dotted the back roads, where I swear the Sloppy Joes and French fries are the best in the world.

"I'm guessing they've been overrun with reporters, bloggers, and self-appointed investigators," Father Leo said.

"You're probably right," I replied, taking my time to savor a great sandwich and fries done to perfection. "And who knows whether or not the Men in Black have been by to scare them into silence?"

He gave me a look. "Next, you'll be telling me that they used their flashy-thingy to make everyone forget."

I shrugged. "Stranger things have happened. You can't deny that if the Occulatum ever got their hands on one of those gadgets, they'd totally use it."

Father Leo didn't argue. He bit into his sandwich and sighed. "This is so good, I might have to mention it at Confession."

Neither of us spoke for a while as we did justice by the meals. That included getting soft-serve cones for dessert. When we finally got back in the car, I felt like lunch meant the day so far had not been wasted.

"What's next?" Father Leo asked.

I handed him my phone's list of suspicious sightings. "I looked at the best-verified reports over the last sixty years. That's not quite a century, but far enough back to have pretty good reporting and the tools to rule out regular comets and satellites. These were the ones that were hard to explain. And if you notice, every place on my short list mentions a sighting in December of 1965."

Father Leo frowned. "What was so special about that incident?"

I pulled back onto the road, taking my phone back so the map program could guide us down the rural routes. "People said they saw a very bright light flash overhead that didn't match aircraft routes—and there wasn't a lot of space junk yet up there to cause problems."

"No, but the Space Race meant what was flying—US or Soviet—was probably classified," he pointed out.

"Maybe. That's where it gets weird. That 1965 sighting is one of the best documented. Lots of people reported it. The arc of sightings would have taken a craft over where we've had disturbances. And legend holds that whatever it was crash-landed in Kecksburg."

"I can't say I've ever been to Kecksburg."

"You and me both, Padre," I replied. "But we're going there today after we check out a few more loose ends."

Fortunately, the next seven stops went quickly, since they were only a few miles apart. Even with Father Leo in his black shirt and clerical collar, folks looked at us suspiciously when we started poking around, asking questions. A few old-timers were willing to talk to us, but they didn't add anything to what I'd learned online. People seemed pretty sure that whatever they'd seen ended up being an ill-fated Soviet satellite.

"You notice how everyone clammed up when we asked if they knew anyone else who'd seen something?" I asked once we were back on the highway.

"Offhand, I'd say someone official came by and scared the daylights out of them."

"Daylights—or something else," I replied. "I don't think they liked strangers, and somehow, I doubt we're welcome to stop by on our way home."

"What that tells me is that whoever handled the clean-up after the incident came down heavy-handed, so I suspect there was something worth hiding," Father Leo said.

That made me worry about what we'd find in Kecksburg.

I wasn't expecting a huge sign on the outskirts proclaiming *"Welcome to Kecksburg! UFO capital of PA!"*

Father Leo and I looked at each other. A nearby billboard promoted the *"Annual UFO Festival and Fish Fry,"* with lurid color drawings of a flaming spaceship and Bigfoot.

"Maybe these folks won't be as hard to talk to," I said, as my truck rumbled down Main Street. We passed a t-shirt shop with a window full of designs featuring bug-eyed aliens and an oddly-shaped ship.

"Mark—look there!" Father Leo said, pointing.

At first, I thought it was a huge, brown acorn lifted high in the air on a sturdy metal support, like the sign for a gas station. Then I realized it was supposed to be a spaceship and that all along the ring at the bottom were strange runes.

Runes that looked entirely too familiar, in a material that, at least from a distance, matched the replica.

"Holy shit," I muttered. "I mean, I read the reports, and I've seen the movies that were made about the incident, but I didn't think they would go all-out like this."

"It's probably the most exciting thing that ever happened in these parts," Father Leo replied, not trying to hide his grin. "And a good excuse for a party every summer."

Kecksburg embraced its UFO the way Salem, Massachusetts, turned its witch trials into a major tourist attraction. Sub shops and pizza parlors featured logos showing their specialties as spaceships. Stores promised their wares were "out of this world." Little green men and more sinister-looking "aliens" with bald heads and big eyes peered at us from every display.

"How about we get dinner, ask around, and then go get a motel?" I suggested. "We can come back late tonight and get a better look at that 'acorn.'"

"Works for me. That diner back there looked like the real deal," Father Leo said. I suspected priests were a little food obsessed to make up for a lack of other pastimes.

I parked near the Cup and Saucer diner, where "saucer" definitely took on a double meaning. But as cheesy as the name and logo were, the old chrome-walled restaurant looked like it had been there forever. I glanced around, unable to shake the feeling that we were being watched, but no one outside seemed to be paying us much attention. That changed when we walked in. Conversation grew quiet as the locals sized us up, probably for tourist potential. Father Leo and I made an odd pair, and even the waitress gave us a second glance as she took us to our booth.

"Everything looks good—like it might be made from family recipes," I said, salivating a little as I read through the large selection of diner comfort foods, and of course, homemade pies, many of which had corny alien-related nicknames.

"We can always come back for breakfast," Father Leo said with a mischievous grin.

"What can I get you, gentlemen?" Kelli, our server asked. I ordered a burger, and Father Leo got fried chicken, promising to save room for dessert.

"Hey, I wondered if you could help us," I said before she had a chance to run off. "We're researching a book about the UFO that crashed near here, and we'd like to talk to someone who was around when it happened."

I guessed I wasn't the first "book researcher" or reporter to ask the question because Kelli hesitated, then nodded. Maybe Father Leo in his clerical collar convinced her we were trustworthy.

"Duane Roache is the go-to guy for that," she said. "He says he had a front-row seat to the crash and also saw the spooky guys who came afterward to clean it up. If Duane likes you, he can connect you to the other folks who will talk about it. You can usually find him over at Cosmic Towing until around eight."

After she was out of hearing range, Father Leo gave me a look. "You didn't need to lie."

"I couldn't exactly tell the truth. Who knows? Maybe I'll write up all my adventures someday and pass it off as fiction," I countered.

The food was as good as the sign promised, so we forgot about conversation and just stuffed our faces. Choosing just one kind of pie was hard with twenty varieties to pick from, which meant breakfast here was guaran-damn-teed. By the time we finished, it was after six.

"I'll call ahead to get us a room, in case it's the busy season," I said as we paid and headed for the truck. "That way, we can still get over to see Duane before he closes up."

I booked us a double at the Blue Moon hotel, and we headed to Cosmic Towing.

"I'm kinda afraid to find out what the high school mascot is," Father Leo mused as we passed neon signs of spaceships, rockets, shooting stars and aliens.

"You know there are towns in PA named Mars and Moon Township, right?"

"There are also towns named Intercourse and Blue Balls, and I worry about their mascots, too."

"And of course, Derry Area High School," I replied. At his confused frown, I prompted, "Say it fast."

"Oh."

Cosmic Towing looked exactly like I pictured it: a cement block garage with two bays and a big sign showing a truck towing a damaged UFO. I was glad that my garage back in Atlantic didn't have to match a hokey theme, but maybe the locals got into the spirit of the story and had fun with it.

We parked at the curb and walked up to the office. I wasn't surprised to find that everyone was in the bays. I only use my office for paperwork. "We're looking for Duane Roache," I said, raising my voice to get their attention above the noise of the pneumatic wrenches.

A white-haired man in coveralls looked up from behind a wrecked Mustang. "Who wants to know?"

"We're researching the UFO crash, and Kelli at the diner said you're the man who knows the most about it," Father Leo jumped in, probably to spare me another venial sin.

Duane snorted. "Mighty nice of her. She's also my granddaughter." He wiped his hands on a rag and ambled over. The other three men went back to work. "I'm trying to finish a job. Can you boys wait in the office while I close up?"

I'm thirty-six, and Father Leo is older than I am, so it's been a while since anyone except Dixie called us "boys," but Duane had us by a good forty years, so I wasn't going to complain. Duane's office was pretty spartan, with the requisite pin-up calendar, plenty of sticky note reminders, and a pile of papers on the worn metal desk. Two uncomfortable plastic chairs provided seating, and a small TV, dog-eared magazines, and an empty coffee maker were the extent of amenities for waiting customers. We passed the time with our phones until Duane joined us, and the other workers packed up and headed home.

"Now, what can I do for you?" Duane asked, eyeing Father Leo's collar. Maybe he didn't see a lot of UFO-investigating priests.

"We'd like to hear your story about what happened the night the UFO fell," I said, pulling out a tablet I brought to look more like a reporter.

Duane sat in his chair behind the desk, and I figured he'd done this a lot. "I was ten years old, out playing with my dog, Chance. All of a sudden, the dog takes off for home like a shot, and I see this bright star falling through the sky. Like a big fireball," he remembered. "The ground shook when it hit, over in the woods at the edge of town. Sent up a plume of blue smoke."

He leaned back and put his feet up on the edge of the desk. "I did what any kid would have done—went right into the woods after it. And there it was, like a huge acorn, half covered with dirt where it knocked down trees and plowed a furrow right into the ground."

"Was it doing anything?" Father Leo asked. "Any lights? Noises? Strange vibes?"

Duane nodded. "It glowed, but then I guess it was still red hot from coming through the atmosphere. And the squiggles all along the edge? Those were lit up almost too bright to look at, white and gold. It hit hard enough that I felt the earth shake."

"Any smoke? Fire?" I prompted.

Duane shook his head. "Nope. But it did look like it had a rough time.

Pieces were missing, like panels had gotten lost. I got to it before anyone else, but I couldn't get close 'cos of the heat. Then real fast, there were sirens, and everything just went crazy with police and firefighters and next thing you knew, the state boys were there and then the Feds." His tone didn't leave much question about what he thought about strangers muscling in on "their" UFO.

"What happened after that?" Father Leo asked, leaning forward.

"I hid in the trees," Duane replied. "No one knew I was there. Nowadays, I'd have had a phone to get photos, video too, but back then..." He shrugged. "I wish I'd had a camera with me. Coulda made a fortune off those photos."

"Tell us about the spaceship," I pressed. "Did it really look like an acorn?"

Duane chuckled. "It looked like the biggest damn acorn you ever did see, yes sirree. About twice as large as the one they've got up on the post on the way into town." He sighed. "Once all the shouting was done between the cops and the Staties and the Feds, the guys in the black suits roped off the area. I hid real good, so they didn't catch me. They took all kinds of readings with fancy instruments, and I guess the outside cooled off because they touched it and nothing happened. It stopped glowing, and the chicken scratch on the edge darkened up. Then they threw a tarp over it and loaded it onto a flatbed once it was dark."

"Any idea where it went?" I didn't really expect him to know.

He shrugged. "Wherever they hide stuff like that. Somewhere out West?"

"So, the replica at the edge of town, who made that?" Father Leo shifted to lean back in his chair.

"Benny Carson, God rest his soul. Died a few years back. Quirky sort, always making art outa things he found along the road." Duane leaned forward. "But I'll tell you something I've never told anyone else. Benny and me, we were drinking buddies. And I was out to his place a couple times while he was making that big acorn. He let me in on a secret. Those government boys didn't find all the pieces. Benny did, and he put them into the material he used to make that there replica."

I didn't make eye contact with Father Leo, but I knew from the way he straightened that we were both thinking the same thing. "What did Benny die of?" I asked.

Duane shook his head. "It was the damnedest thing. I grew up with Benny, and he was healthy as a horse all his life. But after he made that damn acorn, he started getting sick. No one figured out what did him in, but he just wasted away. Hair fell out, got real tired, skin got bad. It was a real shame. Bad way to go."

"Thank you," Father Leo said, standing. I followed his lead. "We've kept you from your dinner. But we really appreciate the information."

"If you mention Benny in your book, you tell people he was a good guy," Duane said. "We wouldn't have none of this UFO festival stuff without his spaceship."

Neither of us spoke until we were back in the car. I still couldn't shake the feeling that someone was watching, but I knew we weren't being tailed. "Tell me what you got from that," Father Leo said.

"The spaceship was real. The Feds—or the Occulatum, or both—took off with it, but they missed pieces. We've probably got the big chunks in that lead box. And I'm thinking Benny likely died from some kind of radiation poisoning, which makes me real glad I stuck the pieces in lead instead of under my seat wrapped up in a towel."

Father Leo nodded. "Yep, that's my take, too. So, I'm wondering what would happen if we put the 'panel' together from the shards when we were near the acorn with its pieces."

"Not keen on getting more X-rays than my doc prescribes," I said.

"We'll be quick about it," he said. "And the shards have had fifty years buried in the dirt to power down. Benny probably handled and lived with pieces that were still 'hot' for weeks or months."

"What do you think is gonna happen?" I didn't like the idea of actually putting the panel together, but I didn't see another choice.

"No idea. Maybe nothing," Father Leo replied. "We know the acorn isn't the real spacecraft, so it's not going to take off for the mothership."

"Aren't you forgetting something? Those shards called up crazy stuff."

"Which means we'll know what to expect." He was too damn calm about it, but I didn't have a better argument, so I shut up. I had kinda figured we were going to do something like that all along.

We went back to the motel and grabbed a nap and a shower to pass the time. Kecksburg didn't look like it had an all-night party scene other than the truck stop by the interstate and the diner, so if we waited for the wee hours, odds should be in our favor that we could check out the acorn without drawing attention.

When we headed back out at three in the morning, I didn't cut on my lights until we were out of the hotel parking lot. The night clerk might think we were skipping out without paying, and we didn't need cops sniffing around. I drove back to where the big acorn-shaped sculpture was a silhouette against the starry sky and pulled off the road.

The feeling of being watched was stronger than ever, and I turned slowly, taking in the shadows beneath the trees and the empty road.

"What's wrong?"

"I can't shake the feeling that there's something out there," I said, wishing that the prickle at the back of my neck would stop.

"There probably is," Father Leo said with a shrug. "And if so, we'll deal with it, like we always do."

He grabbed the gear bag, and I lifted down the heavy lead box. I wasn't convinced that aliens cared about salt lines or iron filings, but if there were other things keeping tabs on us, setting the wardings couldn't hurt. I didn't want to handle the shards more than I had to, so I'd brought a pair of kitchen tongs to move them around. When the tongs didn't melt, I felt a little better. I laid the pieces on the ground, using oven mitts for protection, and pulled out my taped-together mock-up, then lined the shards up on the paper to match. It took a bit of jostling to get the pieces together, but they fit better than I thought they might since they'd been buried for half a century after falling out of the sky. When the panel was assembled, it was about twice the size of the sheet of copy paper I had used for the prototype.

Once the pieces were pushed together in the right order, the damn thing lit up. I yelped and scrambled backward as the tablet began to glow, and the strange markings flared so brightly I had to look away.

An instant later, the runes on the big acorn blazed bright red, and the whole post began to shake.

"Mark, look!"

I raised my head and saw thick fog rolling in from the tree line, where there hadn't been any before. Not fog. Ghosts.

The tablet changed colors, blinking a sequence just like in the damned movie. Whatever bits were inside the acorn sculpture responded, and soon the tablet and the fake spaceship were putting on their own light show.

A glint of red caught my attention. The fog billowed along the edge of the forest, but now I could catch the reflection of the lights in eyes in the shadows, red and yellow—definitely not human. Low growls rose above the sound of crickets, and I heard snuffling and shambling that didn't sound good.

Shit. The shards were waking up every cryptid, zombie, and ghost in the neighborhood, and I did not want to be around for the smackdown.

Meanwhile, the otherworldly light show hadn't let up. In fact, the tablet had synchronized with the sculpture, and they were pulsing together. The ground began to shake, and I could hear the big acorn rattling in its moorings.

A pillar of light burst out of the sculpture, blasting through the top and showering us with debris. A brilliant white flare streaked up into the heavens, and the air around us grew cold enough for us to see our breaths. Every cell in my body seemed to vibrate, and the ghostly fog swirled closer. I could see faces more clearly now in the mist, and I knew that the unquiet dead felt the pull of the tablet and the pulse of the lights.

Father Leo held a shotgun and a canister of salt. I drew my Glock loaded with silver bullets and pulled out a sawed-off to go with it. We stood back to back inside the salt circle, as the shard-tablet grew brighter and brighter.

"Now what?" I yelled above the rumble of the shaking iron pole and the noises of creatures drawing closer in the darkness. We were surrounded, and there was no way the two of us could fight off every-thing, all at once.

"Can we get the tablet back in the box?" Father Leo asked.

I didn't dare look away from the red eyes staring out of the shadows. "That's it? That's your plan?"

"You've got something better?"

I didn't, but we were going to need something quick. Zombies to the right of me, cryptids to the left, there I was. Stuck in the middle with Leo.

Not for the first time, I wished one of us could hurl lightning bolts or smite people with magic. That damn alien acorn had sent out a beacon that called every unnatural creature and restless spirit in the area and riled them up with the radioactive shards.

335

Father Leo began to chant the Last Rites, managing to fire rounds of rock salt into the writhing mist without missing a beat. I took aim, firing two-handed, alternating between shooting the Glock's silver bullets at the red-eyed, shadowy forms and blasting them with iron buckshot from the sawed-off.

Where were the cops when we needed them? Normally, we tried to avoid the boys in blue, but right now, we could use a posse. Surely everyone in town had heard the gunshots, but no one came running, and no flashing lights or sirens suggested that anyone was coming to the rescue.

"Shit," I muttered, reloading. I'd hit several of the creatures, but whether the shots destroyed them or just made them back the hell off, I couldn't tell in the darkness. Nothing—yet—dared to cross the salt line, but the night was young. I had plenty of ammo for our usual clusterfucks, but not enough for a friggin' war. Maybe the monsters were just waiting for us to tire, running down the clock until they could get to us.

Leo transitioned without a hitch from the Last Rites to the exorcism. The gray mist of ghosts had thinned, suggesting that the unwilling spirits had moved on, and only the vengeful ones remained. Exorcism wouldn't dispel regular monsters, and dark shapes slunk around the outside of the salt circle, regarding us with red or yellow eyes that glowed with an unnatural light. Their growls and howls sent chills down my back.

Perhaps that explained why none of the locals were rushing to our defense. I'd seen movies where outsiders were sacrificed to appease the monster in the woods and wondered if we'd served ourselves up as tribute.

A gray, bat-shaped creature as tall as a man, living proof of the Mothman legends, launched itself at us. I fired the Glock, hitting it center mass, and it fell back hissing and howling from the silver. In the next instant, I let loose with the shotgun, spraying buckshot at a cloven-footed, horned goat-man that looked like the PA version of the Jersey Devil.

Father Leo kept on chanting and shooting, and I fought off the creatures that dared to attack, but we couldn't keep this up forever. My granny used to say, "Praise the Lord and pass the ammunition," but I don't think she had a situation quite like this in mind. For all the times I'd thought about ending myself, on nights when memories and failures crowded suffocatingly close, now that the very real possibility of being torn to shreds presented itself, I found I wasn't in a hurry to leave, after all.

"I think we're screwed, Padre," I called over my shoulder. "Put in a good word for me with the Man Upstairs."

A new noise broke through the chaos. It started low; then, it rapidly rose in volume and pitch until I winced and wished I dared to drop the gun to cover my ears. It got louder and higher until my fillings felt like they would vibrate out of my teeth and my bones felt like a xylophone, humming with resonance.

There was no way in hell I should have been able to hear anything over that racket, but I could have sworn I heard a man's deep voice chanting. The words were slippery; I couldn't quite catch or remember them, but they carried a weight and primal force to them that my lizard brain recognized as powerful and dangerous. And then, when the pressure inside my head made me think my eyeballs were about to pop, a weird blue bolt of electricity sizzled from somewhere behind us, zapping the acorn and blowing it to smithereens.

The pillar of light winked out as abruptly as it had turned on, and the tablet suddenly went dark. My eyes took a second to adjust, and I was sure Father Leo and I were about to be mobbed by angry ghosts and hungry shamblers, with a few shady shifters thrown in for good measure.

I tensed, ready to shoot and fight, prepared to go down swinging. Instead, as my vision cleared, I saw an empty field, a darkened patch of woods, and a blackened ruin that had once been the acorn UFO. Everything else was gone, except for the shard-tablet, which lay dark and inert on the grass.

"What the hell just happened?" Father Leo breathed.

"I have no fuckin' idea, Padre."

"You're welcome." We both startled at the new voice. Father Leo and I turned in unison to face this new threat, guns drawn.

"You won't need your weapons. We're on your side."

"Yeah, and next you're gonna try to tell us these weren't the 'droids we were looking for," I muttered. "Who the fuck are you?"

I asked, but I already knew. Two big guys in black suits with dark shades—at night—military haircuts and enough self-importance that they oozed entitlement without ever saying a word. Cue the men in black.

"FBI? CIA? NFL?" I felt like pushing my luck.

"Friends," the taller man replied with a smirk. "Let's not complicate matters. All we want is the tablet."

Father Leo's eyes narrowed, and he said something in Latin. The shorter man appeared rattled by whatever it was and replied in the same dead language. Then, he turned to his arrogant partner and murmured something that wiped the smirk off his face.

"Let me start over," the tall jerk said in a slightly less obnoxious voice. "I'm CIA. He's—"

"Occulatum," the other man replied, and I had the feeling he was the one calling the shots. "We'd been alerted that you might have found and reassembled something related to the ship that crashed here, and we've come to take it off your hands before anyone else gets hurt."

"You're a little late for that," I snapped. I'd been scared out of my wits by the freaky UFO light show, and we'd been fighting our way out of one supernatural mess after another because of those shards. It galled the hell out of me that these two douchebags in suits thought they could waltz in and take over when we'd taken all the risks. "We've been cleaning up your mess all month."

The shorter man had the grace to wince at that. "Yes, sorry. You see, we always wondered what happened to the pieces of the ship that broke off during re-entry, but we never found any, so we weren't sure they existed."

"Until they started causing problems," I replied. "Which we handled. A little back-up would have been nice."

"Mark," Father Leo murmured, warning me to shut up.

"And here we are," the CIA asshole said. "The cavalry coming in over the hill at the last minute, so to speak."

I ignored him since his buddy was obviously in charge. "Now you go home and wash your hands of this whole mess like it never happened," the Occulatum guy continued. "We'll make sure no one here causes trouble, and we'll even arrange to replace the statue after the unfortunate 'lightning strike,'" he said.

"You planning to kill people, or just whammy them?" I asked, because I've never been able to keep my mouth shut, and I didn't want to see Kelli or Duane get a one-way ticket to Gitmo.

"I assure you, no one will get hurt, or...whammied," the Occulatum guy replied. "You've done your part, and you have our gratitude. But now, it's time to hand over the tablet and go get a good night's sleep."

I glanced at Father Leo. "How do we know they're the real deal?"

"I confirmed their identity with my colleague," he replied, and I guessed the Latin was some kind of code word.

"What, no secret handshake?"

Father Leo spared me a tired smile. "No. Not even a priestly decoder ring. I'm going to have to ask you to trust me on this, Mark. They're okay."

I stared at the shard-tablet that had caused so much trouble. For weeks, I couldn't wait to be rid of it, and earlier tonight, I had never wanted to see it again. Now, I felt weird just handing it over, although I certainly didn't have any desire to keep it.

"Fine," I muttered. "But the next time you lose a piece of your space-ship, don't call us, we'll call you." I left the tablet where it lay and stalked past the men to my truck. Father Leo lagged behind, pausing to speak in Latin again to his counterpart before joining me. I was already waiting behind the wheel when he climbed into the cab.

"We won't have any trouble from authorities—local or otherwise," he assured me.

Now that the big alien confrontation was over, I was so tired I could barely keep my eyes open. Although I'd never say it out loud, the two guys in the Fed suits had saved us from getting our asses whupped by all the creepy-crawlies the tablet attracted. And while part of me had hoped a little to get a glimpse of a real alien, I figured that it was probably better, given our track record, that we didn't.

"All right," I conceded. "But tomorrow, I still want breakfast at the diner—and pie."

EPILOGUE

Wonder of wonders, I was actually back in my garage in Atlantic, underneath a car with my sleeves rolled up and my tools beside me. Classic rock blared from the speakers, the shop smelled of sweat, gasoline, and motor oil, and all was right with the world.

So of course, it couldn't stay that way.

"Hey, boss?" Pete, my shop manager, said as his feet appeared in my line of sight. "There're some people here to see you."

"Get them to make an appointment. And if they say I owe them money, they're lying."

"They look kind of official."

I had a sinking feeling. Official-looking was never good. I skidded out on my creeper and wiped my hands on a rag. Sure enough, Tweedledum and Tweedledee, the CIA and Occulatum douches from Kecksburg, were waiting in my office.

"Shouldn't you be busy waterboarding Bigfoot or something?" I asked. I stood just inside the door, arms crossed over my chest, and pointedly did not offer them a seat.

"We need to talk to you."

"Father Leo's church is a couple of miles from here. He's the boss. I'm just the grunt."

The CIA guy smirked as if I'd confirmed something he'd already suspected. I resisted the urge to roll my eyes.

"Headquarters is briefing him as we speak. And I'm quite certain you are far more than just a 'grunt.' In fact, Father Leo insisted that we get your buy-in. We have a problem, and we're counting on the two of you to help find a solution."

A dozen smart remarks came to mind, but I managed not to say any of them. "What's up?"

"There's been a spike in supernatural activity across the northwest corner of the state," the Occulatum guy said. "We originally thought it was due to the Kecksburg shards, but those have been dealt with, and the activity isn't decreasing."

"You think there were more UFOs?"

"We don't know—and that's the problem. We've identified a number of phenomena, and we need you and Father Leo to find out what's going on."

This was big. Usually, Leo and I just got pulled in on a case-by-case basis. "Why us?"

"You're the designated Occulatum hunters in this area," the CIA guy replied, and while he didn't say it, I could hear the "duh" at the end of his sentence.

"We're it?"

The Occulatum guy sighed. "People with your background and skills are difficult to come by, Mr. Wojcik. Most people who encounter monsters don't survive. Those who do are often permanently damaged, or unwilling to tempt fate by going out looking for more. It takes a certain kind of person to do what you do and live through it. Good hunters are in remarkably short supply."

That was almost a compliment, and I saw the CIA guy's jaw twitch as if he were itching to jump in with a jab, but he stayed quiet.

"So, you've got a list of sketchy things you want us to chase down? Do you have any idea what's behind it, so we don't get our asses handed to us?" I'm not a trusting kind of guy, and I had no reason to think these two wouldn't use Father Leo and me as bait in some shady deal.

"We believe someone or something is increasing the frequency and violence of supernatural occurrences," the Occulatum guy replied. "We see the effects, but we need you to examine the evidence and determine the source, so it can be properly dealt with." He paused. "It's possible that the incidents are building to a climax. If that's true, it will be in all of our best interests to stop it before that happens."

"What kind of grand finale are we talking about? End-of-the-world bad, or less-than-extinction bad?"

The Occulatum guy looked at me, and I could feel his stare despite his dark sunglasses. "Worse."

THE END

AFTERWORD

Larry and Gail grew up in the part of Northwestern Pennsylvania that Mark Wojcik calls home. All of the locations in the stories exist, although we've taken creative liberties for story purposes. Many of the places are also reputed to be haunted. Some of the sites are on land our families owned, so it was fun to "invite" Mark to hunt monsters in our backyards!

We have a lot of fun writing these stories, in part because by doing so, we get to share some of our memories and special places with readers. It's also been fun to research the ghost stories and urban legends that we've heard all our lives and find out all kinds of unexpected, interesting, and downright weird stuff about the places we thought we knew. While we moved away from Pennsylvania many years ago, we visit often, and the state will always hold a place in our hearts.

Did you know that all of our urban fantasy series intersect? Mark Wojcik mentions having a resource down in Charleston to get rid of cursed and haunted objects. That's Cassidy Kincaide and her friends in our Deadly Curiosities series. Mark also makes a cameo appearance in our newest urban fantasy novel, Sons of Darkness, and in the series that Gail writes as Morgan Brice (urban fantasy MM paranormal romance), Witchbane and Badlands.

It just made sense to us that people who were hunters and dealt with the supernatural would know each other at some level, and would be resources and backup to each other. So if you like Mark's books, consider checking out the adventures of his friends! And of course, Mark is part of John Hartness's Bubba The Monster Hunter series, so he exists in the same world as John's books and all of the other spin-off series by Falstaff authors, and you'll want to check them out, too!

Stay tuned for Mark and his friends to be back for Season Two, with all-new monsters and pesky government agents!

ABOUT THE AUTHORS

Larry N. Martin is the author of the new sci-fi novel *Salvage Rat*, and co-author of both the *Spells, Salt, and Steel* series and the Steampunk series *Iron and Blood: The Jake Desmet Adventures* (Solaris Books) as well as the related series of short stories/novellas: *The Storm & Fury Adventures*. He has co-authored stories in the anthologies *Clockwork Universe: Steampunk vs. Aliens, The Weird Wild West, The Side of Good/The Side of Evil, Alien Artifacts, Gaslight and Grimm, Space, Contact Light,* and *Robots*.

Gail Z. Martin is the author of *Scourge: A Darkhurst novel*, the first in the new Darkhurst epic fantasy series from Solaris Books. Also new are: *The Shadowed Path,* part of the Chronicles of the Necromancer universe (Solaris Books); *Vendetta: A Deadly Curiosities Novel* in her urban fantasy series set in Charleston, SC (Solaris Books); *Shadow and Flame* the fourth and final book in the Ascendant Kingdoms Saga (Orbit Books); and *Iron and Blood*.

She is also author of *Ice Forged, Reign of Ash* and *War of Shadows* in The Ascendant Kingdoms Saga, The Chronicles of The Necromancer series (*The Summoner, The Blood King, Dark Haven, Dark Lady's Chosen*); The Fallen Kings Cycle (*The Sworn, The Dread*) and the urban fantasy novel *Deadly Curiosities*. Gail writes three short story/novella series: *The Jonmarc Vahanian Adventures, The Deadly Curiosities Adventures* and *The Blaine McFadden Adventures*. *The Storm and Fury Adventures* and *Spells, Salt and Steel*, are co-authored with Larry N. Martin.

Her work has appeared in over 35 US/UK anthologies. Newest

anthologies include: *Hath No Fury, Journeys, #We Are Not This, The Baker Street Irregulars,* and *In a Cat's Eye.*

―――――――――

Find us at www.GailZMartin.com / www.LarryNMartin.com, on Twitter @GailZMartin and @LNMartinAuthor, on Facebook.com/WinterKingdoms, at DisquietingVisions.com blog, on Goodreads https://www.goodreads.com/GailZMartin , on pinterest.com/Gzmartin and read free excerpts on Wattpad http://wattpad.com/GailZMartin.

STAY IN TOUCH

Keep up with all the newest releases and appearance news from Larry & Gail by visiting GailZMartin.com and signing up for their newsletter!

FALSTAFF BOOKS

**Want to know what's new
And coming soon from
Falstaff Books?**

Try This Free Ebook Sampler

https://www.instafreebie.com/free/bsZnl

**Follow the link.
Download the file.
Transfer to your e-reader, phone, tablet, watch, computer, whatever.
Enjoy.**

Made in the USA
Lexington, KY
15 July 2019